THE HARD PLACE™

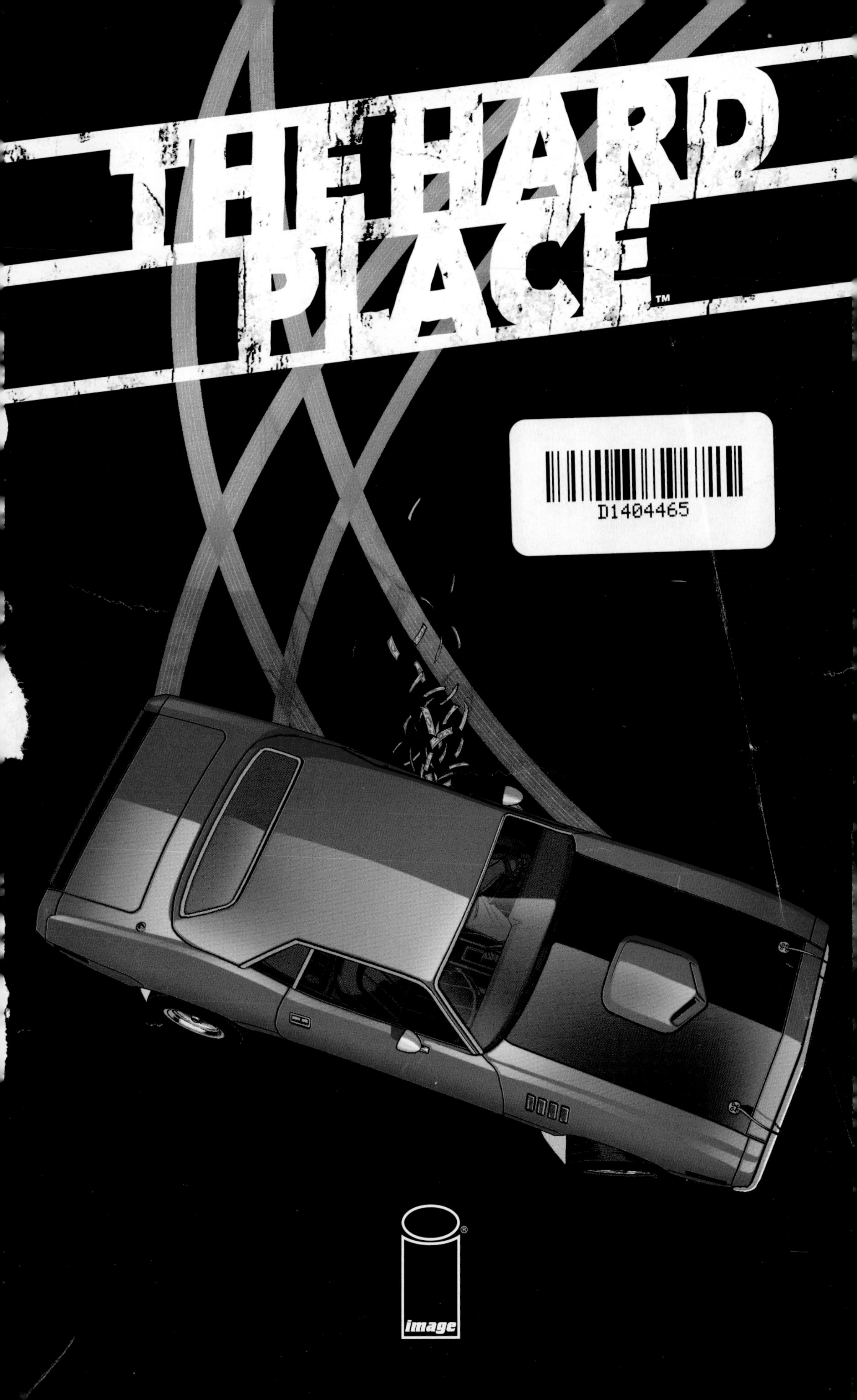

image

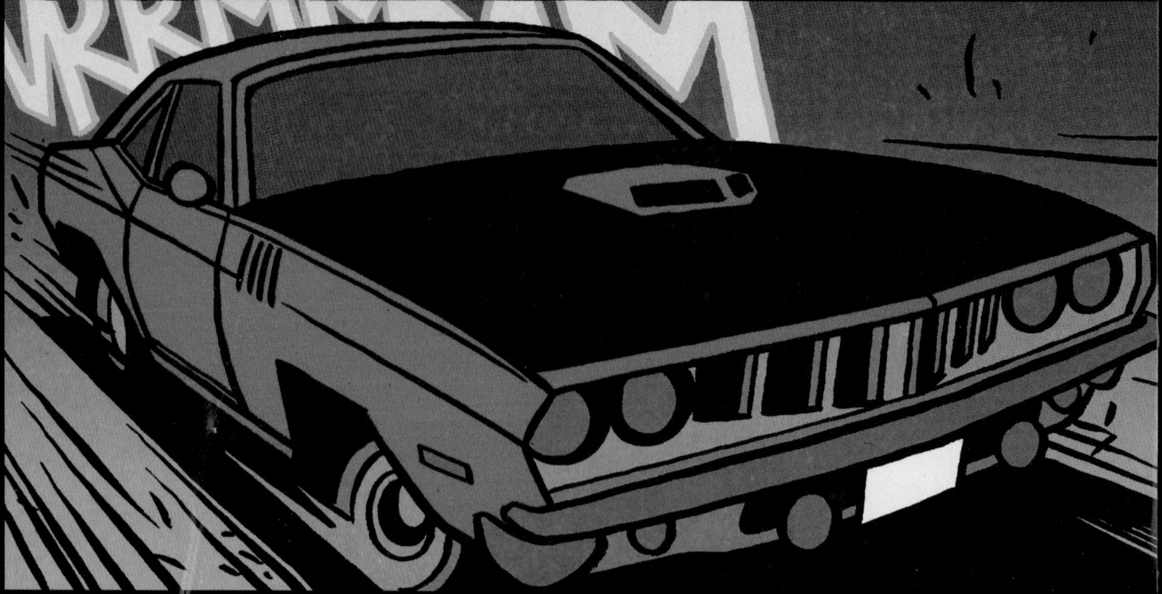

FRANK CVETKOVIC
LETTERS

BRIAN STELFREEZE
COVER

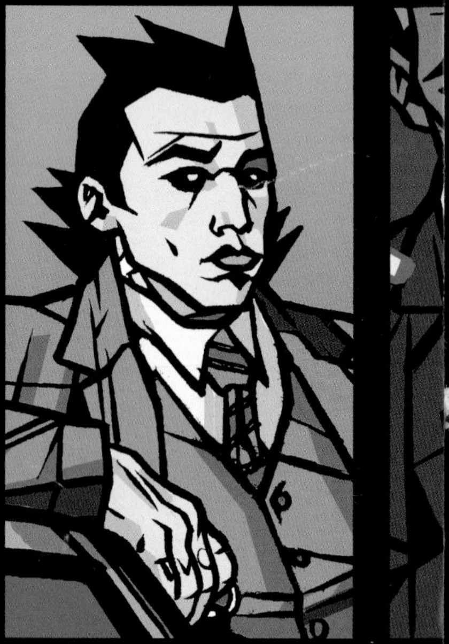

KEVEN GARDNER
EDITOR

EBEN MATTHEWS
LOGO DESIGN

JONATHAN CHAN
BOOK DESIGN

12-GAUGE

FOR 12-GAUGE COMICS
KEVEN GARDNER
DOUG WAGNER
BRIAN STELFREEZE
WWW.12GAUGECOMICS.COM

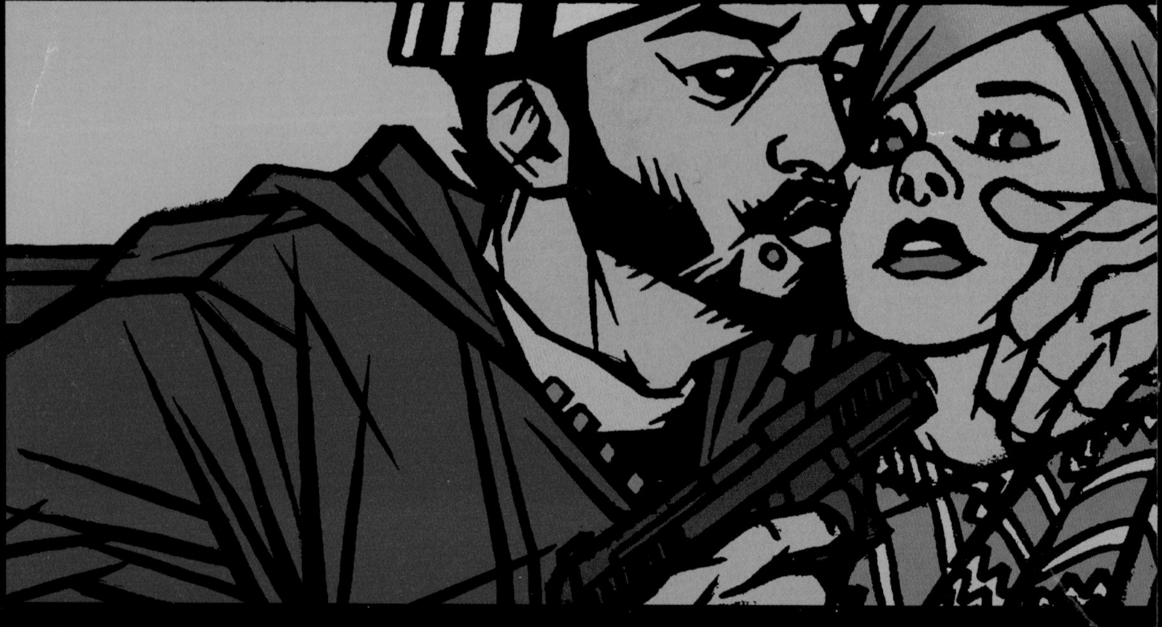

IMAGE COMICS PRESENTS
A 12-GAUGE PRODUCTION

DOUG WAGNER
STORY

NIC RUMMEL
ART

CHARLIE KIRCHOFF
COLORS

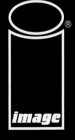

IMAGE COMICS, INC.
ROBERT KIRKMAN - CHIEF OPERATING OFFICER
ERIK LARSEN - CHIEF FINANCIAL OFFICER
TODD MCFARLANE - PRESIDENT
MARC SILVESTRI - CHIEF EXECUTIVE OFFICER
JIM VALENTINO - VICE PRESIDENT
ERIC STEPHENSON - PUBLISHER / CHIEF CREATIVE OFFICER
COREY HART - DIRECTOR OF SALES
JEFF BOISON - DIRECTOR OF PUBLISHING PLANNING & BOOK TRADE SALES
CHRIS ROSS - DIRECTOR OF DIGITAL SALES
JEFF STANG - DIRECTOR OF SPECIALTY SALES
KAT SALAZAR - DIRECTOR OF PR & MARKETING
DREW GILL - ART DIRECTOR
HEATHER DOORNINK - PRODUCTION DIRECTOR
NICOLE LAPALME - CONTROLLER
IMAGECOMICS.COM

CHAPTER ONE

"NOBODY DO NOTHING STUPID!"

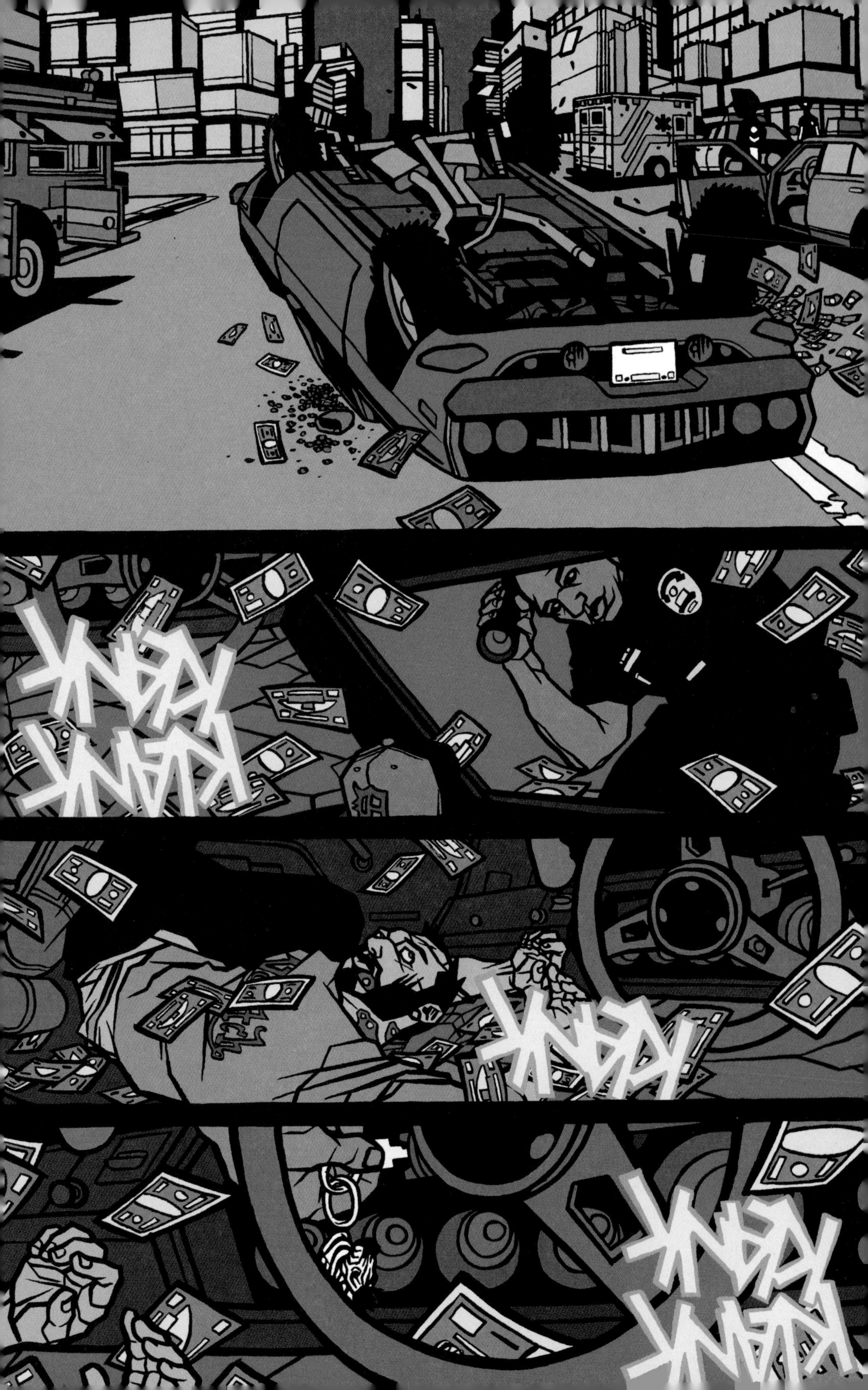

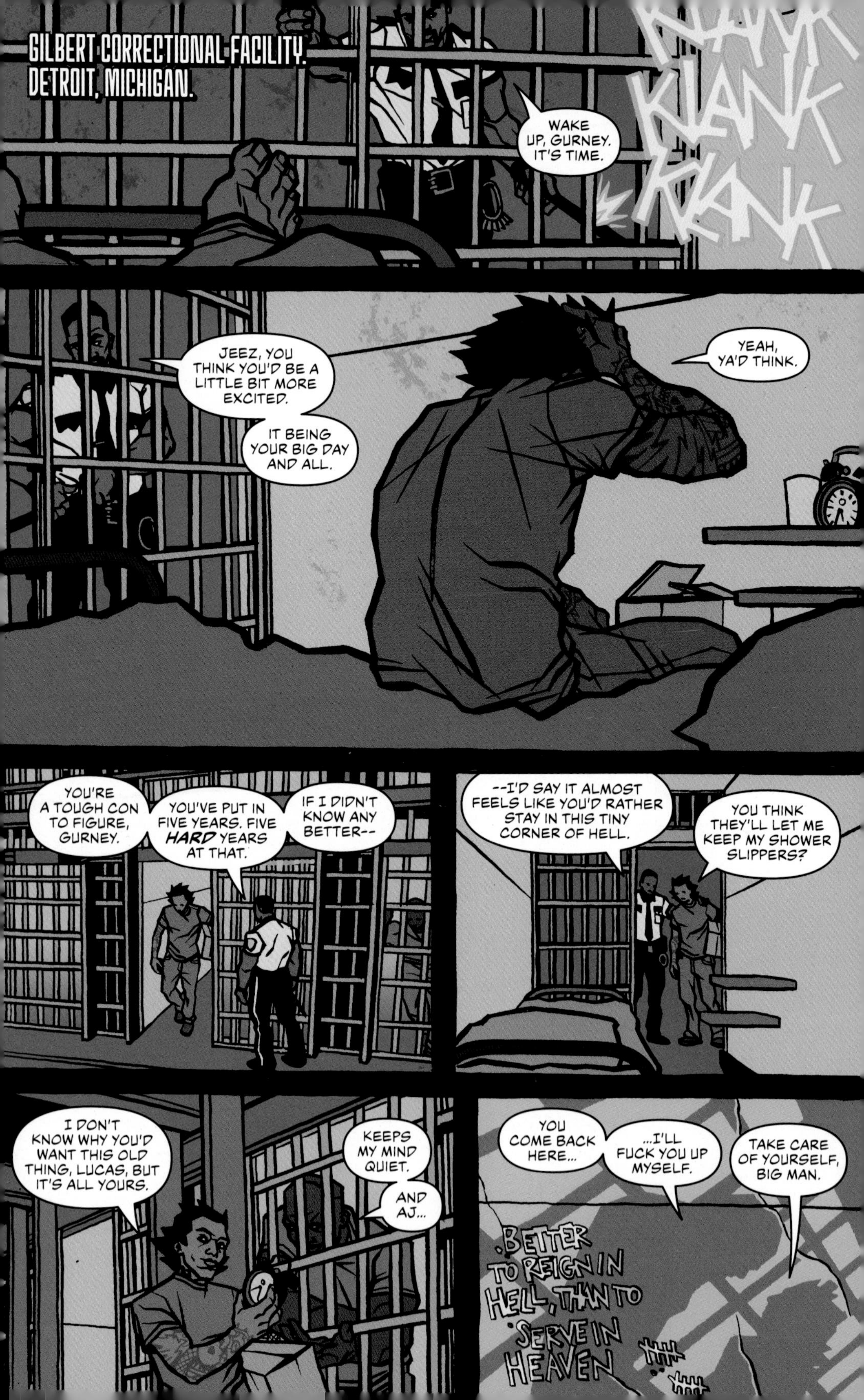
GILBERT CORRECTIONAL FACILITY.
DETROIT, MICHIGAN.
KLANK
KLANK
WAKE UP, GURNEY. IT'S TIME.
JEEZ, YOU THINK YOU'D BE A LITTLE BIT MORE EXCITED.
IT BEING YOUR BIG DAY AND ALL.
YEAH, YA'D THINK.
YOU'RE A TOUGH CON TO FIGURE, GURNEY.
YOU'VE PUT IN FIVE YEARS. FIVE *HARD* YEARS AT THAT.
IF I DIDN'T KNOW ANY BETTER--
--I'D SAY IT ALMOST FEELS LIKE YOU'D RATHER STAY IN THIS TINY CORNER OF HELL.
YOU THINK THEY'LL LET ME KEEP MY SHOWER SLIPPERS?
I DON'T KNOW WHY YOU'D WANT THIS OLD THING, LUCAS, BUT IT'S ALL YOURS.
KEEPS MY MIND QUIET.
AND AJ...
YOU COME BACK HERE...
...I'LL FUCK YOU UP MYSELF.
TAKE CARE OF YOURSELF, BIG MAN.
BETTER TO REIGN IN HELL, THAN TO SERVE IN HEAVEN

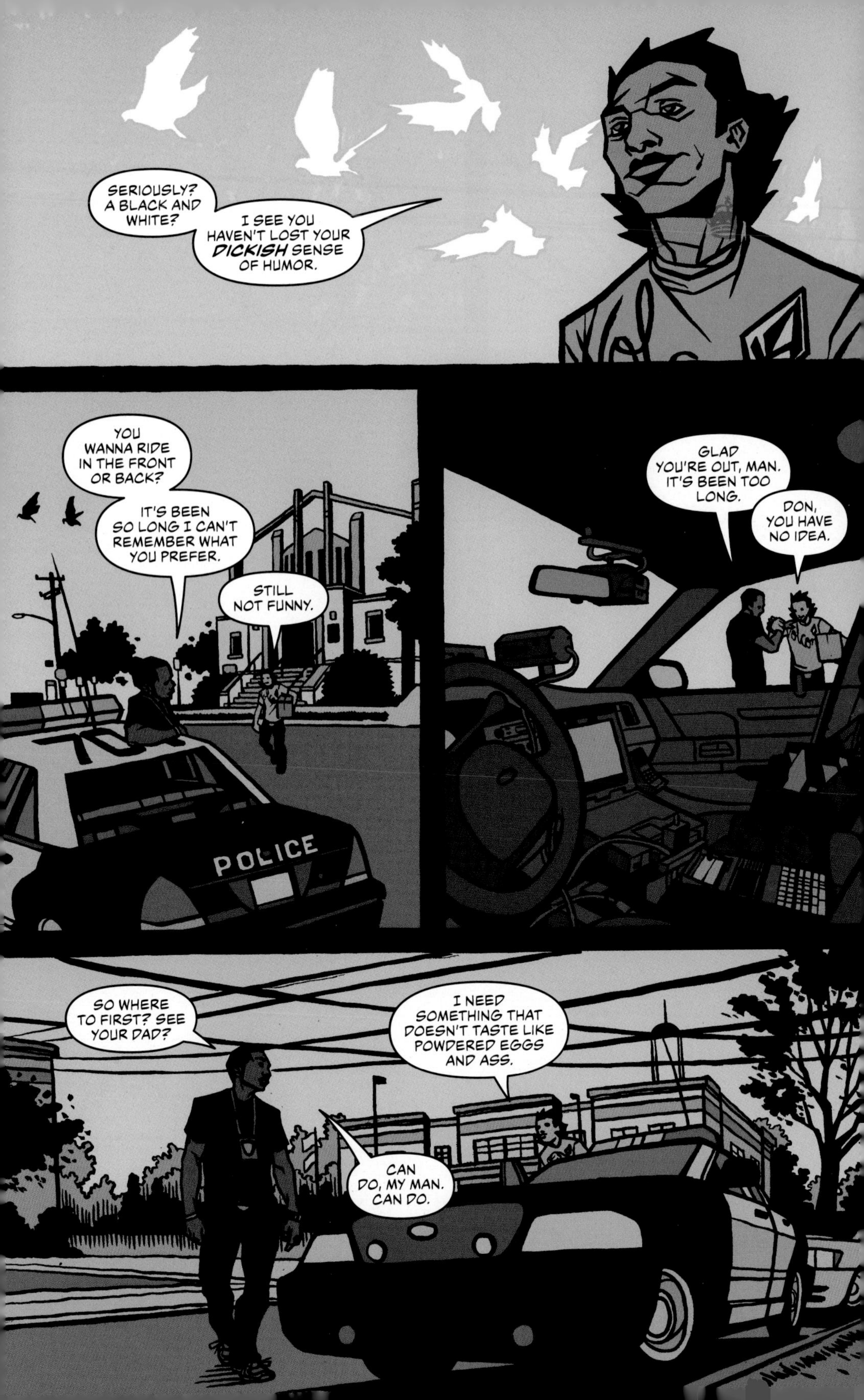
SERIOUSLY? A BLACK AND WHITE?
I SEE YOU HAVEN'T LOST YOUR DICKISH SENSE OF HUMOR.
YOU WANNA RIDE IN THE FRONT OR BACK?
IT'S BEEN SO LONG I CAN'T REMEMBER WHAT YOU PREFER.
STILL NOT FUNNY.
POLICE
GLAD YOU'RE OUT, MAN. IT'S BEEN TOO LONG.
DON, YOU HAVE NO IDEA.
SO WHERE TO FIRST? SEE YOUR DAD?
I NEED SOMETHING THAT DOESN'T TASTE LIKE POWDERED EGGS AND ASS.
CAN DO, MY MAN. CAN DO.

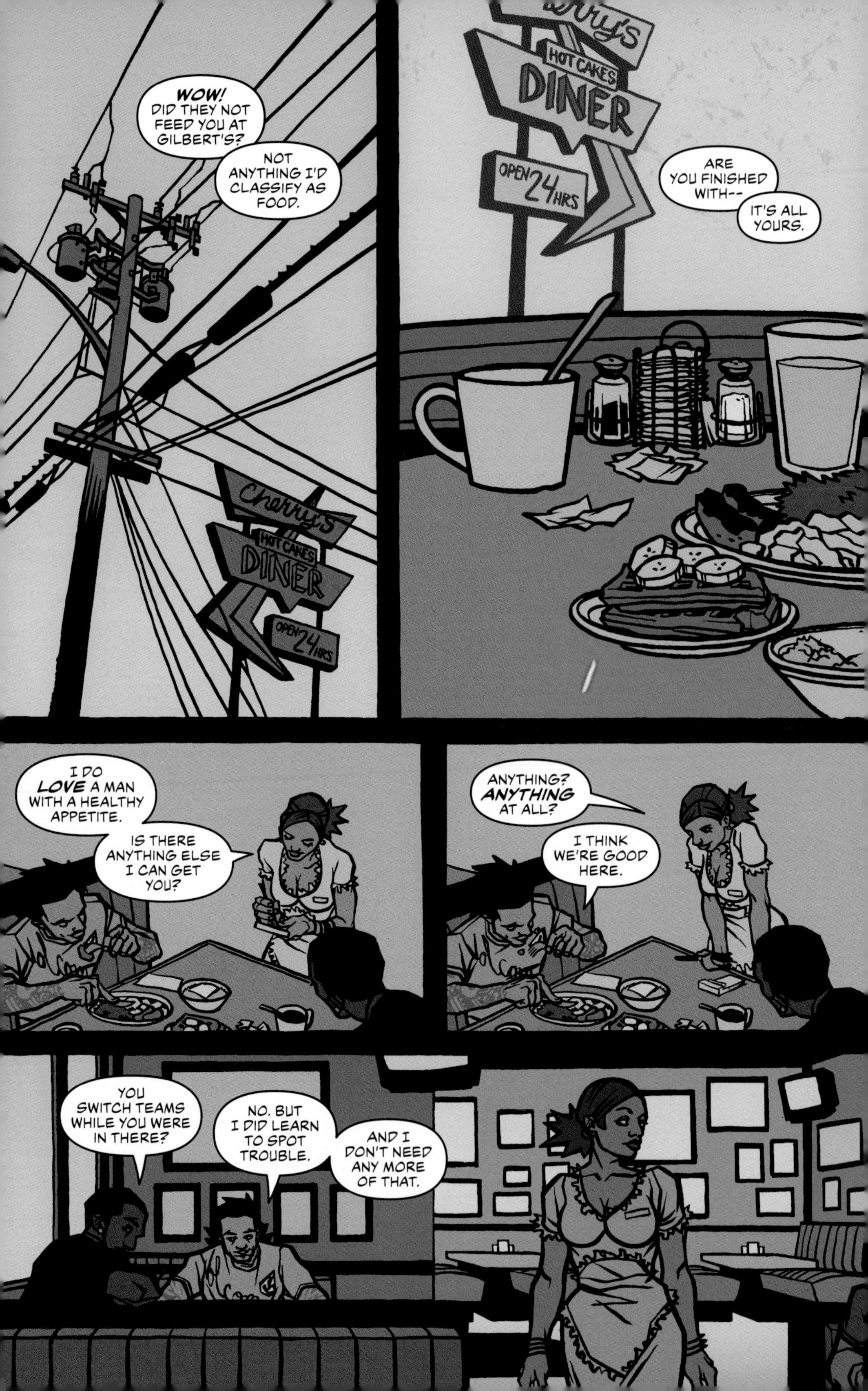
WOW! DID THEY NOT FEED YOU AT GILBERT'S?
NOT ANYTHING I'D CLASSIFY AS FOOD.
Cherry's HOT CAKES DINER OPEN 24 HRS
ARE YOU FINISHED WITH--
IT'S ALL YOURS.
I DO LOVE A MAN WITH A HEALTHY APPETITE.
IS THERE ANYTHING ELSE I CAN GET YOU?
ANYTHING? ANYTHING AT ALL?
I THINK WE'RE GOOD HERE.
YOU SWITCH TEAMS WHILE YOU WERE IN THERE?
NO. BUT I DID LEARN TO SPOT TROUBLE.
AND I DON'T NEED ANY MORE OF THAT.

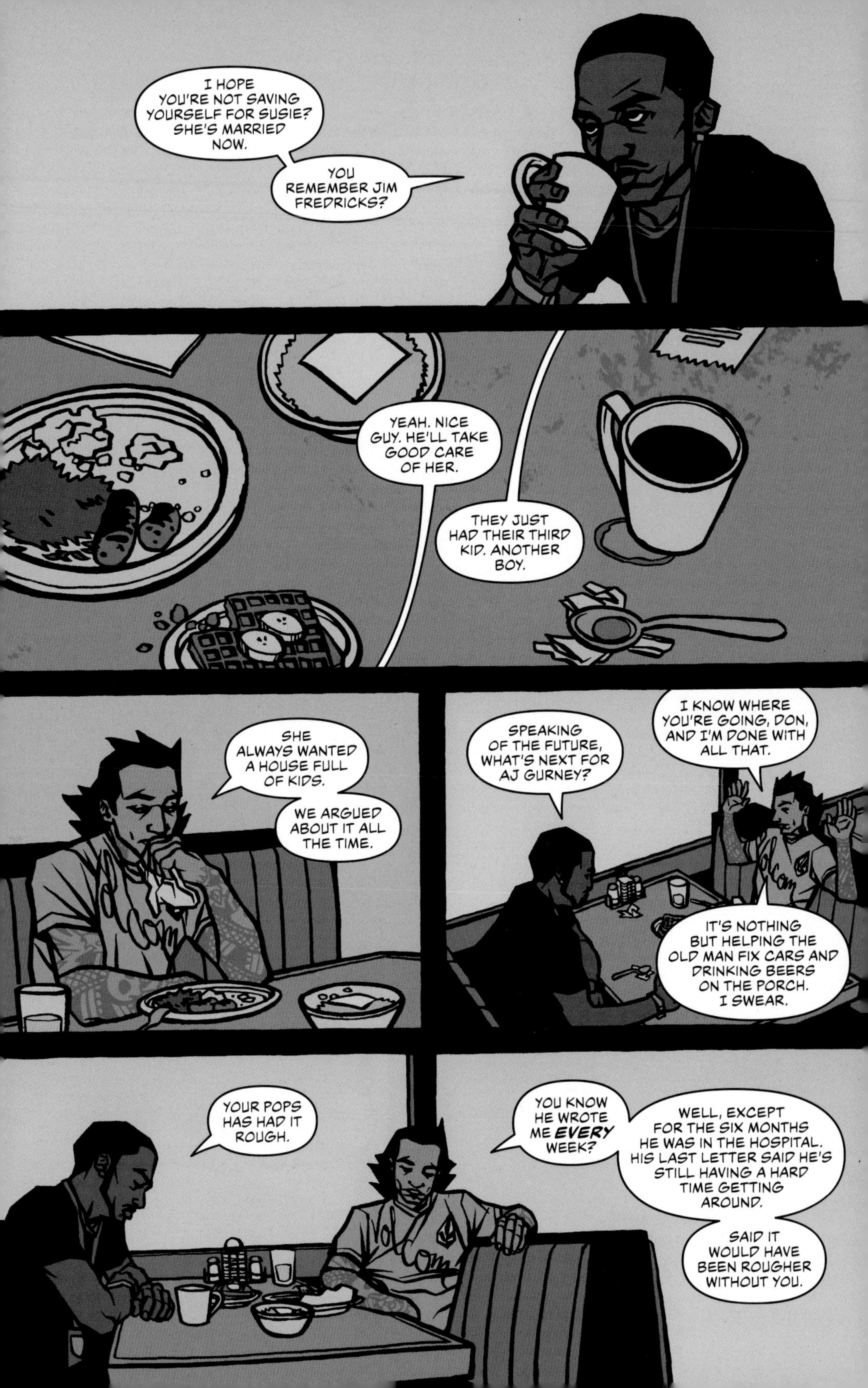
I HOPE YOU'RE NOT SAVING YOURSELF FOR SUSIE? SHE'S MARRIED NOW.
YOU REMEMBER JIM FREDRICKS?
YEAH. NICE GUY. HE'LL TAKE GOOD CARE OF HER.
THEY JUST HAD THEIR THIRD KID. ANOTHER BOY.
SHE ALWAYS WANTED A HOUSE FULL OF KIDS.
WE ARGUED ABOUT IT ALL THE TIME.
SPEAKING OF THE FUTURE, WHAT'S NEXT FOR AJ GURNEY?
I KNOW WHERE YOU'RE GOING, DON, AND I'M DONE WITH ALL THAT.
IT'S NOTHING BUT HELPING THE OLD MAN FIX CARS AND DRINKING BEERS ON THE PORCH. I SWEAR.
YOUR POPS HAS HAD IT ROUGH.
YOU KNOW HE WROTE ME ***EVERY*** WEEK?
WELL, EXCEPT FOR THE SIX MONTHS HE WAS IN THE HOSPITAL. HIS LAST LETTER SAID HE'S STILL HAVING A HARD TIME GETTING AROUND.
SAID IT WOULD HAVE BEEN ROUGHER WITHOUT YOU.

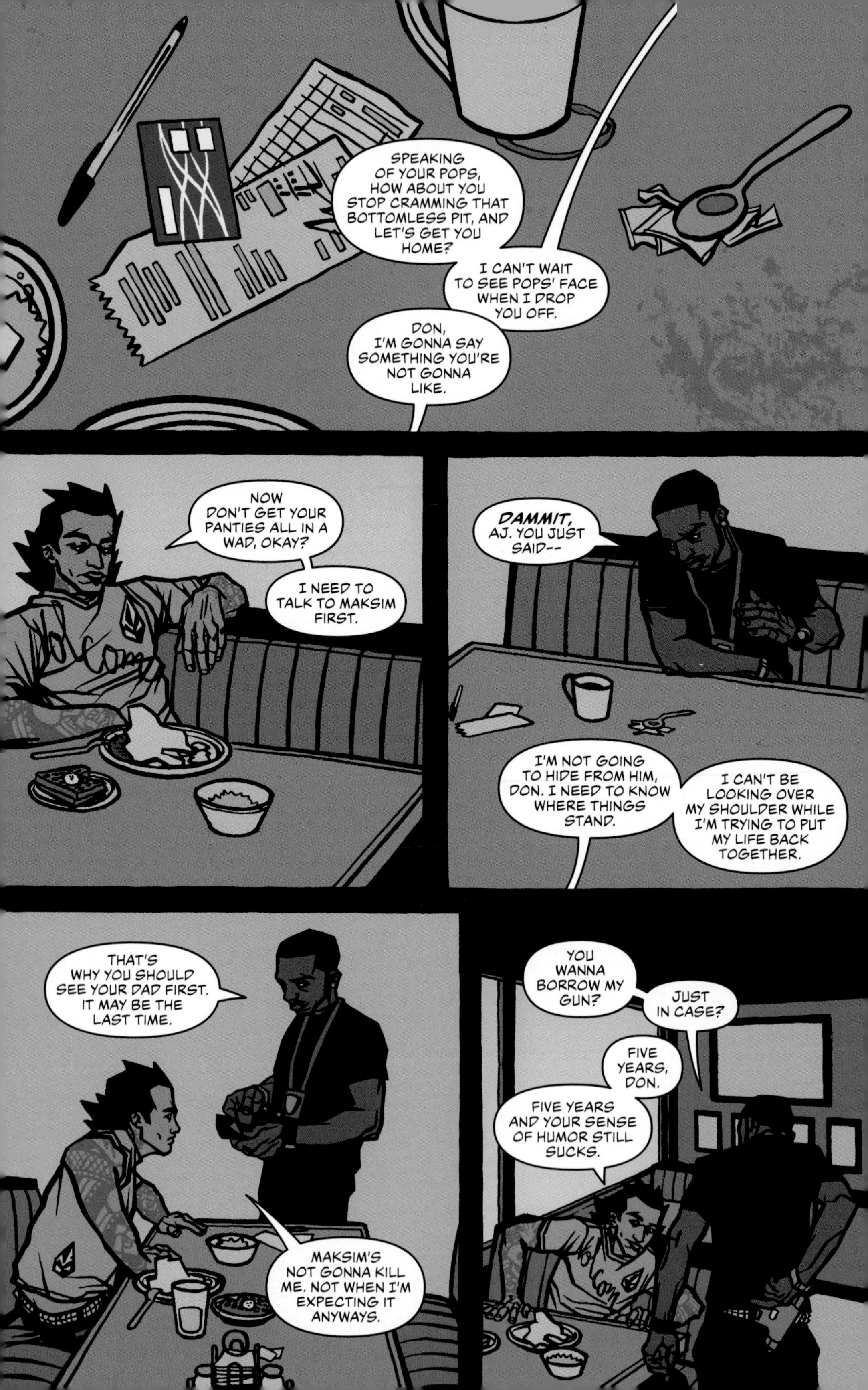
SPEAKING OF YOUR POPS, HOW ABOUT YOU STOP CRAMMING THAT BOTTOMLESS PIT, AND LET'S GET YOU HOME?
I CAN'T WAIT TO SEE POPS' FACE WHEN I DROP YOU OFF.
DON, I'M GONNA SAY SOMETHING YOU'RE NOT GONNA LIKE.
NOW DON'T GET YOUR PANTIES ALL IN A WAD, OKAY?
I NEED TO TALK TO MAKSIM FIRST.
DAMMIT, AJ. YOU JUST SAID--
I'M NOT GOING TO HIDE FROM HIM, DON. I NEED TO KNOW WHERE THINGS STAND.
I CAN'T BE LOOKING OVER MY SHOULDER WHILE I'M TRYING TO PUT MY LIFE BACK TOGETHER.
THAT'S WHY YOU SHOULD SEE YOUR DAD FIRST. IT MAY BE THE LAST TIME.
MAKSIM'S NOT GONNA KILL ME. NOT WHEN I'M EXPECTING IT ANYWAYS.
YOU WANNA BORROW MY GUN?
JUST IN CASE?
FIVE YEARS, DON.
FIVE YEARS AND YOUR SENSE OF HUMOR STILL SUCKS.

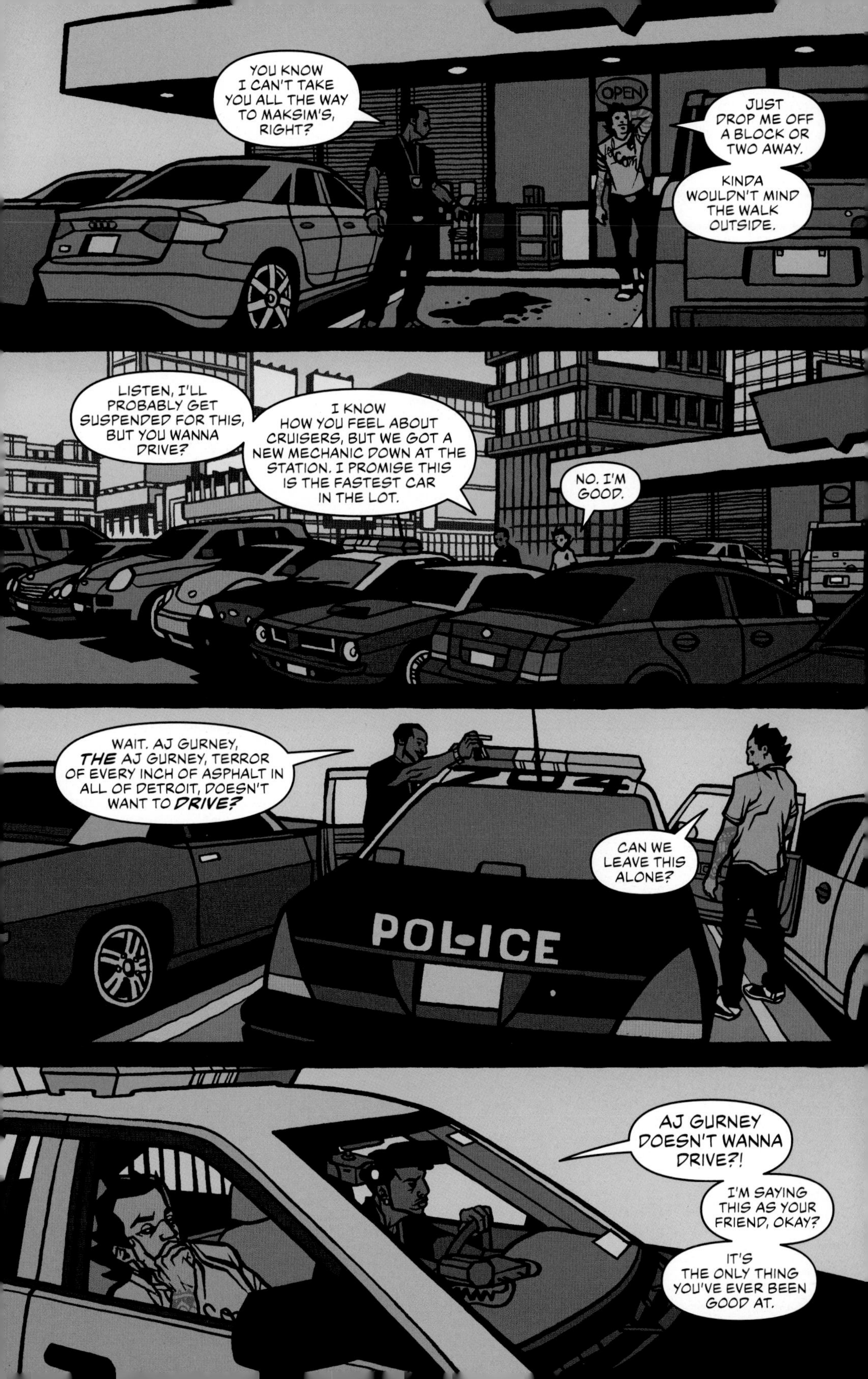

YOU KNOW I CAN'T TAKE YOU ALL THE WAY TO MAKSIM'S, RIGHT?
OPEN
JUST DROP ME OFF A BLOCK OR TWO AWAY.
KINDA WOULDN'T MIND THE WALK OUTSIDE.
LISTEN, I'LL PROBABLY GET SUSPENDED FOR THIS, BUT YOU WANNA DRIVE?
I KNOW HOW YOU FEEL ABOUT CRUISERS, BUT WE GOT A NEW MECHANIC DOWN AT THE STATION. I PROMISE THIS IS THE FASTEST CAR IN THE LOT.
NO. I'M GOOD.
WAIT. AJ GURNEY, *THE* AJ GURNEY, TERROR OF EVERY INCH OF ASPHALT IN ALL OF DETROIT, DOESN'T WANT TO *DRIVE?*
CAN WE LEAVE THIS ALONE?
POLICE
AJ GURNEY DOESN'T WANNA DRIVE?!
I'M SAYING THIS AS YOUR FRIEND, OKAY?
IT'S THE ONLY THING YOU'VE EVER BEEN GOOD AT.

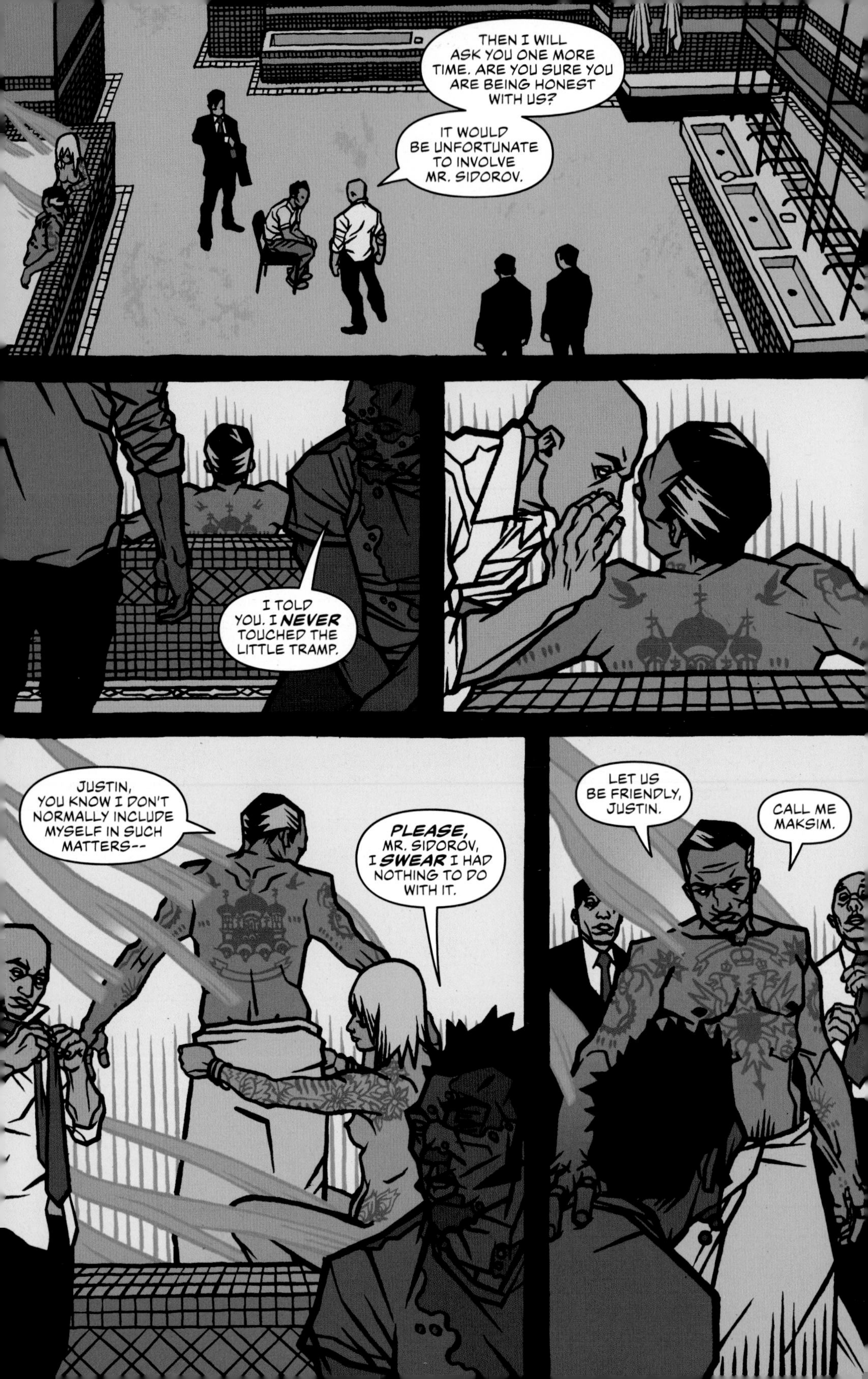
THEN I WILL ASK YOU ONE MORE TIME. ARE YOU SURE YOU ARE BEING HONEST WITH US?
IT WOULD BE UNFORTUNATE TO INVOLVE MR. SIDOROV.
I TOLD YOU. I **NEVER** TOUCHED THE LITTLE TRAMP.
JUSTIN, YOU KNOW I DON'T NORMALLY INCLUDE MYSELF IN SUCH MATTERS--
PLEASE, MR. SIDOROV, I **SWEAR** I HAD NOTHING TO DO WITH IT.
LET US BE FRIENDLY, JUSTIN.
CALL ME MAKSIM.

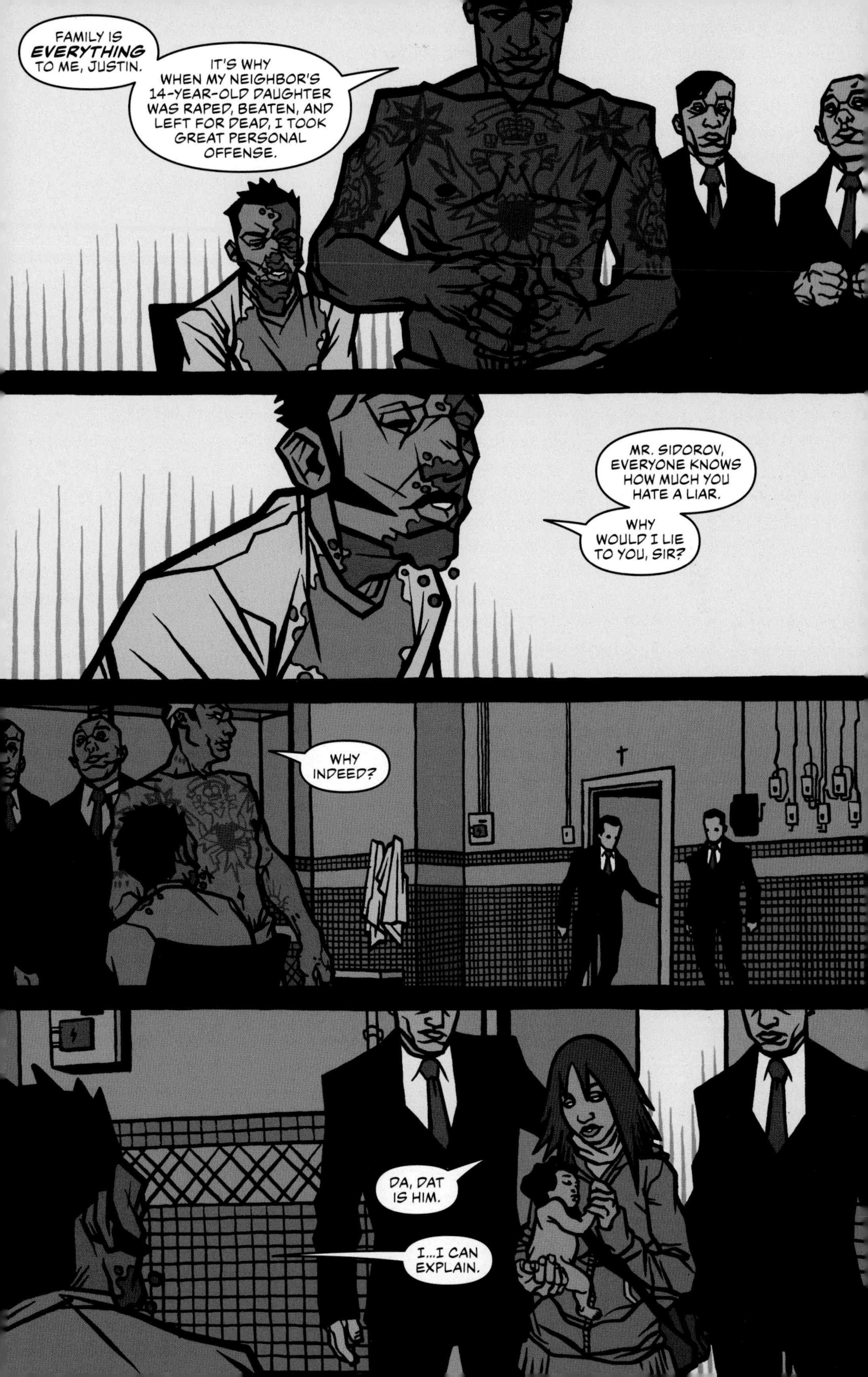
FAMILY IS ***EVERYTHING*** TO ME, JUSTIN.
IT'S WHY WHEN MY NEIGHBOR'S 14-YEAR-OLD DAUGHTER WAS RAPED, BEATEN, AND LEFT FOR DEAD, I TOOK GREAT PERSONAL OFFENSE.
MR. SIDOROV, EVERYONE KNOWS HOW MUCH YOU HATE A LIAR.
WHY WOULD I LIE TO YOU, SIR?
WHY INDEED?
DA, DAT IS HIM.
I...I CAN EXPLAIN.

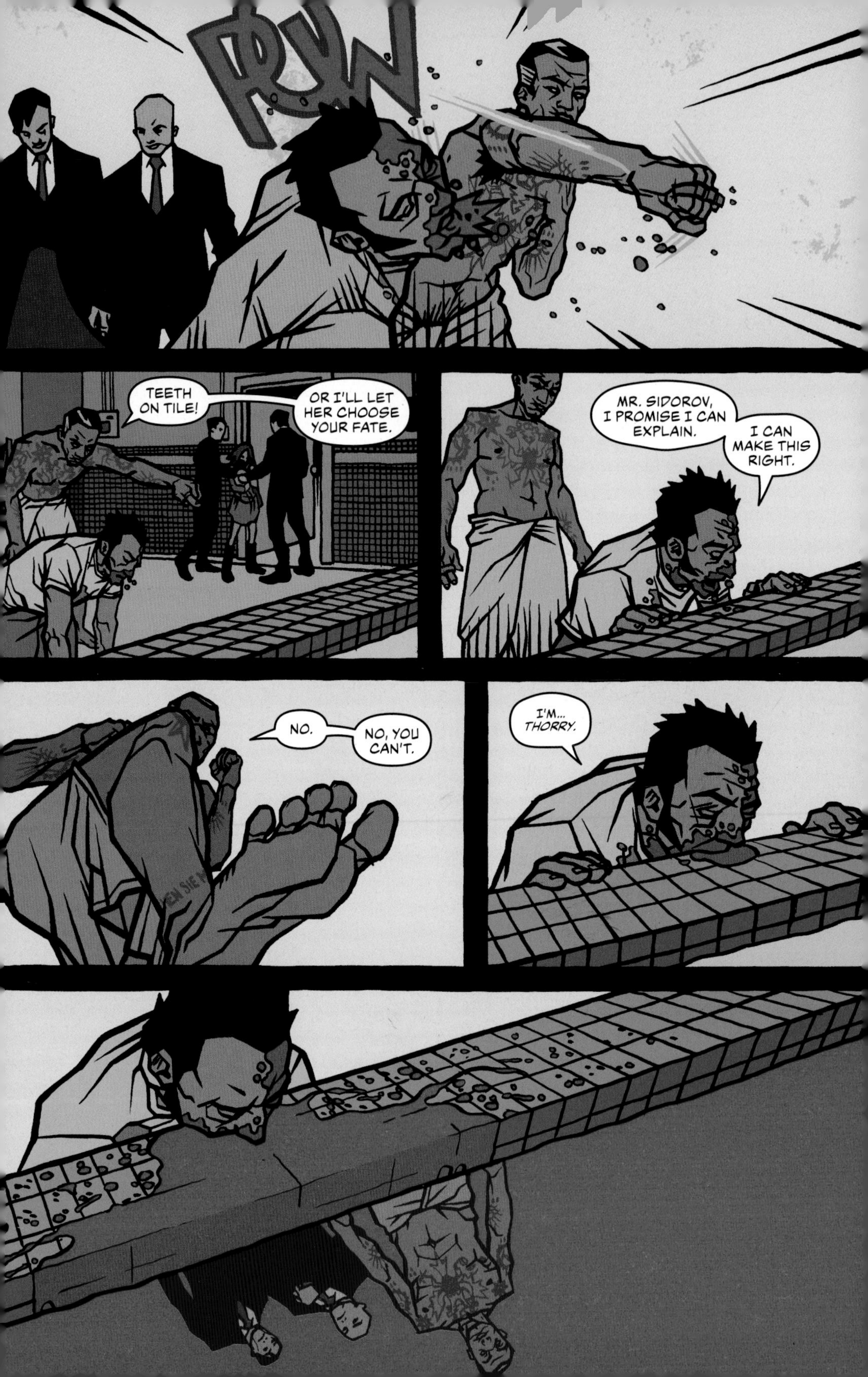
POW
TEETH ON TILE!
OR I'LL LET HER CHOOSE YOUR FATE.
MR. SIDOROV, I PROMISE I CAN EXPLAIN.
I CAN MAKE THIS RIGHT.
NO.
NO, YOU CAN'T.
I'M... THORRY.

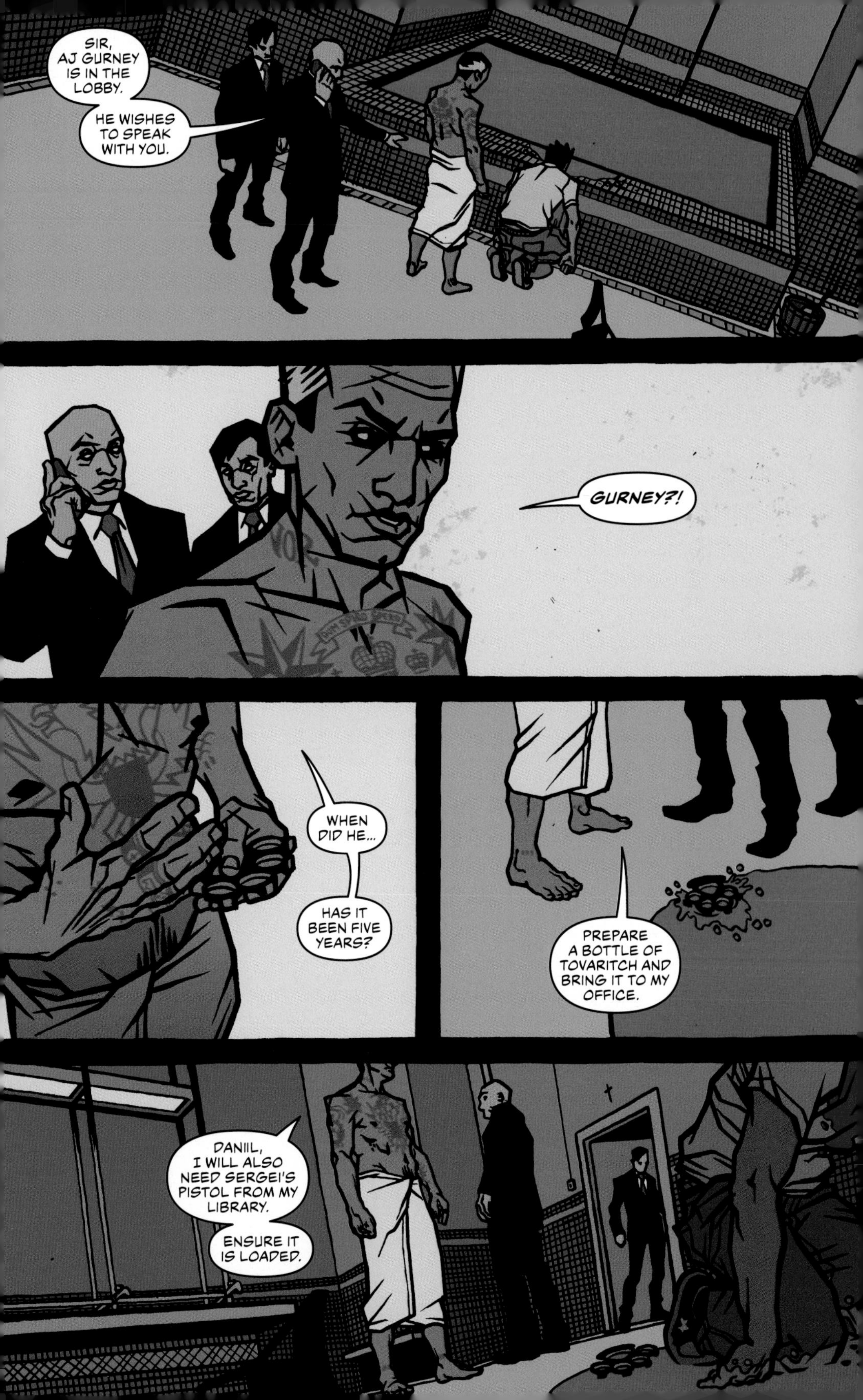
SIR, AJ GURNEY IS IN THE LOBBY.
HE WISHES TO SPEAK WITH YOU.
GURNEY?!
WHEN DID HE...
HAS IT BEEN FIVE YEARS?
PREPARE A BOTTLE OF TOVARITCH AND BRING IT TO MY OFFICE.
DANIIL, I WILL ALSO NEED SERGEI'S PISTOL FROM MY LIBRARY.
ENSURE IT IS LOADED.

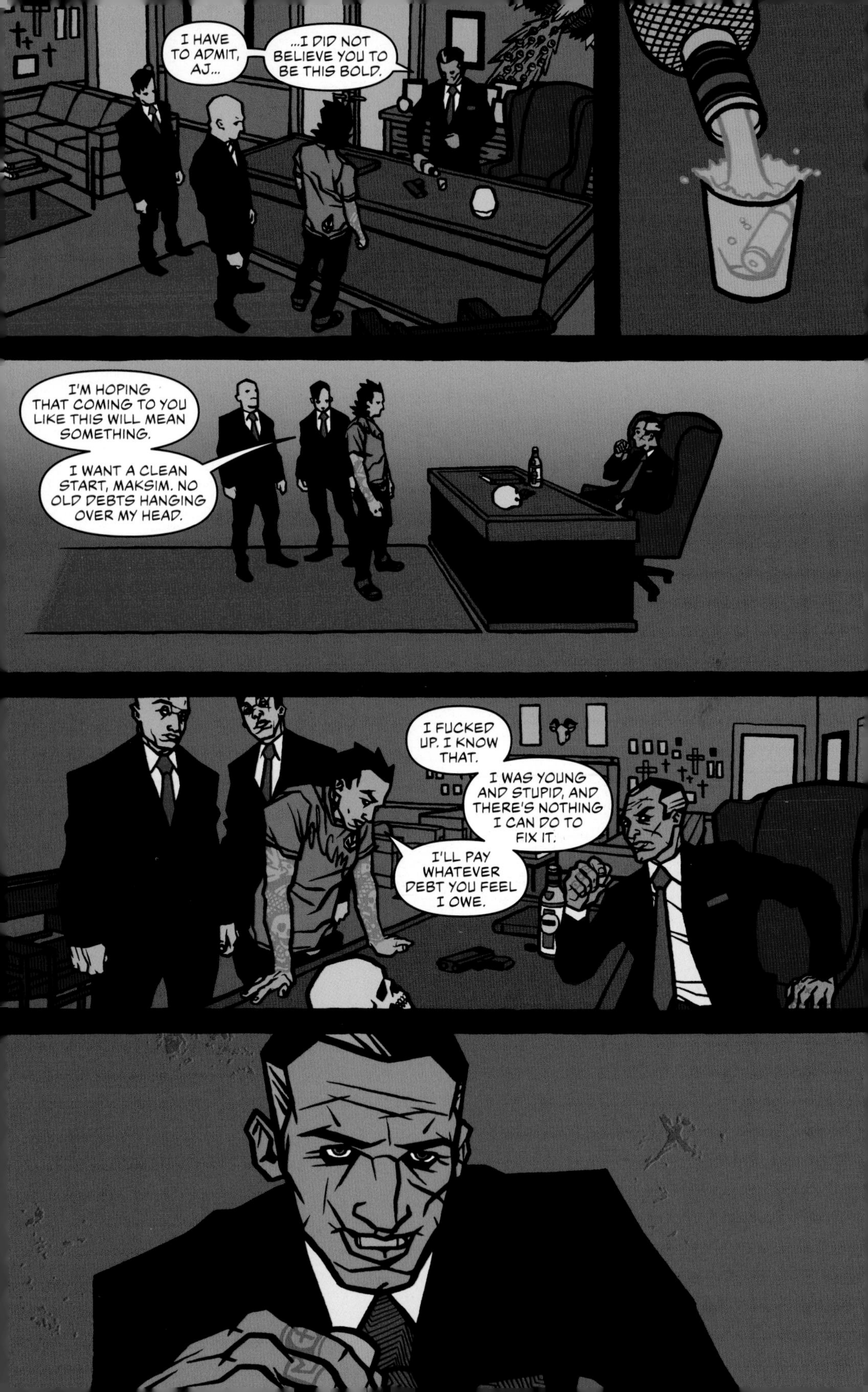
I HAVE TO ADMIT, AJ...
...I DID NOT BELIEVE YOU TO BE THIS BOLD.
I'M HOPING THAT COMING TO YOU LIKE THIS WILL MEAN SOMETHING.
I WANT A CLEAN START, MAKSIM. NO OLD DEBTS HANGING OVER MY HEAD.
I FUCKED UP. I KNOW THAT.
I WAS YOUNG AND STUPID, AND THERE'S NOTHING I CAN DO TO FIX IT.
I'LL PAY WHATEVER DEBT YOU FEEL I OWE.

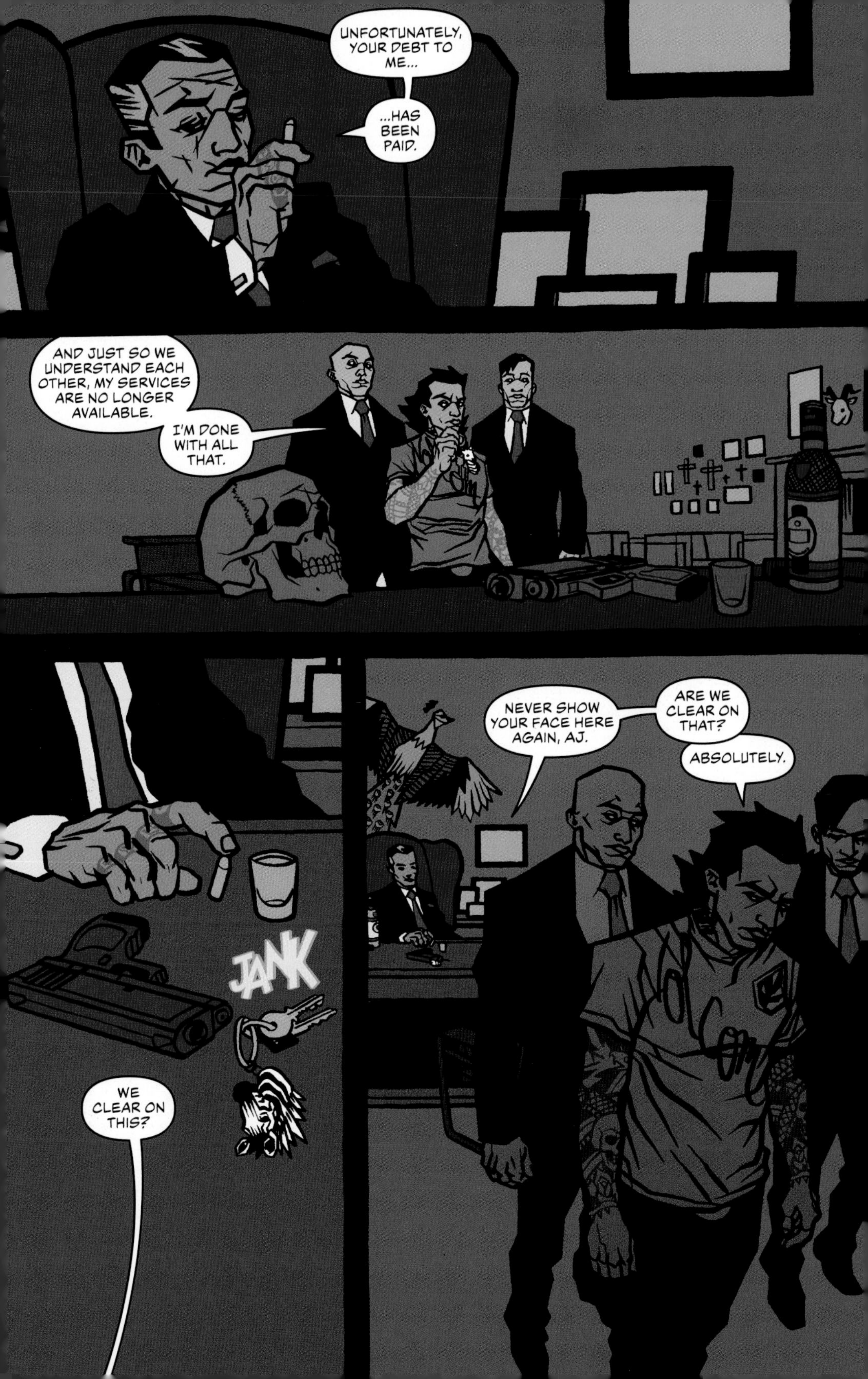
UNFORTUNATELY, YOUR DEBT TO ME...
...HAS BEEN PAID.
AND JUST SO WE UNDERSTAND EACH OTHER, MY SERVICES ARE NO LONGER AVAILABLE.
I'M DONE WITH ALL THAT.
JANK
WE CLEAR ON THIS?
NEVER SHOW YOUR FACE HERE AGAIN, AJ.
ARE WE CLEAR ON THAT?
ABSOLUTELY.

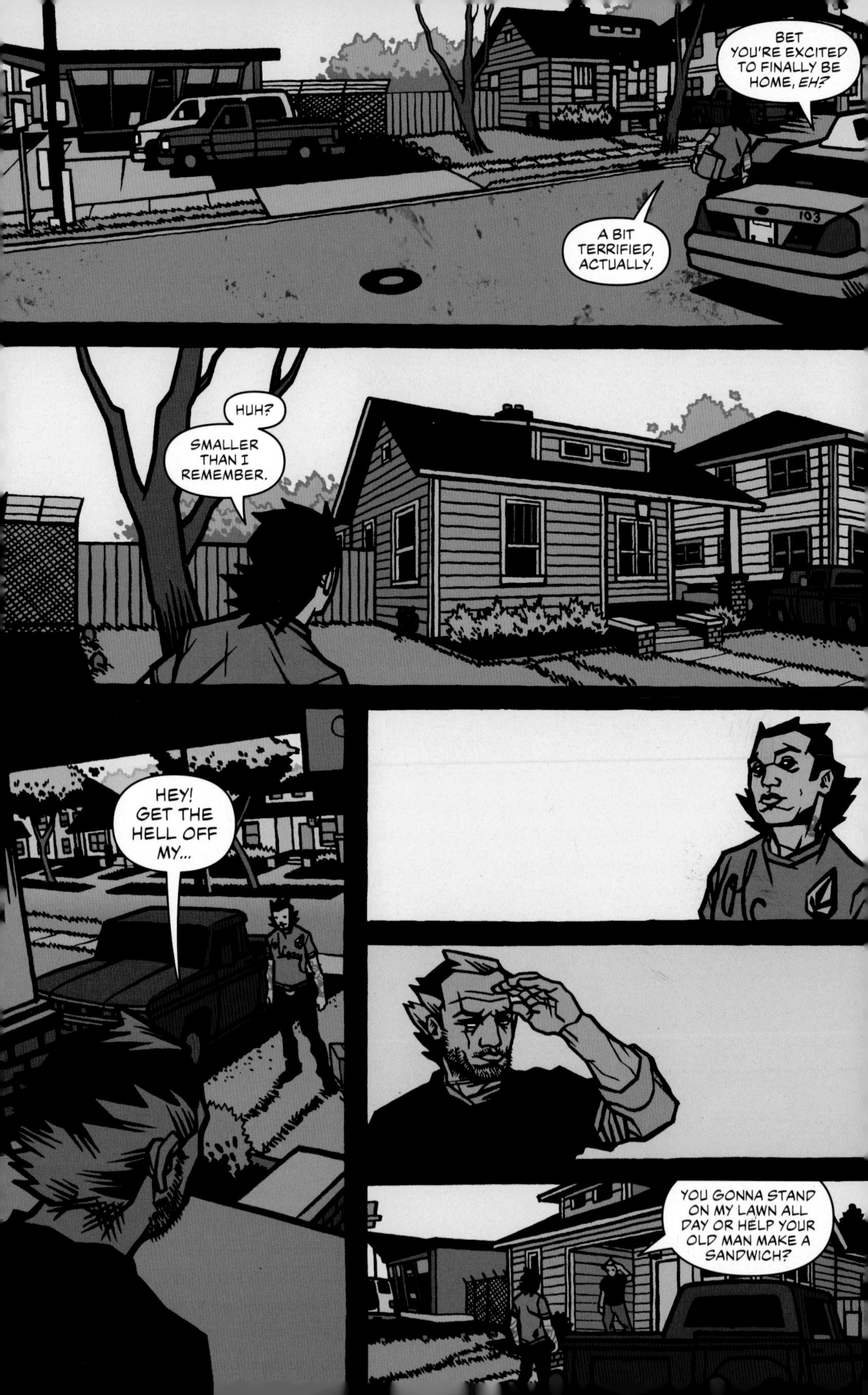
BET YOU'RE EXCITED TO FINALLY BE HOME, EH?
A BIT TERRIFIED, ACTUALLY.
HUH?
SMALLER THAN I REMEMBER.
HEY! GET THE HELL OFF MY...
YOU GONNA STAND ON MY LAWN ALL DAY OR HELP YOUR OLD MAN MAKE A SANDWICH?

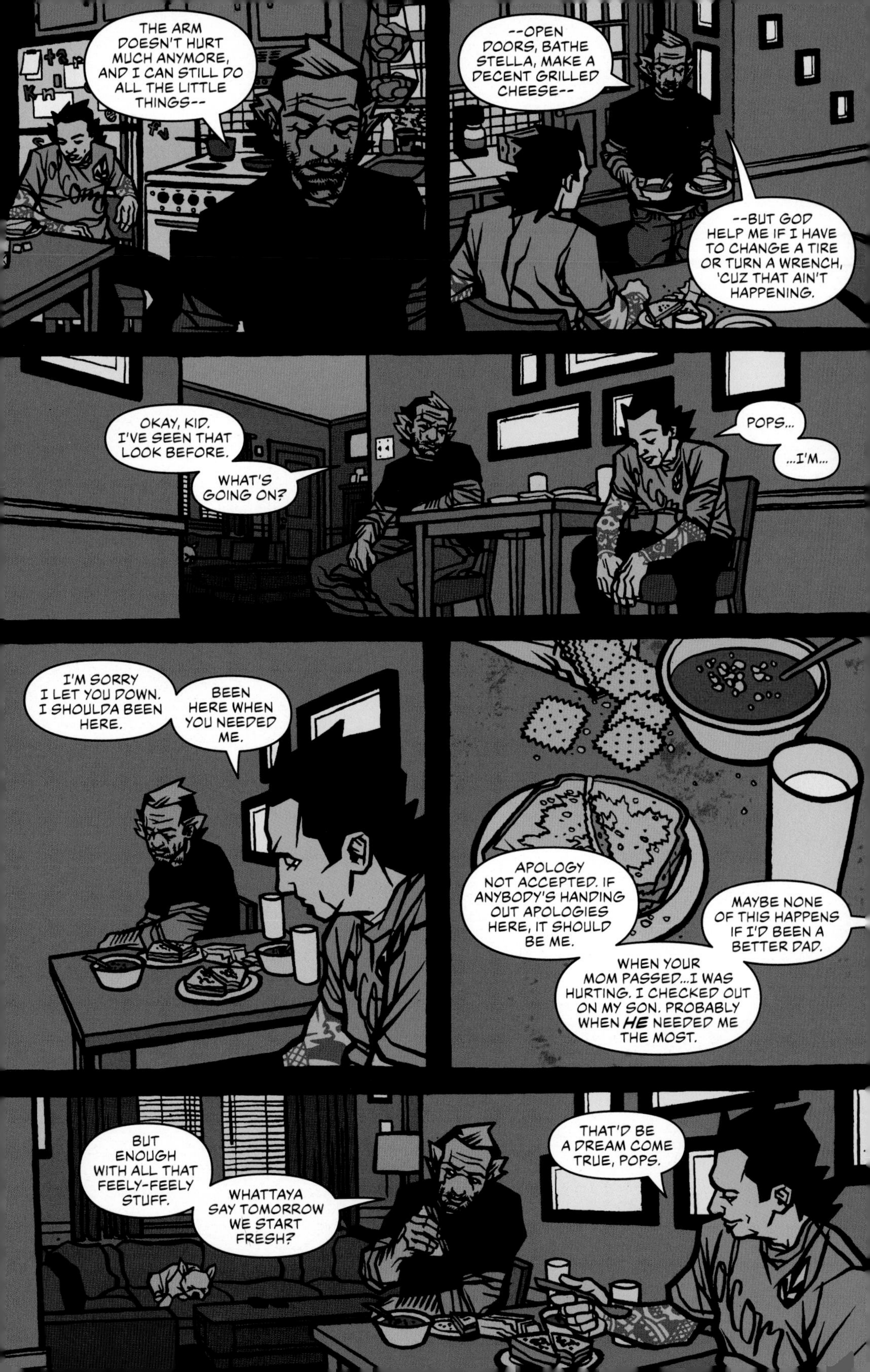
THE ARM DOESN'T HURT MUCH ANYMORE, AND I CAN STILL DO ALL THE LITTLE THINGS--
--OPEN DOORS, BATHE STELLA, MAKE A DECENT GRILLED CHEESE--
--BUT GOD HELP ME IF I HAVE TO CHANGE A TIRE OR TURN A WRENCH, 'CUZ THAT AIN'T HAPPENING.
OKAY, KID. I'VE SEEN THAT LOOK BEFORE.
WHAT'S GOING ON?
POPS...
...I'M...
I'M SORRY I LET YOU DOWN. I SHOULDA BEEN HERE.
BEEN HERE WHEN YOU NEEDED ME.
APOLOGY NOT ACCEPTED. IF ANYBODY'S HANDING OUT APOLOGIES HERE, IT SHOULD BE ME.
MAYBE NONE OF THIS HAPPENS IF I'D BEEN A BETTER DAD.
WHEN YOUR MOM PASSED...I WAS HURTING. I CHECKED OUT ON MY SON. PROBABLY WHEN *HE* NEEDED ME THE MOST.
BUT ENOUGH WITH ALL THAT FEELY-FEELY STUFF.
WHATTAYA SAY TOMORROW WE START FRESH?
THAT'D BE A DREAM COME TRUE, POPS.

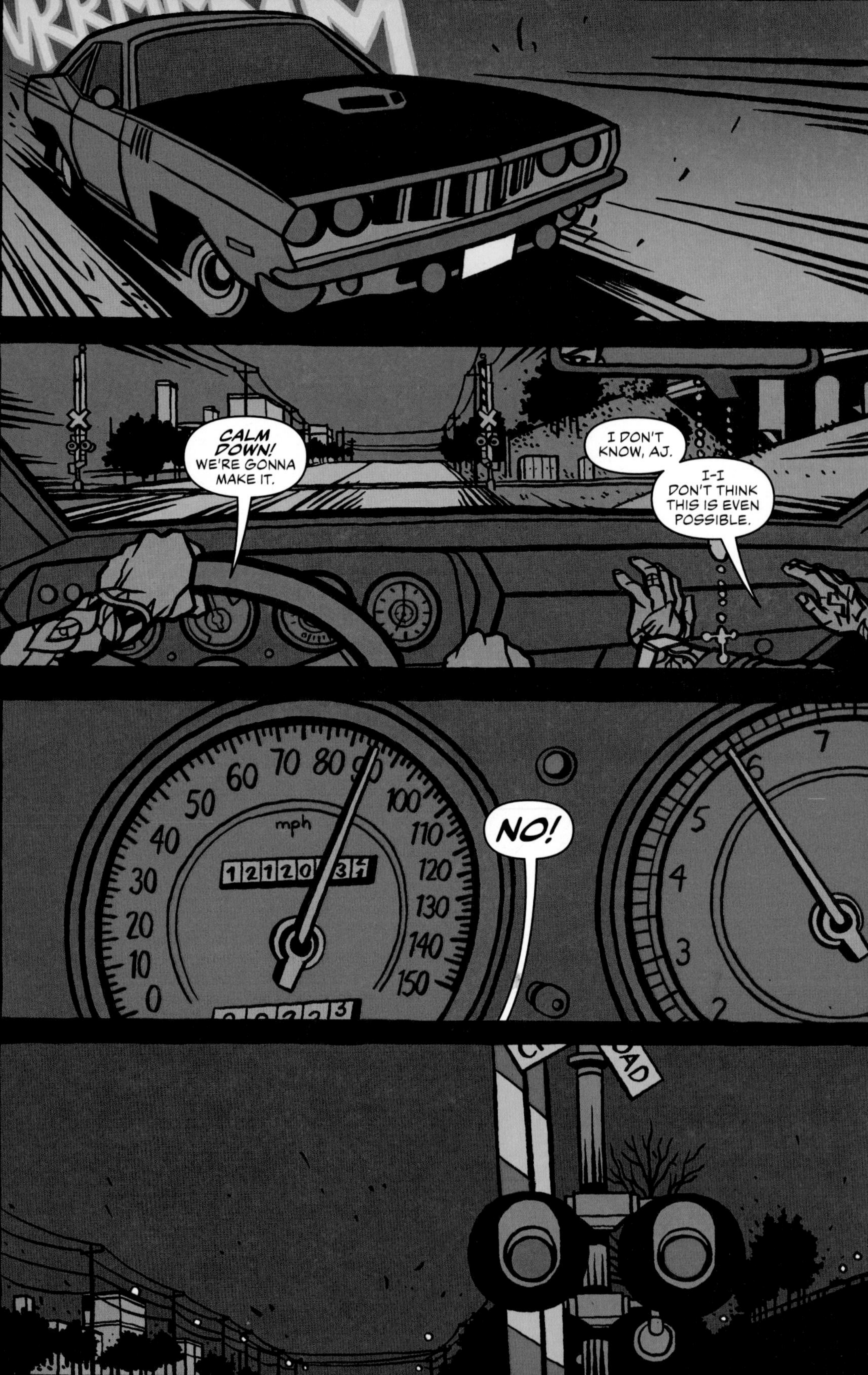

CALM DOWN! WE'RE GONNA MAKE IT.
I DON'T KNOW, AJ.
I-I DON'T THINK THIS IS EVEN POSSIBLE.
NO!

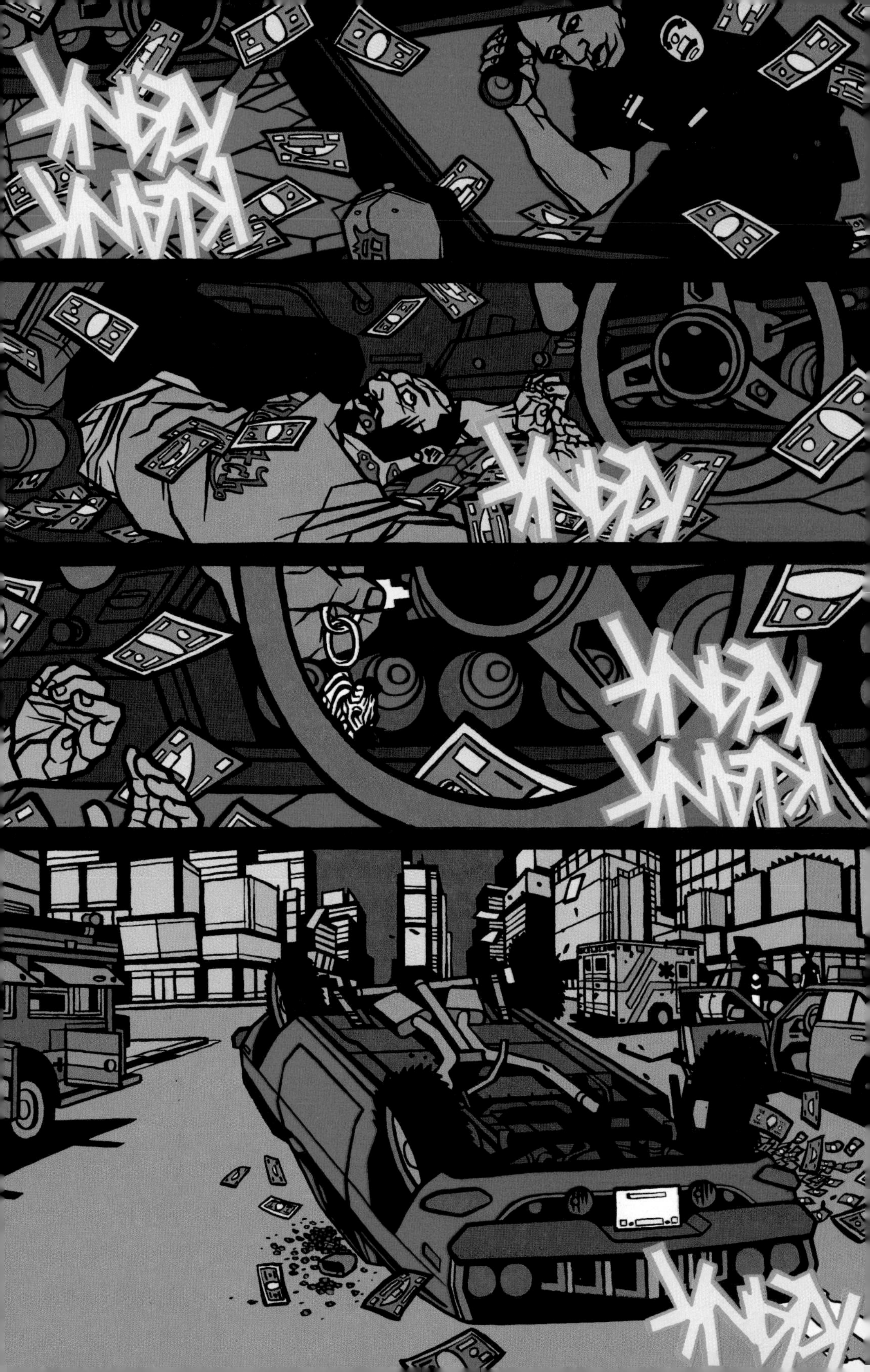
KLANK KLANK
KLANK
KLANK KLANK
KLANK

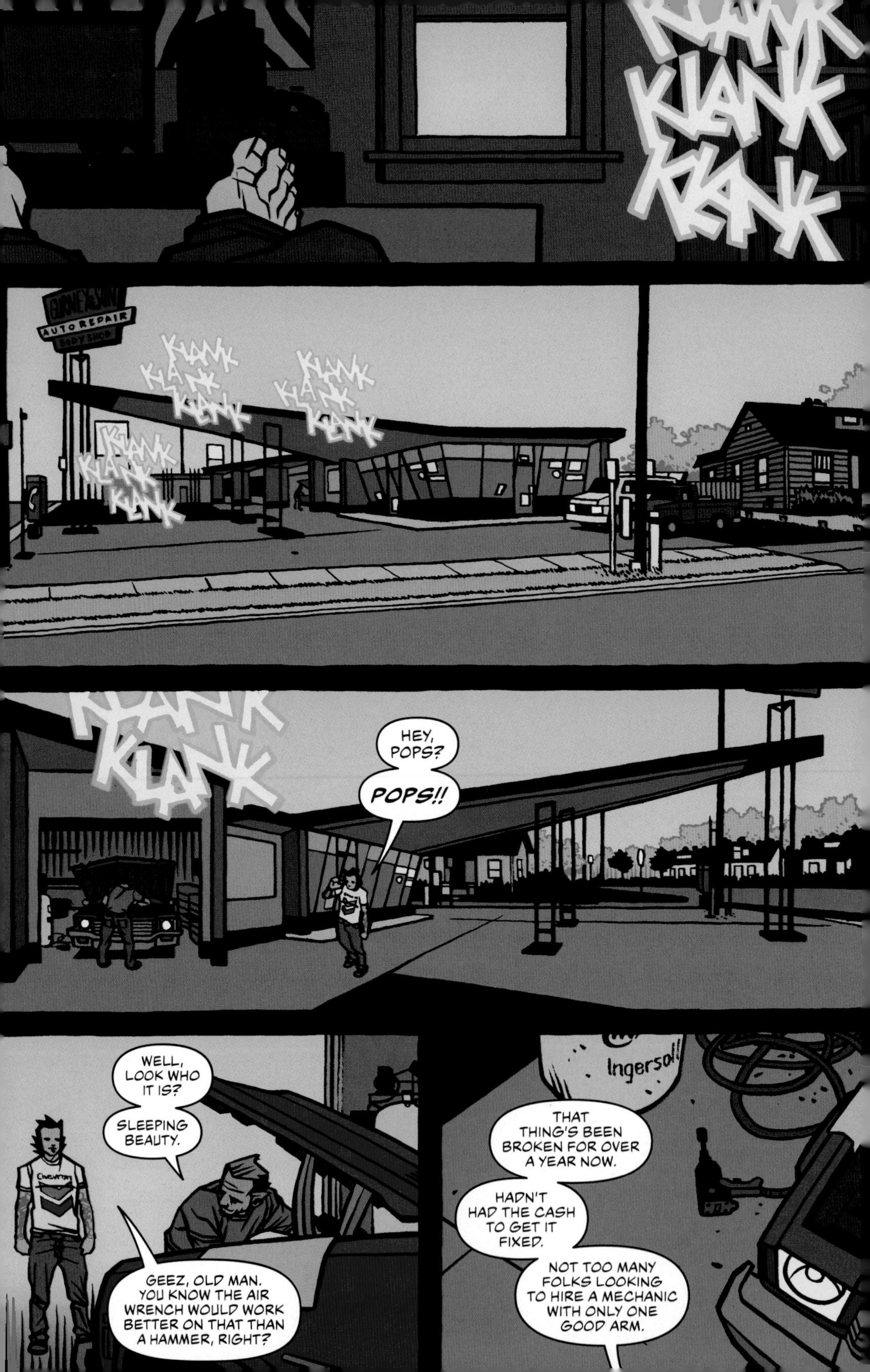
KLANK
KLANK
KLANK
AUTO REPAIR
BODY SHOP
KLANK
KLANK
KLANK
KLANK
KLANK
KLANK
KLANK
KLANK
KLANK
KLANK
KLANK
HEY, POPS?
POPS!!
WELL, LOOK WHO IT IS?
SLEEPING BEAUTY.
GEEZ, OLD MAN. YOU KNOW THE AIR WRENCH WOULD WORK BETTER ON THAT THAN A HAMMER, RIGHT?
Ingersoll
THAT THING'S BEEN BROKEN FOR OVER A YEAR NOW.
HADN'T HAD THE CASH TO GET IT FIXED.
NOT TOO MANY FOLKS LOOKING TO HIRE A MECHANIC WITH ONLY ONE GOOD ARM.

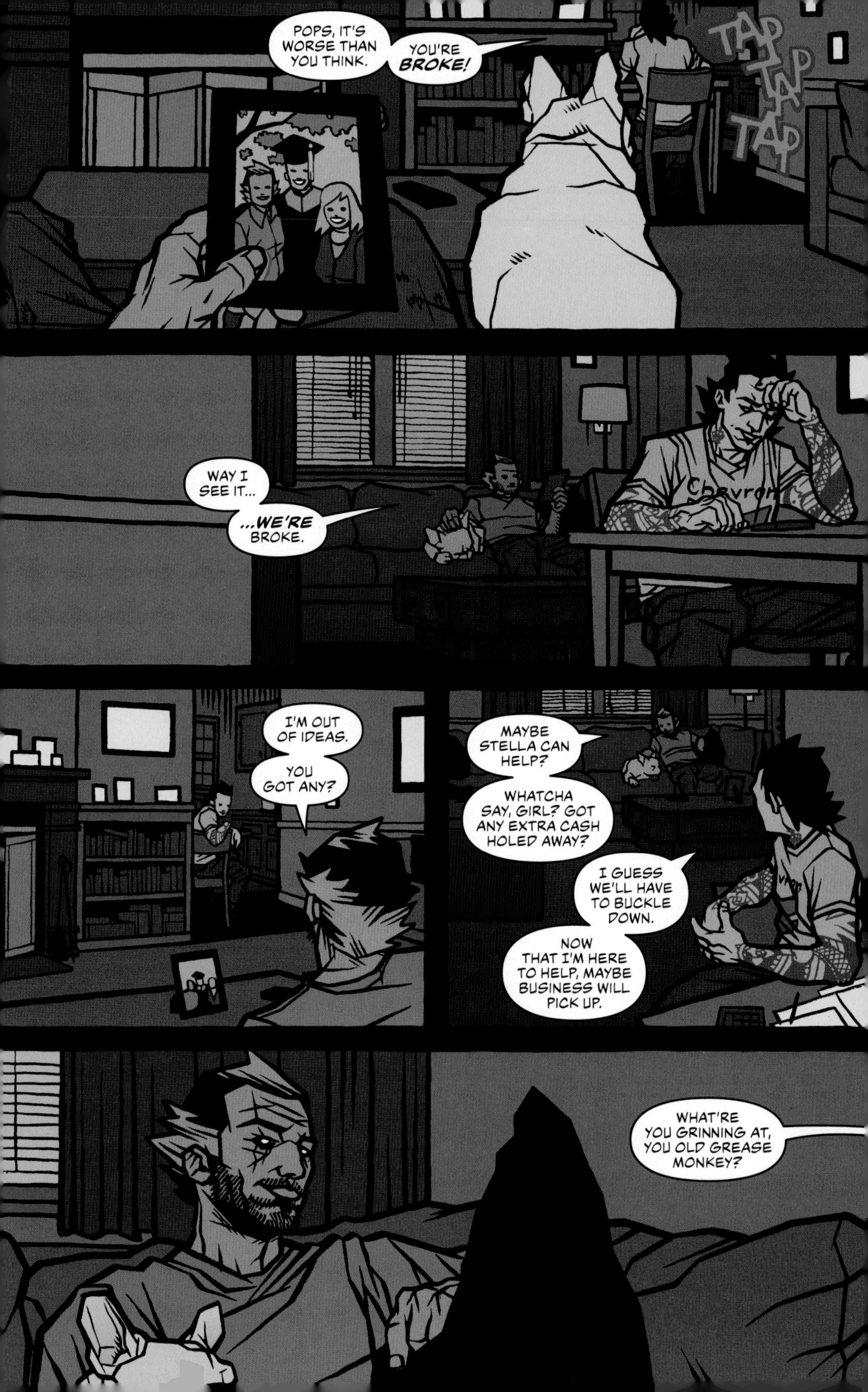
POPS, IT'S WORSE THAN YOU THINK.
YOU'RE **BROKE!**
TAP TAP TAP TAP
WAY I SEE IT...
...WE'RE BROKE.
I'M OUT OF IDEAS.
YOU GOT ANY?
MAYBE STELLA CAN HELP?
WHATCHA SAY, GIRL? GOT ANY EXTRA CASH HOLED AWAY?
I GUESS WE'LL HAVE TO BUCKLE DOWN.
NOW THAT I'M HERE TO HELP, MAYBE BUSINESS WILL PICK UP.
WHAT'RE YOU GRINNING AT, YOU OLD GREASE MONKEY?

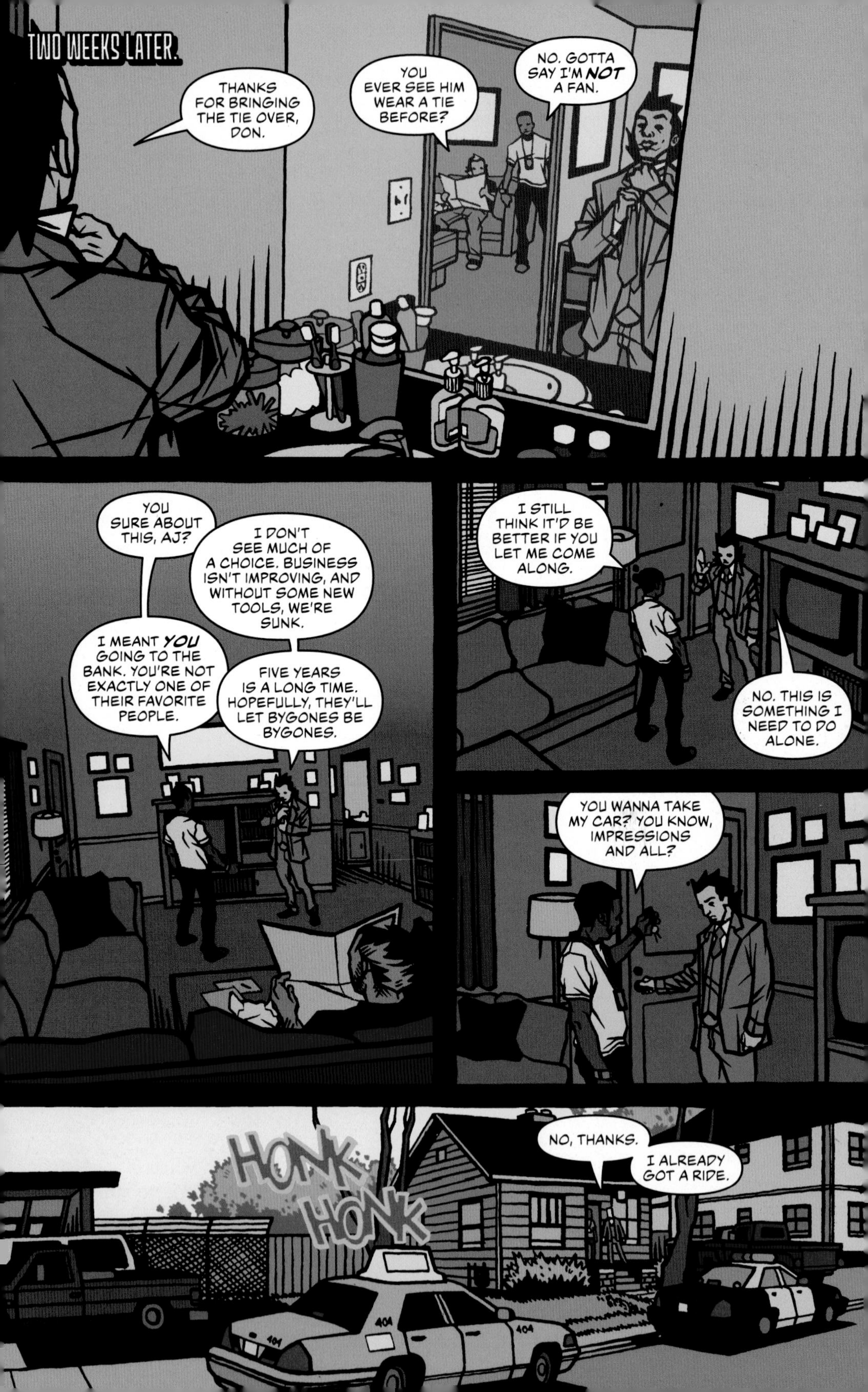
TWO WEEKS LATER.
THANKS FOR BRINGING THE TIE OVER, DON.
YOU EVER SEE HIM WEAR A TIE BEFORE?
NO. GOTTA SAY I'M NOT A FAN.
YOU SURE ABOUT THIS, AJ?
I DON'T SEE MUCH OF A CHOICE. BUSINESS ISN'T IMPROVING, AND WITHOUT SOME NEW TOOLS, WE'RE SUNK.
I MEANT YOU GOING TO THE BANK. YOU'RE NOT EXACTLY ONE OF THEIR FAVORITE PEOPLE.
FIVE YEARS IS A LONG TIME. HOPEFULLY, THEY'LL LET BYGONES BE BYGONES.
I STILL THINK IT'D BE BETTER IF YOU LET ME COME ALONG.
NO. THIS IS SOMETHING I NEED TO DO ALONE.
YOU WANNA TAKE MY CAR? YOU KNOW, IMPRESSIONS AND ALL?
HONK HONK
NO, THANKS.
I ALREADY GOT A RIDE.

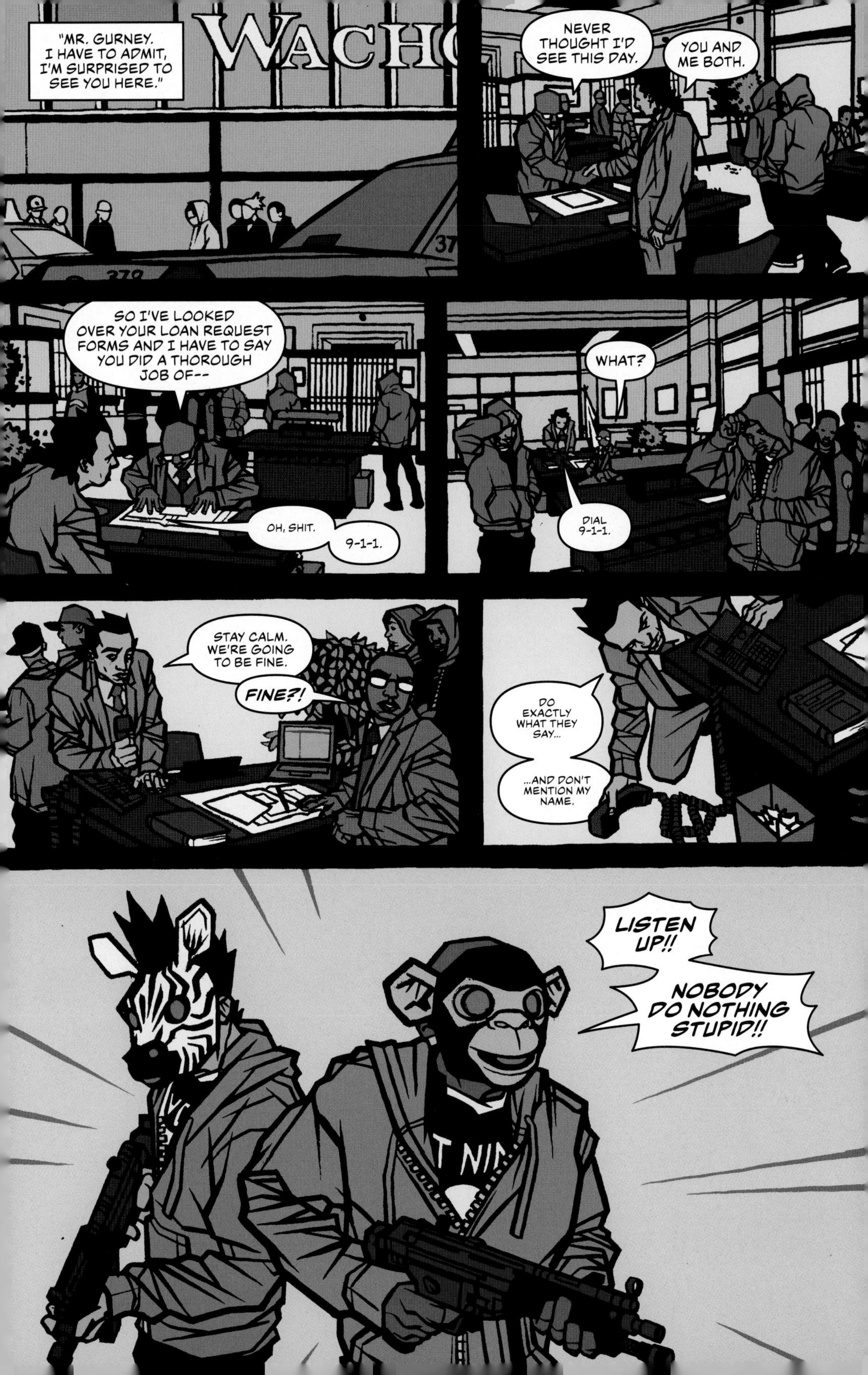
"MR. GURNEY. I HAVE TO ADMIT, I'M SURPRISED TO SEE YOU HERE."
WACHO
NEVER THOUGHT I'D SEE THIS DAY.
YOU AND ME BOTH.
SO I'VE LOOKED OVER YOUR LOAN REQUEST FORMS AND I HAVE TO SAY YOU DID A THOROUGH JOB OF--
OH, SHIT.
9-1-1.
WHAT?
DIAL 9-1-1.
STAY CALM. WE'RE GOING TO BE FINE.
FINE?!
DO EXACTLY WHAT THEY SAY...
...AND DON'T MENTION MY NAME.
LISTEN UP!!
NOBODY DO NOTHING STUPID!!

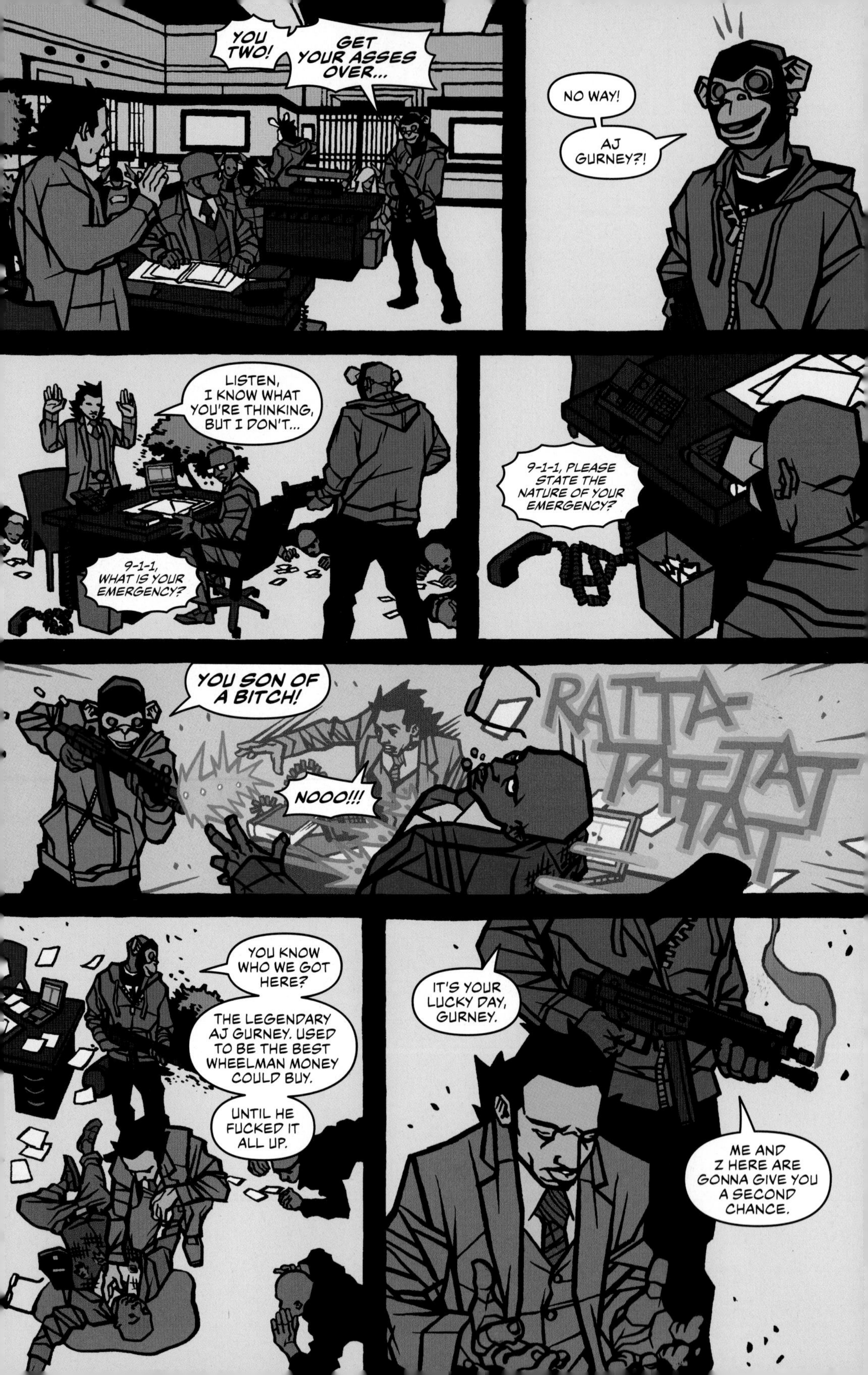
YOU TWO!
GET YOUR ASSES OVER...
NO WAY!
AJ GURNEY?!
LISTEN, I KNOW WHAT YOU'RE THINKING, BUT I DON'T...
9-1-1, WHAT IS YOUR EMERGENCY?
9-1-1, PLEASE STATE THE NATURE OF YOUR EMERGENCY?
YOU SON OF A BITCH!
NOOO!!!
RATTA-TAT-TAT-TAT
YOU KNOW WHO WE GOT HERE?
THE LEGENDARY AJ GURNEY. USED TO BE THE BEST WHEELMAN MONEY COULD BUY.
UNTIL HE FUCKED IT ALL UP.
IT'S YOUR LUCKY DAY, GURNEY.
ME AND Z HERE ARE GONNA GIVE YOU A SECOND CHANCE.

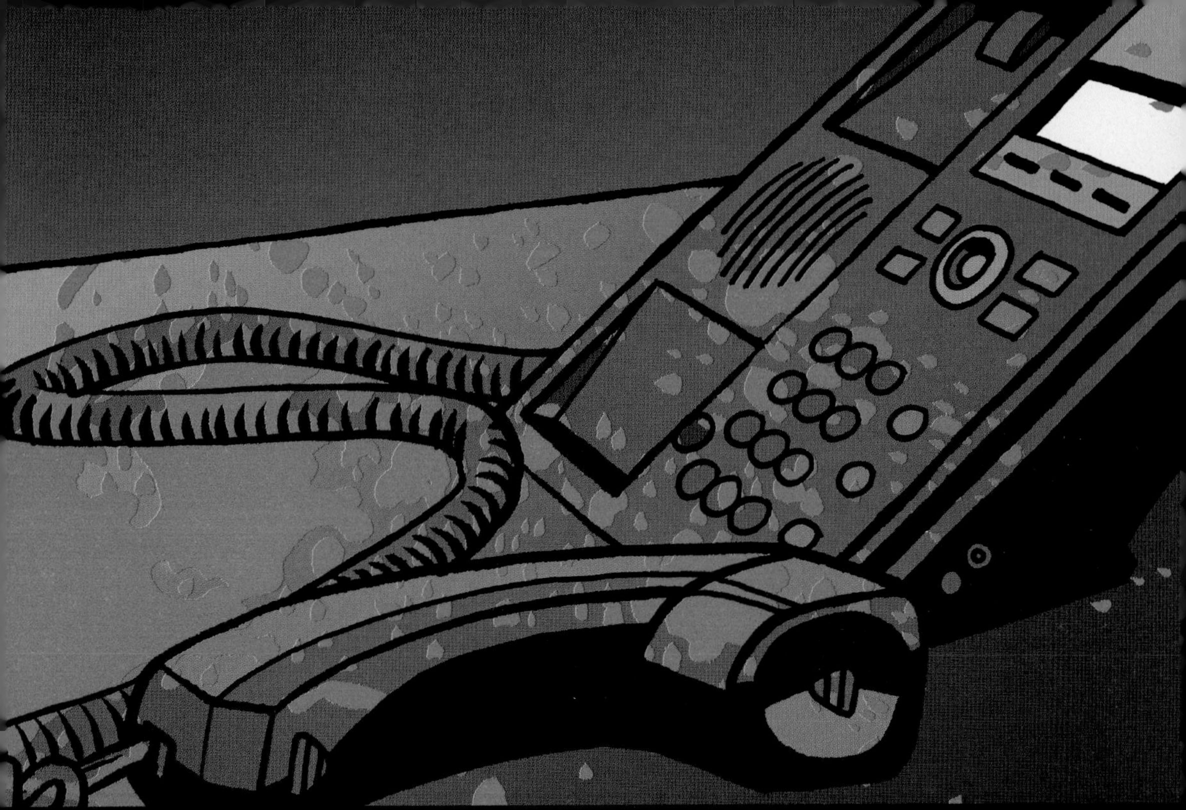

I'm traveling a one-way road, and I'm not fooling myself as to what the end will be.
- John Dillinger

CHAPTER TWO

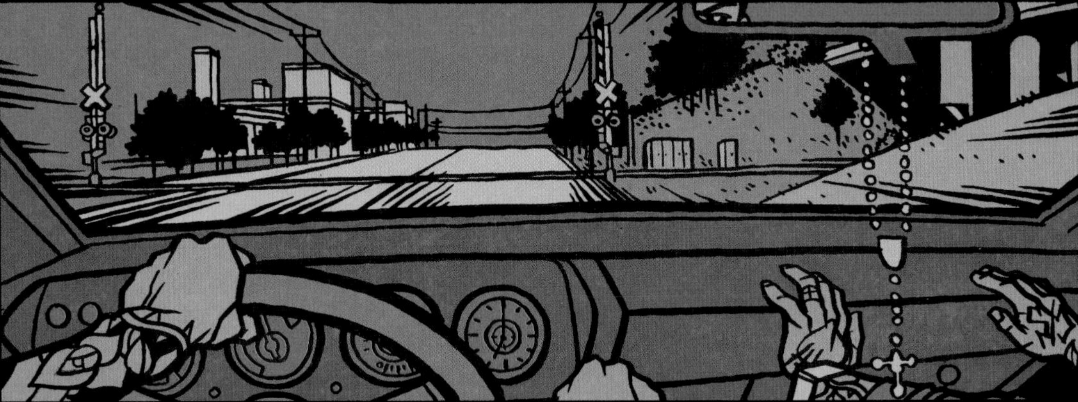

"COME OUT WITH YOUR HANDS UP!"

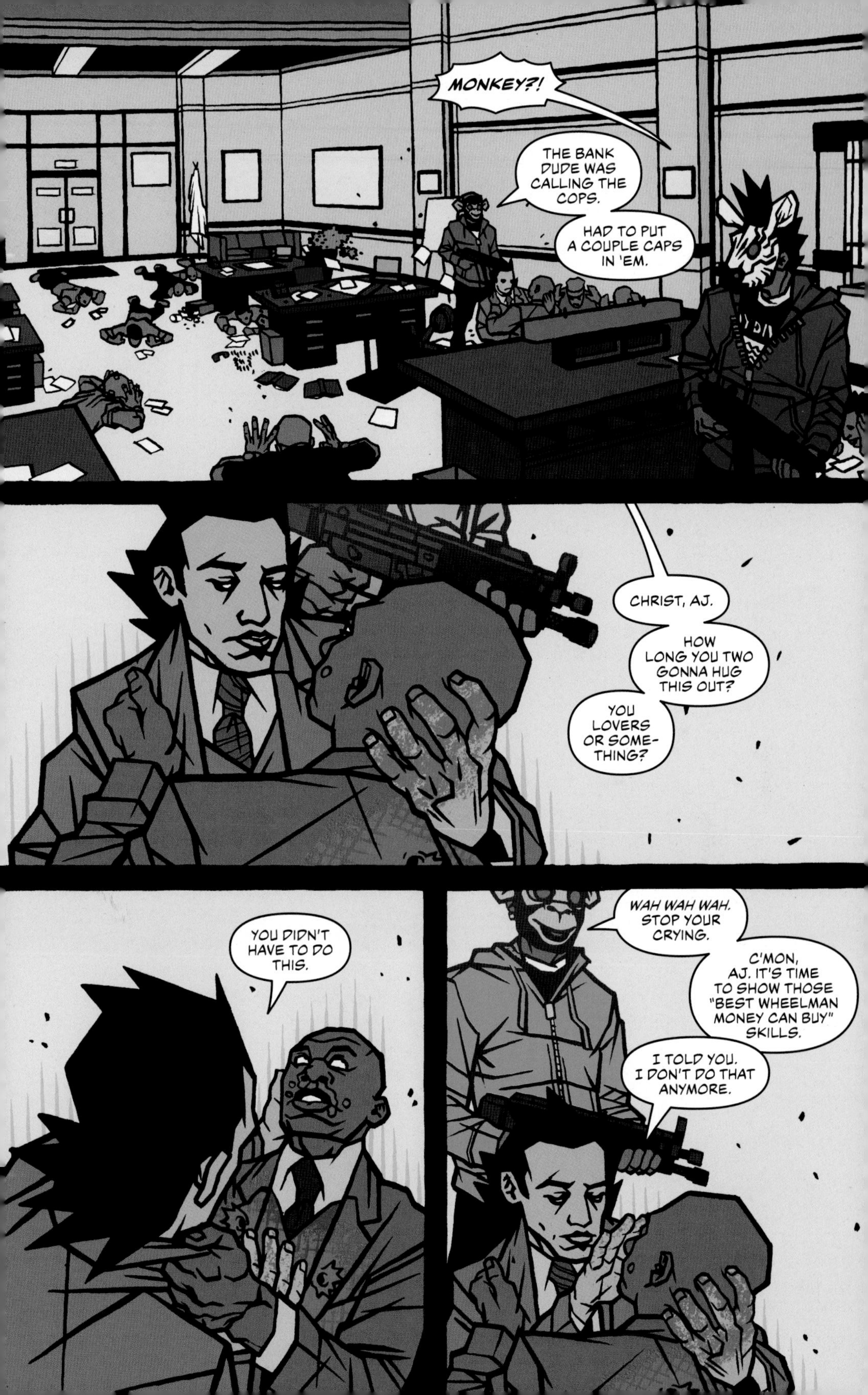
MONKEY?!
THE BANK DUDE WAS CALLING THE COPS.
HAD TO PUT A COUPLE CAPS IN 'EM.
CHRIST, AJ.
HOW LONG YOU TWO GONNA HUG THIS OUT?
YOU LOVERS OR SOME-THING?
YOU DIDN'T HAVE TO DO THIS.
WAH WAH WAH. STOP YOUR CRYING.
C'MON, AJ. IT'S TIME TO SHOW THOSE "BEST WHEELMAN MONEY CAN BUY" SKILLS.
I TOLD YOU. I DON'T DO THAT ANYMORE.

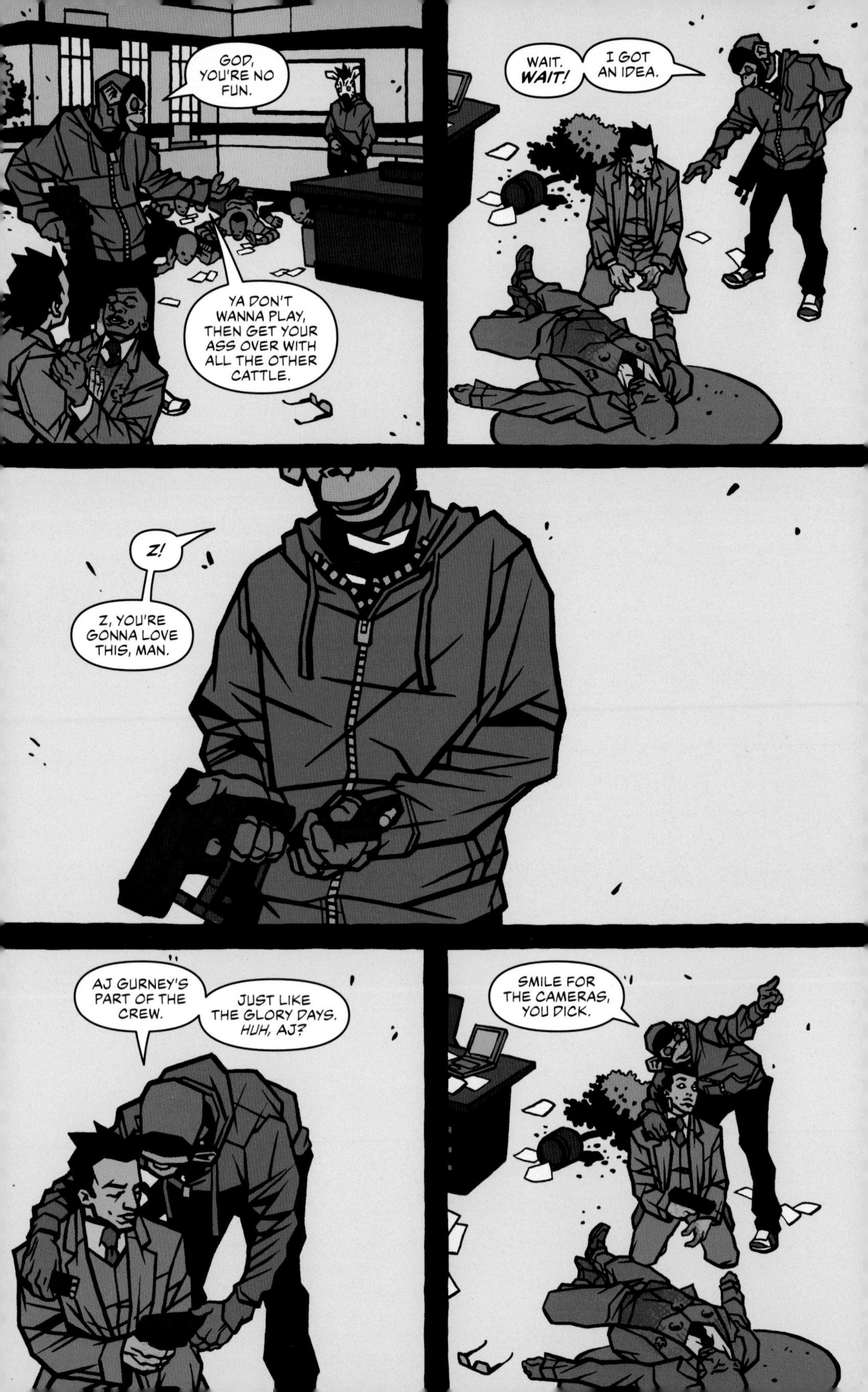
GOD, YOU'RE NO FUN.
YA DON'T WANNA PLAY, THEN GET YOUR ASS OVER WITH ALL THE OTHER CATTLE.
WAIT. *WAIT!*
I GOT AN IDEA.
Z!
Z, YOU'RE GONNA LOVE THIS, MAN.
AJ GURNEY'S PART OF THE CREW.
JUST LIKE THE GLORY DAYS. *HUH, AJ?*
SMILE FOR THE CAMERAS, YOU DICK.

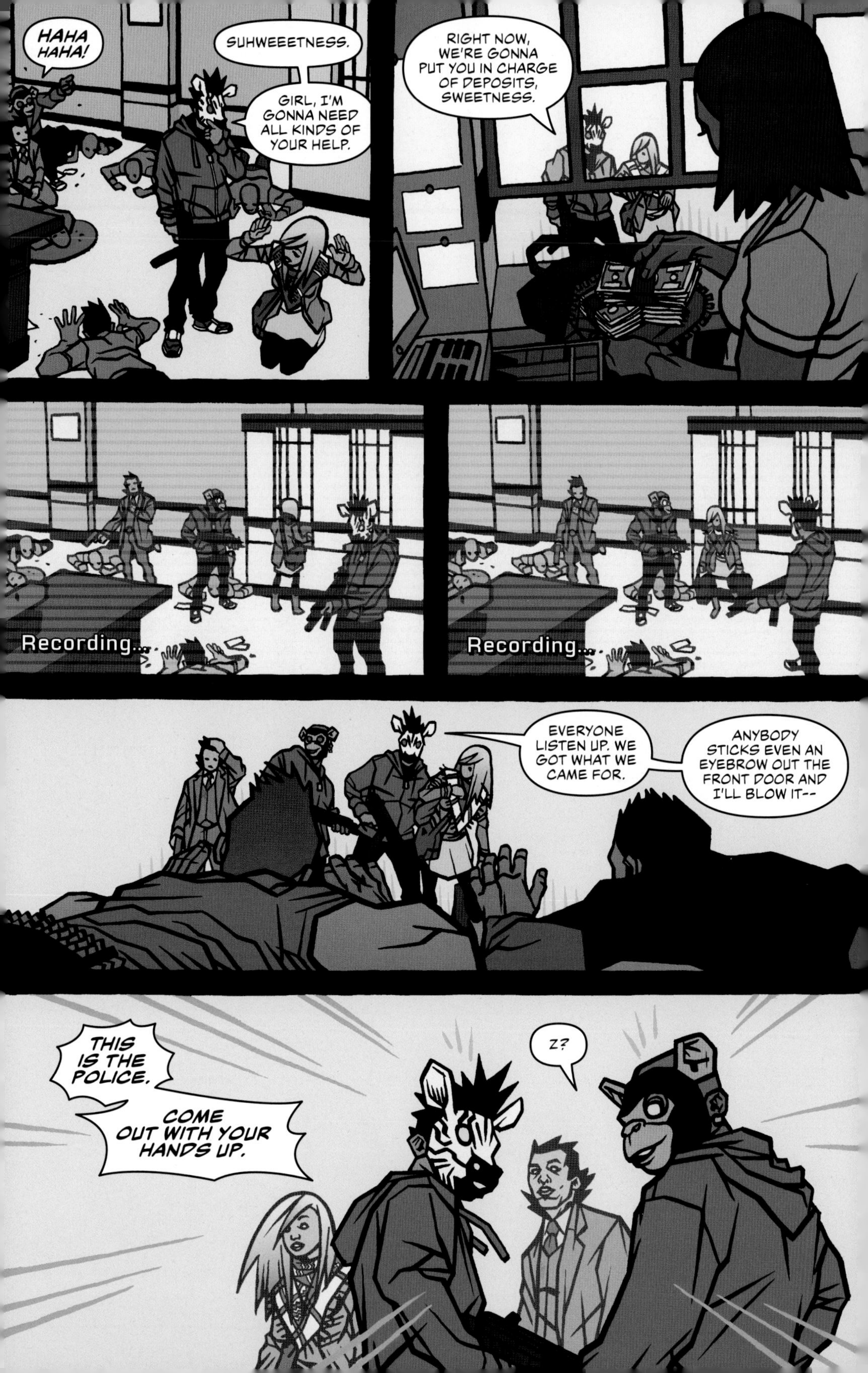
HAHA HAHA!
SUHWEEETNESS.
GIRL, I'M GONNA NEED ALL KINDS OF YOUR HELP.
RIGHT NOW, WE'RE GONNA PUT YOU IN CHARGE OF DEPOSITS, SWEETNESS.
Recording...
Recording...
EVERYONE LISTEN UP. WE GOT WHAT WE CAME FOR.
ANYBODY STICKS EVEN AN EYEBROW OUT THE FRONT DOOR AND I'LL BLOW IT--
THIS IS THE POLICE.
COME OUT WITH YOUR HANDS UP.
Z?

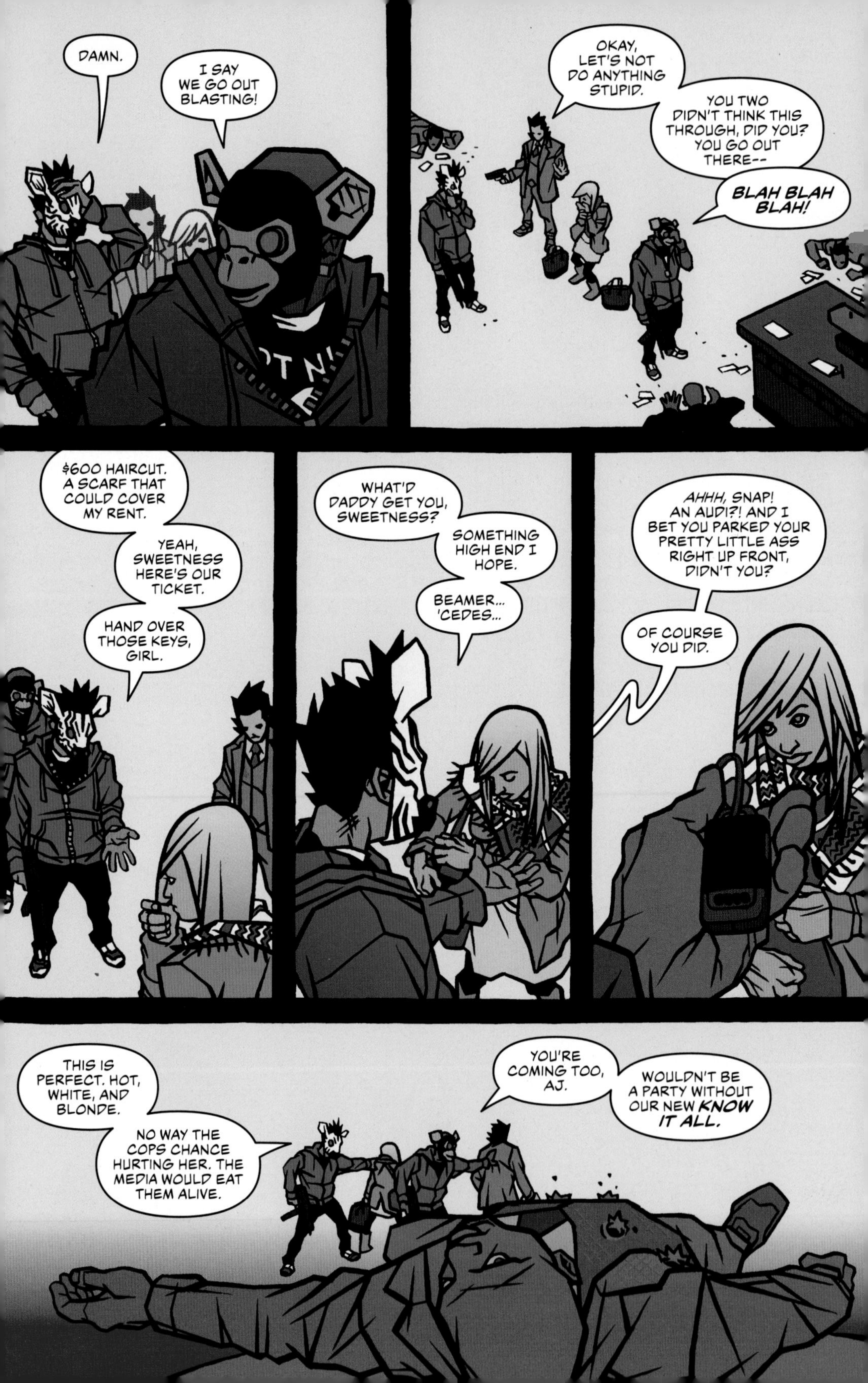
DAMN.
I SAY WE GO OUT BLASTING!
OKAY, LET'S NOT DO ANYTHING STUPID.
YOU TWO DIDN'T THINK THIS THROUGH, DID YOU? YOU GO OUT THERE--
BLAH BLAH BLAH!
$600 HAIRCUT. A SCARF THAT COULD COVER MY RENT.
YEAH, SWEETNESS HERE'S OUR TICKET.
HAND OVER THOSE KEYS, GIRL.
WHAT'D DADDY GET YOU, SWEETNESS?
SOMETHING HIGH END I HOPE.
BEAMER... 'CEDES...
AHHH, SNAP! AN AUDI?! AND I BET YOU PARKED YOUR PRETTY LITTLE ASS RIGHT UP FRONT, DIDN'T YOU?
OF COURSE YOU DID.
THIS IS PERFECT. HOT, WHITE, AND BLONDE.
NO WAY THE COPS CHANCE HURTING HER. THE MEDIA WOULD EAT THEM ALIVE.
YOU'RE COMING TOO, AJ.
WOULDN'T BE A PARTY WITHOUT OUR NEW KNOW IT ALL.

ANYBODY EVEN LOOK AT US FUNNY AND I SWEAR TO GOD!

PUT GURNEY IN THE DRIVER'S SEAT.

YOU THINK WE'LL MAKE THE NEWS, AJ?

MAYBE WE'LL GO VIRAL... BE ON ONE OF THEM VIRAL SHOWS.

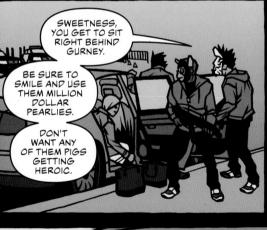

SWEETNESS, YOU GET TO SIT RIGHT BEHIND GURNEY.

BE SURE TO SMILE AND USE THEM MILLION DOLLAR PEARLIES.

DON'T WANT ANY OF THEM PIGS GETTING HEROIC.

START 'ER UP.

SLAM

GURNEY, YOU DO **NOT** WANT TO PLAY GAMES WITH ME.

START THE CAR!

Z?

THEY... THEY CAN'T SHOOT BACK, RIGHT?

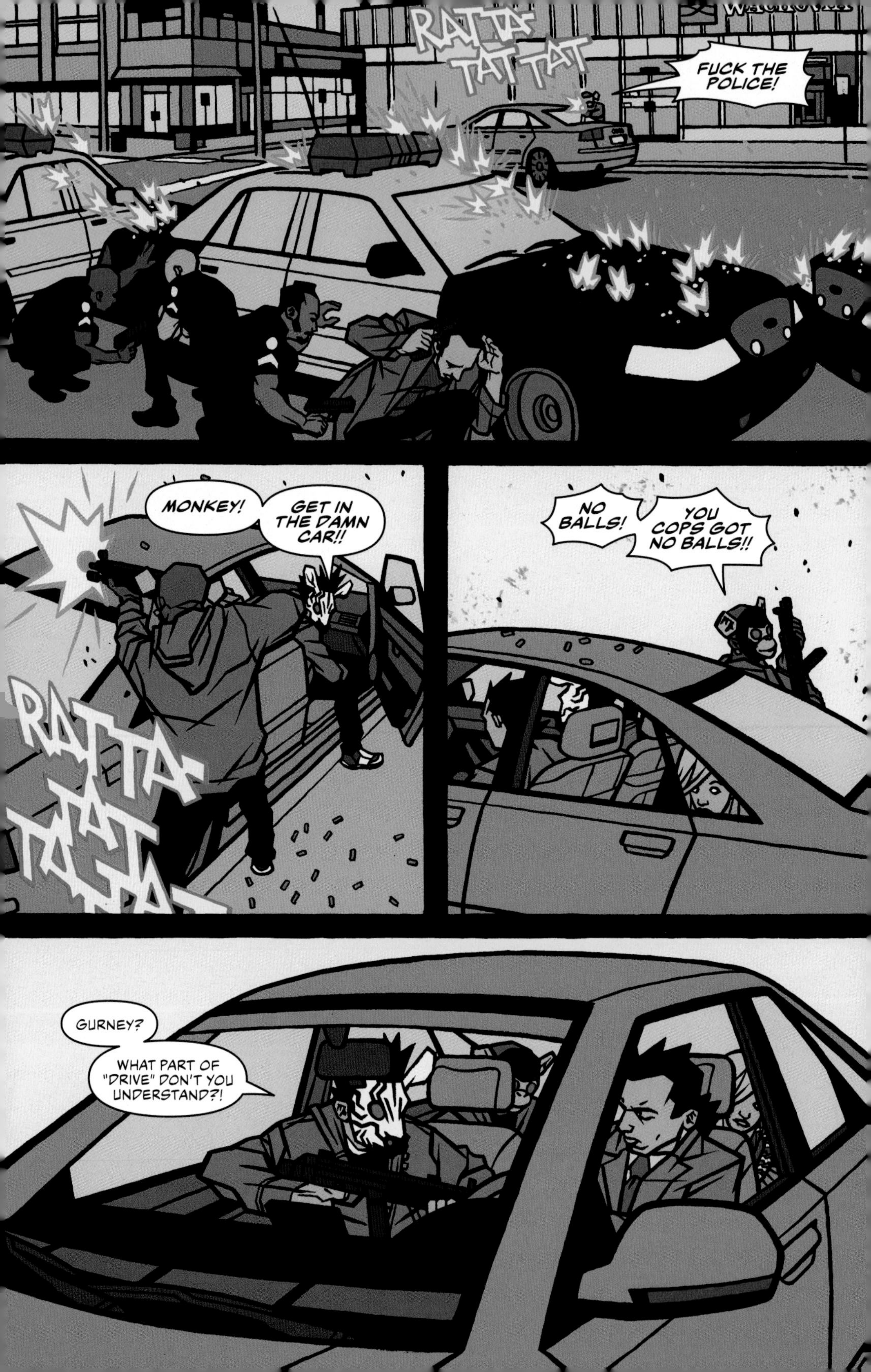
RATTA-TAT TAT
FUCK THE POLICE!
MONKEY!
GET IN THE DAMN CAR!!
RATTA-TAT
NO BALLS!
YOU COPS GOT NO BALLS!!
GURNEY?
WHAT PART OF "DRIVE" DON'T YOU UNDERSTAND?!

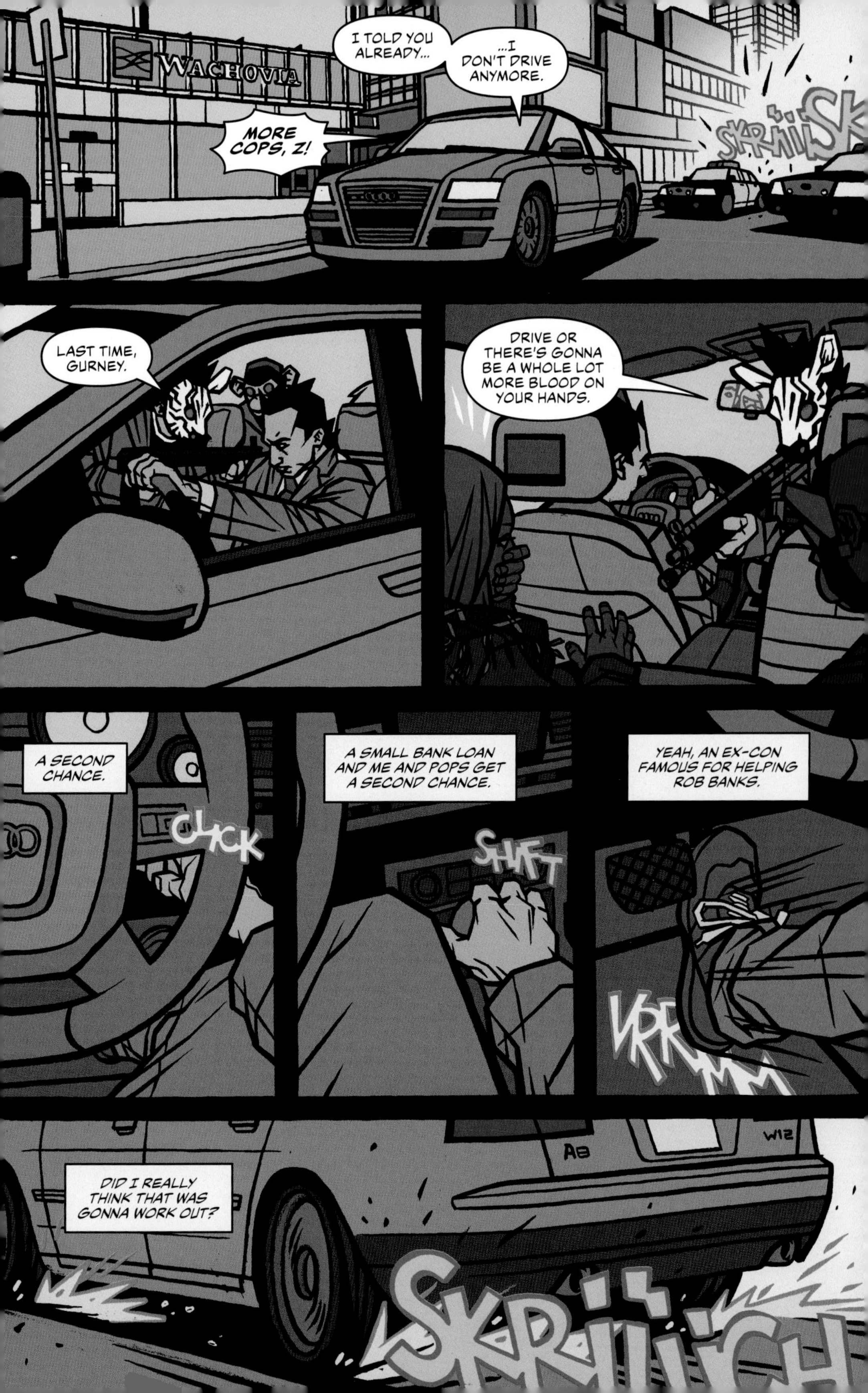
WACHOVIA
I TOLD YOU ALREADY...
...I DON'T DRIVE ANYMORE.
MORE COPS, Z!
SKRIIISK
LAST TIME, GURNEY.
DRIVE OR THERE'S GONNA BE A WHOLE LOT MORE BLOOD ON YOUR HANDS.
A SECOND CHANCE.
CLICK
A SMALL BANK LOAN AND ME AND POPS GET A SECOND CHANCE.
SHIFT
YEAH, AN EX-CON FAMOUS FOR HELPING ROB BANKS.
VRRMMM
W12
A8
DID I REALLY THINK THAT WAS GONNA WORK OUT?
SKRIIICH

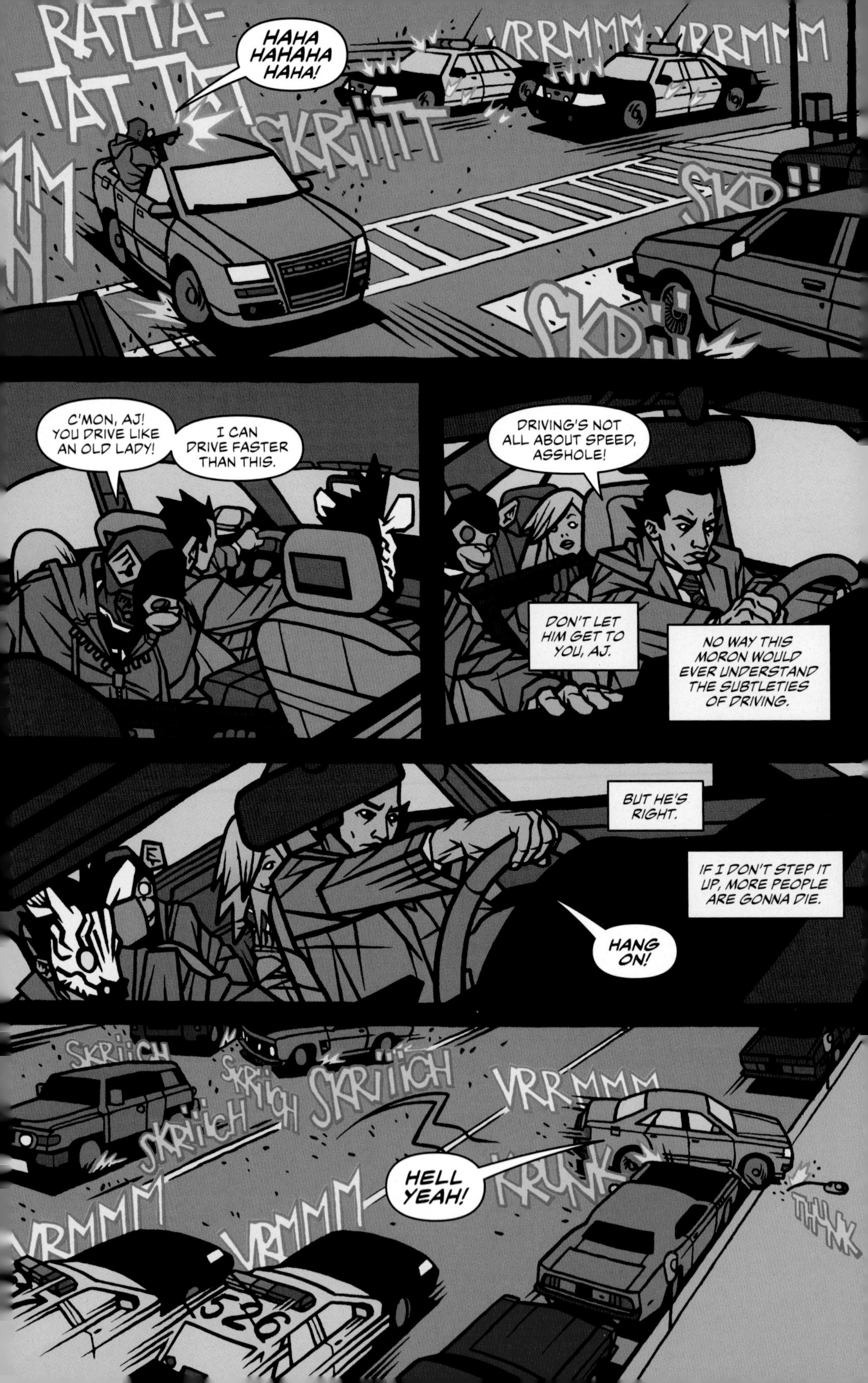
RATTA-TAT TAT
HAHA HAHAHA HAHA!
VRRMMM VRRMMM
SKRIIITT
SKD!!
SKD!!
C'MON, AJ! YOU DRIVE LIKE AN OLD LADY!
I CAN DRIVE FASTER THAN THIS.
DRIVING'S NOT ALL ABOUT SPEED, ASSHOLE!
DON'T LET HIM GET TO YOU, AJ.
NO WAY THIS MORON WOULD EVER UNDERSTAND THE SUBTLETIES OF DRIVING.
BUT HE'S RIGHT.
IF I DON'T STEP IT UP, MORE PEOPLE ARE GONNA DIE.
HANG ON!
SKRIICH
SKRIICH
SKRIICH
SKRIICH
VRRMMM
HELL YEAH!
KRUNK
THUNK
VRMMM
VRMMM

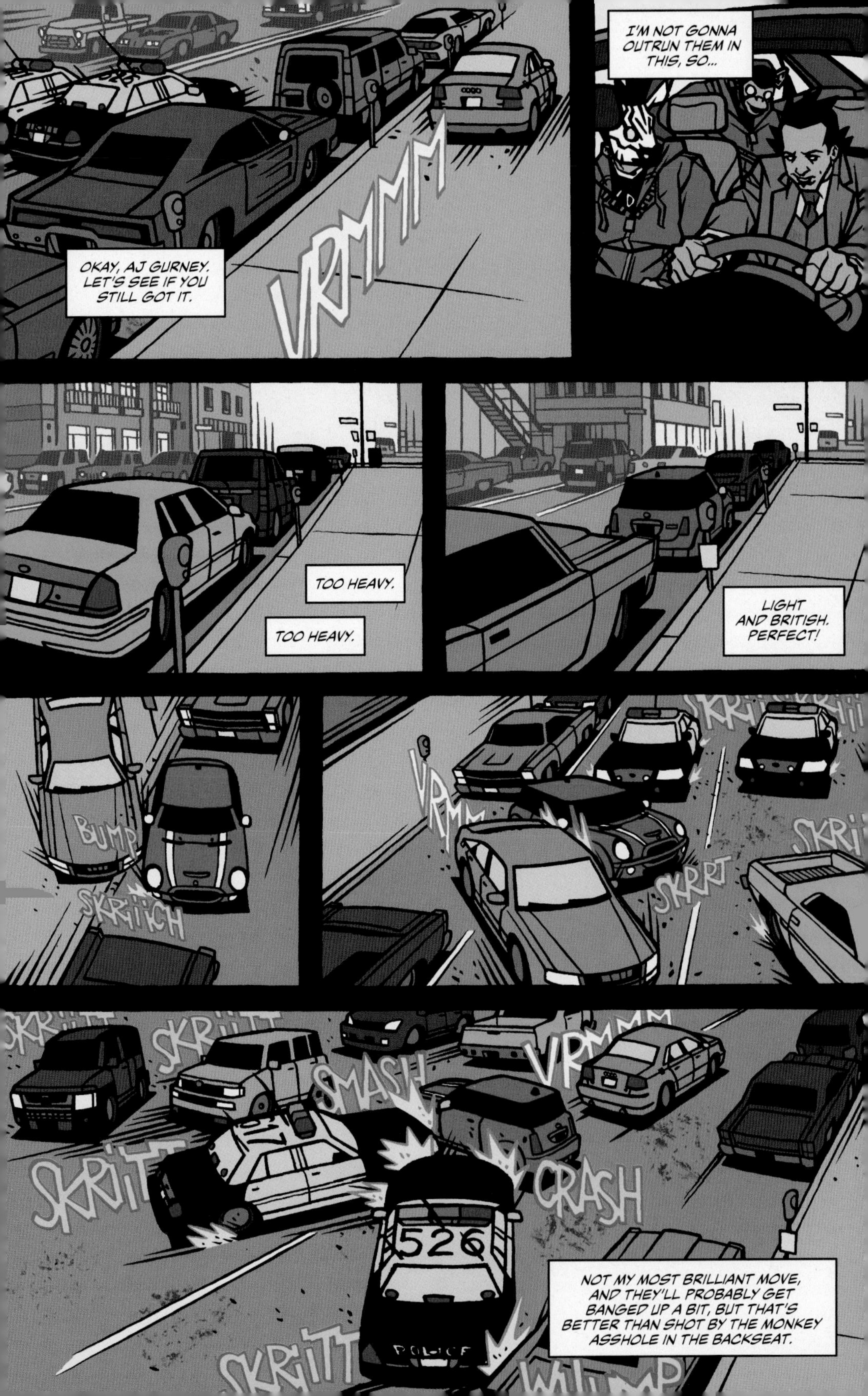
OKAY, AJ GURNEY. LET'S SEE IF YOU STILL GOT IT.
VRMMM
I'M NOT GONNA OUTRUN THEM IN THIS, SO...
TOO HEAVY.
TOO HEAVY.
LIGHT AND BRITISH. PERFECT!
BUMP
SKRiiTCH
VRMM
SKRRT
SKRiiTT
SMASH
VRMMM
SKRiiTT
CRASH
526
NOT MY MOST BRILLIANT MOVE, AND THEY'LL PROBABLY GET BANGED UP A BIT, BUT THAT'S BETTER THAN SHOT BY THE MONKEY ASSHOLE IN THE BACKSEAT.

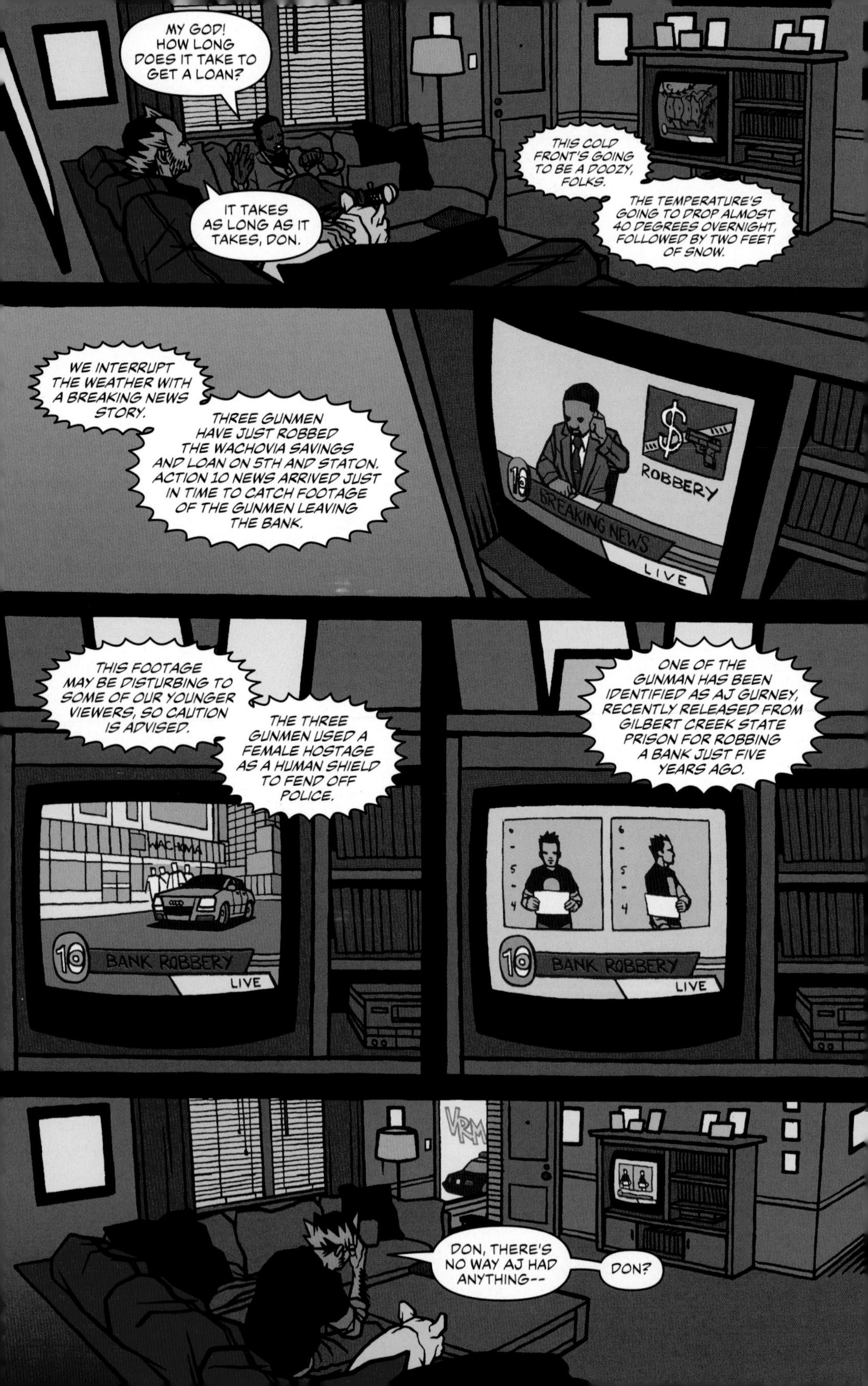
MY GOD! HOW LONG DOES IT TAKE TO GET A LOAN?
IT TAKES AS LONG AS IT TAKES, DON.
THIS COLD FRONT'S GOING TO BE A DOOZY, FOLKS.
THE TEMPERATURE'S GOING TO DROP ALMOST 40 DEGREES OVERNIGHT, FOLLOWED BY TWO FEET OF SNOW.
WE INTERRUPT THE WEATHER WITH A BREAKING NEWS STORY.
THREE GUNMEN HAVE JUST ROBBED THE WACHOVIA SAVINGS AND LOAN ON 5TH AND STATON. ACTION 10 NEWS ARRIVED JUST IN TIME TO CATCH FOOTAGE OF THE GUNMEN LEAVING THE BANK.
ROBBERY
BREAKING NEWS
LIVE
THIS FOOTAGE MAY BE DISTURBING TO SOME OF OUR YOUNGER VIEWERS, SO CAUTION IS ADVISED.
THE THREE GUNMEN USED A FEMALE HOSTAGE AS A HUMAN SHIELD TO FEND OFF POLICE.
BANK ROBBERY
LIVE
ONE OF THE GUNMAN HAS BEEN IDENTIFIED AS AJ GURNEY, RECENTLY RELEASED FROM GILBERT CREEK STATE PRISON FOR ROBBING A BANK JUST FIVE YEARS AGO.
BANK ROBBERY
LIVE
VRM
DON, THERE'S NO WAY AJ HAD ANYTHING--
DON?

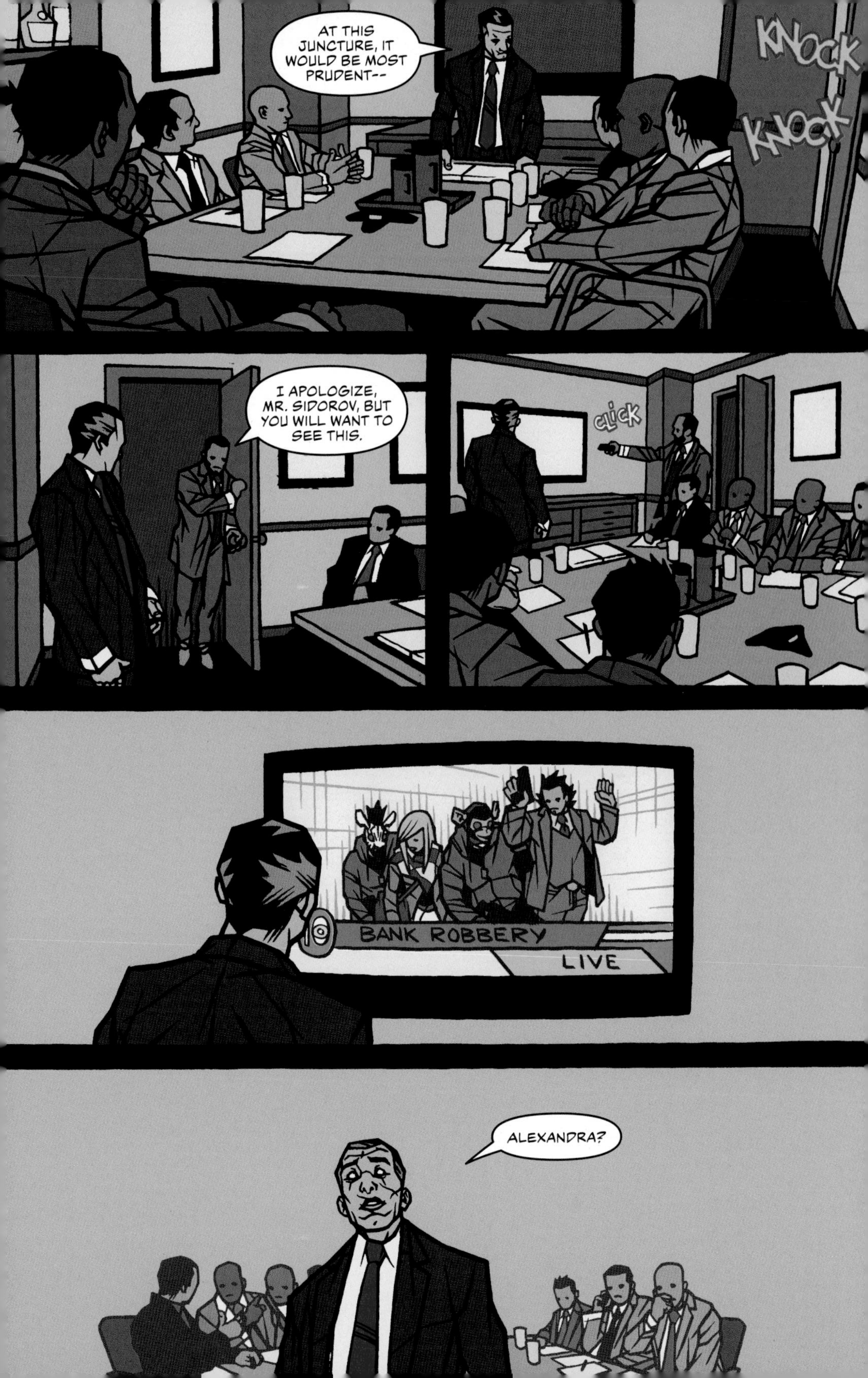
AT THIS JUNCTURE, IT WOULD BE MOST PRUDENT--
KNOCK
KNOCK
I APOLOGIZE, MR. SIDOROV, BUT YOU WILL WANT TO SEE THIS.
CLICK
BANK ROBBERY
LIVE
ALEXANDRA?

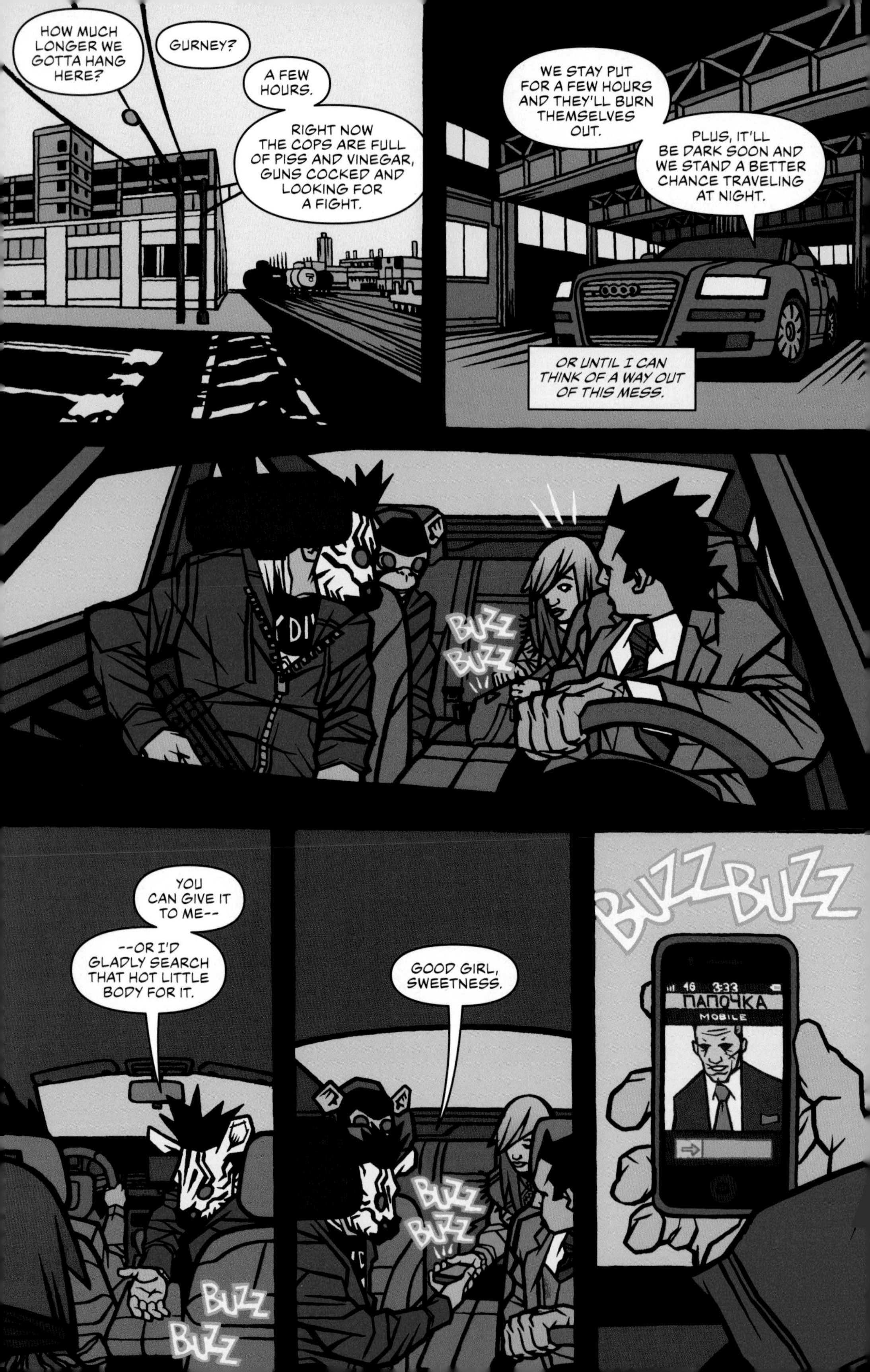
HOW MUCH LONGER WE GOTTA HANG HERE?
GURNEY?
A FEW HOURS.
RIGHT NOW THE COPS ARE FULL OF PISS AND VINEGAR, GUNS COCKED AND LOOKING FOR A FIGHT.
WE STAY PUT FOR A FEW HOURS AND THEY'LL BURN THEMSELVES OUT.
PLUS, IT'LL BE DARK SOON AND WE STAND A BETTER CHANCE TRAVELING AT NIGHT.
OR UNTIL I CAN THINK OF A WAY OUT OF THIS MESS.
BUZZ BUZZ
YOU CAN GIVE IT TO ME--
--OR I'D GLADLY SEARCH THAT HOT LITTLE BODY FOR IT.
BUZZ BUZZ
GOOD GIRL, SWEETNESS.
BUZZ BUZZ
BUZZ BUZZ
3:33
ПАПОЧКА
MOBILE

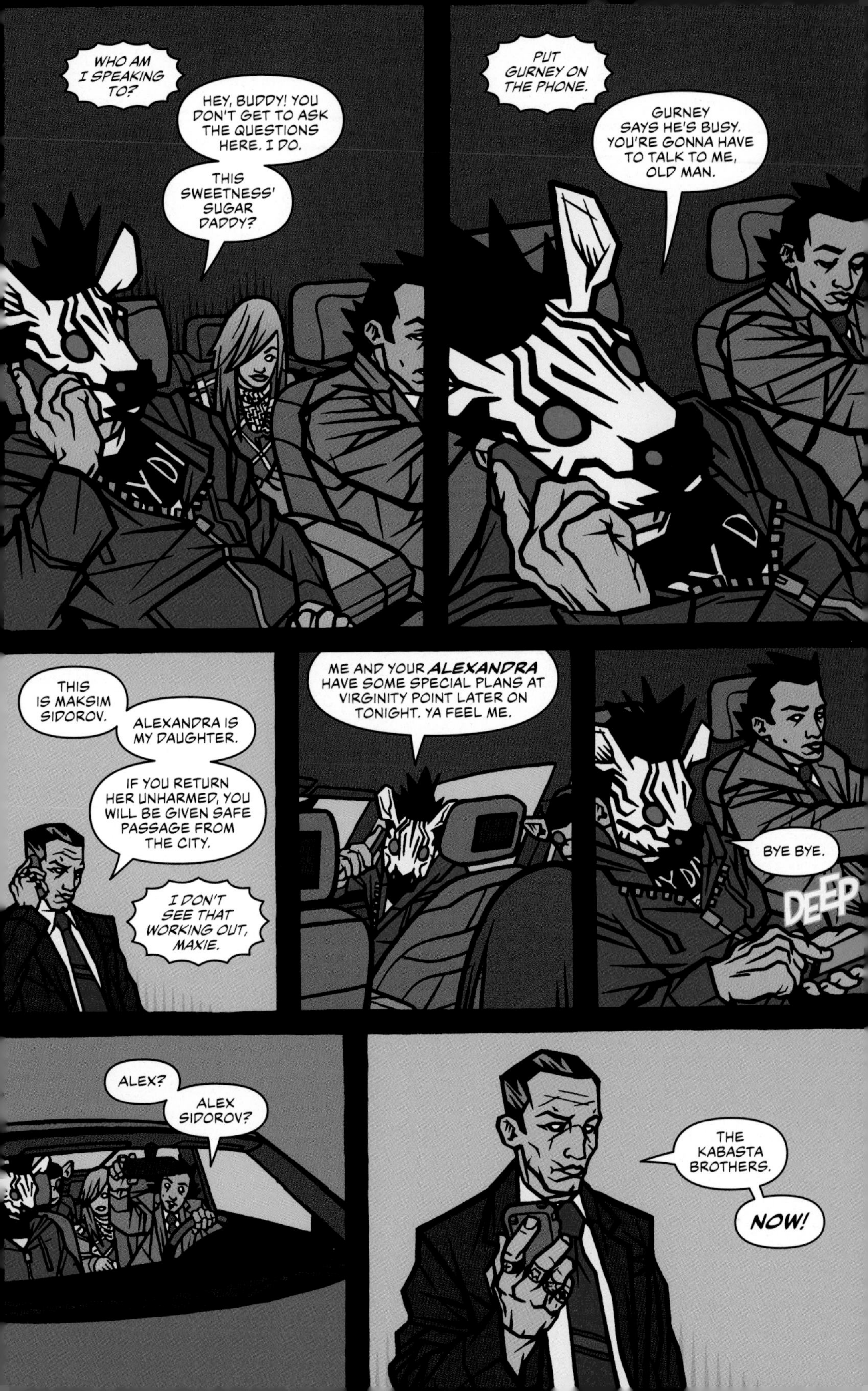
WHO AM I SPEAKING TO?
HEY, BUDDY! YOU DON'T GET TO ASK THE QUESTIONS HERE. I DO.
THIS SWEETNESS' SUGAR DADDY?
PUT GURNEY ON THE PHONE.
GURNEY SAYS HE'S BUSY. YOU'RE GONNA HAVE TO TALK TO ME, OLD MAN.
THIS IS MAKSIM SIDOROV.
ALEXANDRA IS MY DAUGHTER.
IF YOU RETURN HER UNHARMED, YOU WILL BE GIVEN SAFE PASSAGE FROM THE CITY.
I DON'T SEE THAT WORKING OUT, MAXIE.
ME AND YOUR ALEXANDRA HAVE SOME SPECIAL PLANS AT VIRGINITY POINT LATER ON TONIGHT. YA FEEL ME.
BYE BYE.
DEEP
ALEX?
ALEX SIDOROV?
THE KABASTA BROTHERS.
NOW!

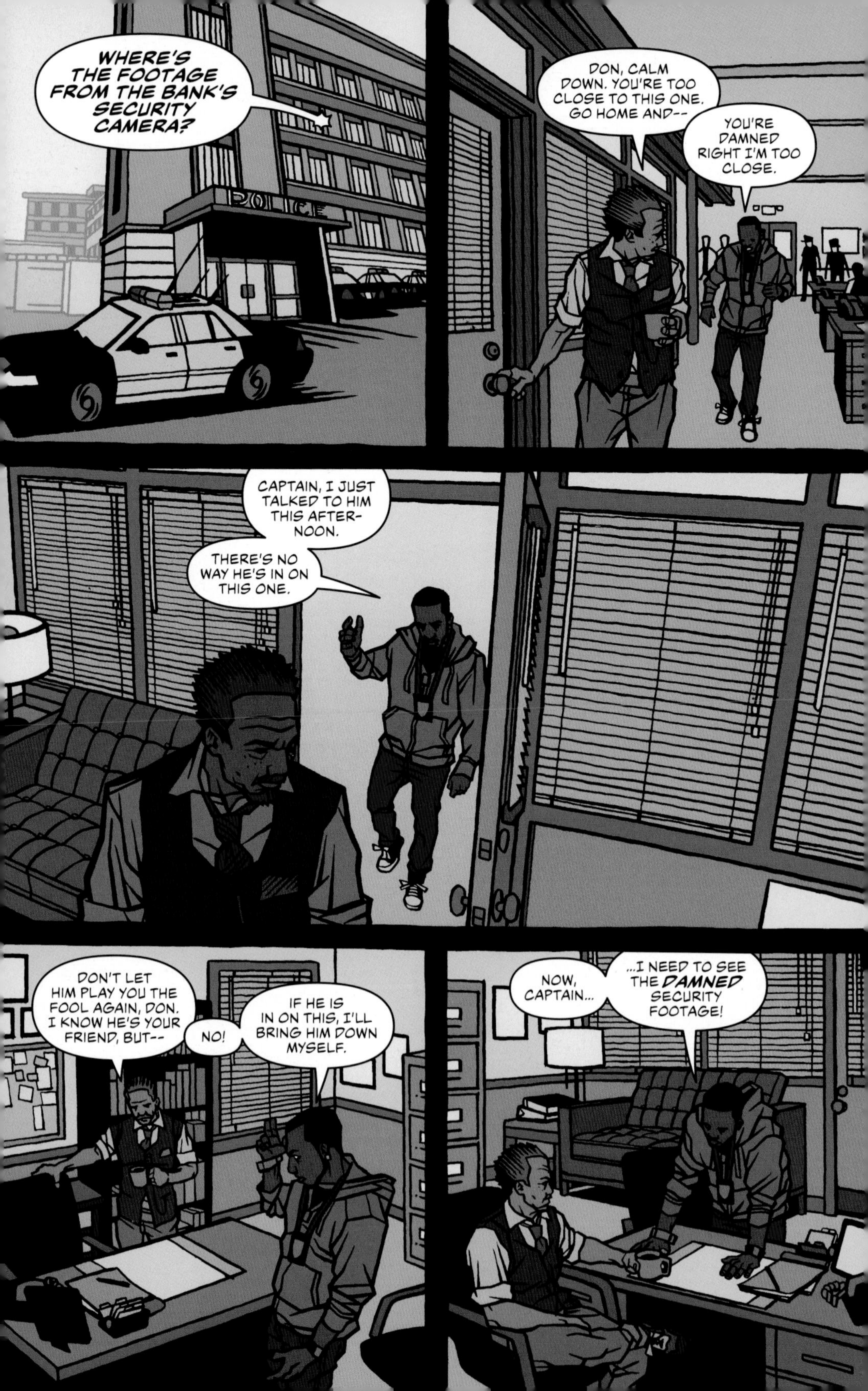
WHERE'S THE FOOTAGE FROM THE BANK'S SECURITY CAMERA?
POLICE
DON, CALM DOWN. YOU'RE TOO CLOSE TO THIS ONE. GO HOME AND--
YOU'RE DAMNED RIGHT I'M TOO CLOSE.
CAPTAIN, I JUST TALKED TO HIM THIS AFTER-NOON.
THERE'S NO WAY HE'S IN ON THIS ONE.
DON'T LET HIM PLAY YOU THE FOOL AGAIN, DON. I KNOW HE'S YOUR FRIEND, BUT--
NO!
IF HE IS IN ON THIS, I'LL BRING HIM DOWN MYSELF.
NOW, CAPTAIN...
...I NEED TO SEE THE *DAMNED* SECURITY FOOTAGE!

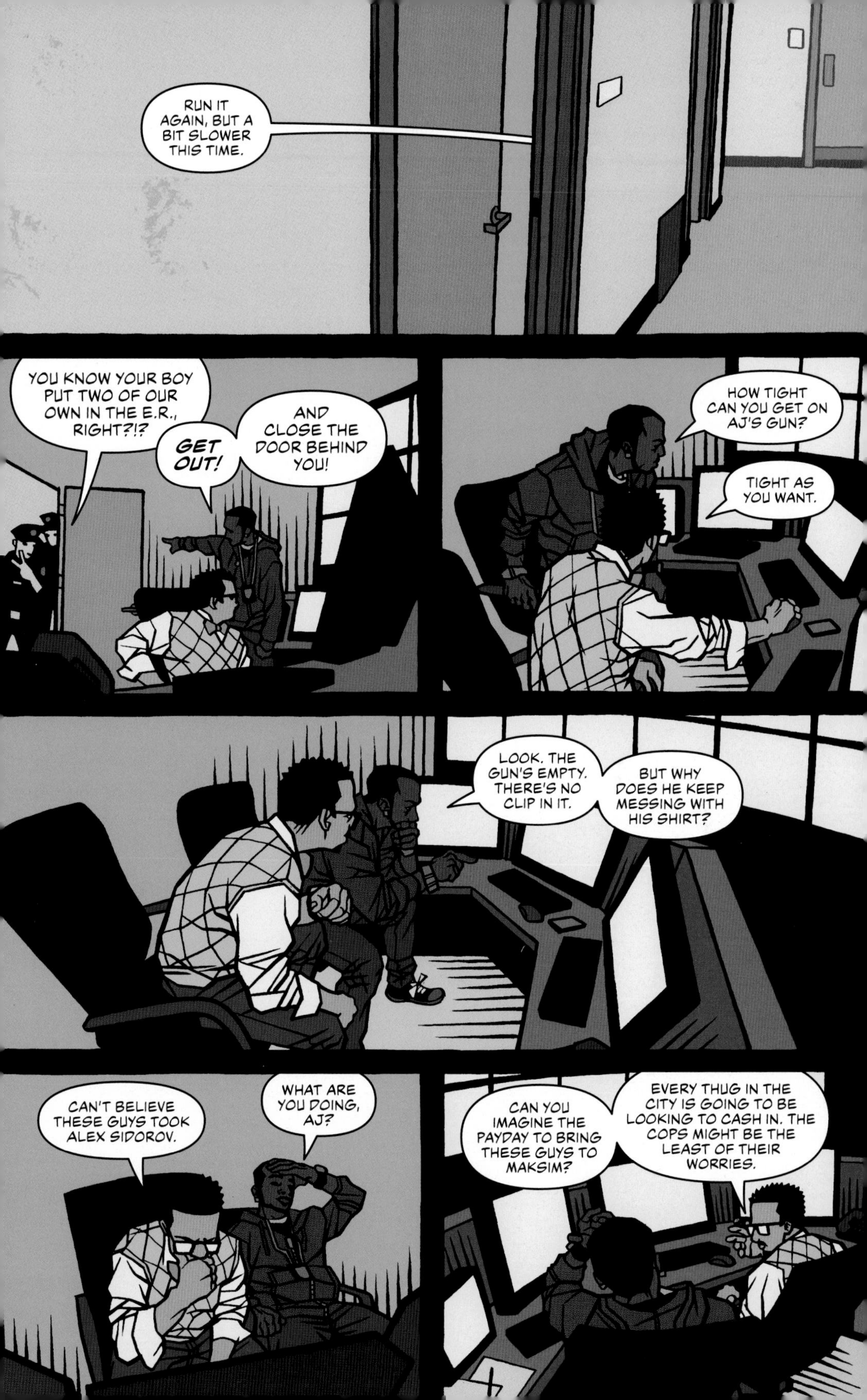
RUN IT AGAIN, BUT A BIT SLOWER THIS TIME.
YOU KNOW YOUR BOY PUT TWO OF OUR OWN IN THE E.R., RIGHT?!?
GET OUT!
AND CLOSE THE DOOR BEHIND YOU!
HOW TIGHT CAN YOU GET ON AJ'S GUN?
TIGHT AS YOU WANT.
LOOK. THE GUN'S EMPTY. THERE'S NO CLIP IN IT.
BUT WHY DOES HE KEEP MESSING WITH HIS SHIRT?
CAN'T BELIEVE THESE GUYS TOOK ALEX SIDOROV.
WHAT ARE YOU DOING, AJ?
CAN YOU IMAGINE THE PAYDAY TO BRING THESE GUYS TO MAKSIM?
EVERY THUG IN THE CITY IS GOING TO BE LOOKING TO CASH IN. THE COPS MIGHT BE THE LEAST OF THEIR WORRIES.

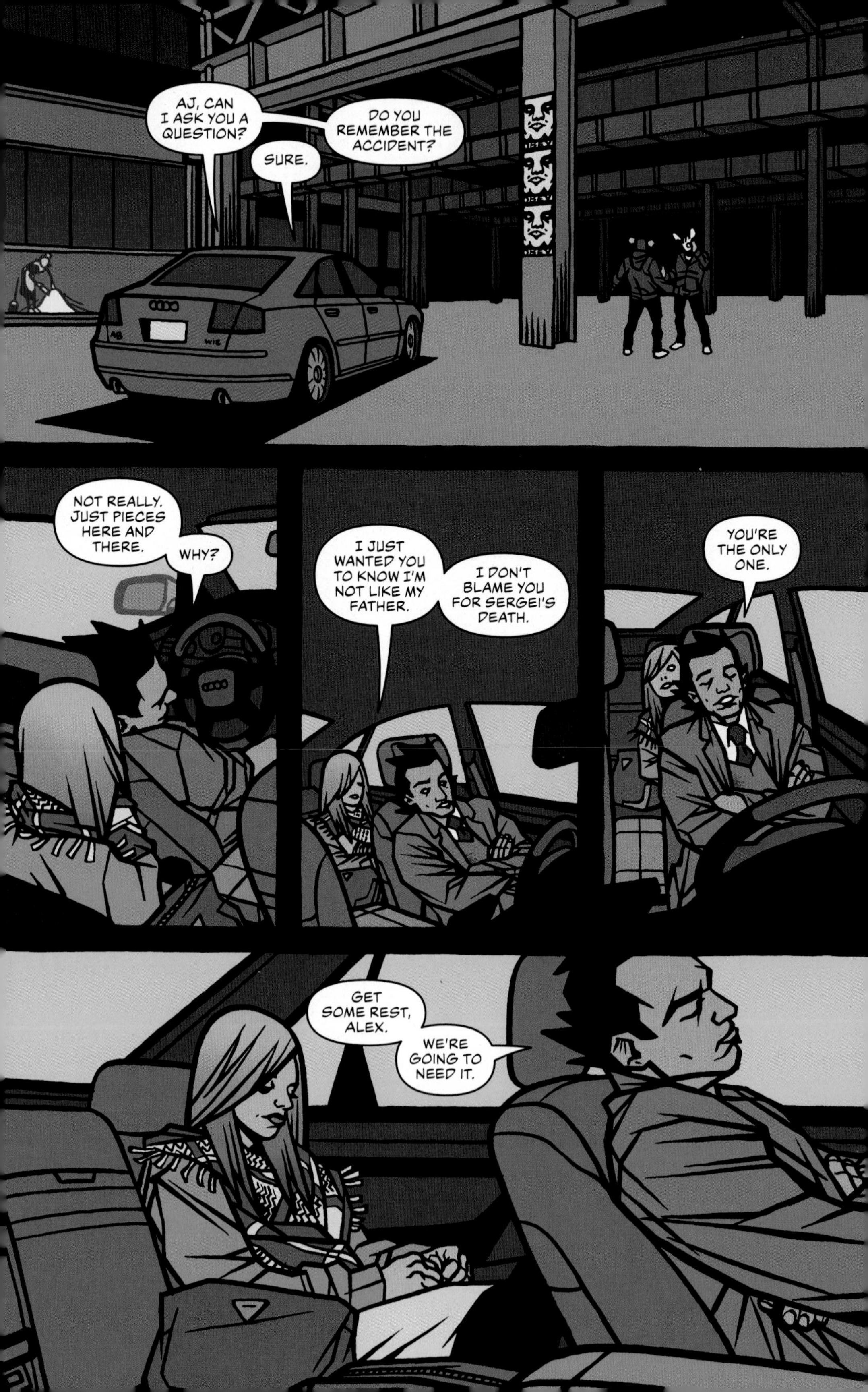
AJ, CAN I ASK YOU A QUESTION?
SURE.
DO YOU REMEMBER THE ACCIDENT?
NOT REALLY. JUST PIECES HERE AND THERE.
WHY?
I JUST WANTED YOU TO KNOW I'M NOT LIKE MY FATHER.
I DON'T BLAME YOU FOR SERGEI'S DEATH.
YOU'RE THE ONLY ONE.
GET SOME REST, ALEX.
WE'RE GOING TO NEED IT.

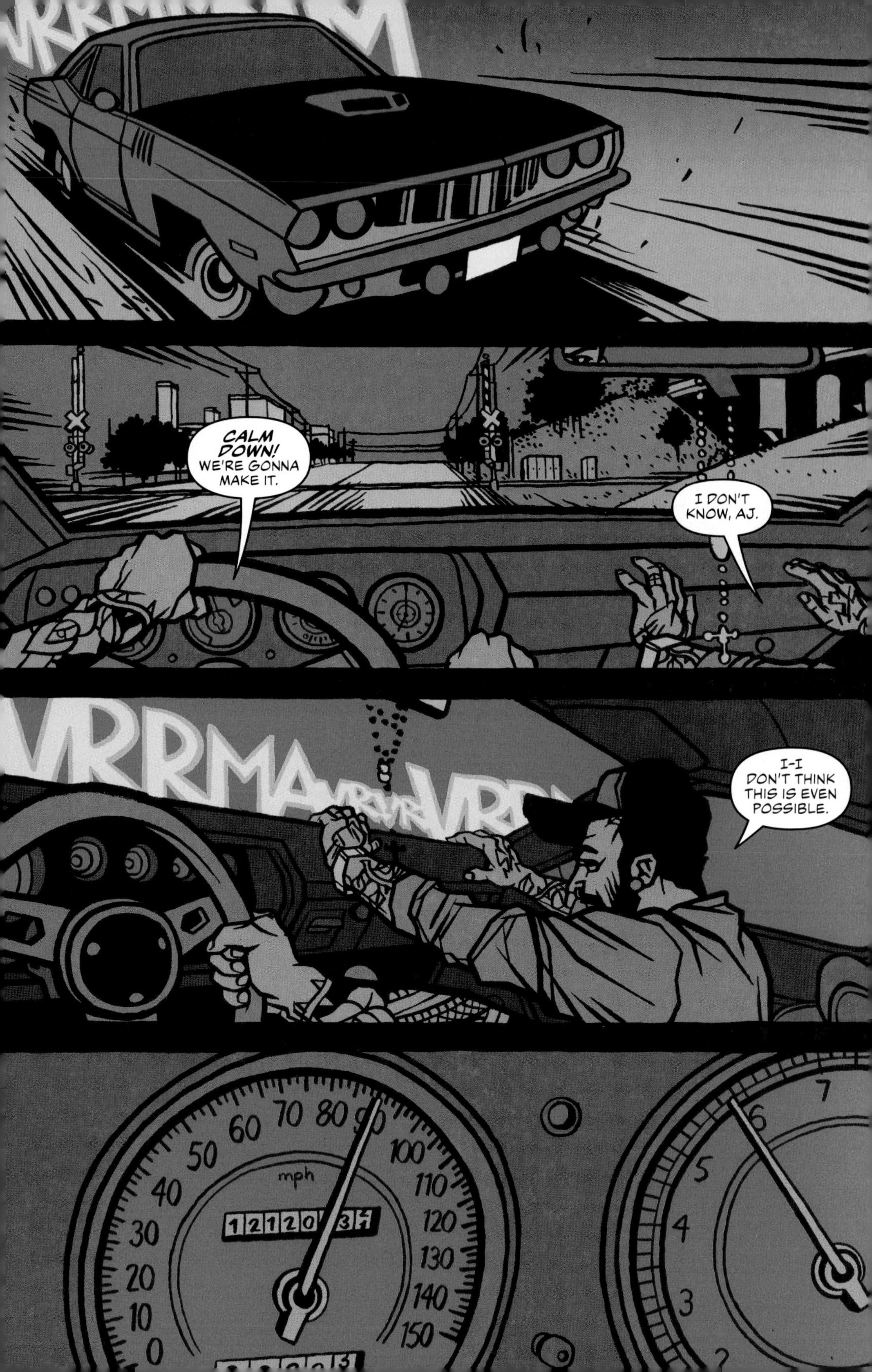
CALM DOWN! WE'RE GONNA MAKE IT.
I DON'T KNOW, AJ.
I-I DON'T THINK THIS IS EVEN POSSIBLE.
mph

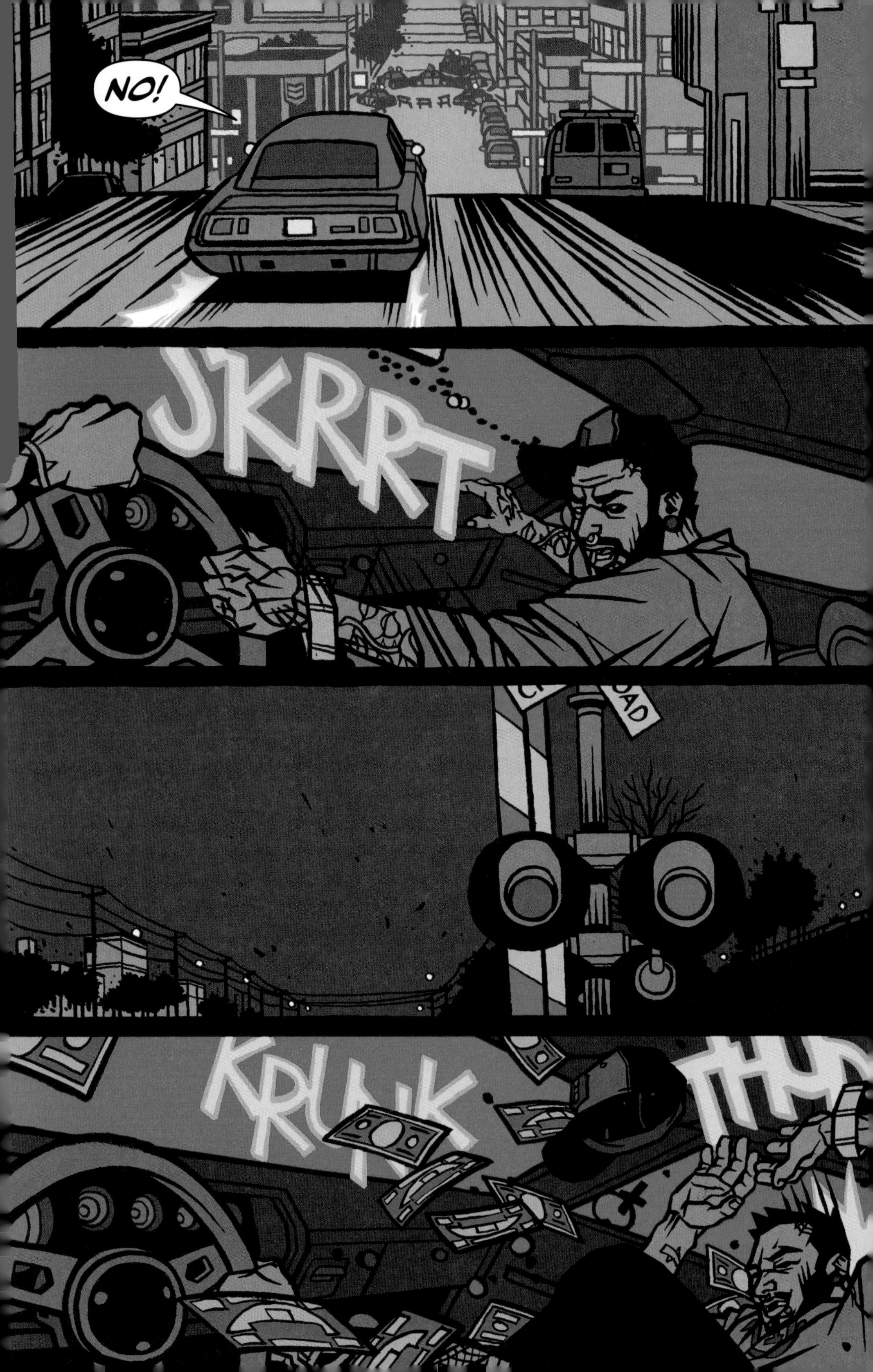
NO!
SKRRT
KRUNK

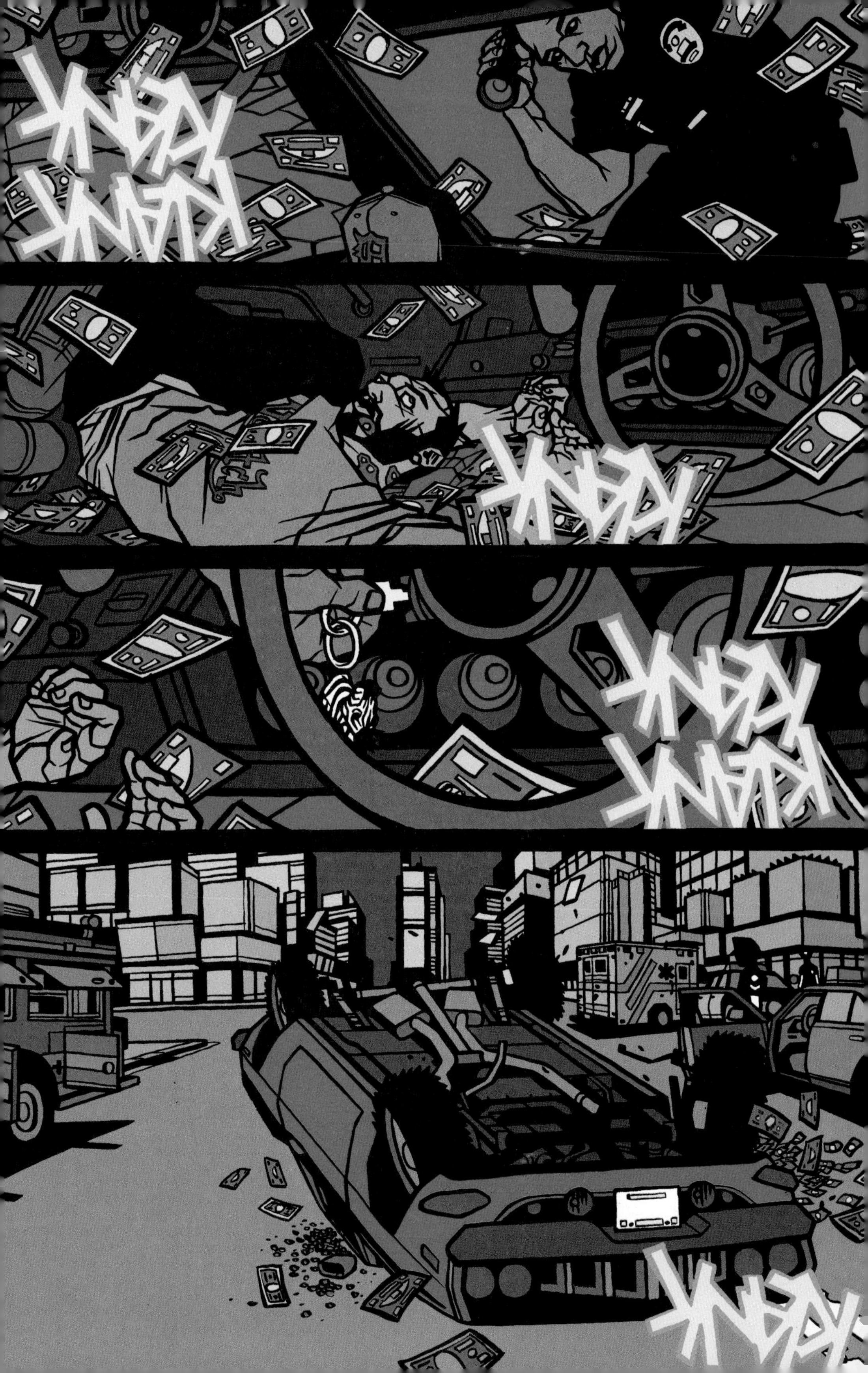

KLANK
KLANK
KLANK
KLANK
KLANK
KLANK

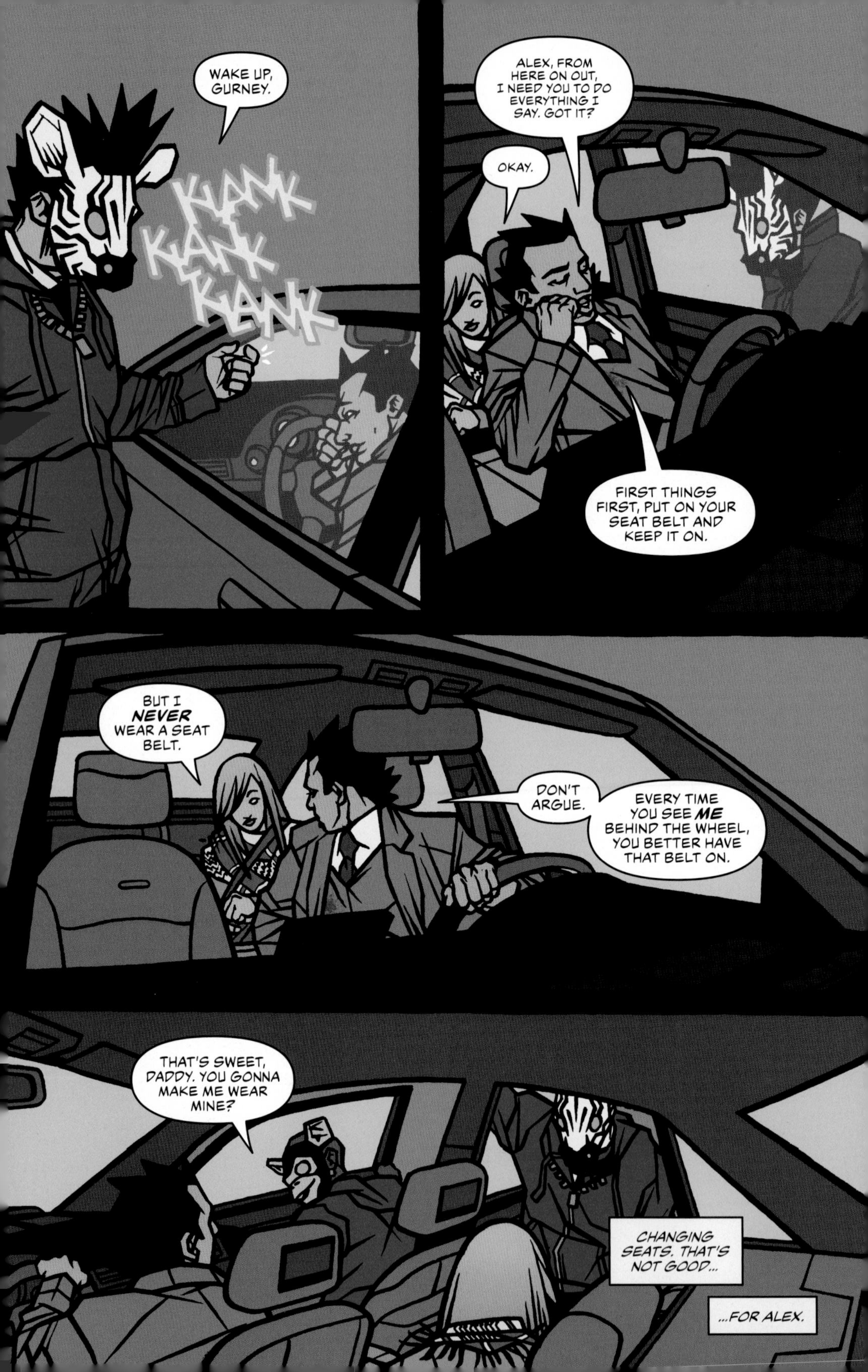

WAKE UP, GURNEY.
KLANK KLANK KLANK
ALEX, FROM HERE ON OUT, I NEED YOU TO DO EVERYTHING I SAY. GOT IT?
OKAY.
FIRST THINGS FIRST, PUT ON YOUR SEAT BELT AND KEEP IT ON.
BUT I ***NEVER*** WEAR A SEAT BELT.
DON'T ARGUE.
EVERY TIME YOU SEE ***ME*** BEHIND THE WHEEL, YOU BETTER HAVE THAT BELT ON.
THAT'S SWEET, DADDY. YOU GONNA MAKE ME WEAR MINE?
CHANGING SEATS. THAT'S NOT GOOD...
...FOR ALEX.

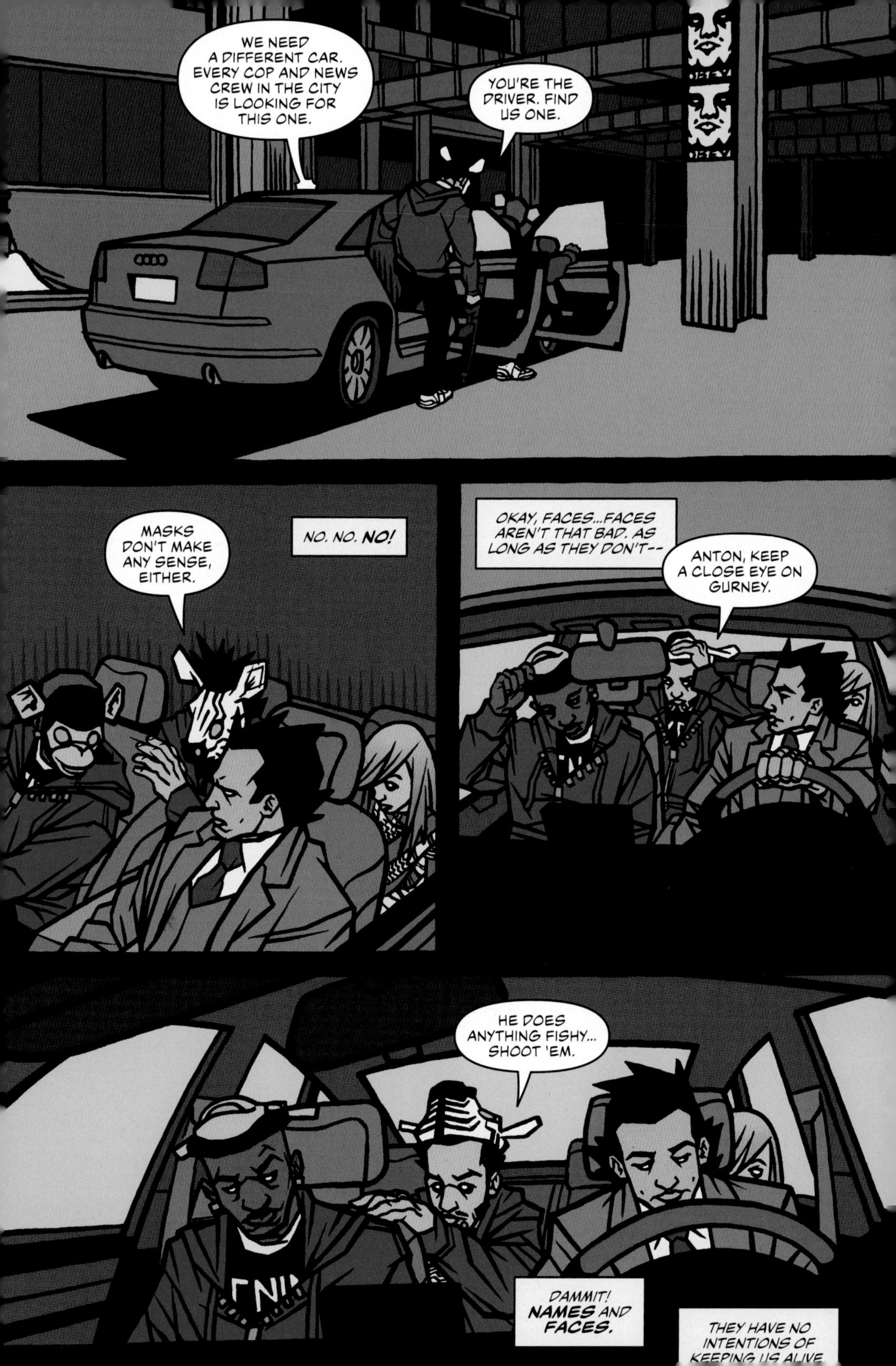
WE NEED A DIFFERENT CAR. EVERY COP AND NEWS CREW IN THE CITY IS LOOKING FOR THIS ONE.
YOU'RE THE DRIVER. FIND US ONE.
OBEY
OBEY
MASKS DON'T MAKE ANY SENSE, EITHER.
NO. NO. NO!
OKAY, FACES...FACES AREN'T THAT BAD. AS LONG AS THEY DON'T--
ANTON, KEEP A CLOSE EYE ON GURNEY.
HE DOES ANYTHING FISHY... SHOOT 'EM.
DAMMIT! NAMES AND FACES.
THEY HAVE NO INTENTIONS OF KEEPING US ALIVE

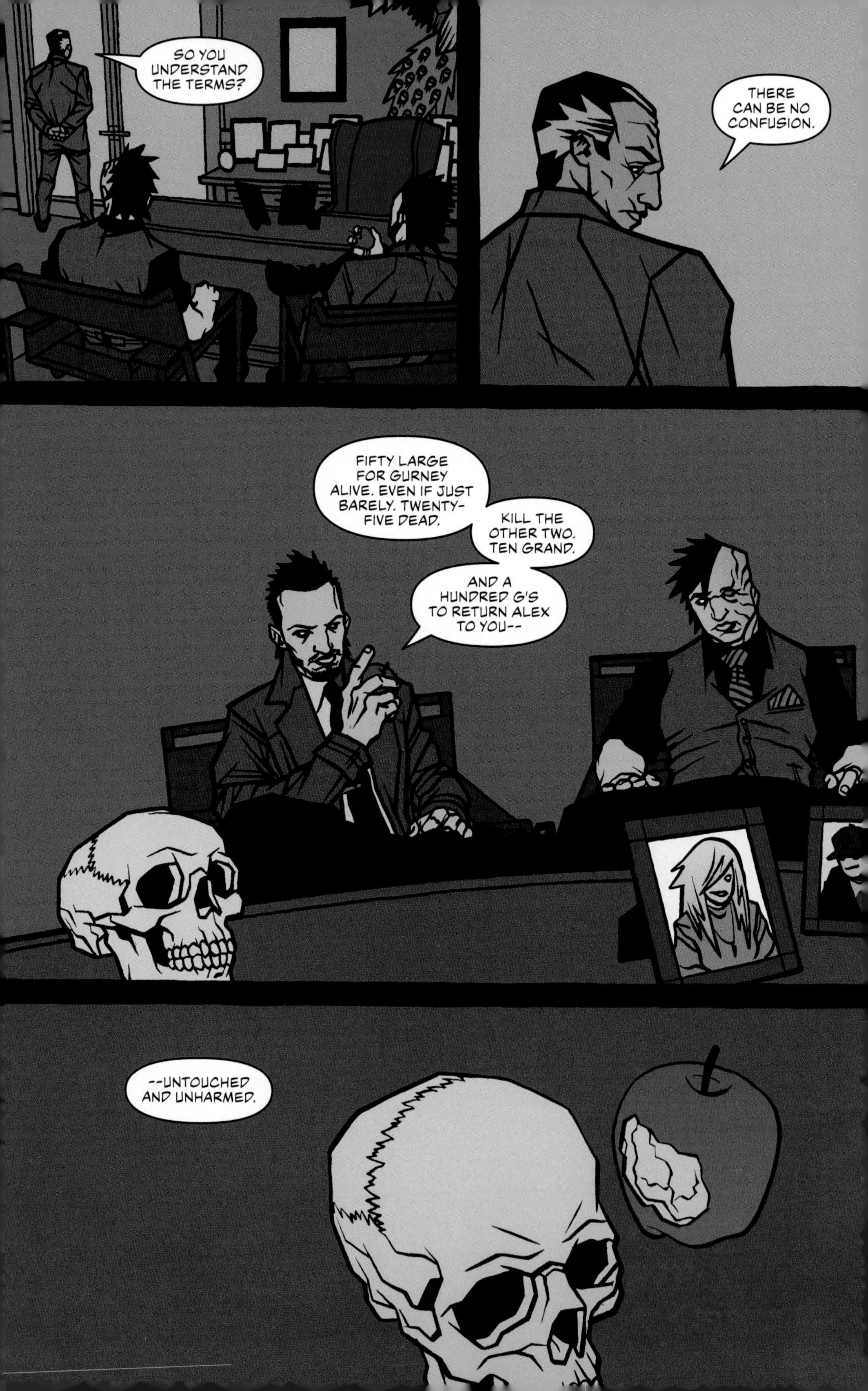
SO YOU UNDERSTAND THE TERMS?
THERE CAN BE NO CONFUSION.
FIFTY LARGE FOR GURNEY ALIVE. EVEN IF JUST BARELY. TWENTY-FIVE DEAD.
KILL THE OTHER TWO. TEN GRAND.
AND A HUNDRED G'S TO RETURN ALEX TO YOU--
--UNTOUCHED AND UNHARMED.

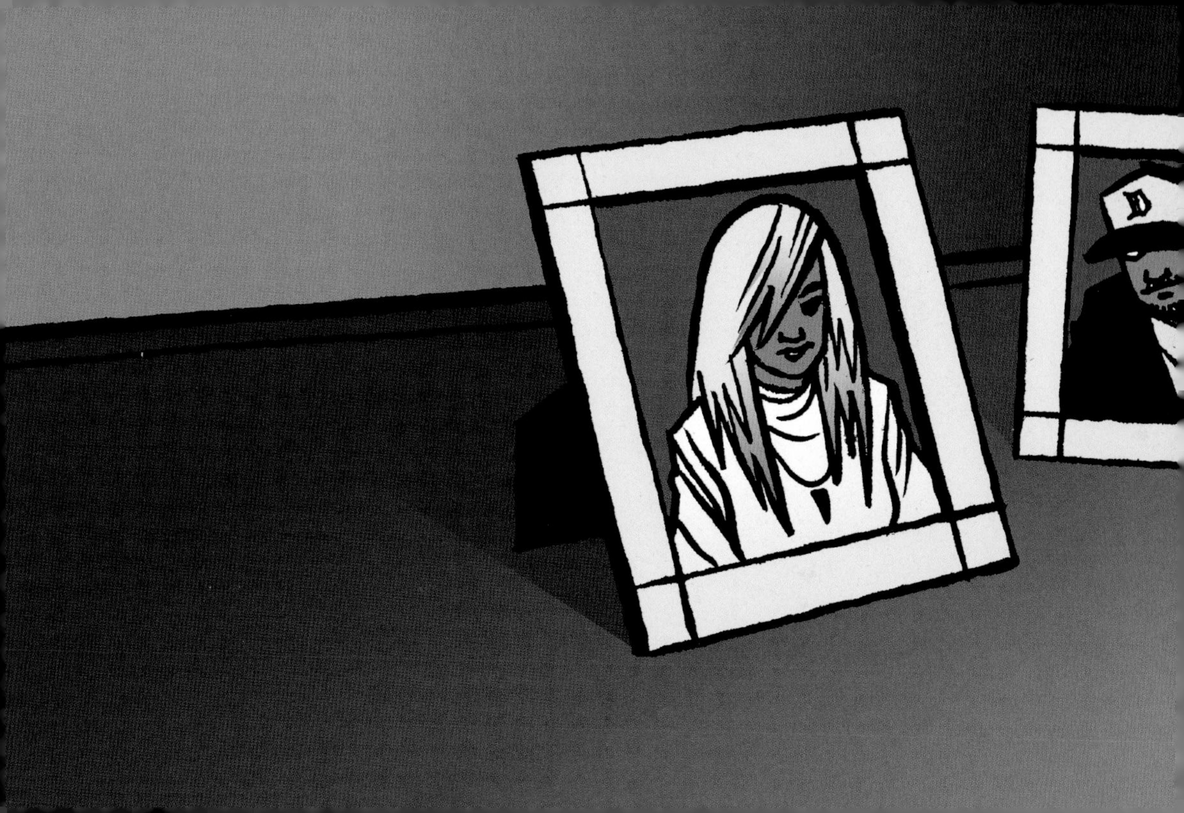

CHAPTER THREE

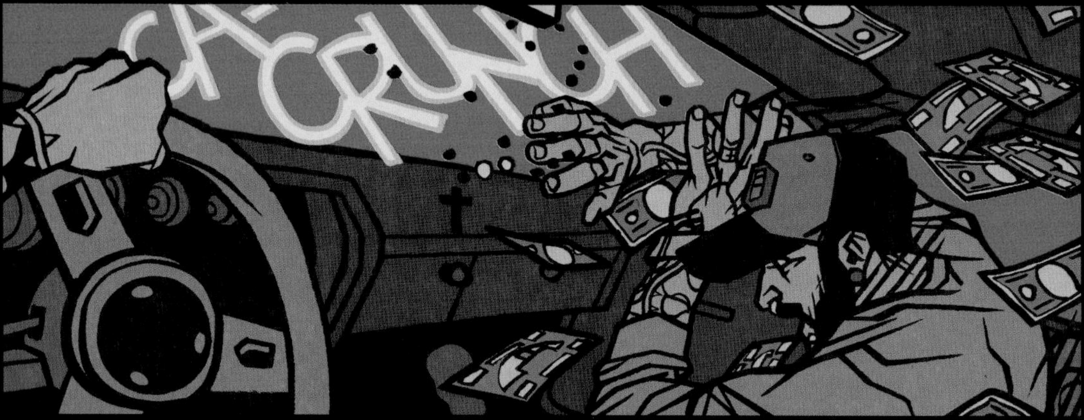
CA-CRUNCH

"BANG!"

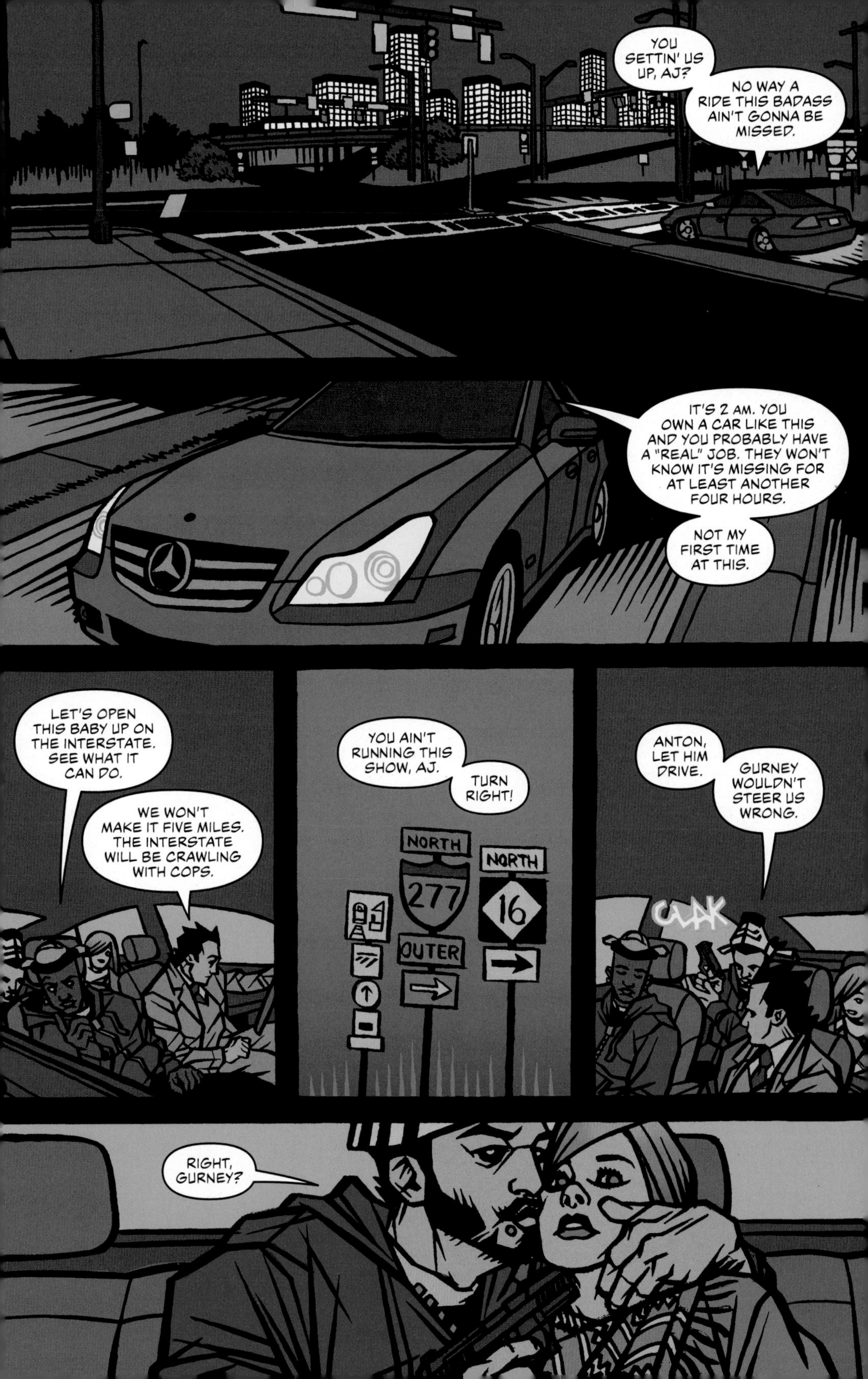
YOU SETTIN' US UP, AJ?
NO WAY A RIDE THIS BADASS AIN'T GONNA BE MISSED.
IT'S 2 AM. YOU OWN A CAR LIKE THIS AND YOU PROBABLY HAVE A "REAL" JOB. THEY WON'T KNOW IT'S MISSING FOR AT LEAST ANOTHER FOUR HOURS.
NOT MY FIRST TIME AT THIS.
LET'S OPEN THIS BABY UP ON THE INTERSTATE. SEE WHAT IT CAN DO.
WE WON'T MAKE IT FIVE MILES. THE INTERSTATE WILL BE CRAWLING WITH COPS.
YOU AIN'T RUNNING THIS SHOW, AJ.
TURN RIGHT!
NORTH
277
OUTER
NORTH
16
ANTON, LET HIM DRIVE.
GURNEY WOULDN'T STEER US WRONG.
CLAK
RIGHT, GURNEY?

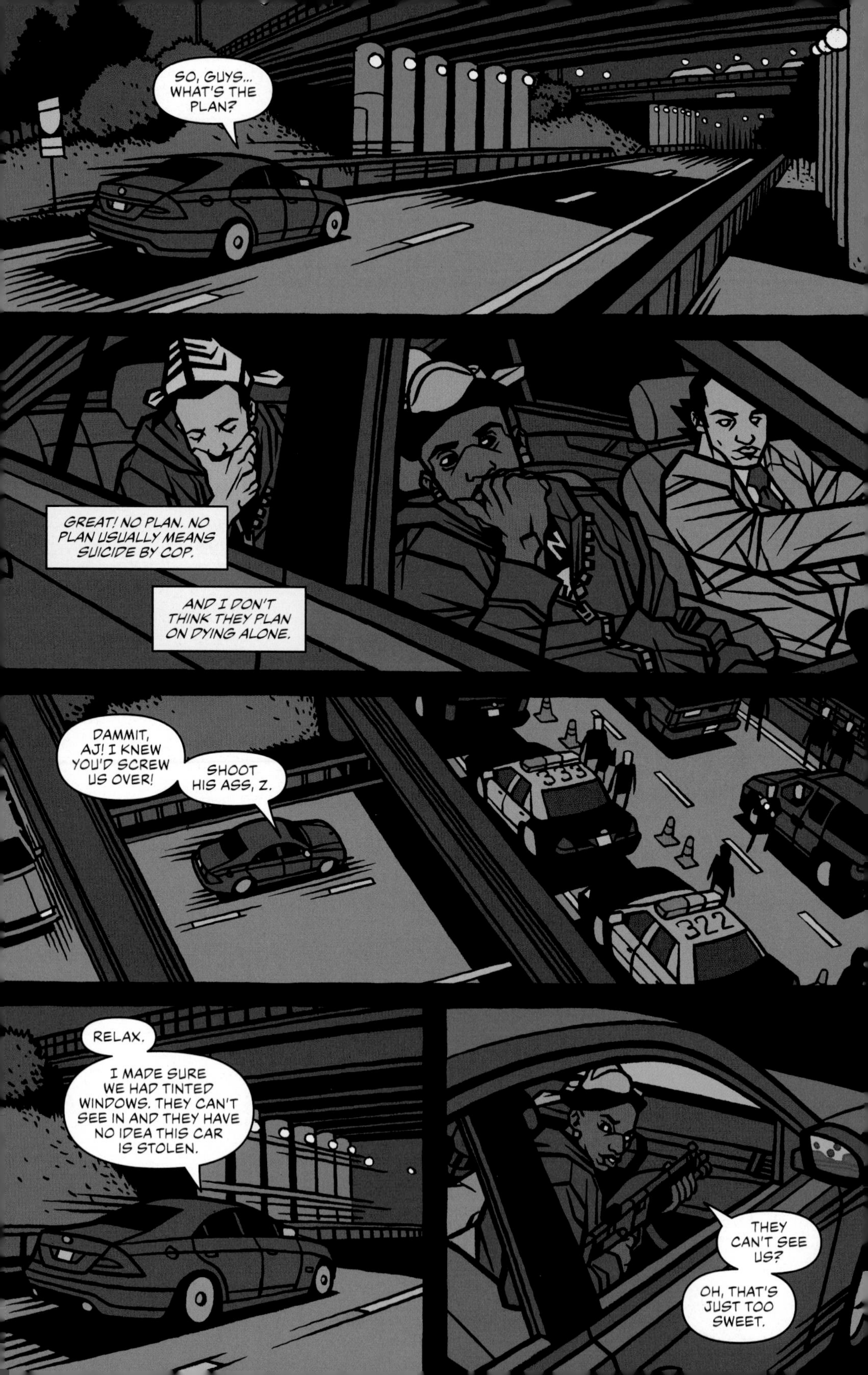
SO, GUYS... WHAT'S THE PLAN?
GREAT! NO PLAN. NO PLAN USUALLY MEANS SUICIDE BY COP.
AND I DON'T THINK THEY PLAN ON DYING ALONE.
DAMMIT, AJ! I KNEW YOU'D SCREW US OVER!
SHOOT HIS ASS, Z.
333
322
RELAX.
I MADE SURE WE HAD TINTED WINDOWS. THEY CAN'T SEE IN AND THEY HAVE NO IDEA THIS CAR IS STOLEN.
THEY CAN'T SEE US?
OH, THAT'S JUST TOO SWEET.

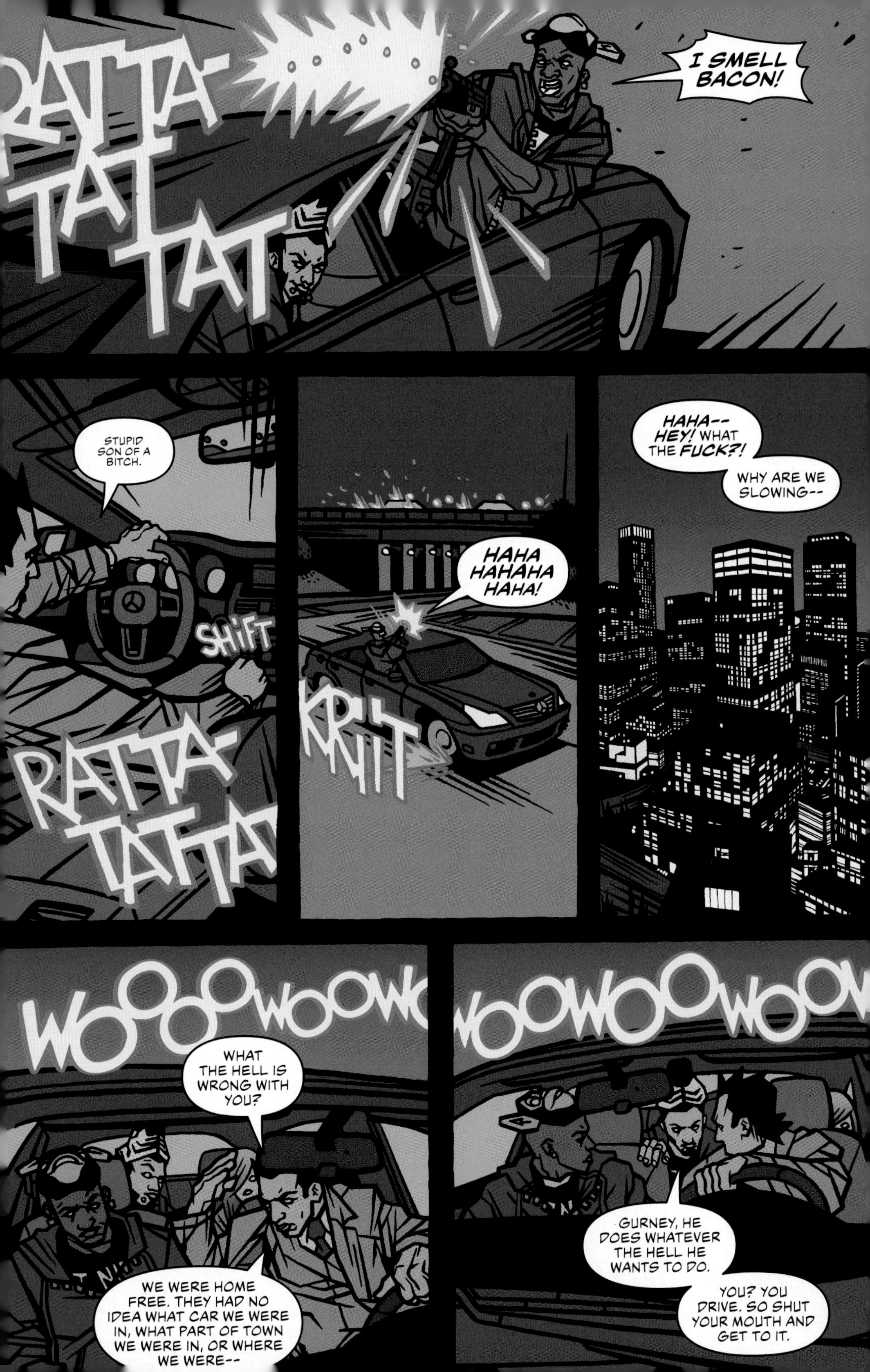
RATTA-TAT TAT
I SMELL BACON!
STUPID SON OF A BITCH.
SHIFT
RATTA-TATTAT
HAHA HAHAHA HAHA!
KRITT
HAHA-- HEY! WHAT THE FUCK?!
WHY ARE WE SLOWING--
WOOOOWOOWO
WHAT THE HELL IS WRONG WITH YOU?
WE WERE HOME FREE. THEY HAD NO IDEA WHAT CAR WE WERE IN, WHAT PART OF TOWN WE WERE IN, OR WHERE WE WERE--
WOOWOOWOOW
GURNEY, HE DOES WHATEVER THE HELL HE WANTS TO DO.
YOU? YOU DRIVE. SO SHUT YOUR MOUTH AND GET TO IT.

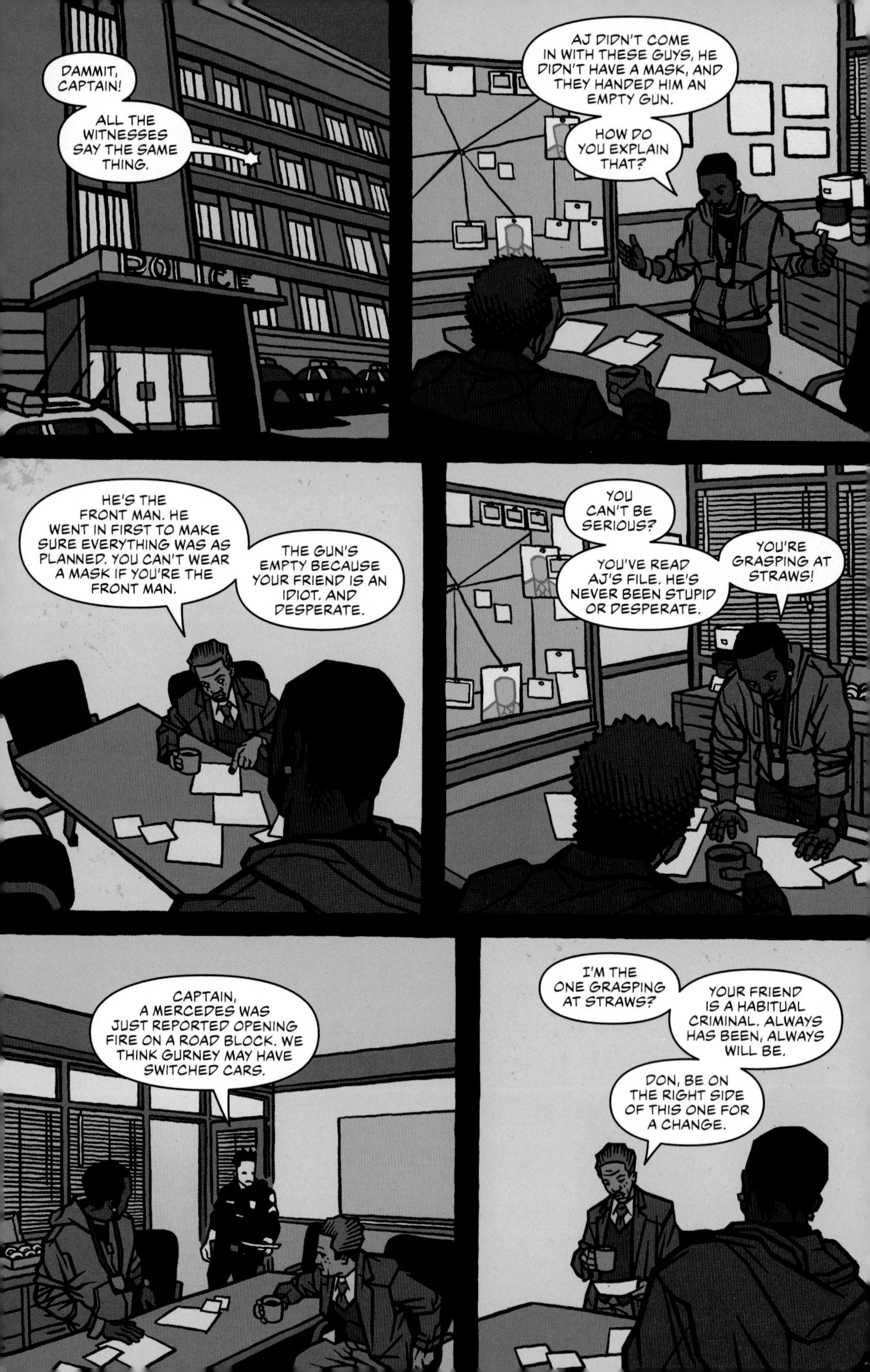
DAMMIT, CAPTAIN!
ALL THE WITNESSES SAY THE SAME THING.
POLICE
AJ DIDN'T COME IN WITH THESE GUYS, HE DIDN'T HAVE A MASK, AND THEY HANDED HIM AN EMPTY GUN.
HOW DO YOU EXPLAIN THAT?
HE'S THE FRONT MAN. HE WENT IN FIRST TO MAKE SURE EVERYTHING WAS AS PLANNED. YOU CAN'T WEAR A MASK IF YOU'RE THE FRONT MAN.
THE GUN'S EMPTY BECAUSE YOUR FRIEND IS AN IDIOT. AND DESPERATE.
YOU CAN'T BE SERIOUS?
YOU'VE READ AJ'S FILE. HE'S NEVER BEEN STUPID OR DESPERATE.
YOU'RE GRASPING AT STRAWS!
CAPTAIN, A MERCEDES WAS JUST REPORTED OPENING FIRE ON A ROAD BLOCK. WE THINK GURNEY MAY HAVE SWITCHED CARS.
I'M THE ONE GRASPING AT STRAWS?
YOUR FRIEND IS A HABITUAL CRIMINAL. ALWAYS HAS BEEN, ALWAYS WILL BE.
DON, BE ON THE RIGHT SIDE OF THIS ONE FOR A CHANGE.

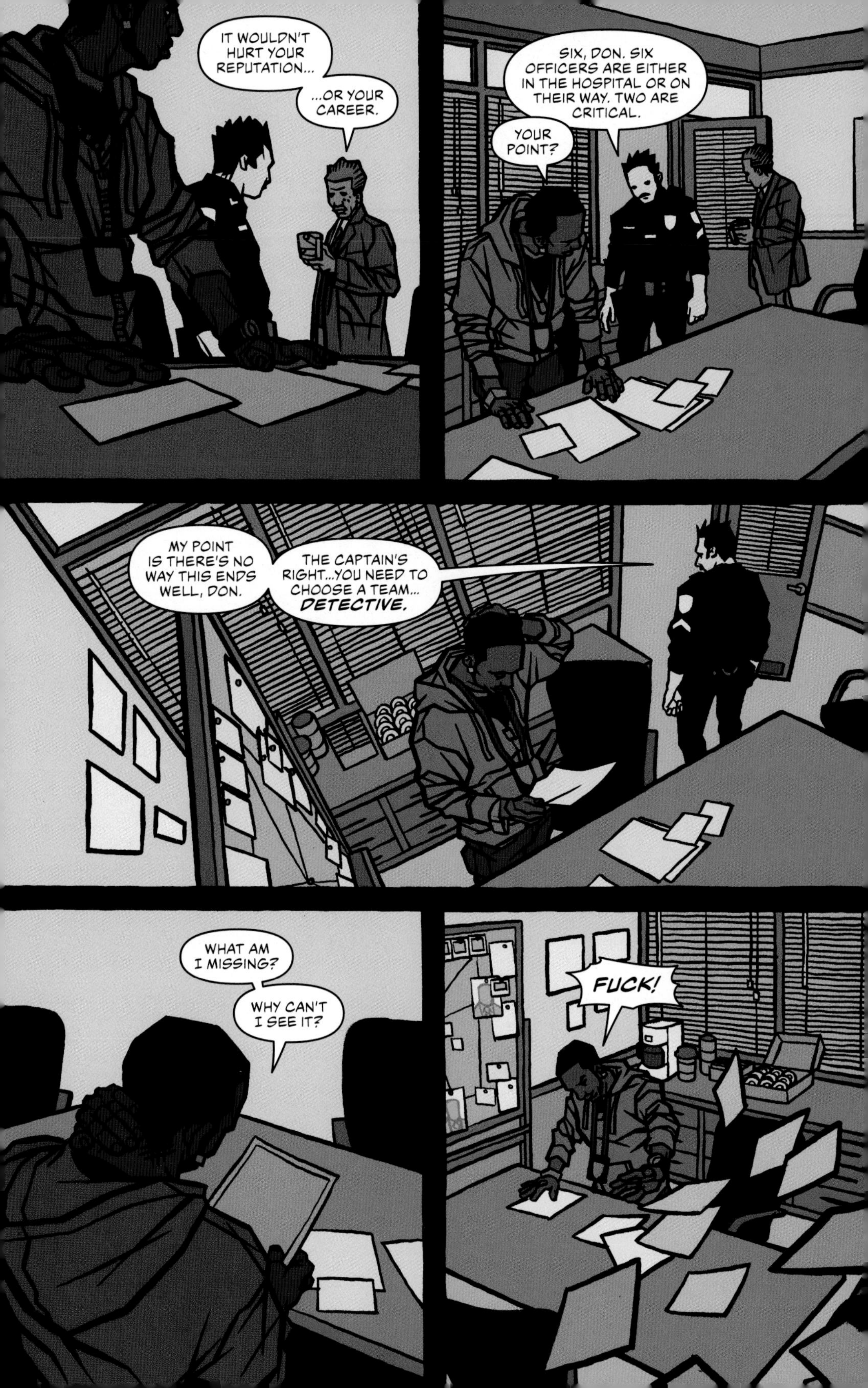
IT WOULDN'T HURT YOUR REPUTATION...
...OR YOUR CAREER.
SIX, DON. SIX OFFICERS ARE EITHER IN THE HOSPITAL OR ON THEIR WAY. TWO ARE CRITICAL.
YOUR POINT?
MY POINT IS THERE'S NO WAY THIS ENDS WELL, DON.
THE CAPTAIN'S RIGHT...YOU NEED TO CHOOSE A TEAM... *DETECTIVE.*
WHAT AM I MISSING?
WHY CAN'T I SEE IT?
FUCK!

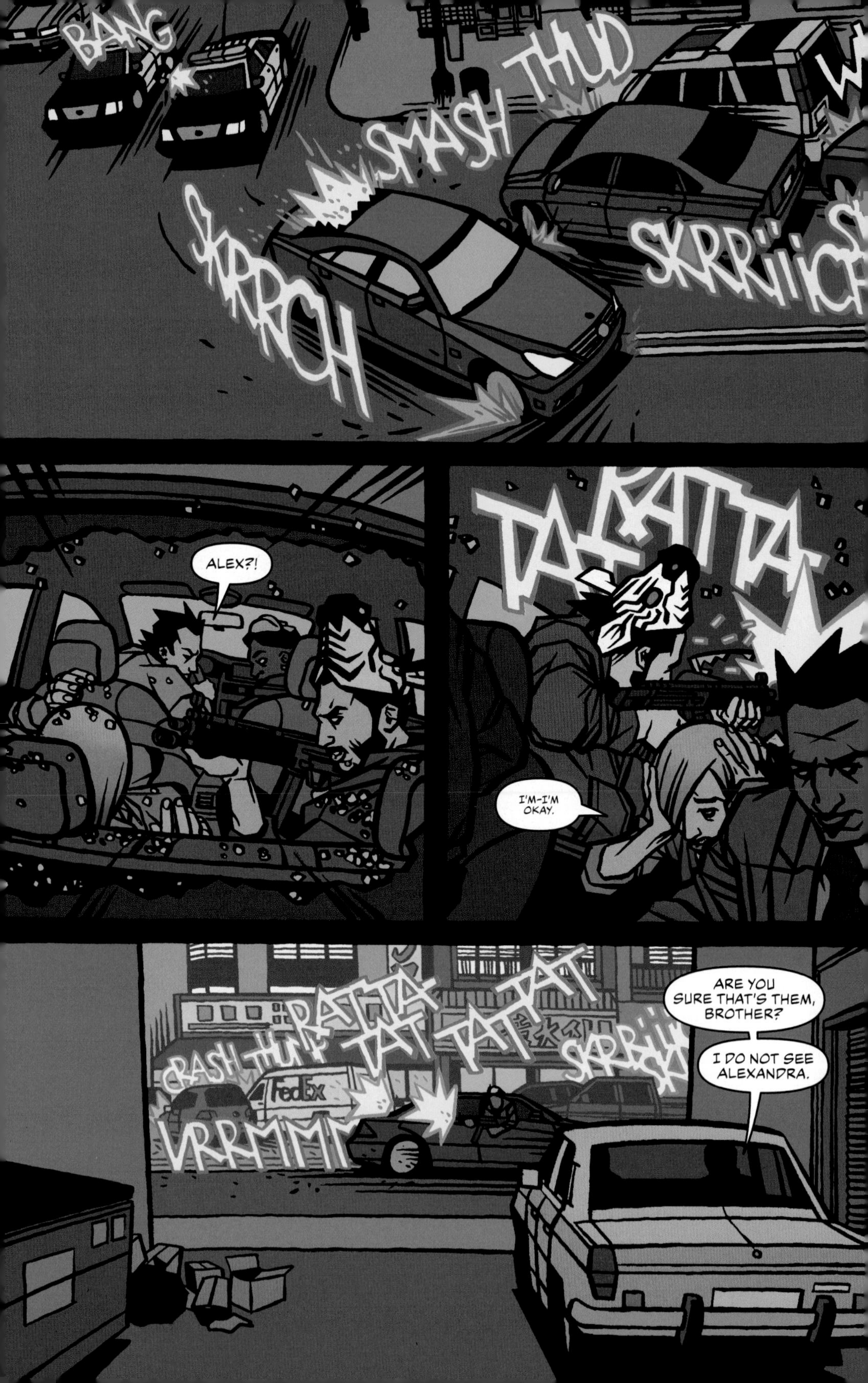
BANG
SMASH THUD
SKRRCH
SKRRIIICH
ALEX?!
TATATTA
I'M-I'M OKAY.
CRASH THUF RATTA TAT TATAT
SKRRIIISK
VRRMMM
ARE YOU SURE THAT'S THEM, BROTHER?
I DO NOT SEE ALEXANDRA.

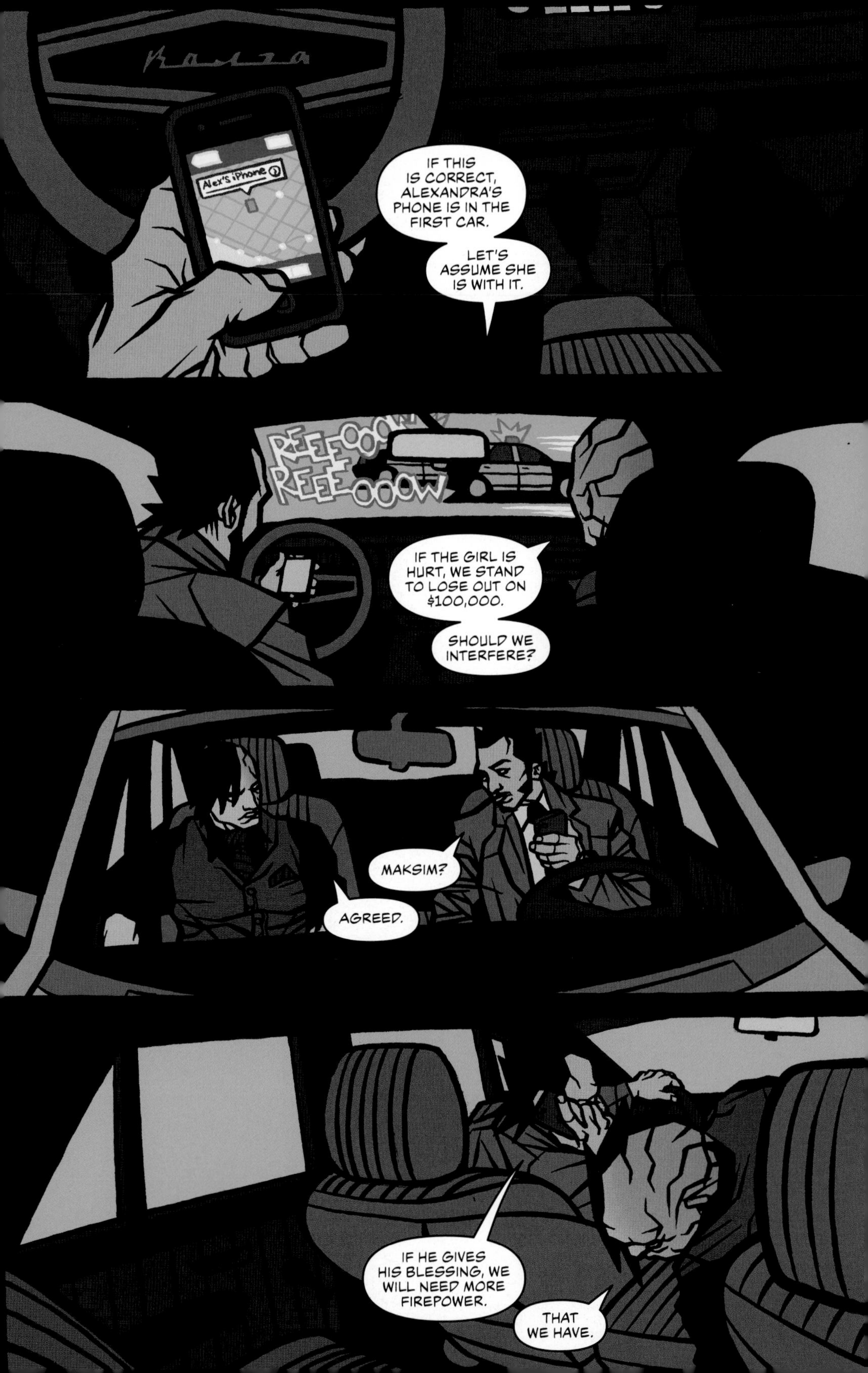
Alex's iPhone
IF THIS IS CORRECT, ALEXANDRA'S PHONE IS IN THE FIRST CAR.
LET'S ASSUME SHE IS WITH IT.
REEEOOOW REEEOOOW
IF THE GIRL IS HURT, WE STAND TO LOSE OUT ON $100,000.
SHOULD WE INTERFERE?
MAKSIM?
AGREED.
IF HE GIVES HIS BLESSING, WE WILL NEED MORE FIREPOWER.
THAT WE HAVE.

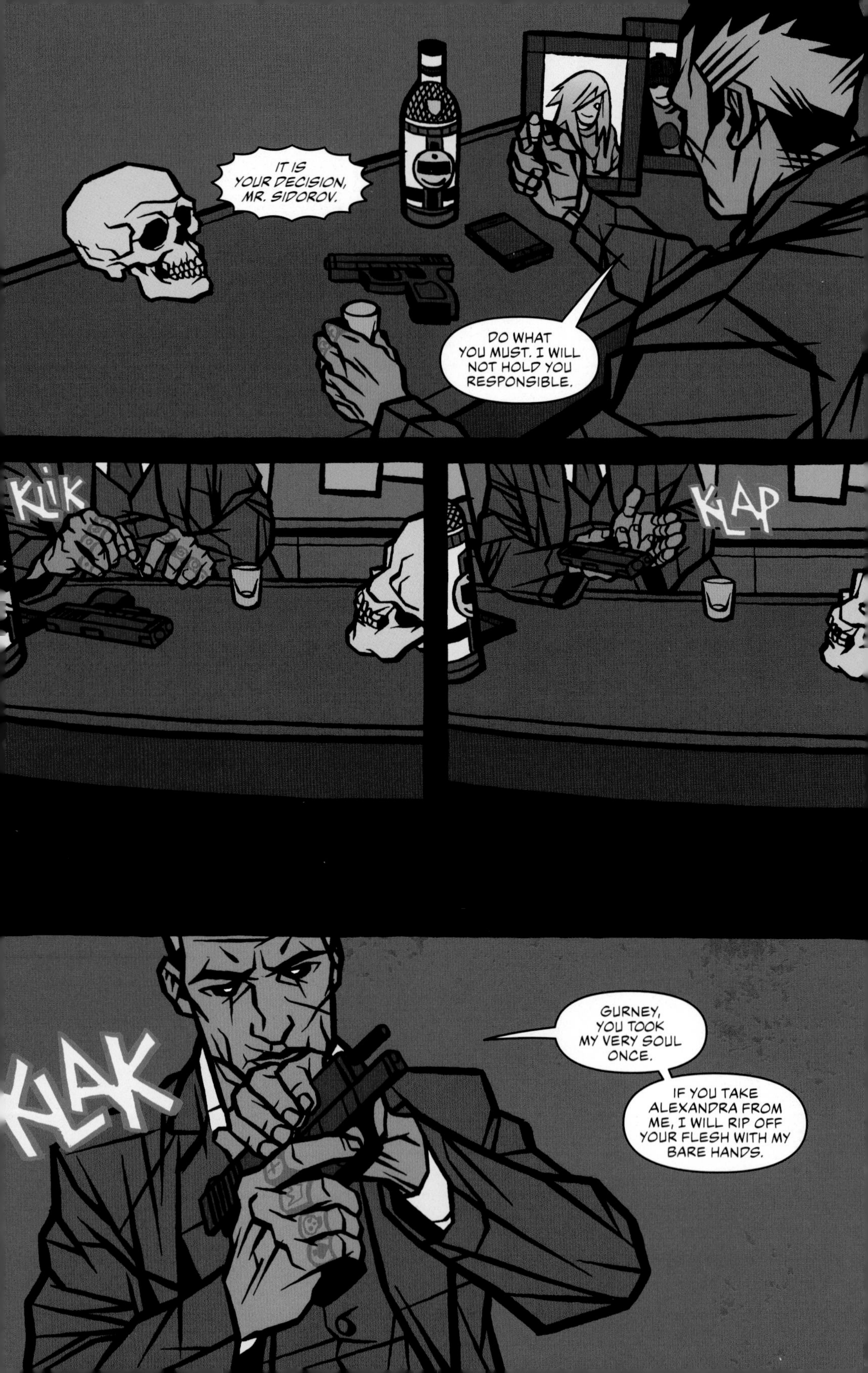
IT IS YOUR DECISION, MR. SIDOROV.
DO WHAT YOU MUST. I WILL NOT HOLD YOU RESPONSIBLE.
KLIK
KLAP
KLAK
GURNEY, YOU TOOK MY VERY SOUL ONCE.
IF YOU TAKE ALEXANDRA FROM ME, I WILL RIP OFF YOUR FLESH WITH MY BARE HANDS.

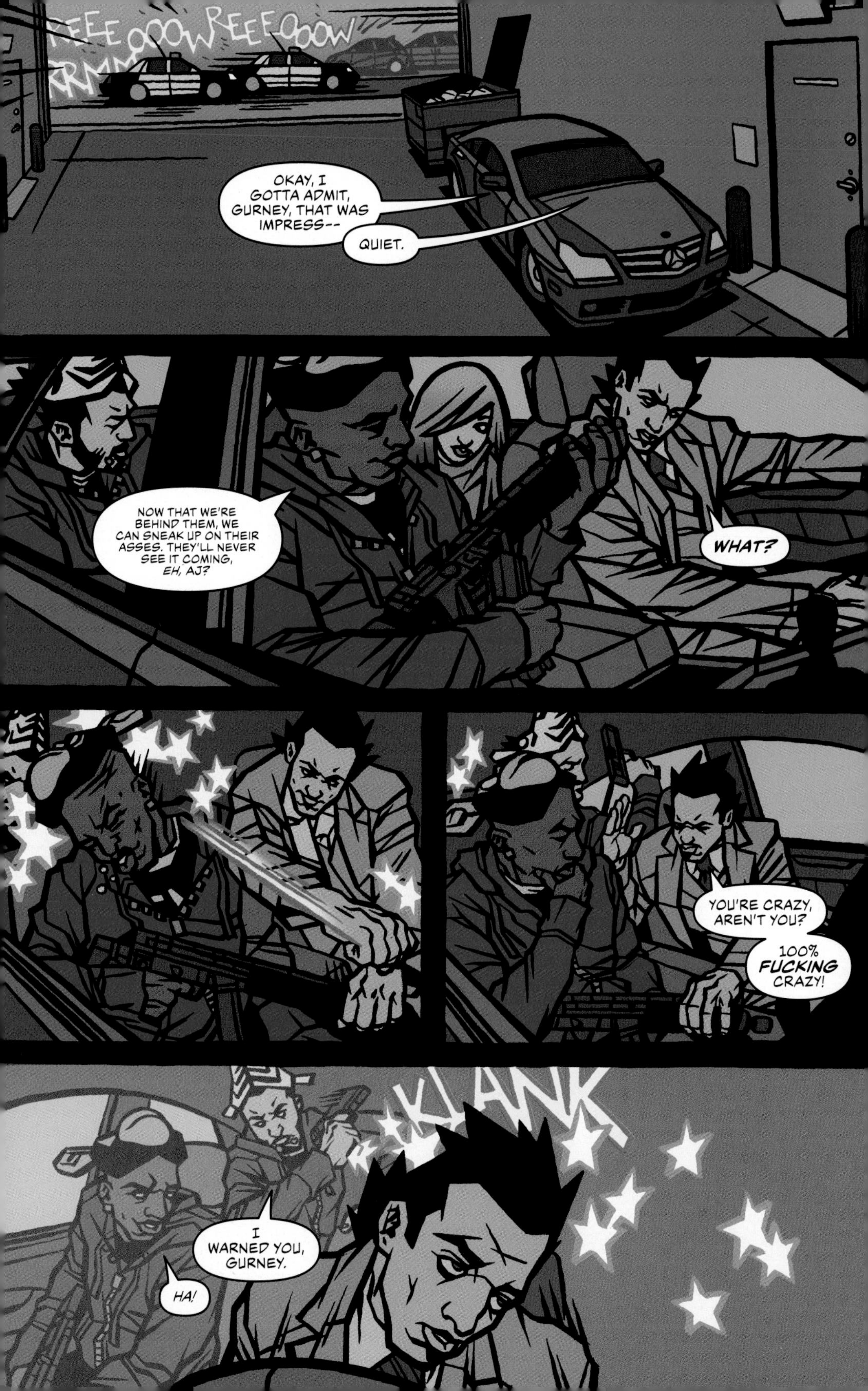
REEE-OOOW REEE-OOOW
RRMM
OKAY, I GOTTA ADMIT, GURNEY, THAT WAS IMPRESS--
QUIET.
NOW THAT WE'RE BEHIND THEM, WE CAN SNEAK UP ON THEIR ASSES. THEY'LL NEVER SEE IT COMING, EH, AJ?
WHAT?
YOU'RE CRAZY, AREN'T YOU?
100% FUCKING CRAZY!
KLANK
I WARNED YOU, GURNEY.
HA!

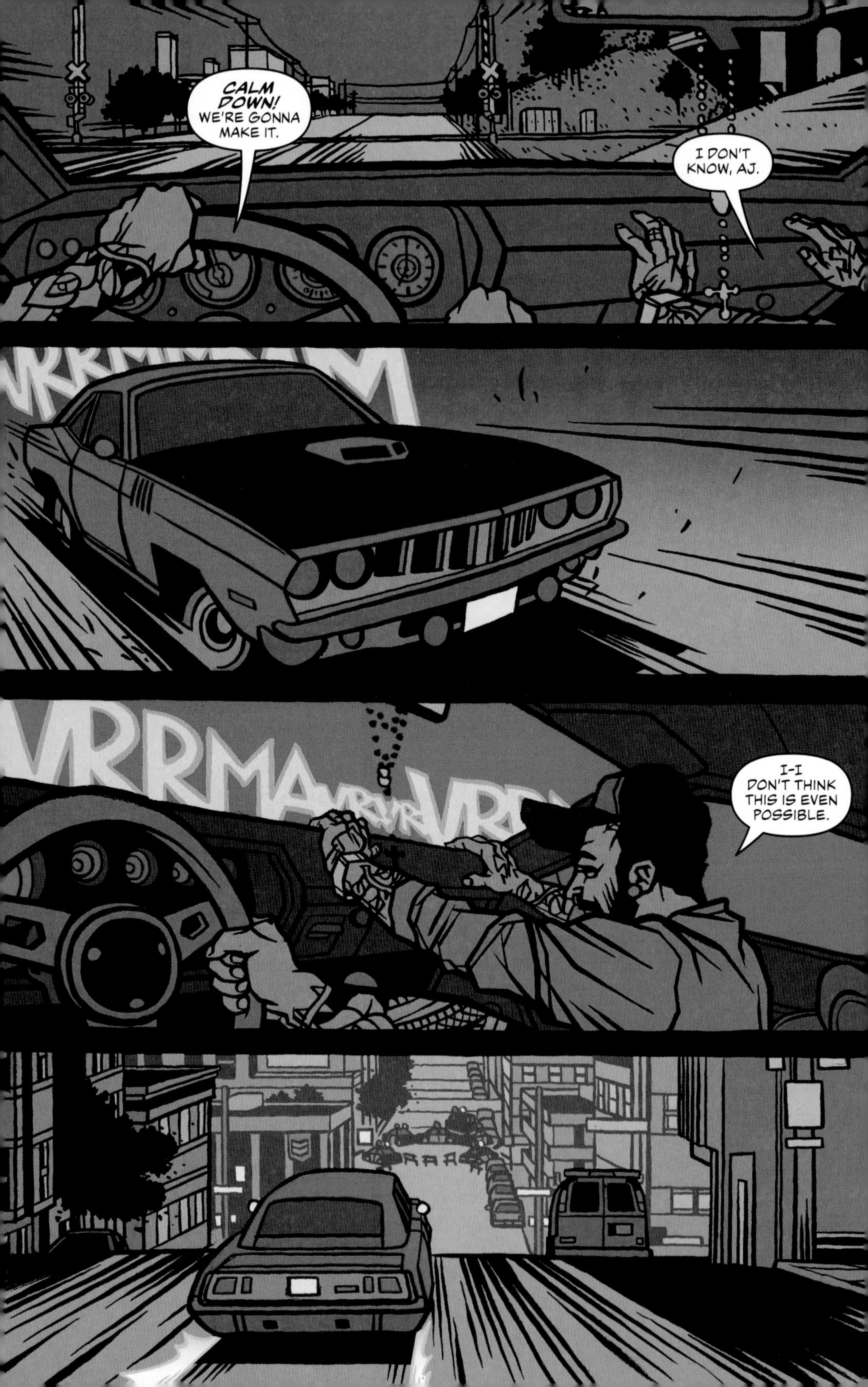

CALM DOWN! WE'RE GONNA MAKE IT.
I DON'T KNOW, AJ.
VRRMMM
VRRMAVRVRVRR
I-I DON'T THINK THIS IS EVEN POSSIBLE.

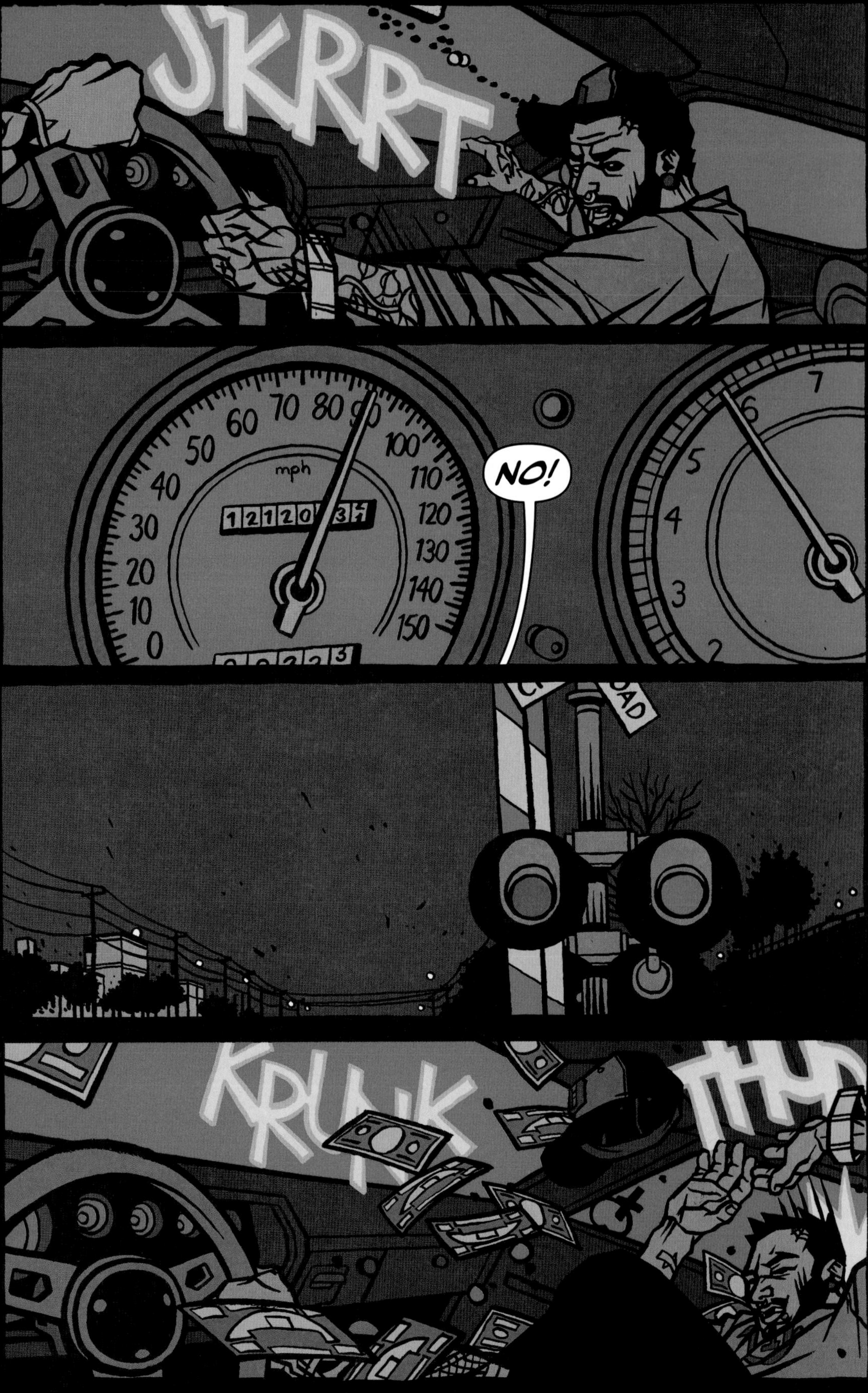
JKRRT
NO!
KRUNK

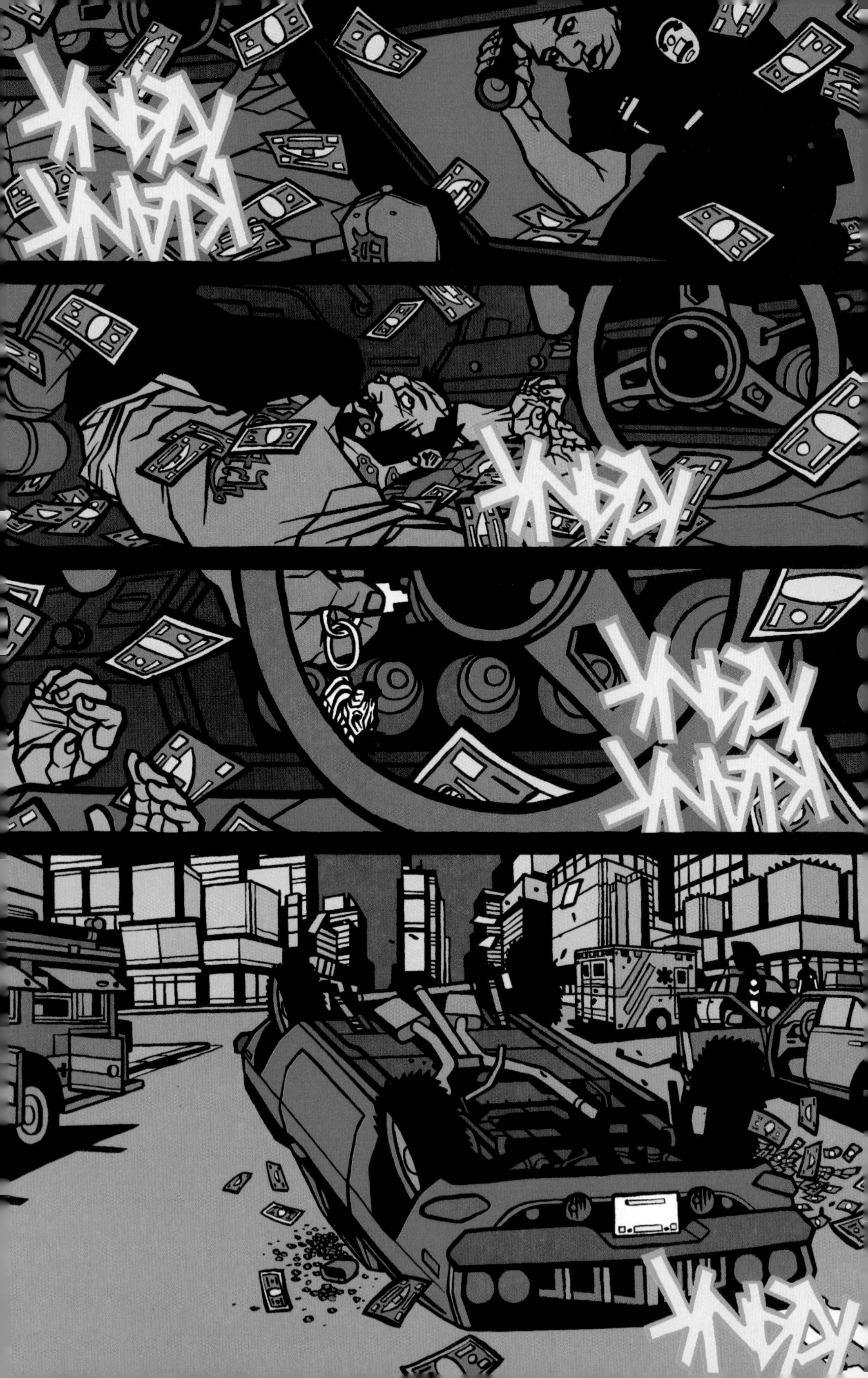
KRANK
KRAK
KRAK
KRANK
KRAK
KRAK

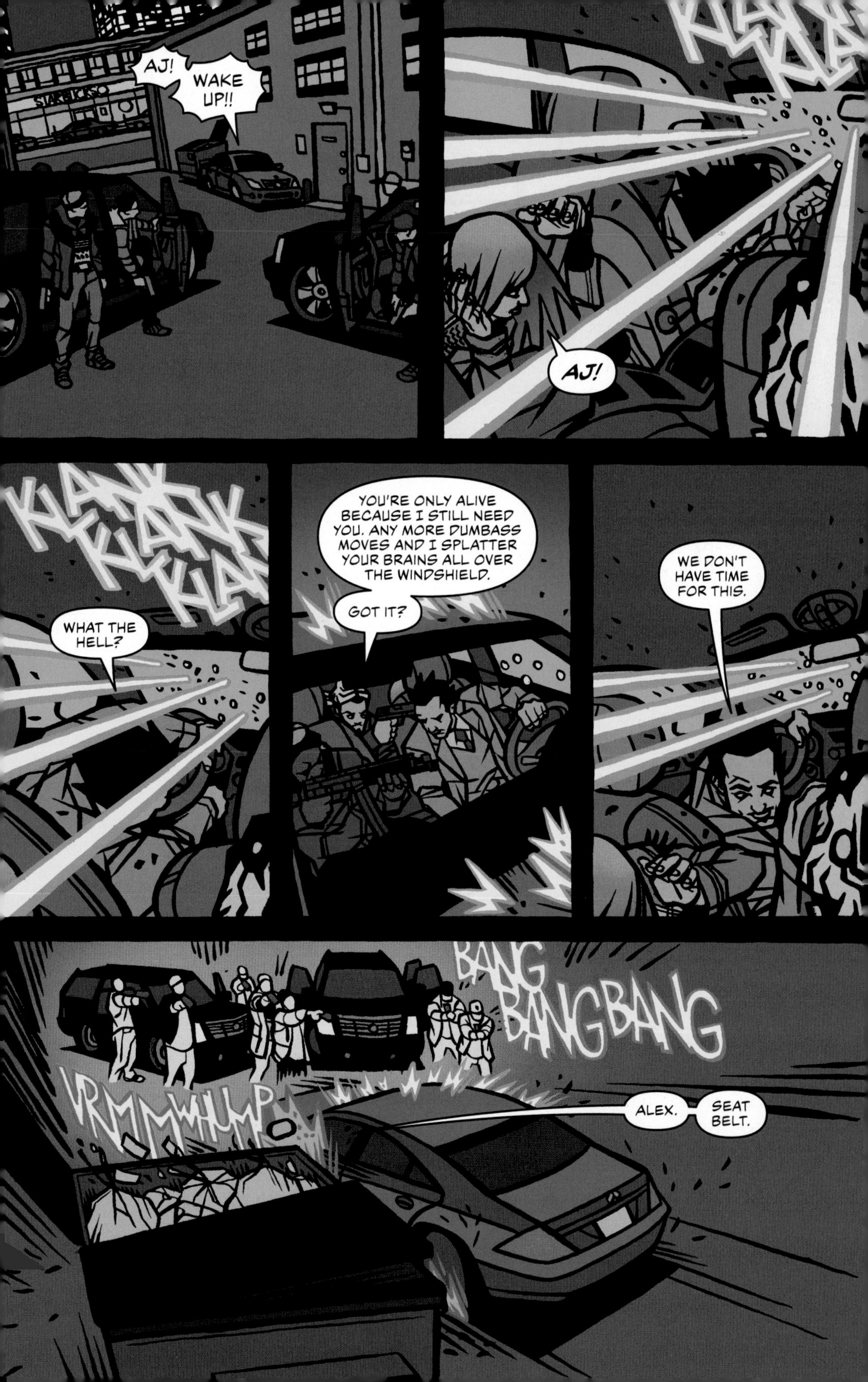
AJ!
WAKE UP!!
AJ!
WHAT THE HELL?
YOU'RE ONLY ALIVE BECAUSE I STILL NEED YOU. ANY MORE DUMBASS MOVES AND I SPLATTER YOUR BRAINS ALL OVER THE WINDSHIELD.
GOT IT?
WE DON'T HAVE TIME FOR THIS.
BANG BANG BANG BANG
VRMMWHUMP
ALEX.
SEAT BELT.

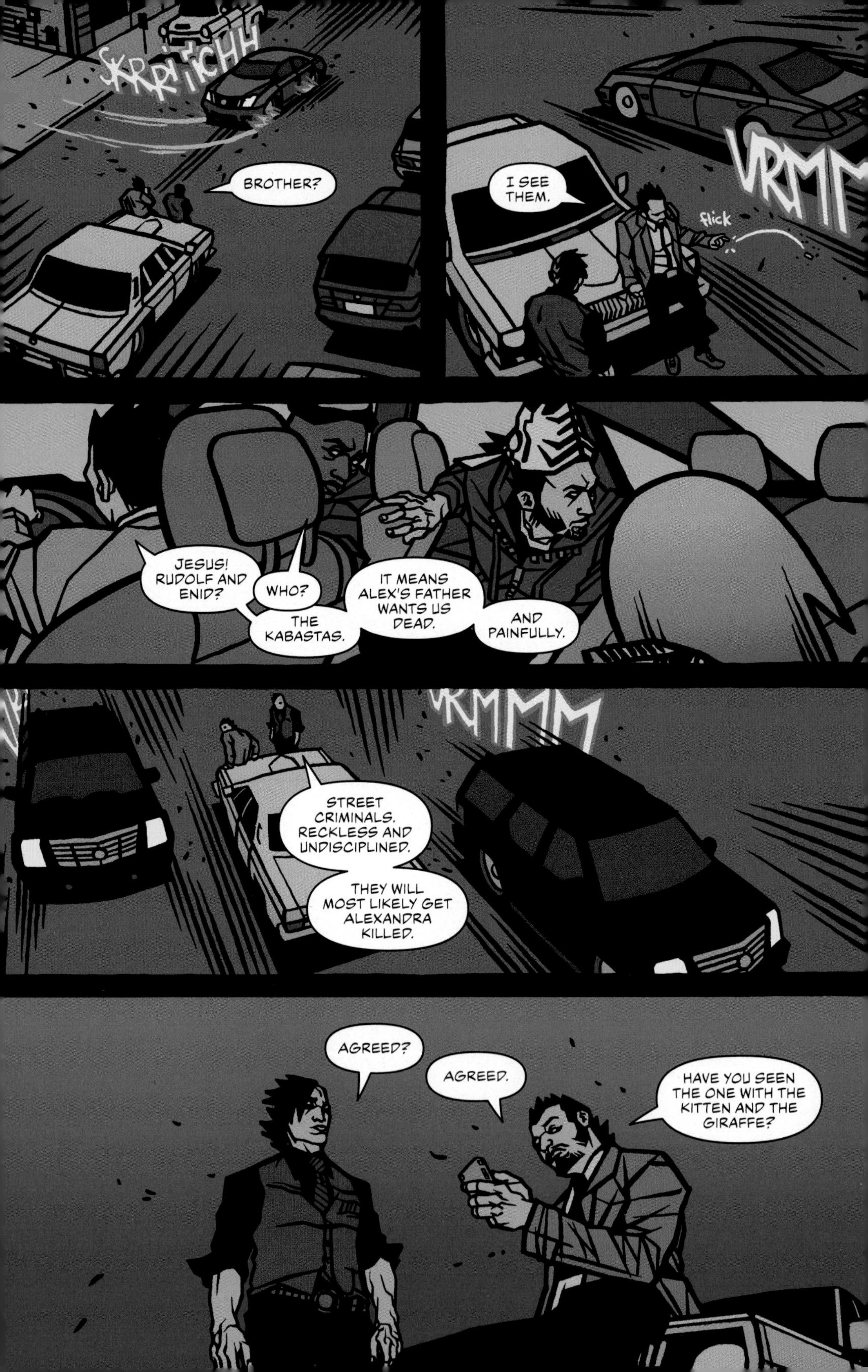
SKRRITCHH
BROTHER?
I SEE THEM.
VRMM
flick
JESUS! RUDOLF AND ENID?
WHO?
THE KABASTAS.
IT MEANS ALEX'S FATHER WANTS US DEAD.
AND PAINFULLY.
VRMMM
STREET CRIMINALS. RECKLESS AND UNDISCIPLINED.
THEY WILL MOST LIKELY GET ALEXANDRA KILLED.
AGREED?
AGREED.
HAVE YOU SEEN THE ONE WITH THE KITTEN AND THE GIRAFFE?

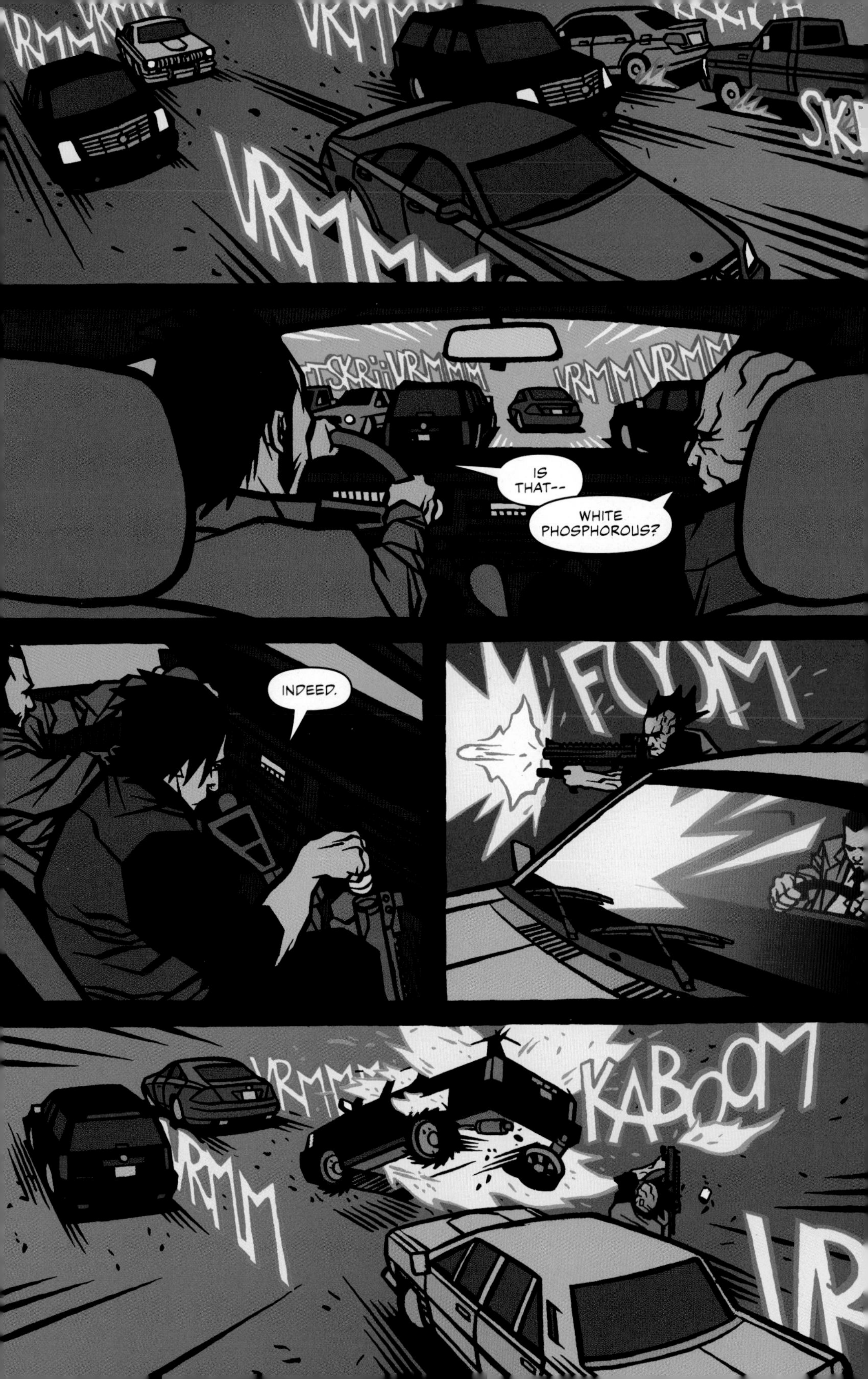
VRMM VRMM
VRMMM
SKRRGH
SKR
VRMMMM
SKRii VRMMM
VRMM VRMM
IS THAT--
WHITE PHOSPHOROUS?
INDEED.
FOOM
VRMM
KABOOM
VRMM
VR

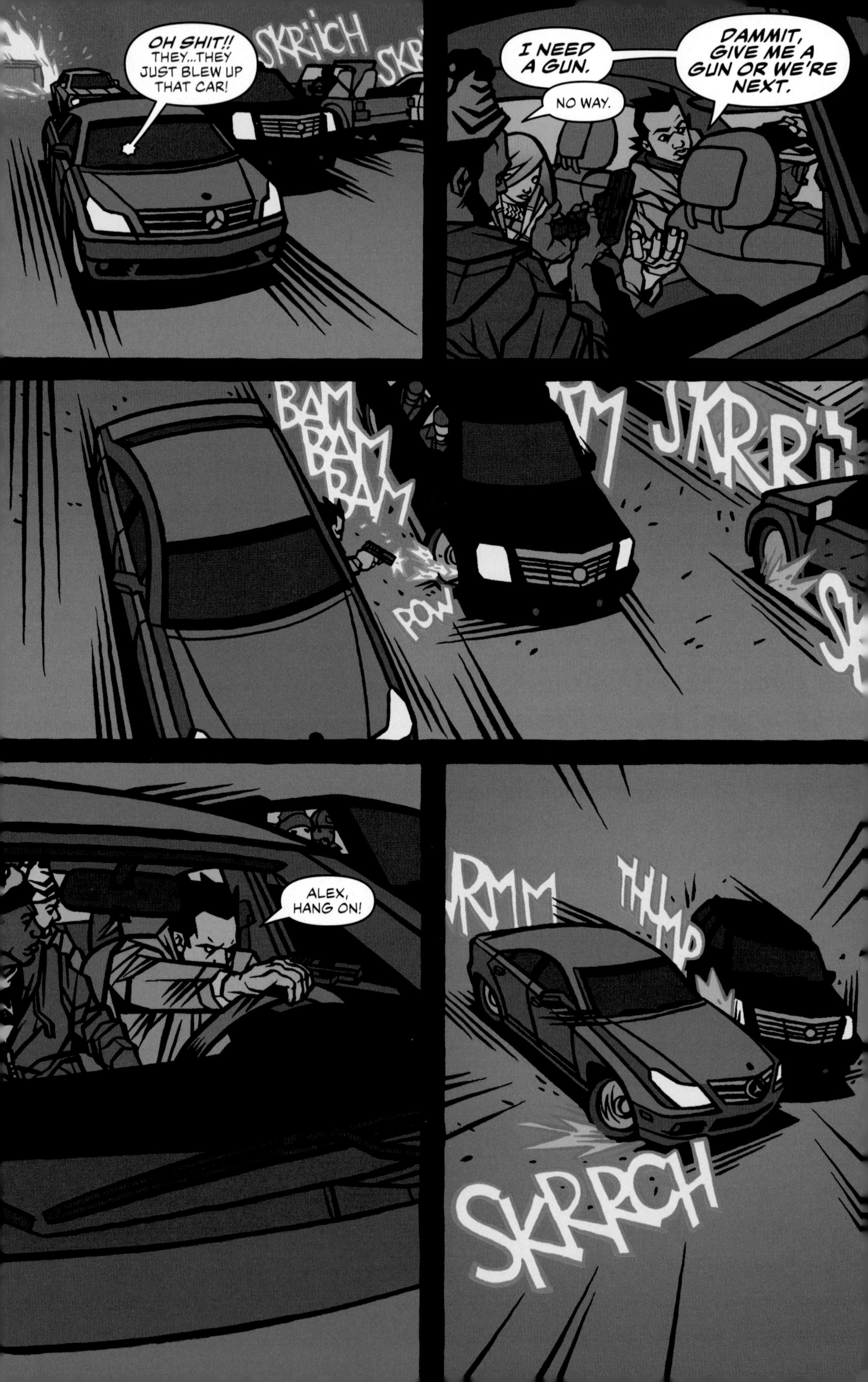
OH SHIT!! THEY...THEY JUST BLEW UP THAT CAR!
SKRICH
I NEED A GUN.
DAMMIT, GIVE ME A GUN OR WE'RE NEXT.
NO WAY.
BAM BAM BAM BAM
POW
SKRR
ALEX, HANG ON!
RMM
THUMP
SKRRCH

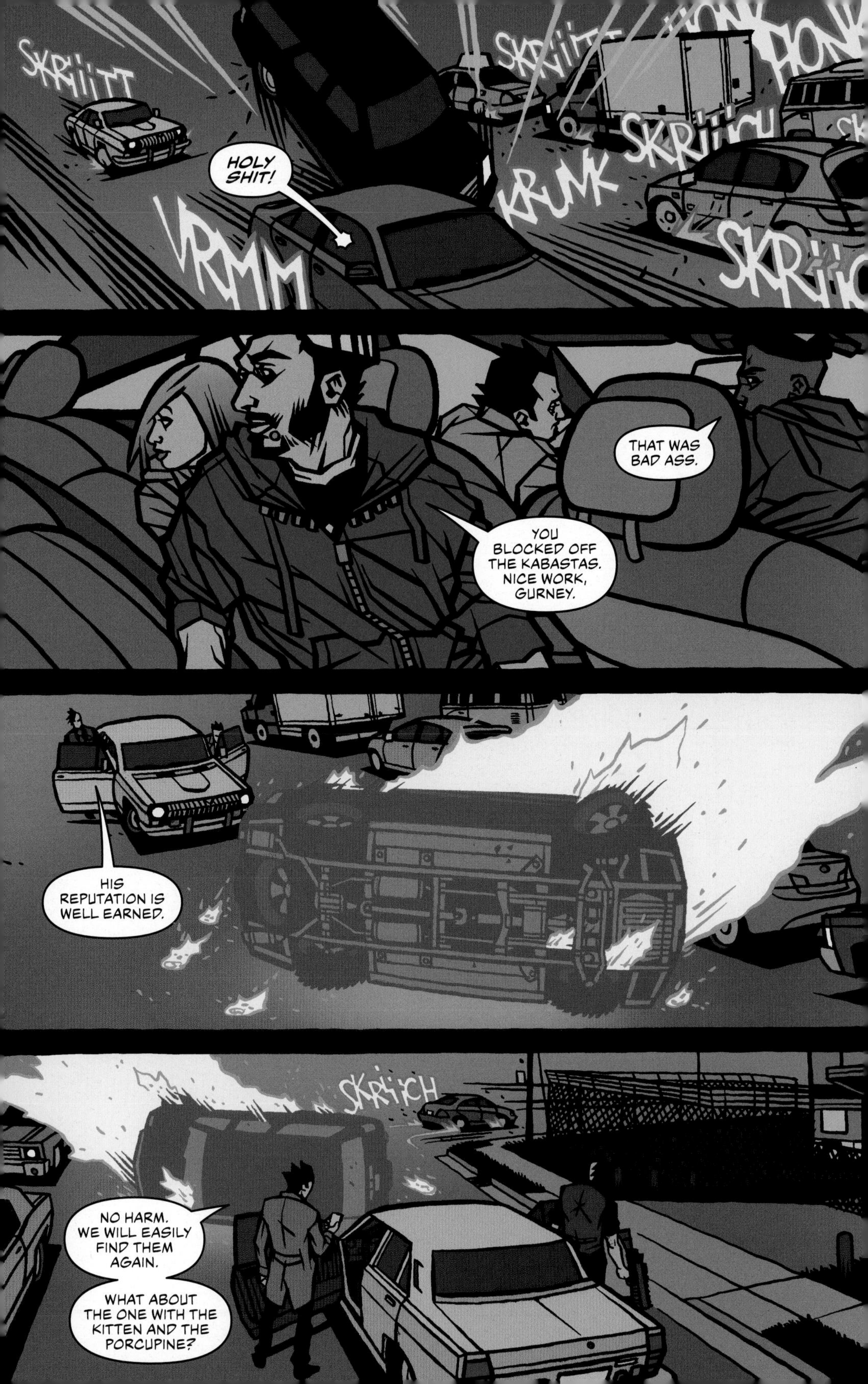
SKRIITT
SKRIITT
HONK HONK
SKRIIICH
KRUNK
HOLY SHIT!
VRMM
SKRIIICH
THAT WAS BAD ASS.
YOU BLOCKED OFF THE KABASTAS. NICE WORK, GURNEY.
HIS REPUTATION IS WELL EARNED.
SKRIICH
NO HARM. WE WILL EASILY FIND THEM AGAIN.
WHAT ABOUT THE ONE WITH THE KITTEN AND THE PORCUPINE?

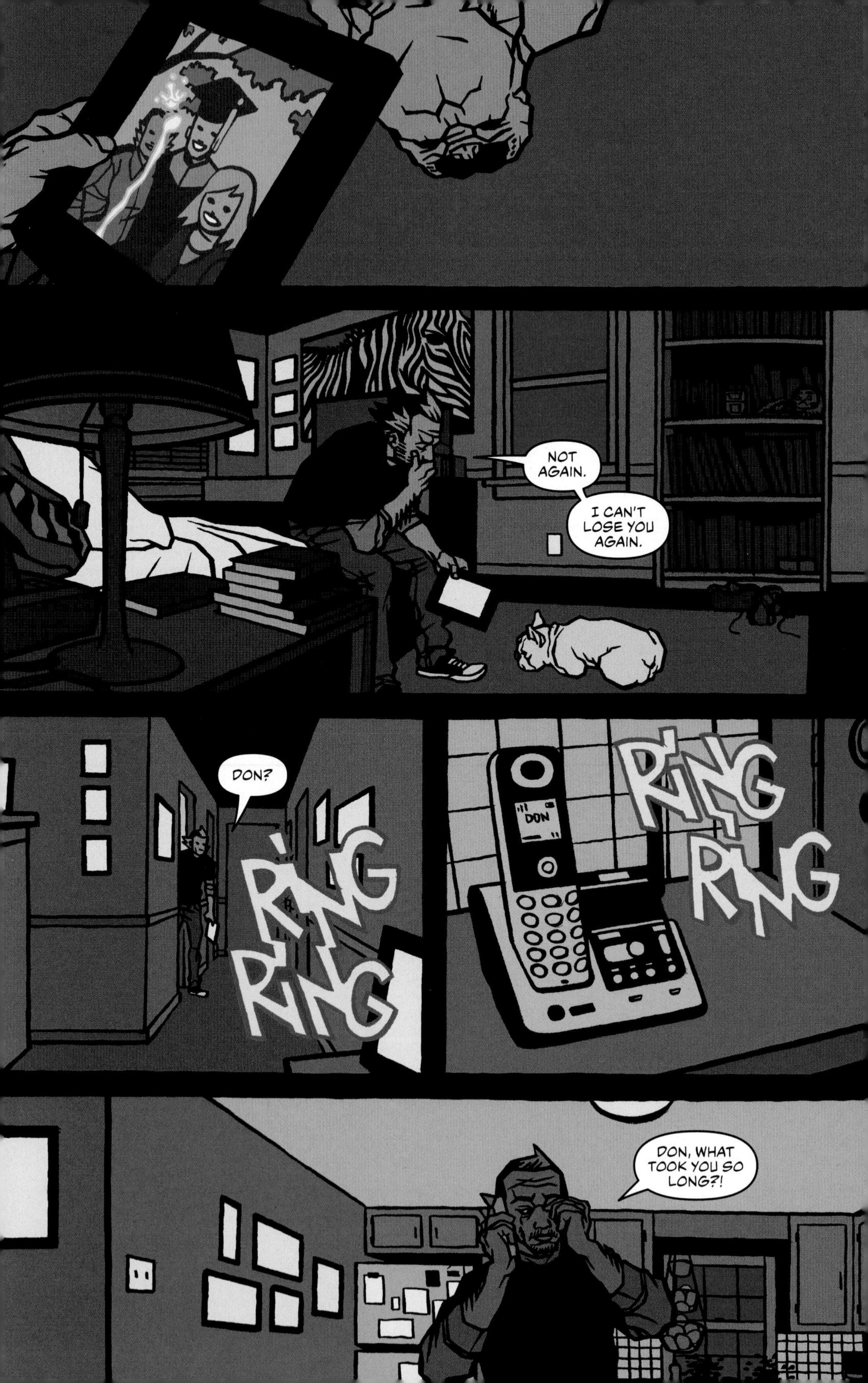
NOT AGAIN.
I CAN'T LOSE YOU AGAIN.
DON?
RING RING
DON
RING RING
DON, WHAT TOOK YOU SO LONG?!

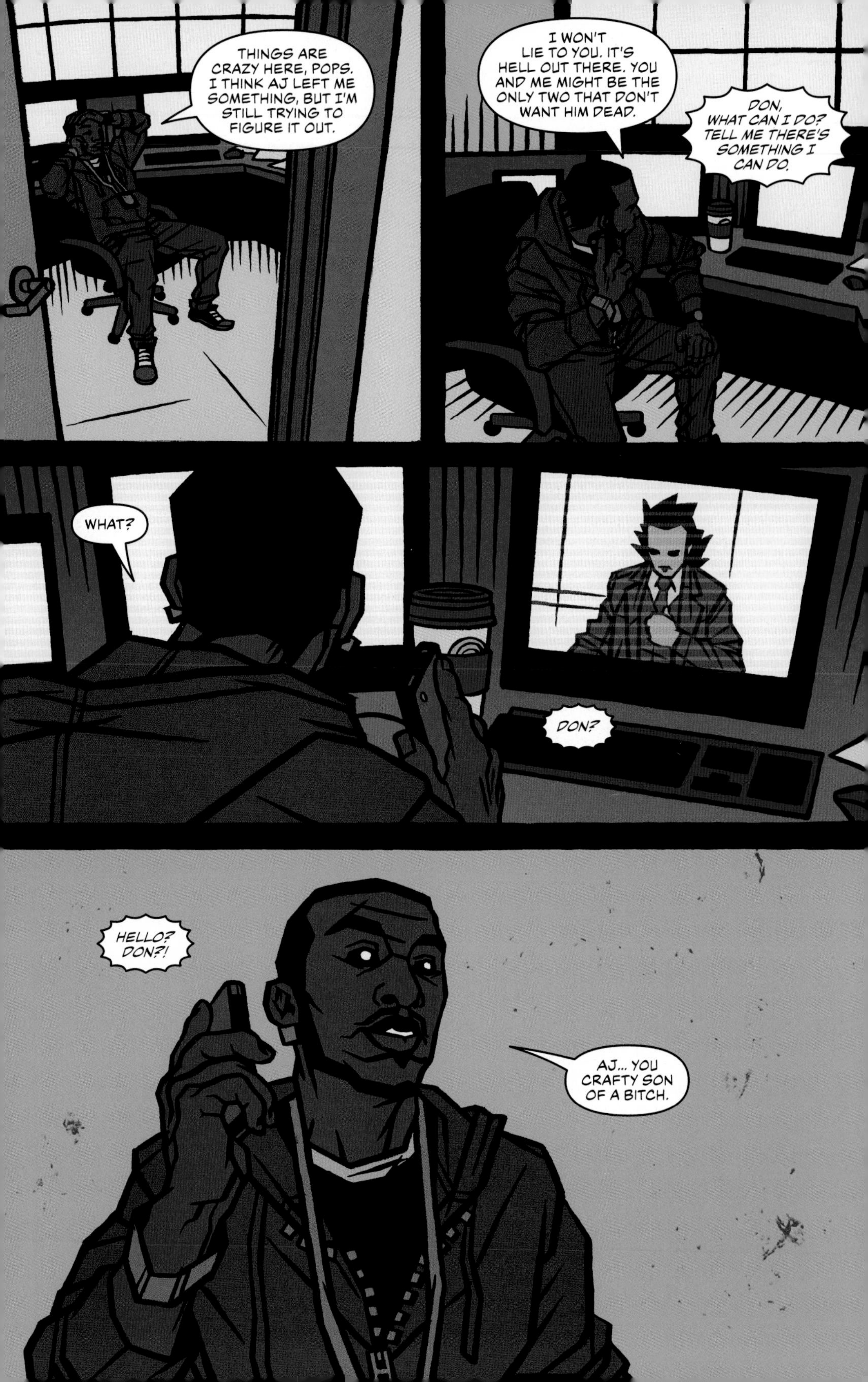
THINGS ARE CRAZY HERE, POPS. I THINK AJ LEFT ME SOMETHING, BUT I'M STILL TRYING TO FIGURE IT OUT.
I WON'T LIE TO YOU. IT'S HELL OUT THERE. YOU AND ME MIGHT BE THE ONLY TWO THAT DON'T WANT HIM DEAD.
DON, WHAT CAN I DO? TELL ME THERE'S SOMETHING I CAN DO.
WHAT?
DON?
HELLO? DON?!
AJ... YOU CRAFTY SON OF A BITCH.

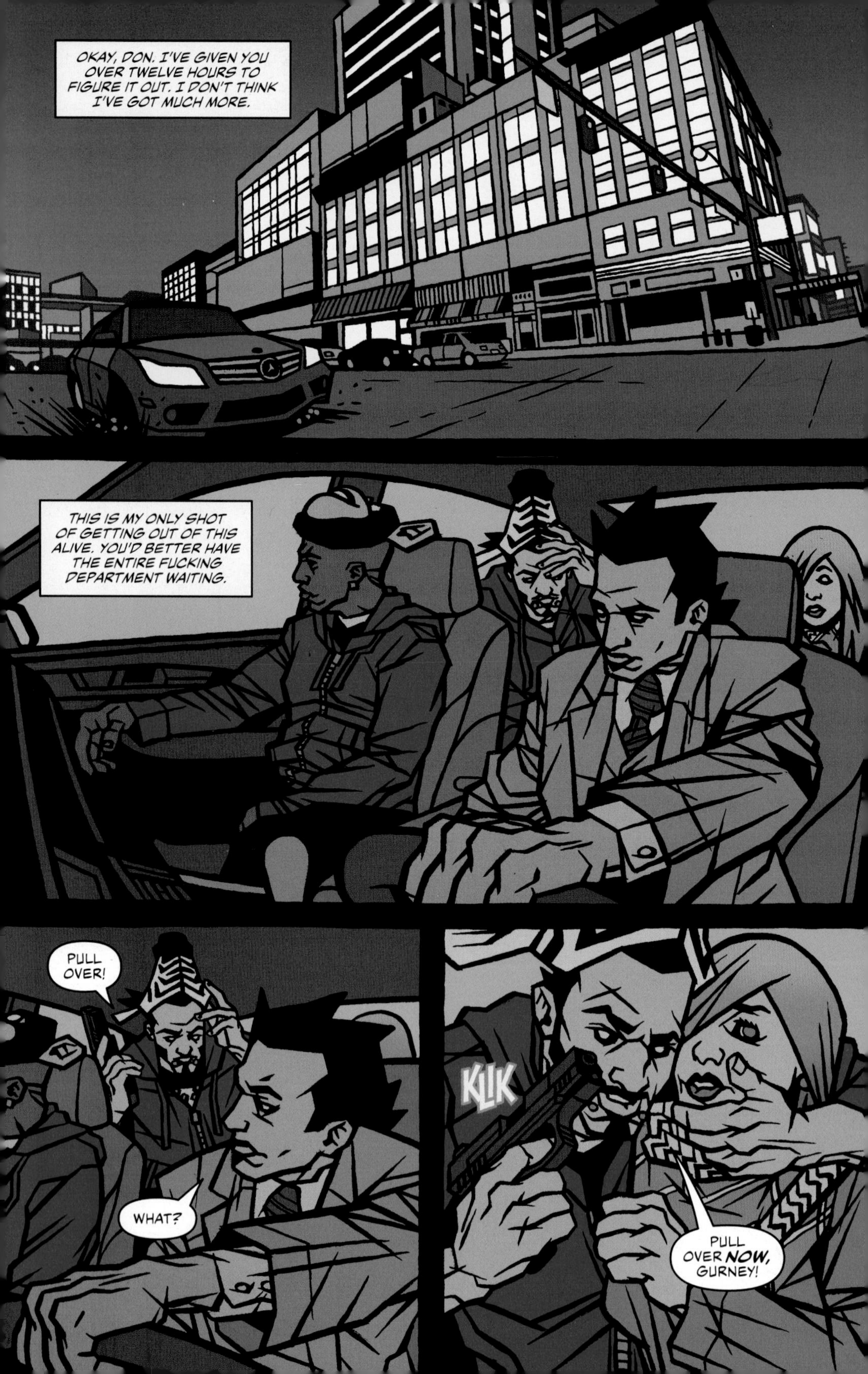
OKAY, DON. I'VE GIVEN YOU OVER TWELVE HOURS TO FIGURE IT OUT. I DON'T THINK I'VE GOT MUCH MORE.
THIS IS MY ONLY SHOT OF GETTING OUT OF THIS ALIVE. YOU'D BETTER HAVE THE ENTIRE FUCKING DEPARTMENT WAITING.
PULL OVER!
WHAT?
KLIK
PULL OVER NOW, GURNEY!

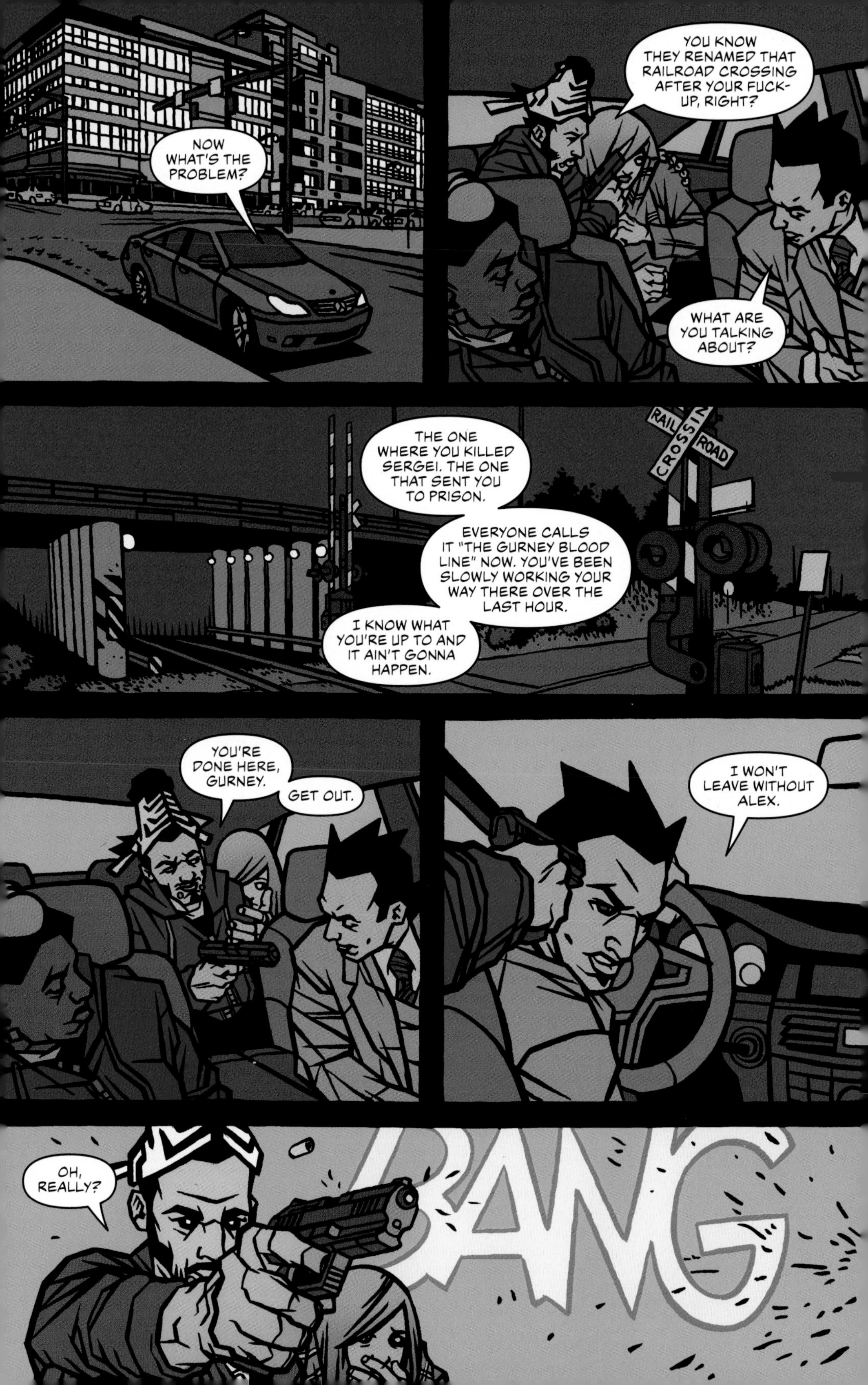
NOW WHAT'S THE PROBLEM?
YOU KNOW THEY RENAMED THAT RAILROAD CROSSING AFTER YOUR FUCK-UP, RIGHT?
WHAT ARE YOU TALKING ABOUT?
RAILROAD CROSSING
THE ONE WHERE YOU KILLED SERGEI. THE ONE THAT SENT YOU TO PRISON.
EVERYONE CALLS IT "THE GURNEY BLOOD LINE" NOW. YOU'VE BEEN SLOWLY WORKING YOUR WAY THERE OVER THE LAST HOUR.
I KNOW WHAT YOU'RE UP TO AND IT AIN'T GONNA HAPPEN.
YOU'RE DONE HERE, GURNEY.
GET OUT.
I WON'T LEAVE WITHOUT ALEX.
OH, REALLY?
BANG

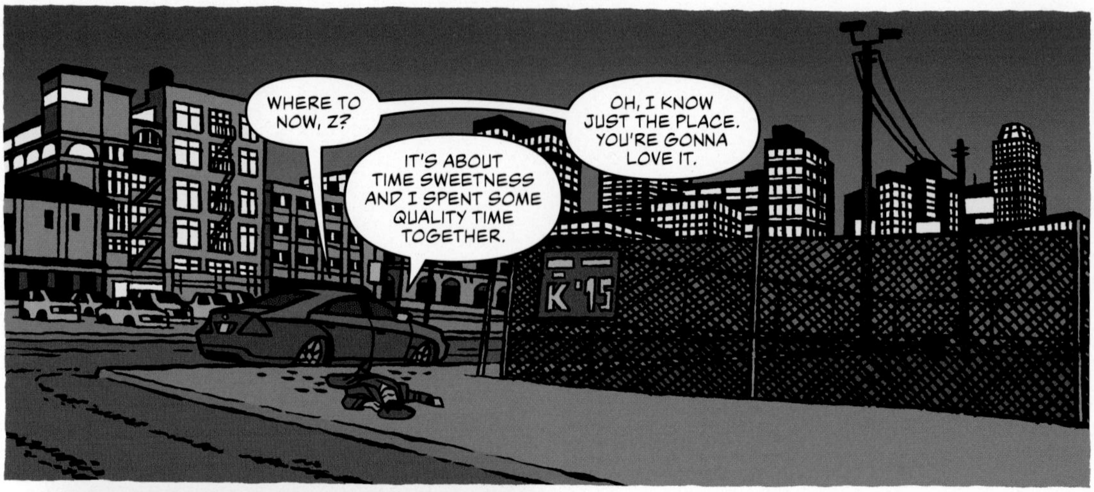
WHERE TO NOW, Z?
IT'S ABOUT TIME SWEETNESS AND I SPENT SOME QUALITY TIME TOGETHER.
OH, I KNOW JUST THE PLACE. YOU'RE GONNA LOVE IT.
K '15

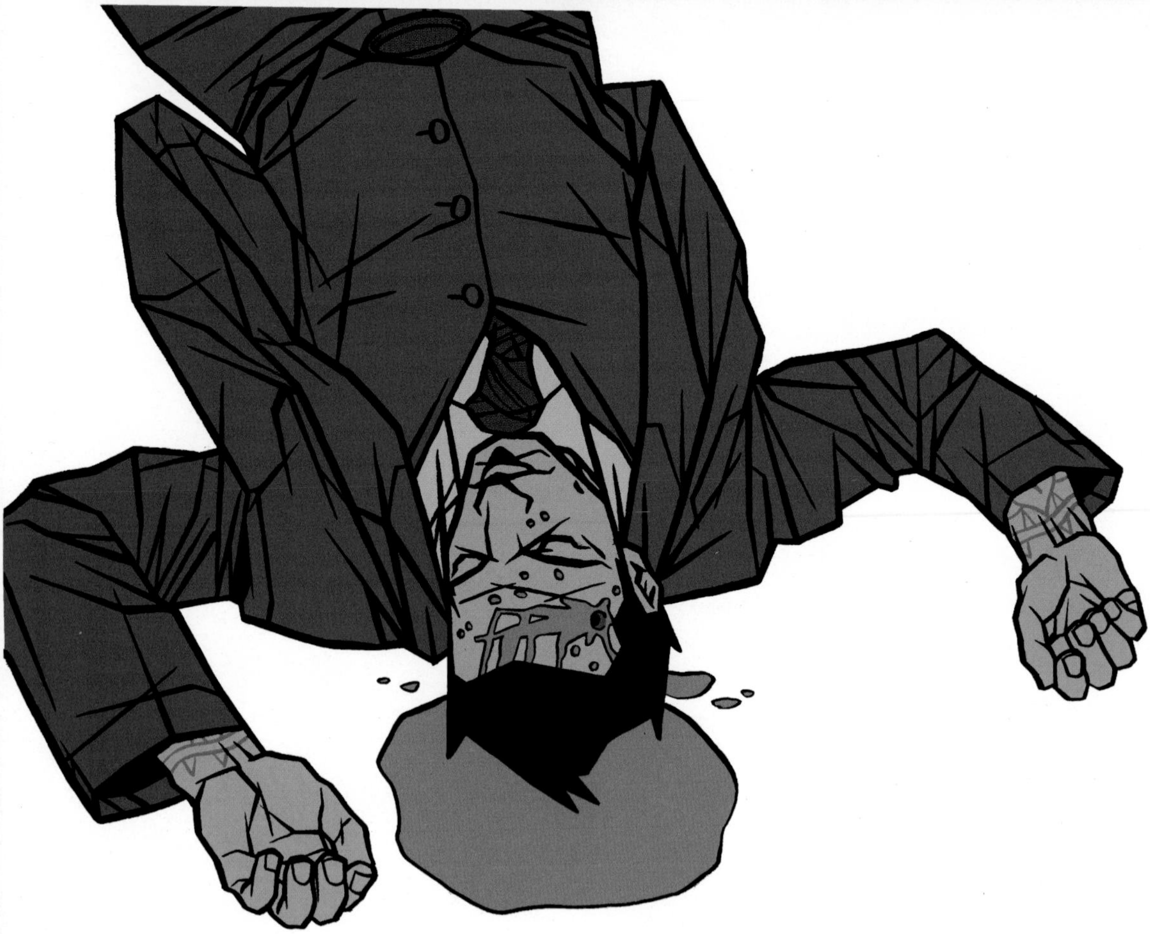

You drive. I've been hit.

- George "Baby Face" Nelson

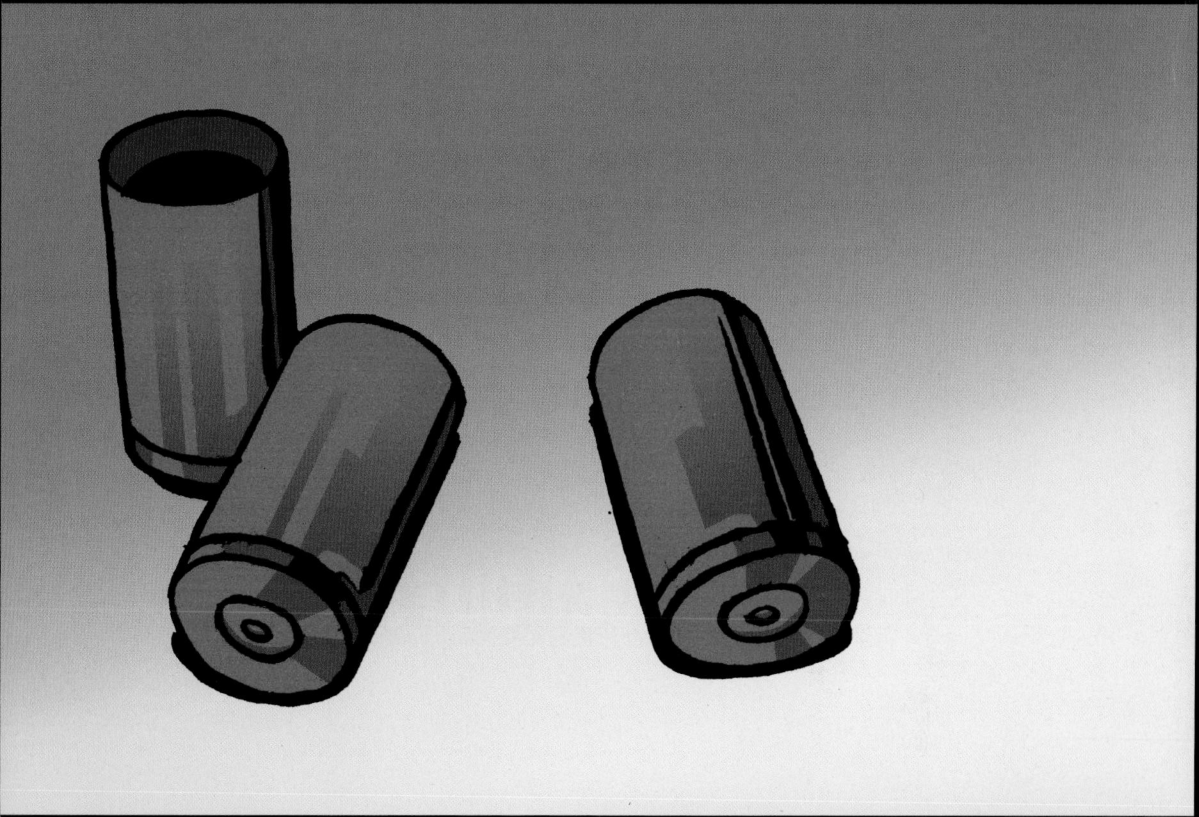

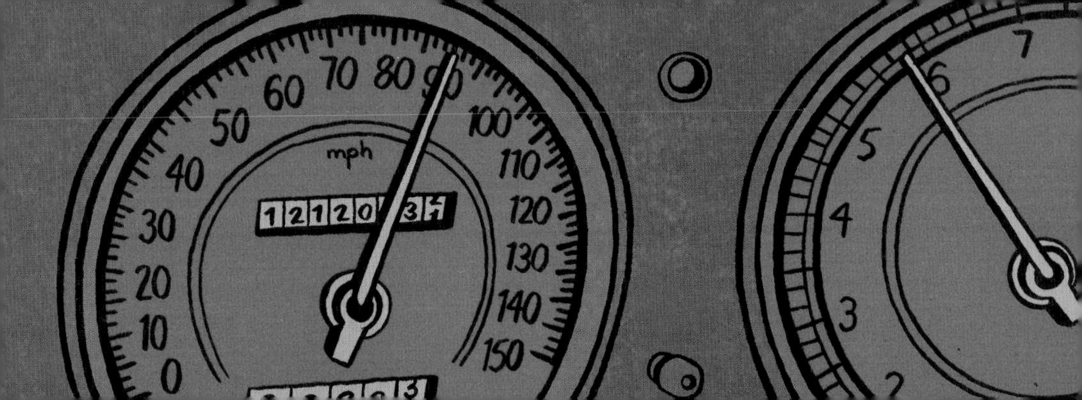

0
10
20
30
40
50
60
70
80
90
100
110
120
130
140
150
mph
2
3
4
5
6
7

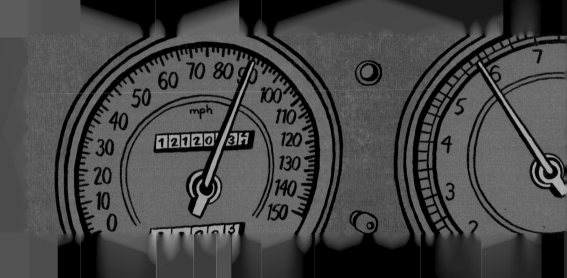

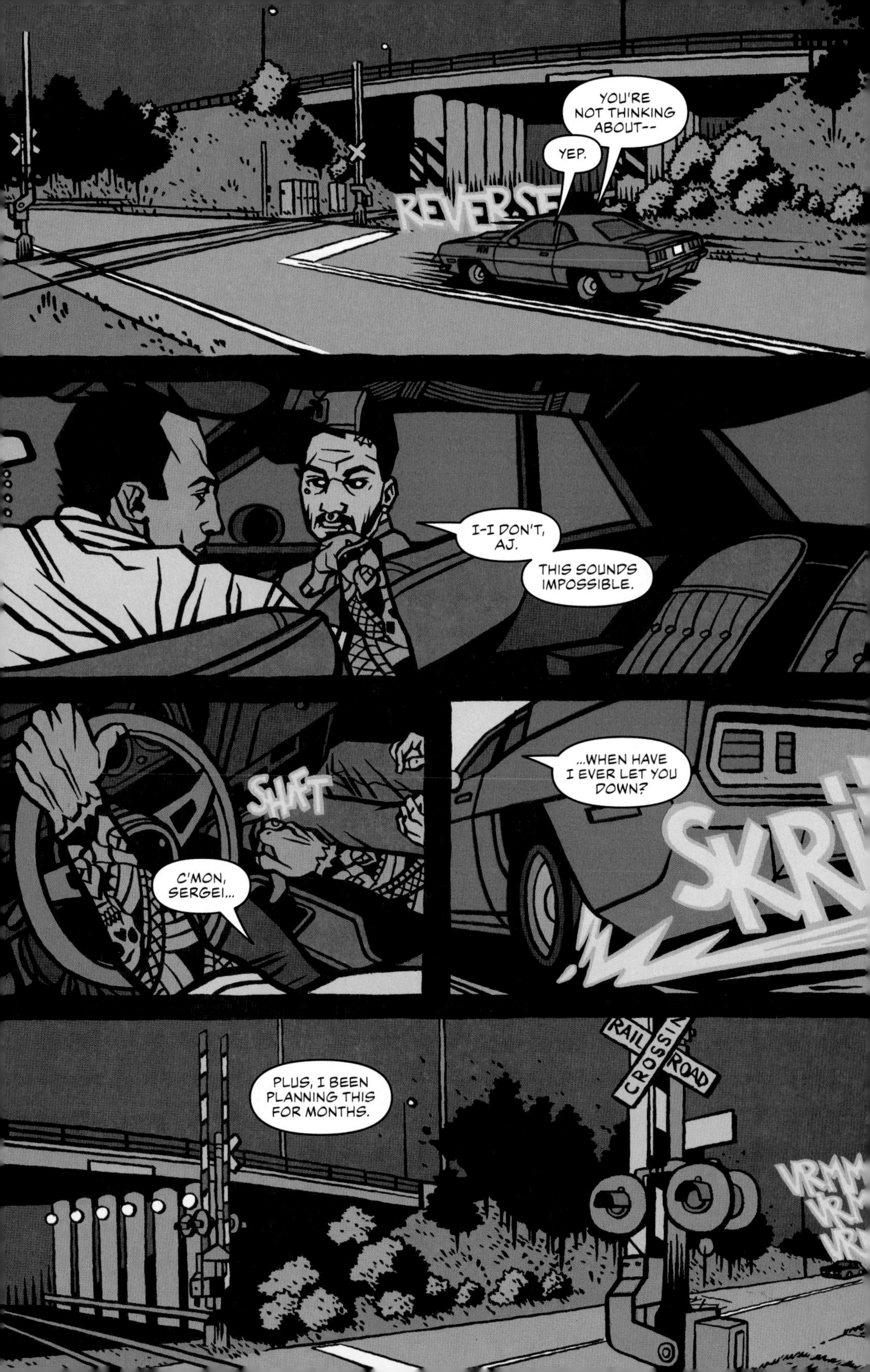

REVERSE
YOU'RE NOT THINKING ABOUT--
YEP.
I-I DON'T, AJ.
THIS SOUNDS IMPOSSIBLE.
SHIFT
C'MON, SERGEI...
...WHEN HAVE I EVER LET YOU DOWN?
SKRI
RAIL ROAD CROSSING
PLUS, I BEEN PLANNING THIS FOR MONTHS.

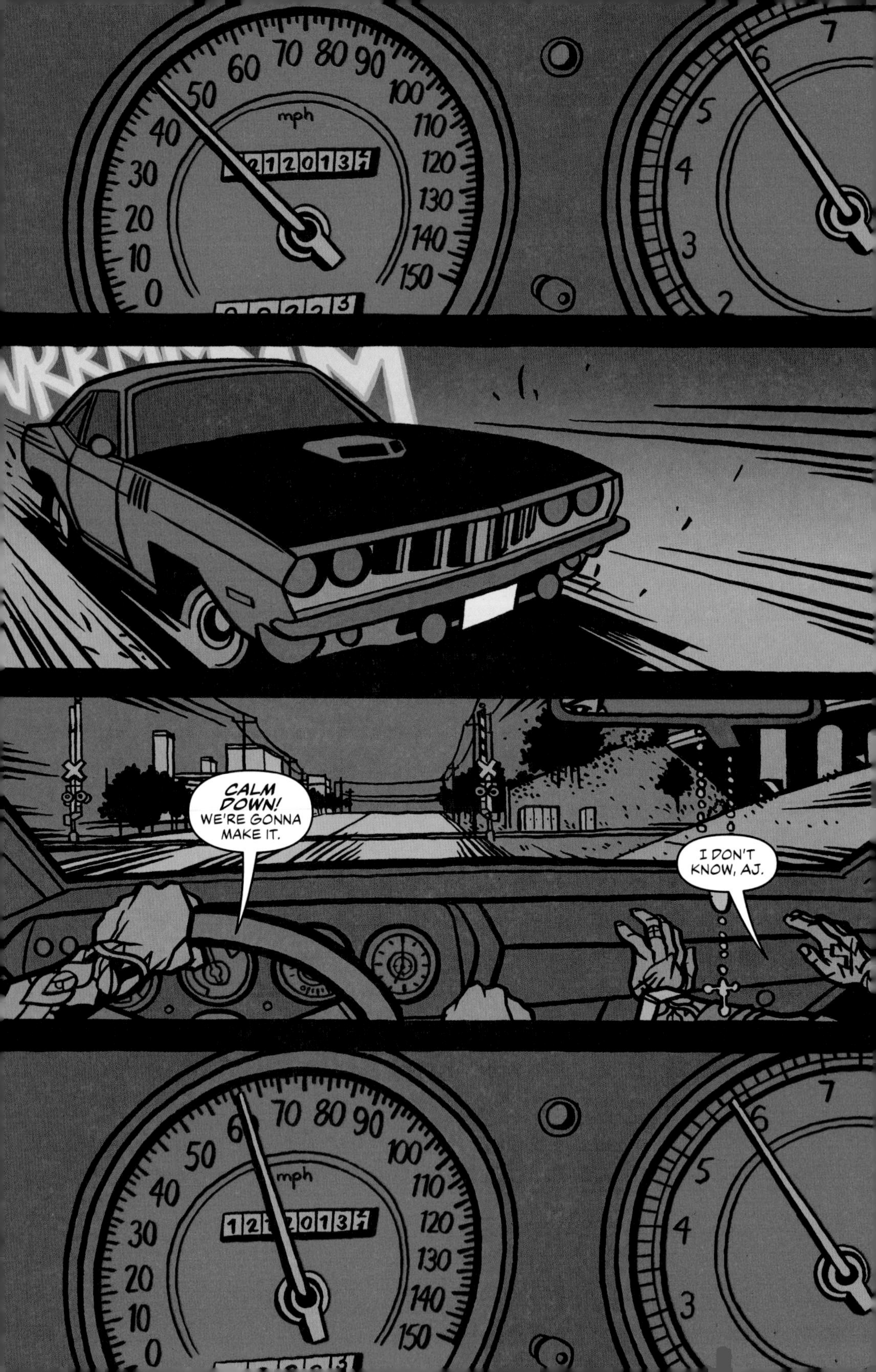
CALM DOWN! WE'RE GONNA MAKE IT.
I DON'T KNOW, AJ.

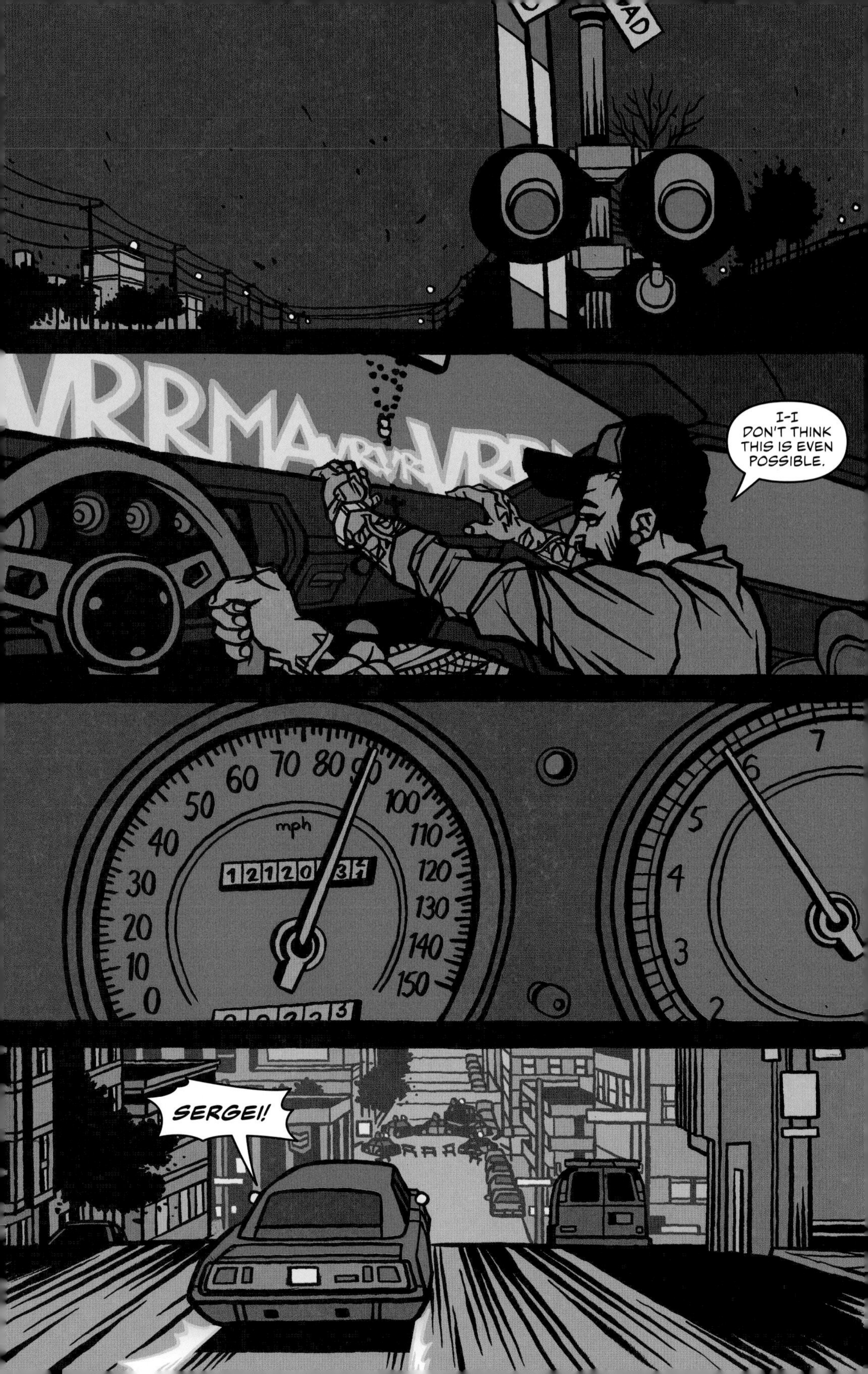
VRRMAvrvrVRR
I-I DON'T THINK THIS IS EVEN POSSIBLE.
SERGEI!

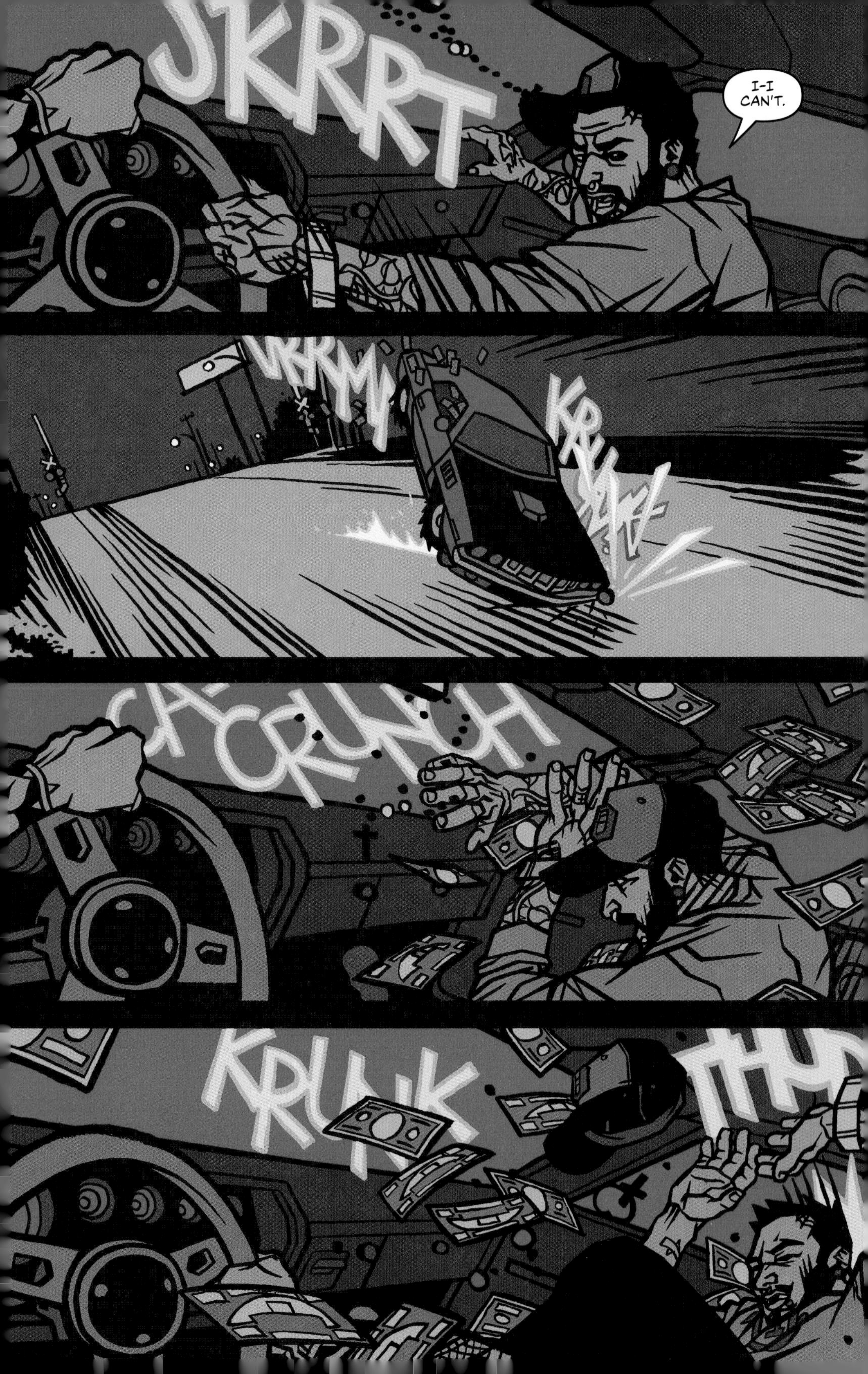
JKRRT
I-I CAN'T.
VRRM
CA-CRUNCH
KRUNK

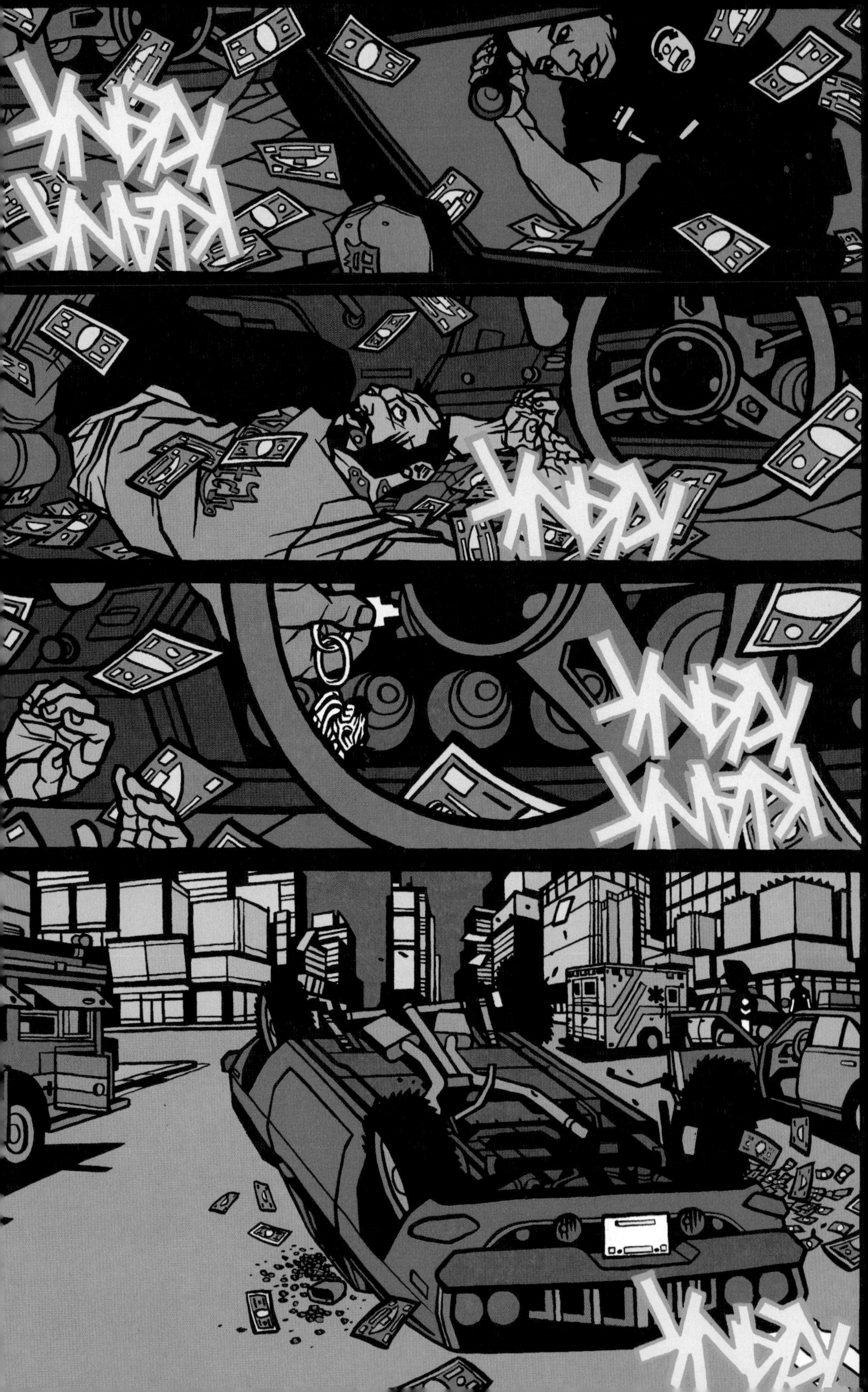
KRAK
KLANK
KRAK
KRAK
KLANK
KRAK

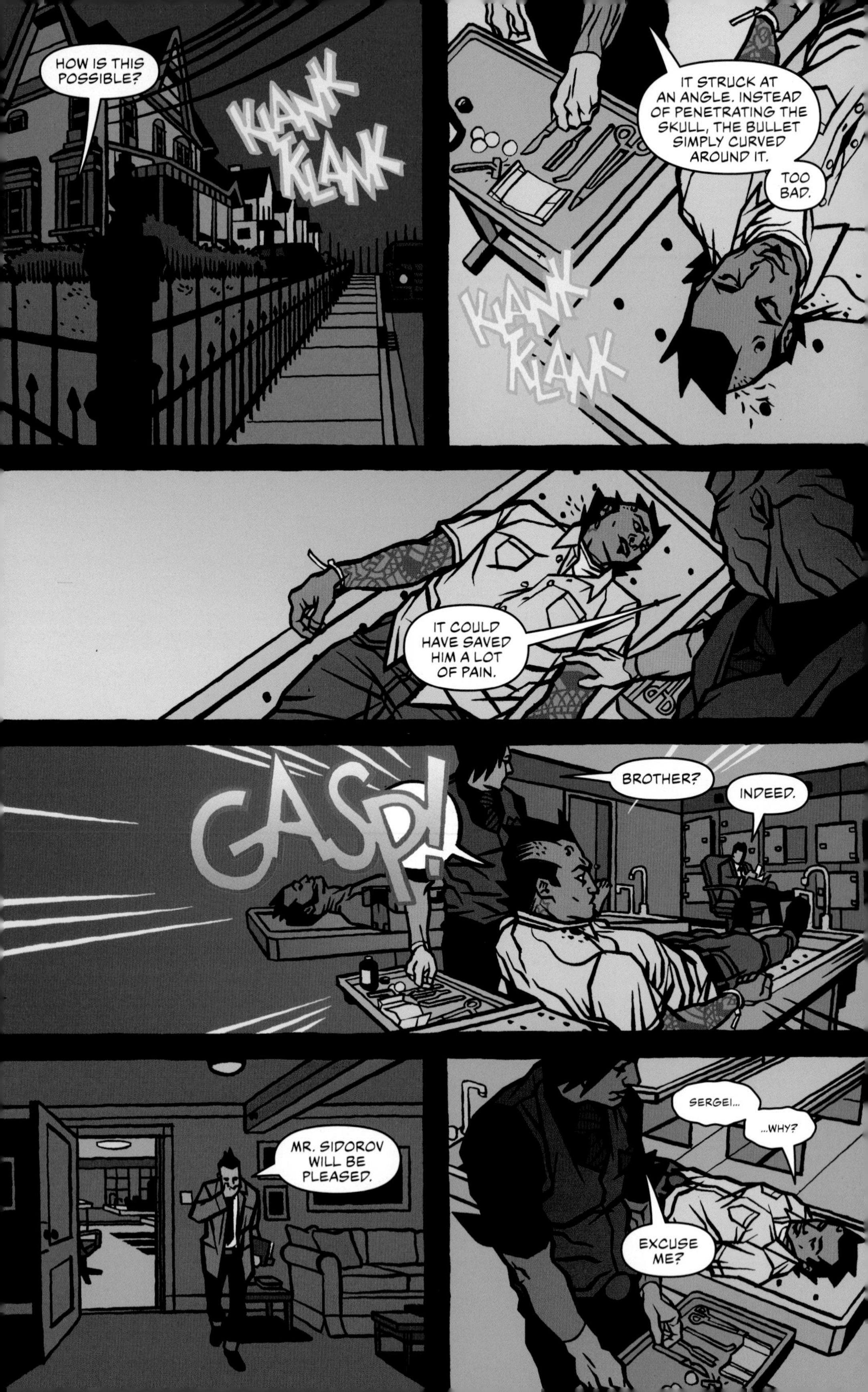
HOW IS THIS POSSIBLE?
KLANK KLANK
IT STRUCK AT AN ANGLE. INSTEAD OF PENETRATING THE SKULL, THE BULLET SIMPLY CURVED AROUND IT.
TOO BAD.
KLANK KLANK
IT COULD HAVE SAVED HIM A LOT OF PAIN.
GASP!
BROTHER?
INDEED.
MR. SIDOROV WILL BE PLEASED.
SERGEI...
...WHY?
EXCUSE ME?

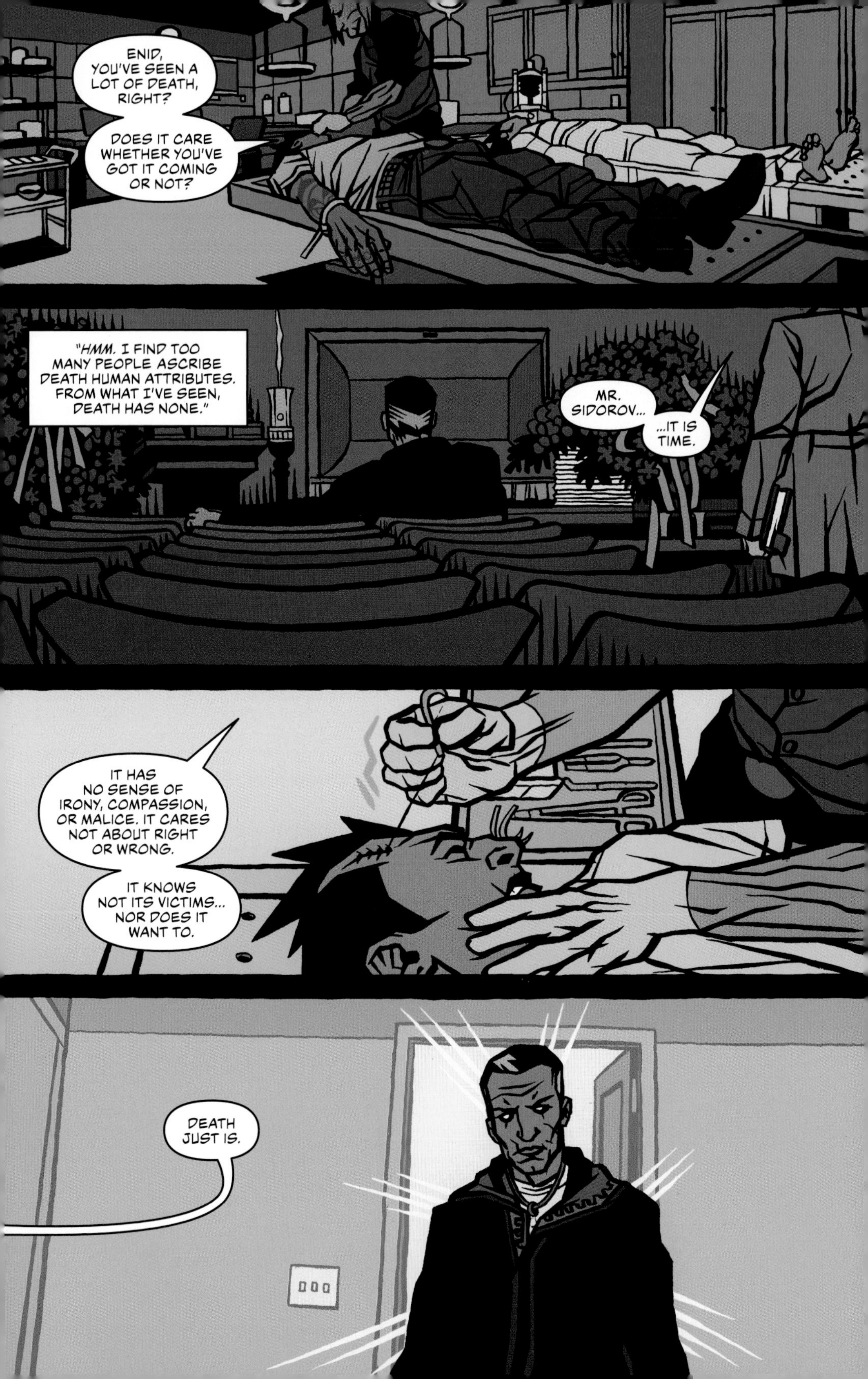
ENID, YOU'VE SEEN A LOT OF DEATH, RIGHT?
DOES IT CARE WHETHER YOU'VE GOT IT COMING OR NOT?
"HMM. I FIND TOO MANY PEOPLE ASCRIBE DEATH HUMAN ATTRIBUTES. FROM WHAT I'VE SEEN, DEATH HAS NONE."
MR. SIDOROV...
...IT IS TIME.
IT HAS NO SENSE OF IRONY, COMPASSION, OR MALICE. IT CARES NOT ABOUT RIGHT OR WRONG.
IT KNOWS NOT ITS VICTIMS... NOR DOES IT WANT TO.
DEATH JUST IS.

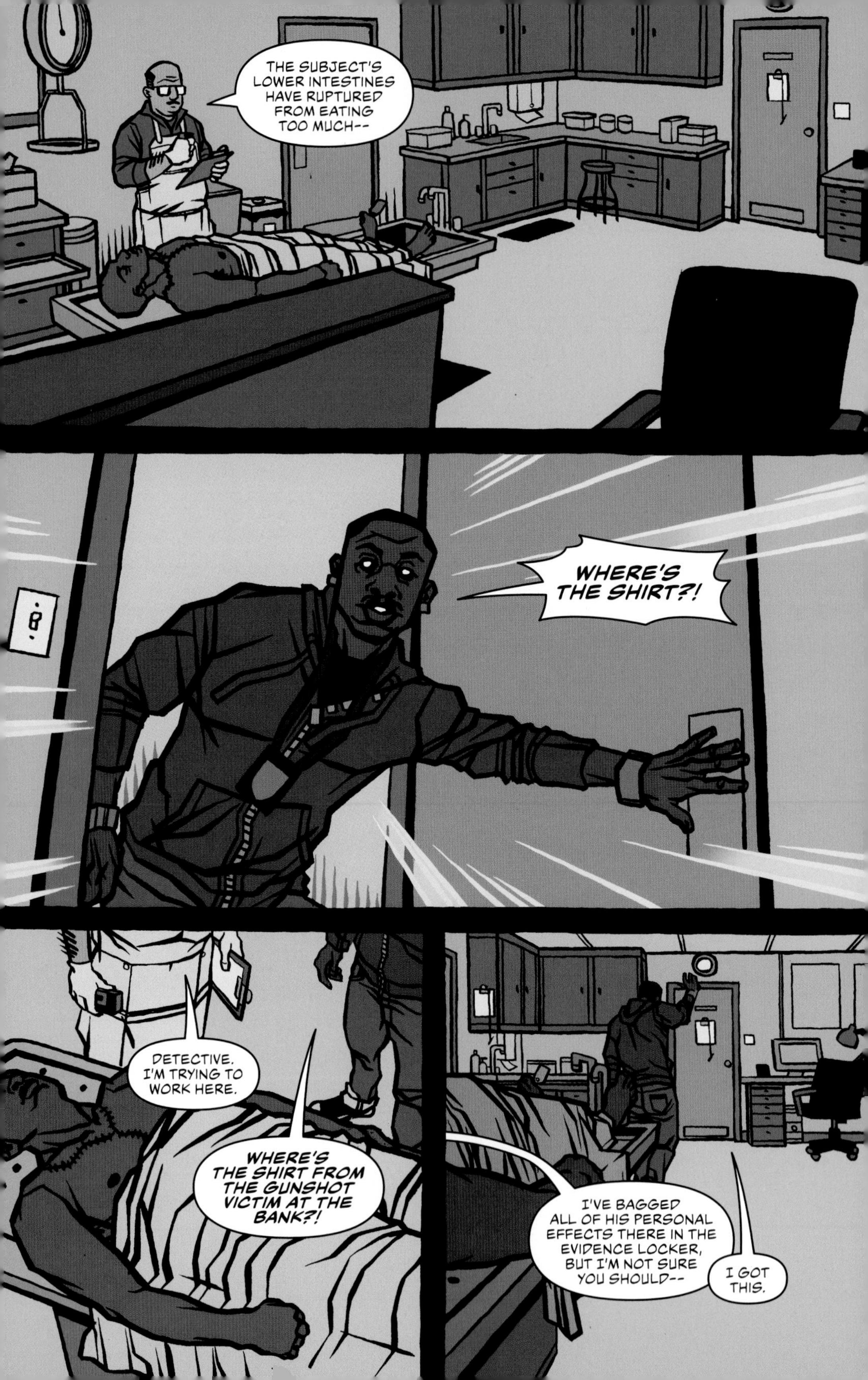
THE SUBJECT'S LOWER INTESTINES HAVE RUPTURED FROM EATING TOO MUCH--
WHERE'S THE SHIRT?!
DETECTIVE. I'M TRYING TO WORK HERE.
WHERE'S THE SHIRT FROM THE GUNSHOT VICTIM AT THE BANK?!
I'VE BAGGED ALL OF HIS PERSONAL EFFECTS THERE IN THE EVIDENCE LOCKER, BUT I'M NOT SURE YOU SHOULD--
I GOT THIS.

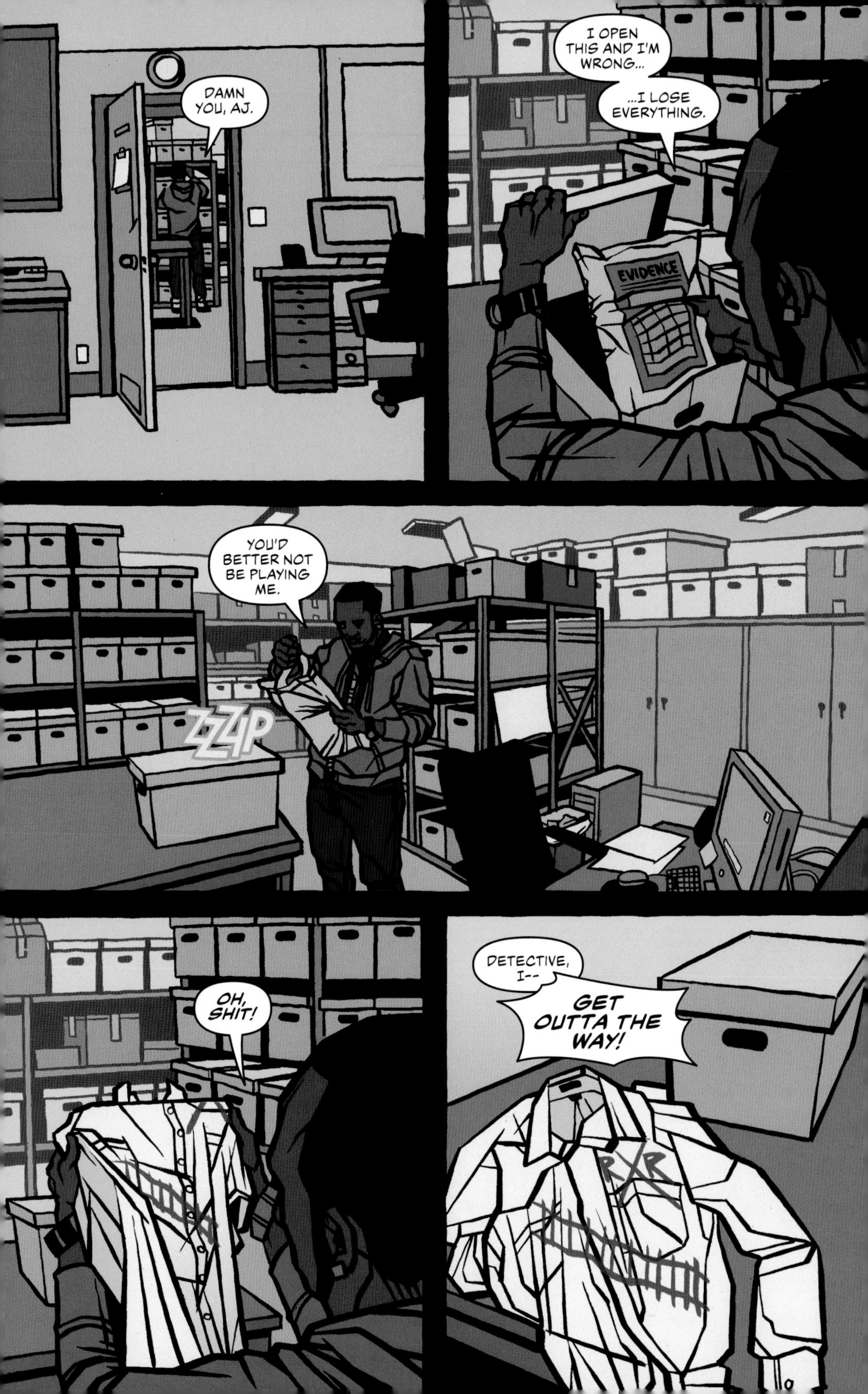
DAMN YOU, AJ.
I OPEN THIS AND I'M WRONG...
...I LOSE EVERYTHING.
EVIDENCE
YOU'D BETTER NOT BE PLAYING ME.
ZZZAP
OH, SHIT!
DETECTIVE, I--
GET OUTTA THE WAY!

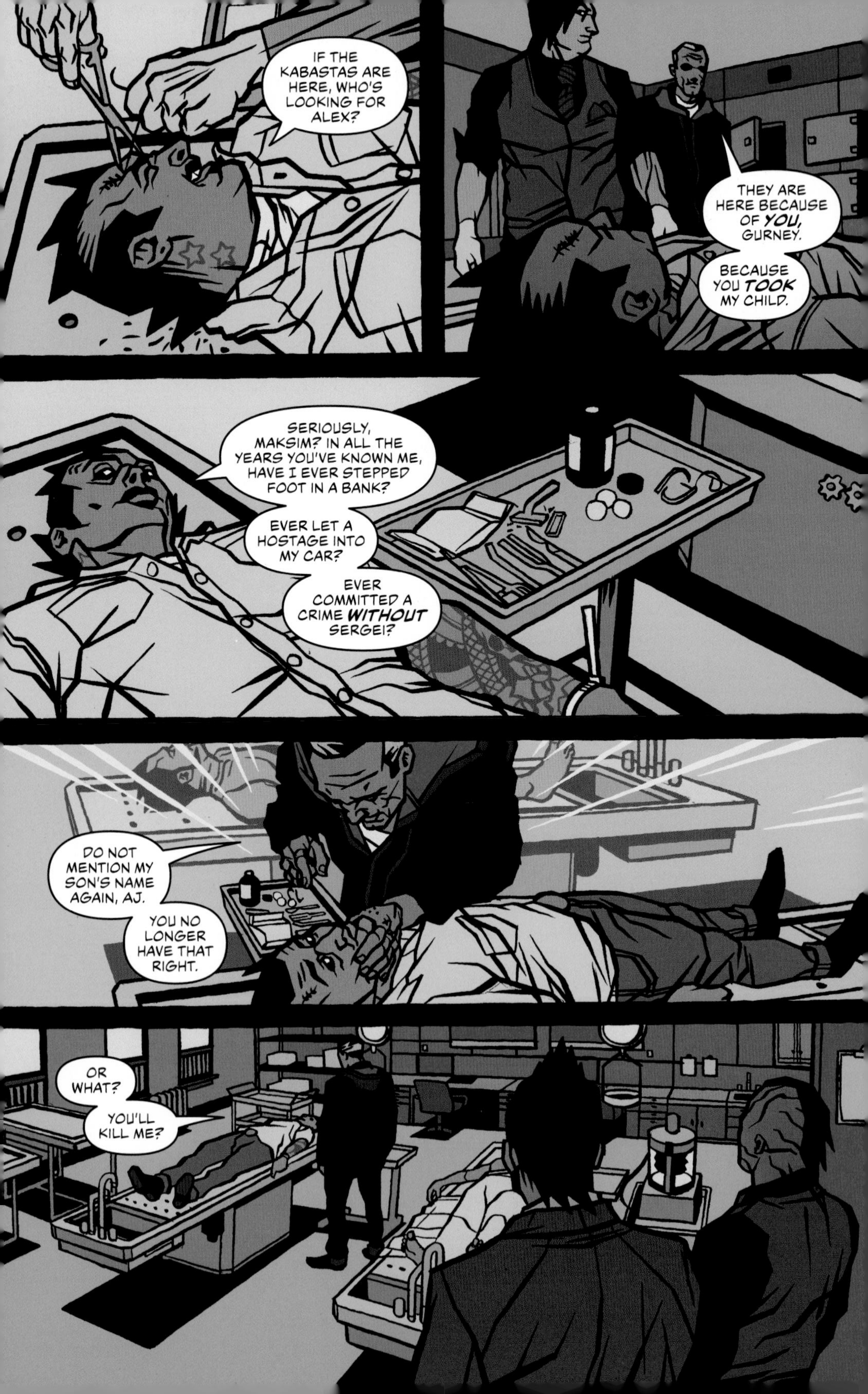
IF THE KABASTAS ARE HERE, WHO'S LOOKING FOR ALEX?
THEY ARE HERE BECAUSE OF *YOU*, GURNEY.
BECAUSE YOU *TOOK* MY CHILD.
SERIOUSLY, MAKSIM? IN ALL THE YEARS YOU'VE KNOWN ME, HAVE I EVER STEPPED FOOT IN A BANK?
EVER LET A HOSTAGE INTO MY CAR?
EVER COMMITTED A CRIME *WITHOUT* SERGEI?
DO NOT MENTION MY SON'S NAME AGAIN, AJ.
YOU NO LONGER HAVE THAT RIGHT.
OR WHAT?
YOU'LL KILL ME?

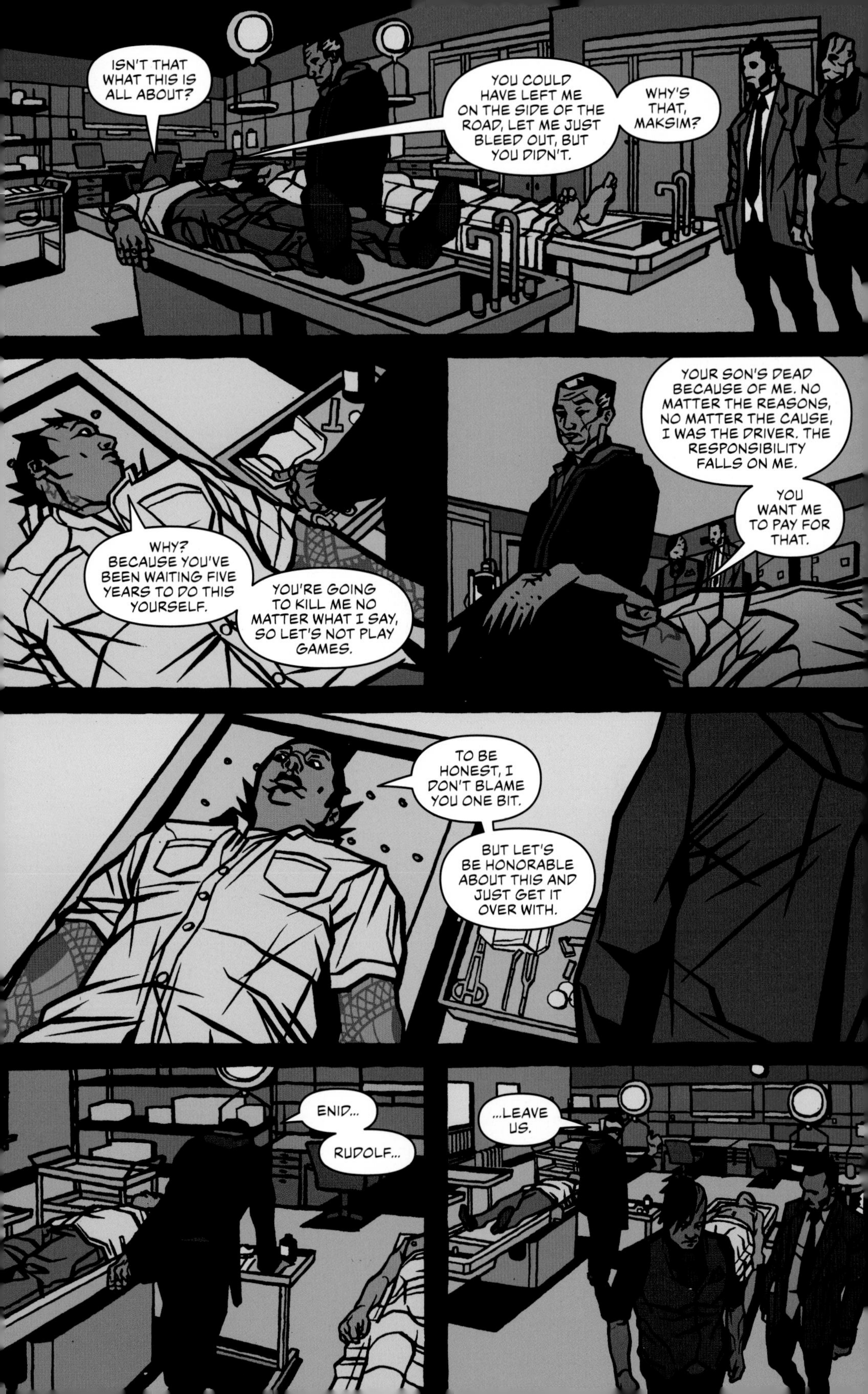
ISN'T THAT WHAT THIS IS ALL ABOUT?
YOU COULD HAVE LEFT ME ON THE SIDE OF THE ROAD, LET ME JUST BLEED OUT, BUT YOU DIDN'T.
WHY'S THAT, MAKSIM?
WHY? BECAUSE YOU'VE BEEN WAITING FIVE YEARS TO DO THIS YOURSELF.
YOU'RE GOING TO KILL ME NO MATTER WHAT I SAY, SO LET'S NOT PLAY GAMES.
YOUR SON'S DEAD BECAUSE OF ME. NO MATTER THE REASONS, NO MATTER THE CAUSE, I WAS THE DRIVER. THE RESPONSIBILITY FALLS ON ME.
YOU WANT ME TO PAY FOR THAT.
TO BE HONEST, I DON'T BLAME YOU ONE BIT.
BUT LET'S BE HONORABLE ABOUT THIS AND JUST GET IT OVER WITH.
ENID...
RUDOLF...
...LEAVE US.

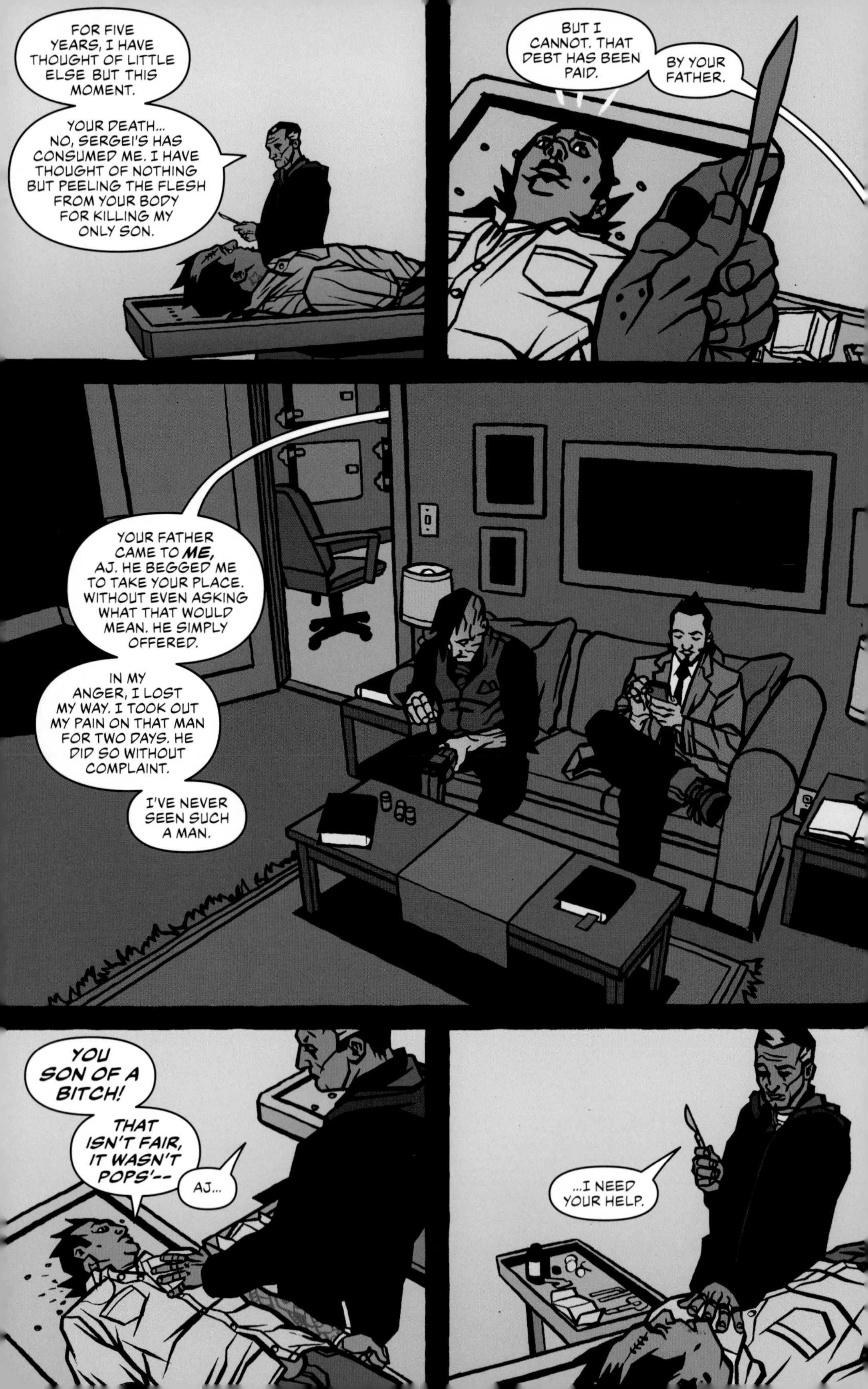
FOR FIVE YEARS, I HAVE THOUGHT OF LITTLE ELSE BUT THIS MOMENT.
YOUR DEATH... NO, SERGEI'S HAS CONSUMED ME. I HAVE THOUGHT OF NOTHING BUT PEELING THE FLESH FROM YOUR BODY FOR KILLING MY ONLY SON.
BUT I CANNOT. THAT DEBT HAS BEEN PAID.
BY YOUR FATHER.
YOUR FATHER CAME TO ME, AJ. HE BEGGED ME TO TAKE YOUR PLACE. WITHOUT EVEN ASKING WHAT THAT WOULD MEAN. HE SIMPLY OFFERED.
IN MY ANGER, I LOST MY WAY. I TOOK OUT MY PAIN ON THAT MAN FOR TWO DAYS. HE DID SO WITHOUT COMPLAINT.
I'VE NEVER SEEN SUCH A MAN.
YOU SON OF A BITCH!
THAT ISN'T FAIR, IT WASN'T POPS'--
AJ...
...I NEED YOUR HELP.

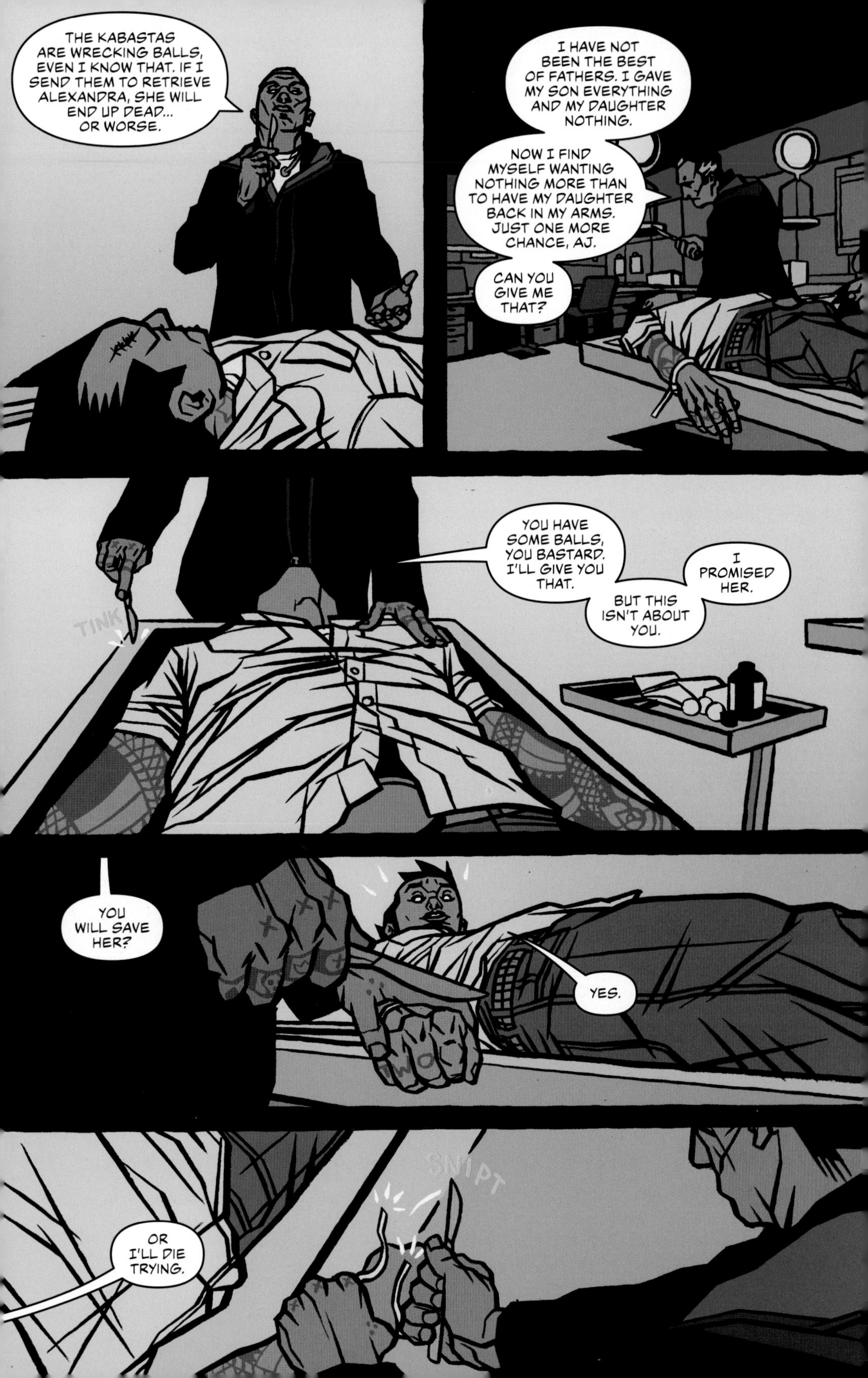
THE KABASTAS ARE WRECKING BALLS, EVEN I KNOW THAT. IF I SEND THEM TO RETRIEVE ALEXANDRA, SHE WILL END UP DEAD... OR WORSE.
I HAVE NOT BEEN THE BEST OF FATHERS. I GAVE MY SON EVERYTHING AND MY DAUGHTER NOTHING.
NOW I FIND MYSELF WANTING NOTHING MORE THAN TO HAVE MY DAUGHTER BACK IN MY ARMS. JUST ONE MORE CHANCE, AJ.
CAN YOU GIVE ME THAT?
TINK
YOU HAVE SOME BALLS, YOU BASTARD. I'LL GIVE YOU THAT.
BUT THIS ISN'T ABOUT YOU.
I PROMISED HER.
YOU WILL SAVE HER?
YES.
SNIPT
OR I'LL DIE TRYING.

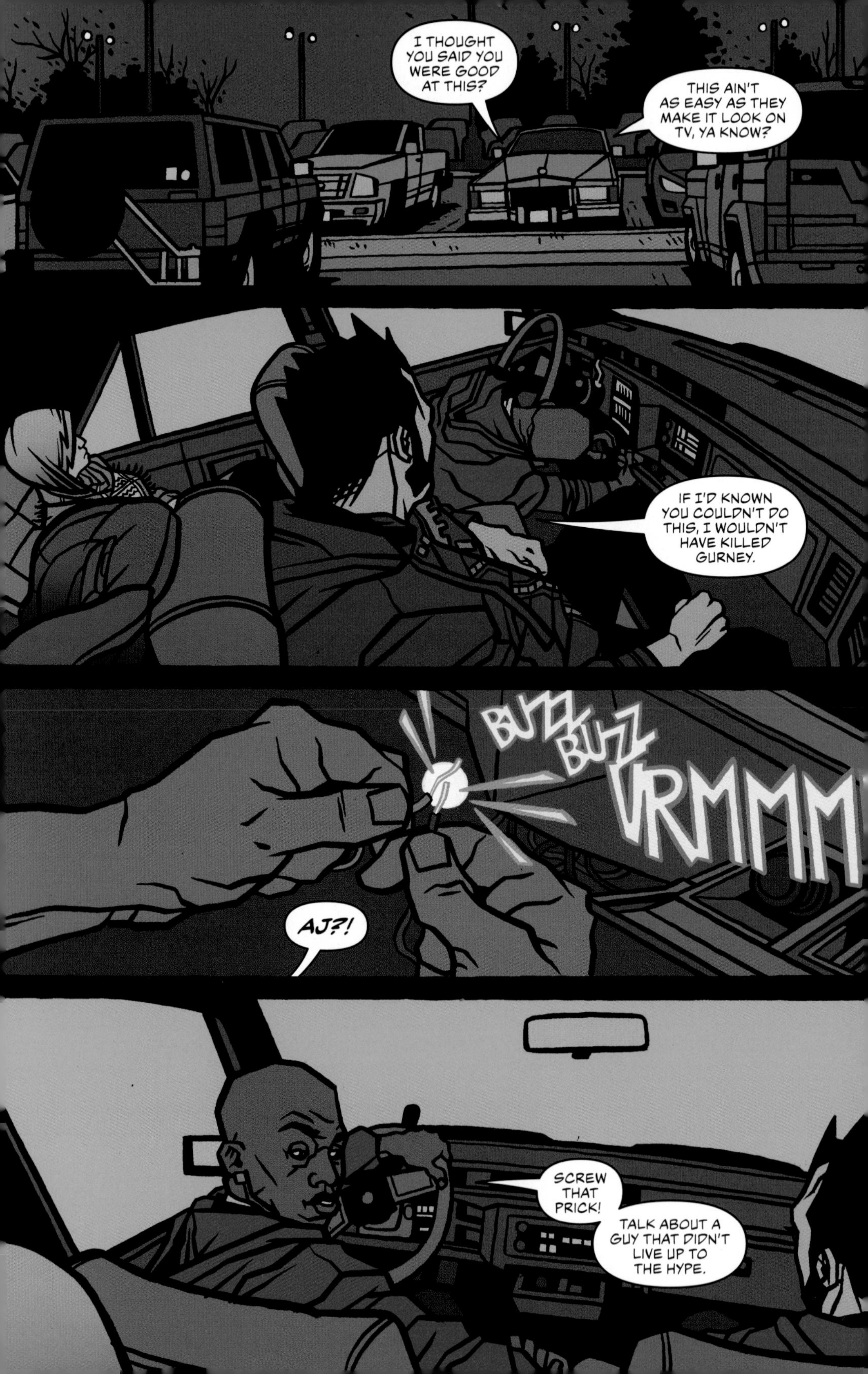
I THOUGHT YOU SAID YOU WERE GOOD AT THIS?
THIS AIN'T AS EASY AS THEY MAKE IT LOOK ON TV, YA KNOW?
IF I'D KNOWN YOU COULDN'T DO THIS, I WOULDN'T HAVE KILLED GURNEY.
BUZZ BUZZ
VRMMM
AJ?!
SCREW THAT PRICK!
TALK ABOUT A GUY THAT DIDN'T LIVE UP TO THE HYPE.

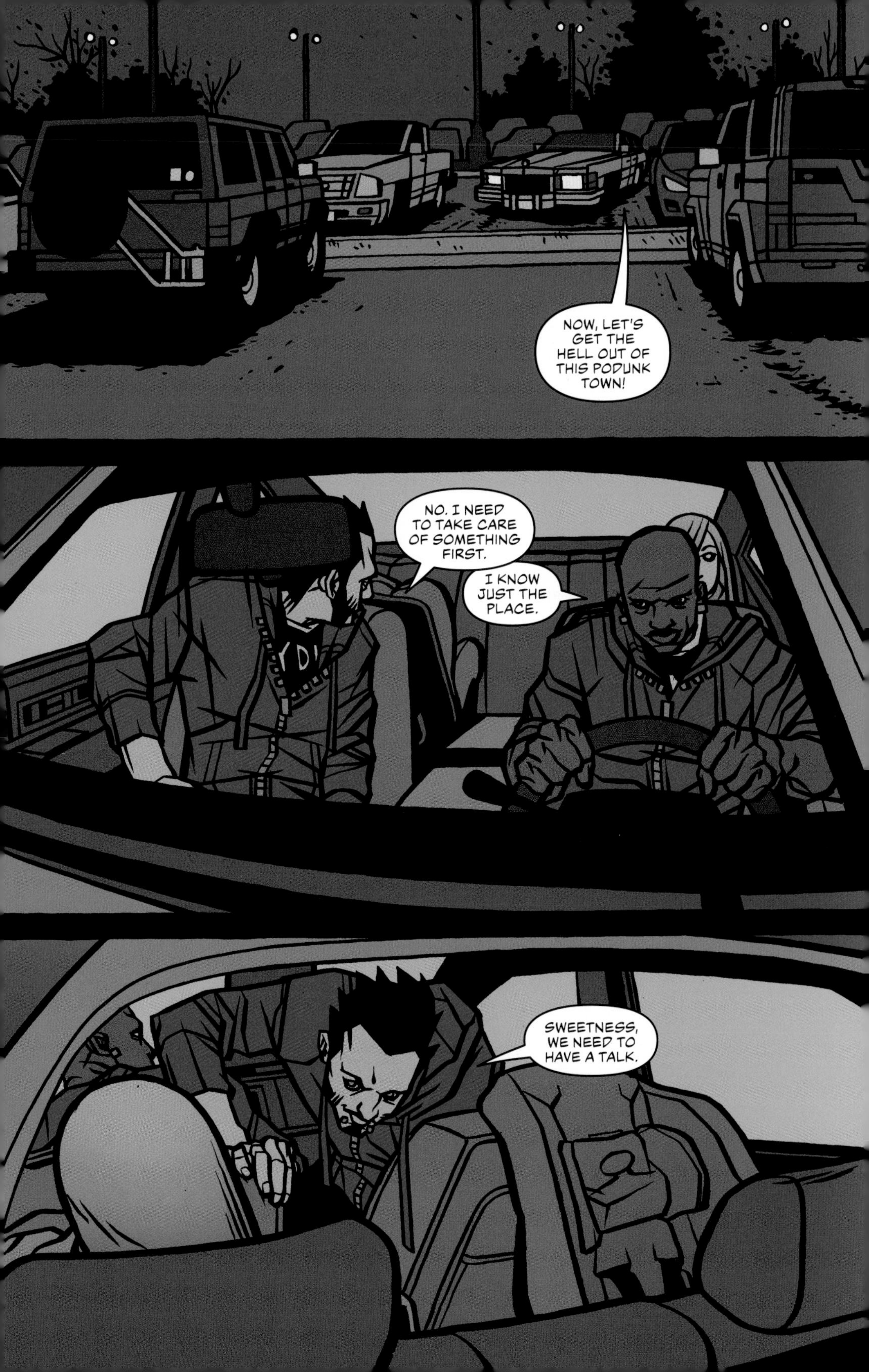
NOW, LET'S GET THE HELL OUT OF THIS PODUNK TOWN!
NO. I NEED TO TAKE CARE OF SOMETHING FIRST.
I KNOW JUST THE PLACE.
SWEETNESS, WE NEED TO HAVE A TALK.

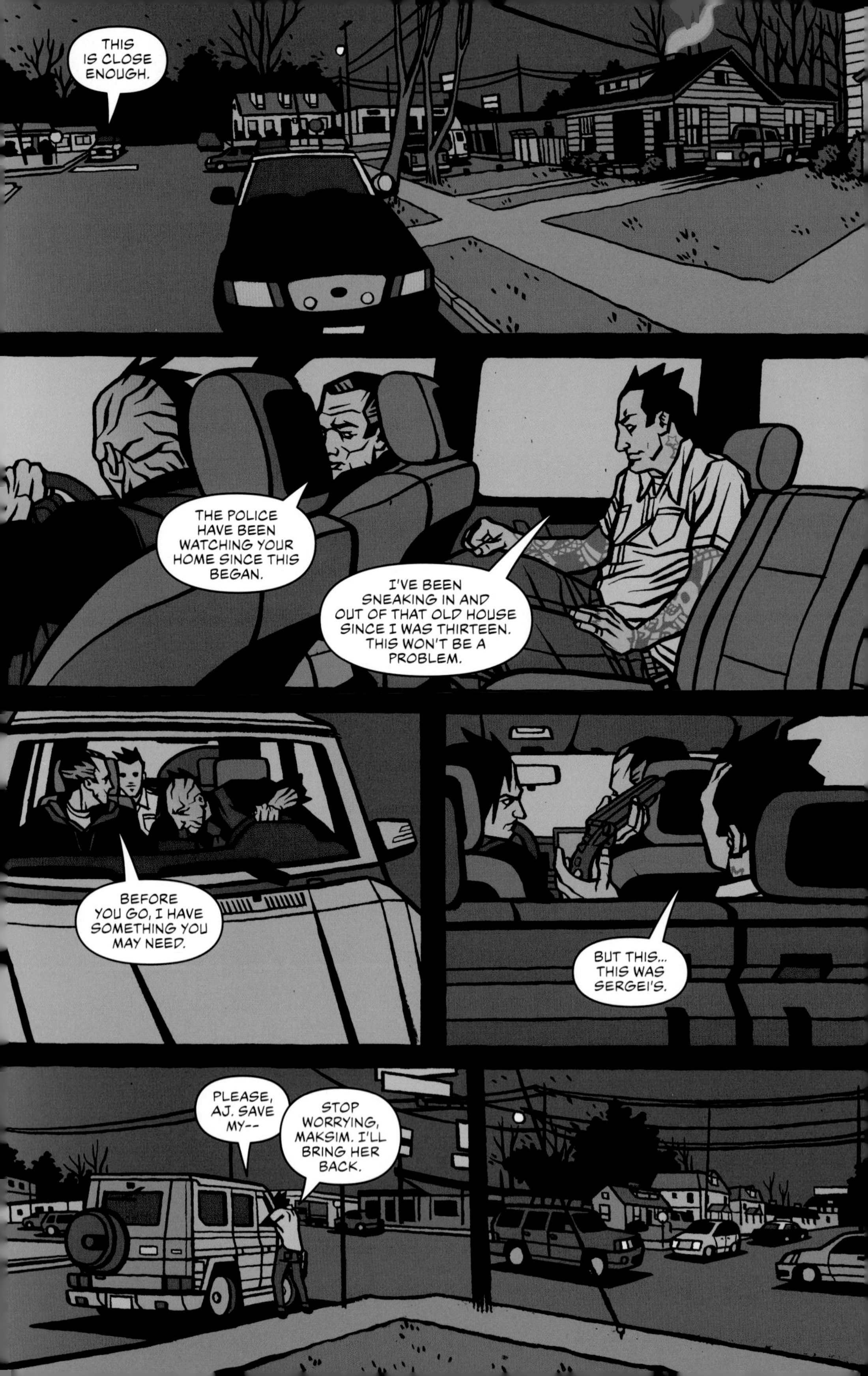
THIS IS CLOSE ENOUGH.
THE POLICE HAVE BEEN WATCHING YOUR HOME SINCE THIS BEGAN.
I'VE BEEN SNEAKING IN AND OUT OF THAT OLD HOUSE SINCE I WAS THIRTEEN. THIS WON'T BE A PROBLEM.
BEFORE YOU GO, I HAVE SOMETHING YOU MAY NEED.
BUT THIS... THIS WAS SERGEI'S.
PLEASE, AJ. SAVE MY--
STOP WORRYING, MAKSIM. I'LL BRING HER BACK.

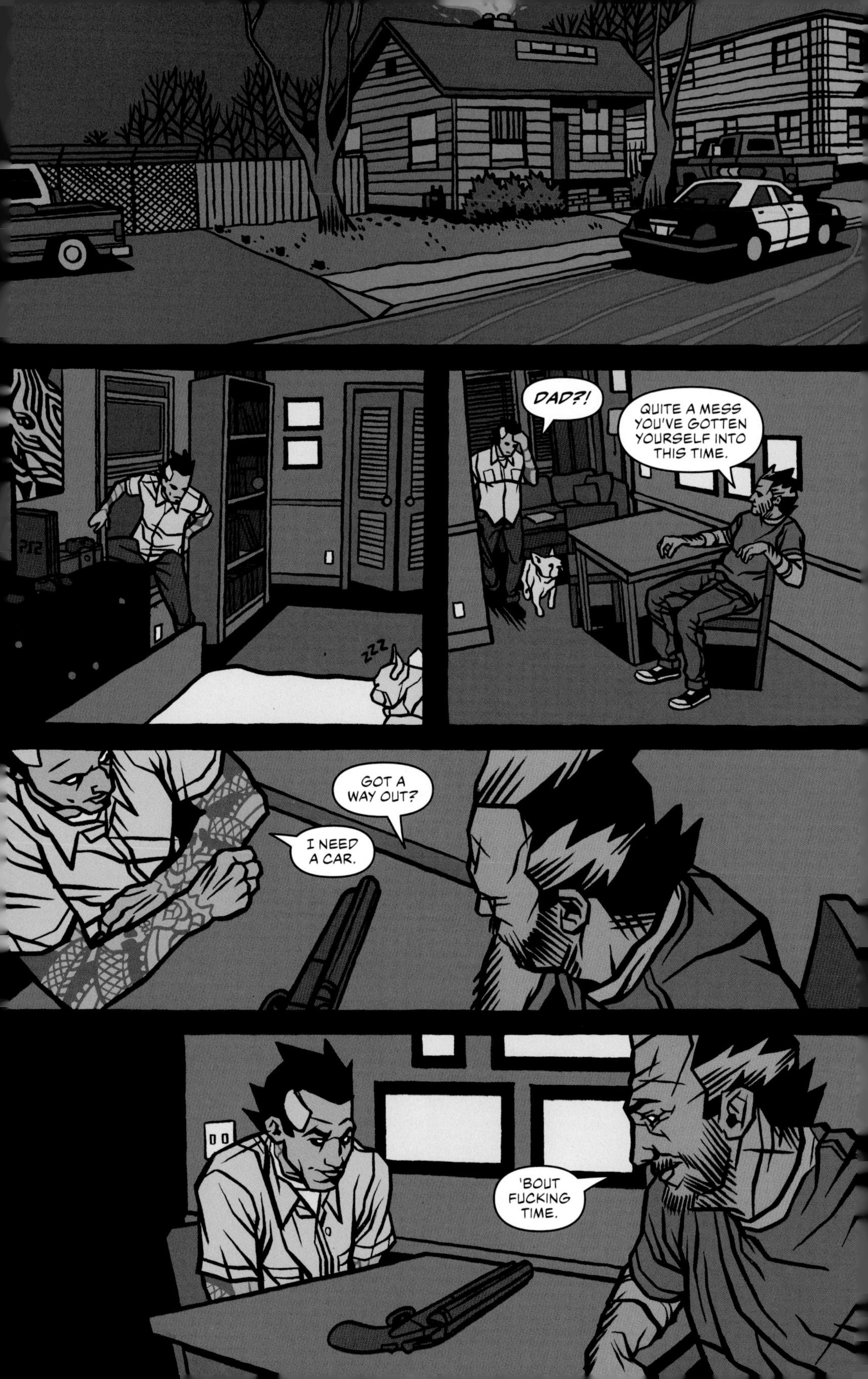
ZZZ
DAD?!
QUITE A MESS YOU'VE GOTTEN YOURSELF INTO THIS TIME.
I NEED A CAR.
GOT A WAY OUT?
'BOUT FUCKING TIME.

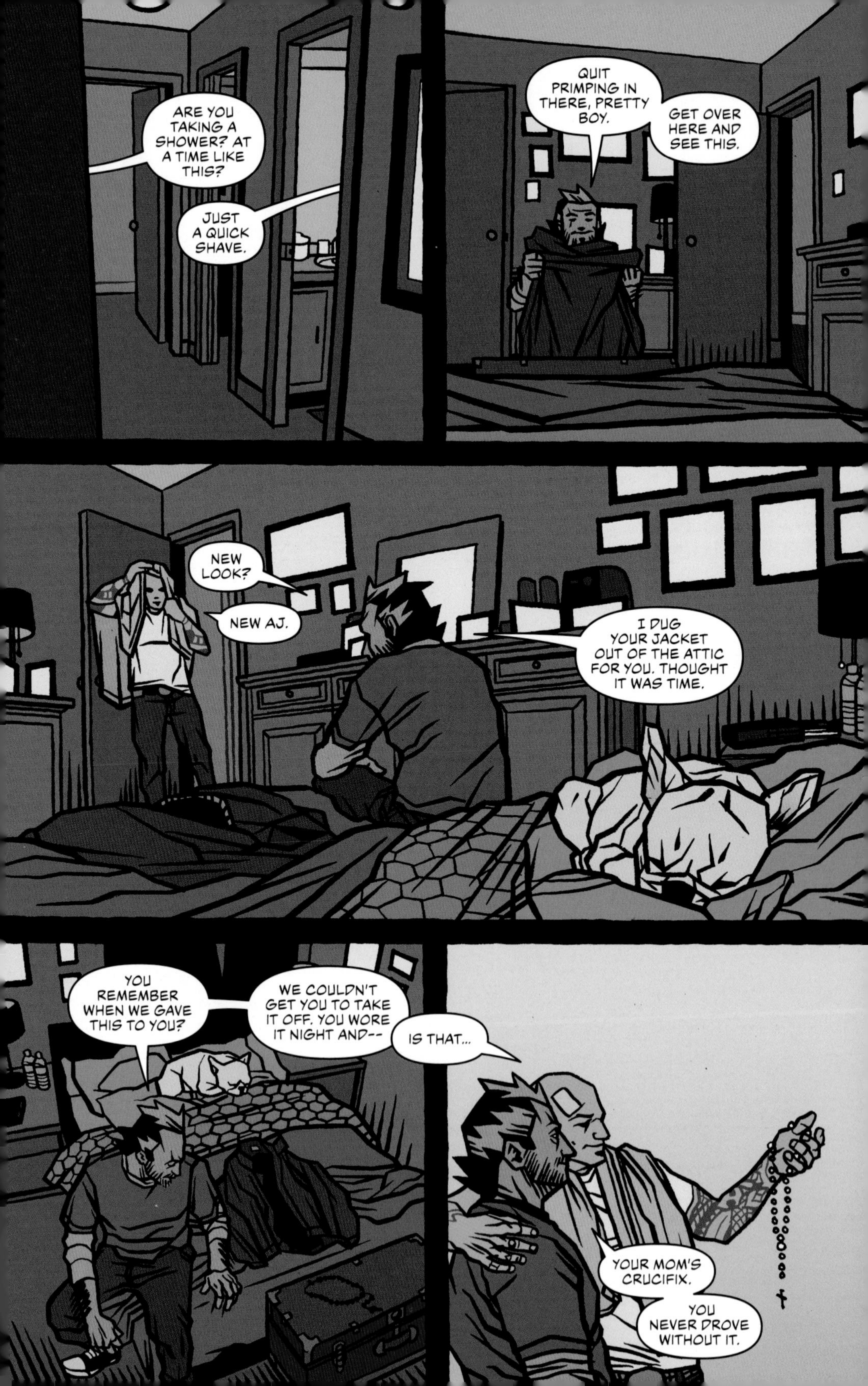
ARE YOU TAKING A SHOWER? AT A TIME LIKE THIS?
JUST A QUICK SHAVE.
QUIT PRIMPING IN THERE, PRETTY BOY.
GET OVER HERE AND SEE THIS.
NEW LOOK?
NEW AJ.
I DUG YOUR JACKET OUT OF THE ATTIC FOR YOU. THOUGHT IT WAS TIME.
YOU REMEMBER WHEN WE GAVE THIS TO YOU?
WE COULDN'T GET YOU TO TAKE IT OFF. YOU WORE IT NIGHT AND--
IS THAT...
YOUR MOM'S CRUCIFIX.
YOU NEVER DROVE WITHOUT IT.

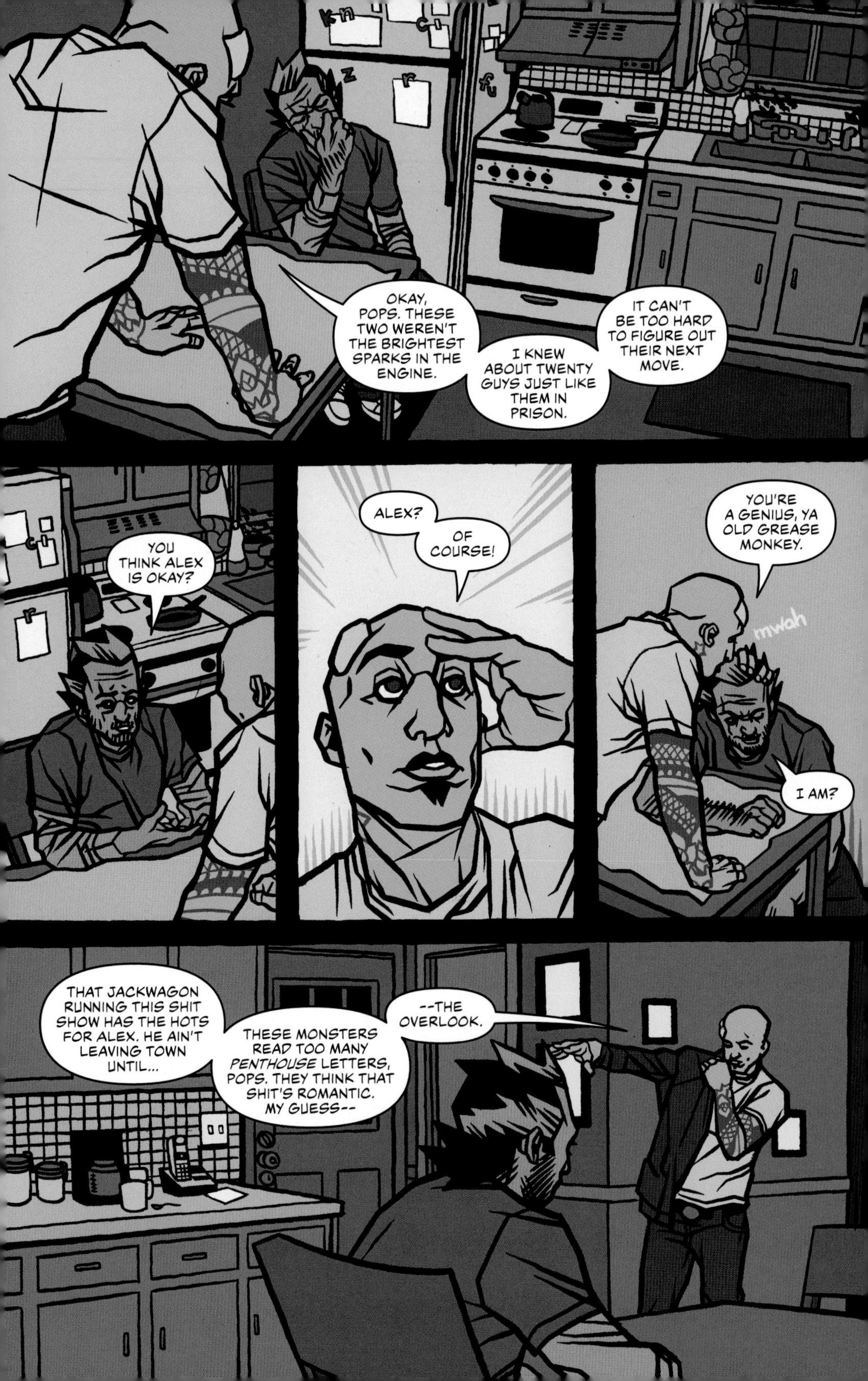
OKAY, POPS. THESE TWO WEREN'T THE BRIGHTEST SPARKS IN THE ENGINE.
I KNEW ABOUT TWENTY GUYS JUST LIKE THEM IN PRISON.
IT CAN'T BE TOO HARD TO FIGURE OUT THEIR NEXT MOVE.
YOU THINK ALEX IS OKAY?
ALEX?
OF COURSE!
YOU'RE A GENIUS, YA OLD GREASE MONKEY.
mwah
I AM?
THAT JACKWAGON RUNNING THIS SHIT SHOW HAS THE HOTS FOR ALEX. HE AIN'T LEAVING TOWN UNTIL...
THESE MONSTERS READ TOO MANY PENTHOUSE LETTERS, POPS. THEY THINK THAT SHIT'S ROMANTIC. MY GUESS--
--THE OVERLOOK.

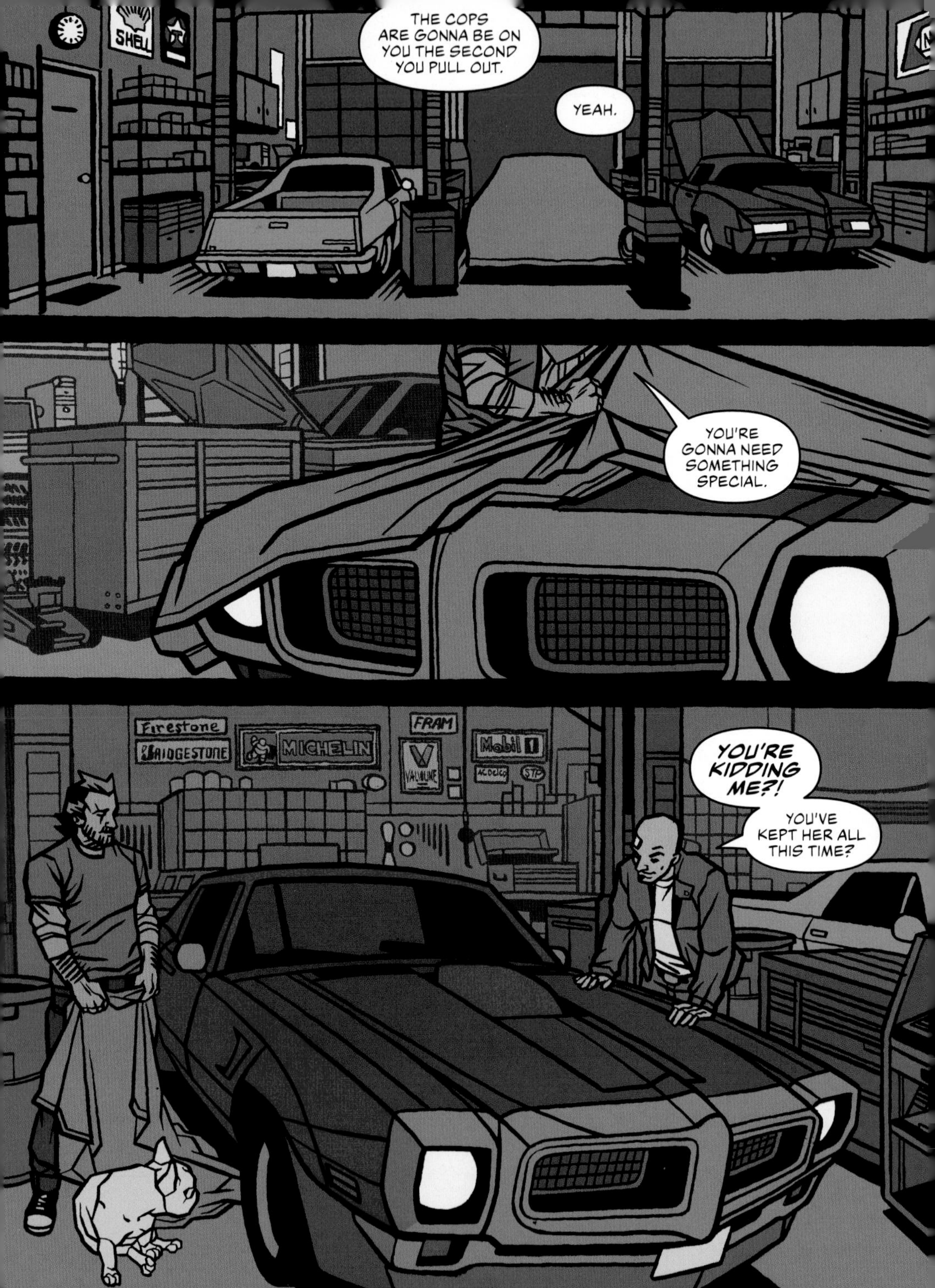
SHELL
THE COPS ARE GONNA BE ON YOU THE SECOND YOU PULL OUT.
YEAH.
YOU'RE GONNA NEED SOMETHING SPECIAL.
Firestone
BRIDGESTONE
MICHELIN
FRAM
VALVOLINE
Mobil 1
ACDelco
STP
YOU'RE KIDDING ME?!
YOU'VE KEPT HER ALL THIS TIME?

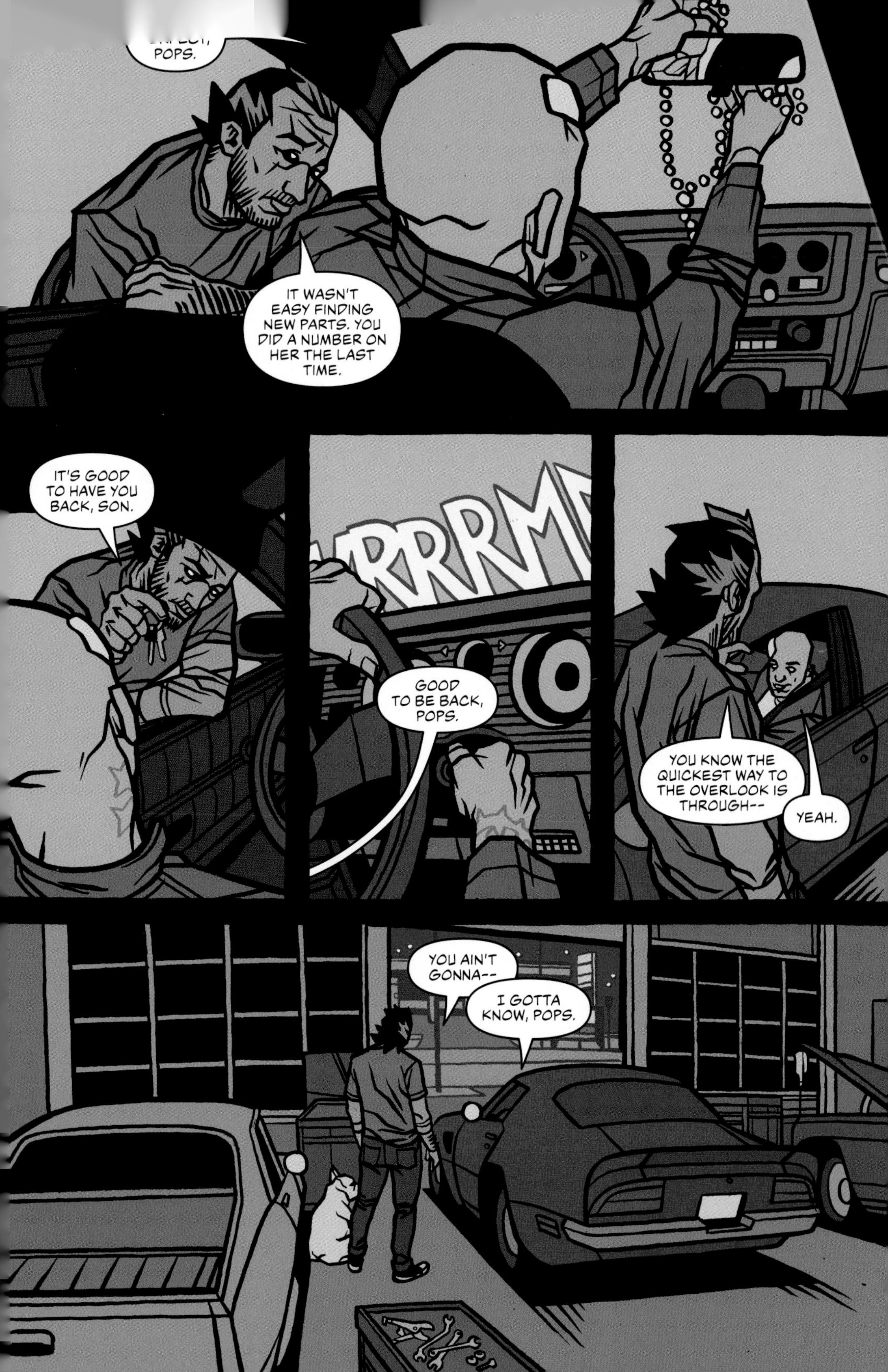
POPS.
IT WASN'T EASY FINDING NEW PARTS. YOU DID A NUMBER ON HER THE LAST TIME.
IT'S GOOD TO HAVE YOU BACK, SON.
GOOD TO BE BACK, POPS.
YOU KNOW THE QUICKEST WAY TO THE OVERLOOK IS THROUGH--
YEAH.
YOU AIN'T GONNA--
I GOTTA KNOW, POPS.

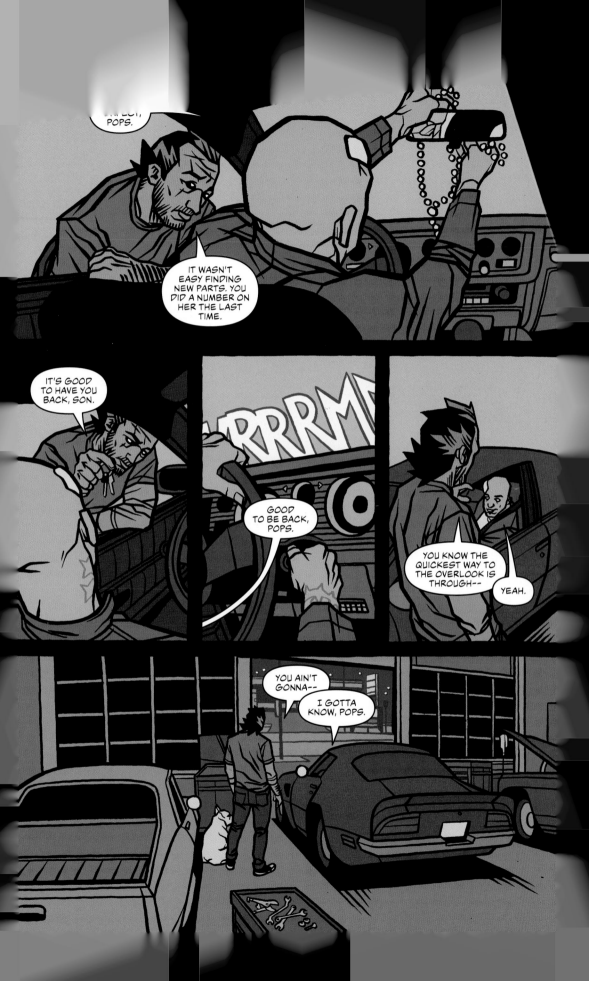

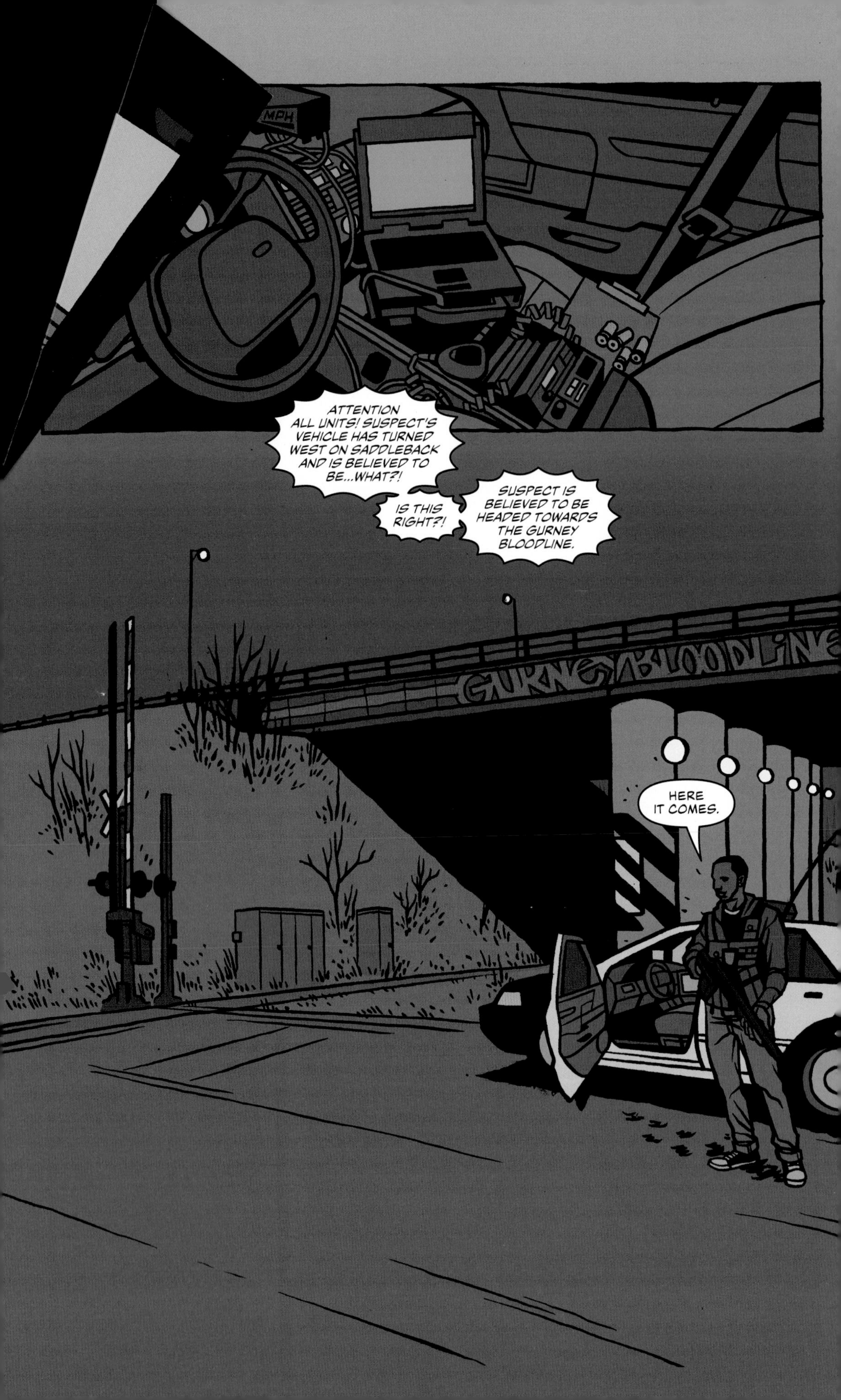
MPH
ATTENTION ALL UNITS! SUSPECT'S VEHICLE HAS TURNED WEST ON SADDLEBACK AND IS BELIEVED TO BE...WHAT?!
IS THIS RIGHT?!
SUSPECT IS BELIEVED TO BE HEADED TOWARDS THE GURNEY BLOODLINE.
GURNEY BLOODLINE
HERE IT COMES.

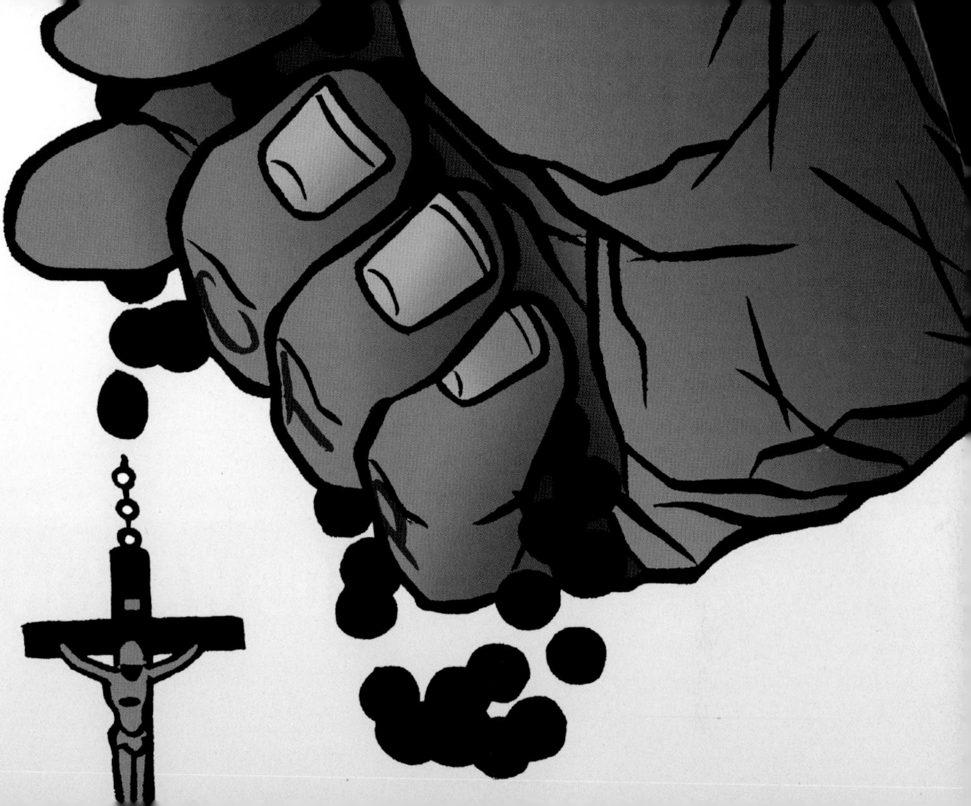

CHAPTER FIVE

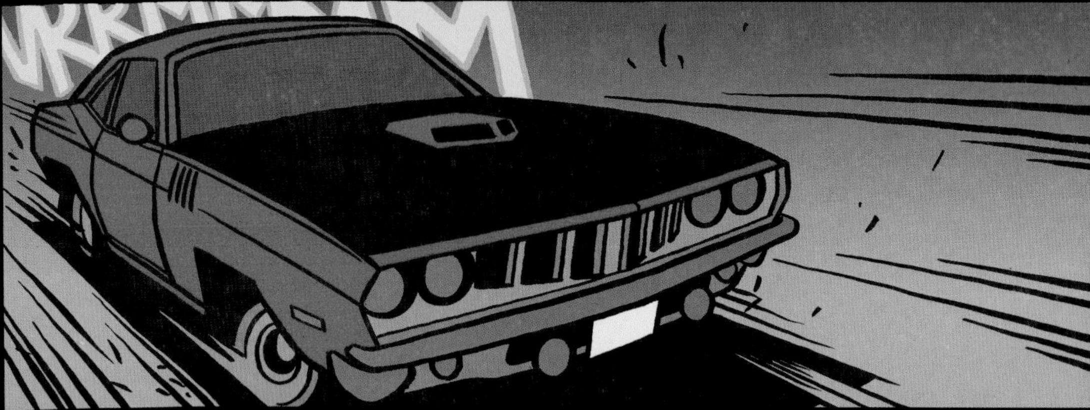

"I SAW YOU WALK IN HERE!"

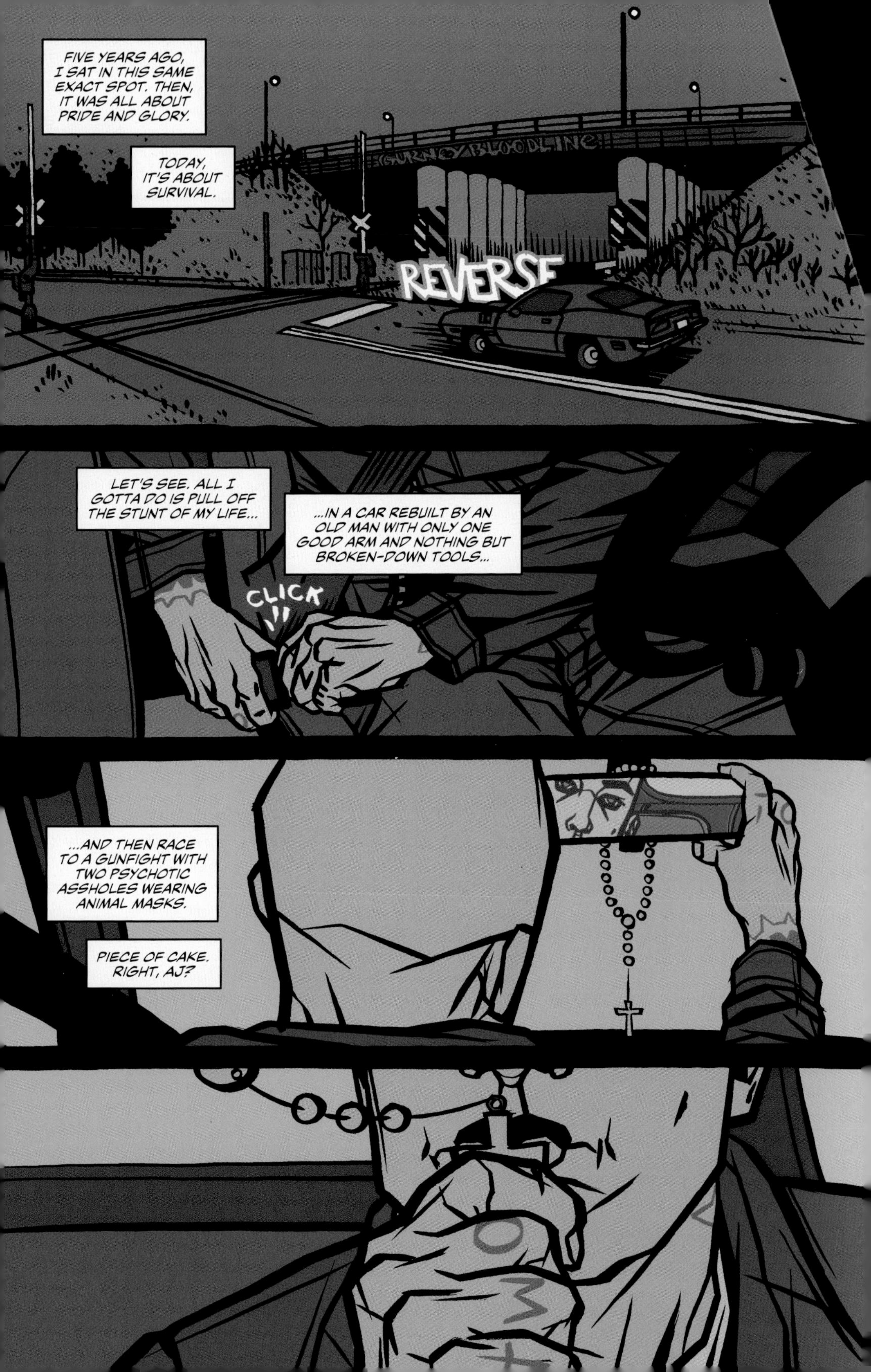
FIVE YEARS AGO, I SAT IN THIS SAME EXACT SPOT. THEN, IT WAS ALL ABOUT PRIDE AND GLORY.
TODAY, IT'S ABOUT SURVIVAL.
REVERSE
LET'S SEE. ALL I GOTTA DO IS PULL OFF THE STUNT OF MY LIFE...
...IN A CAR REBUILT BY AN OLD MAN WITH ONLY ONE GOOD ARM AND NOTHING BUT BROKEN-DOWN TOOLS...
CLICK
...AND THEN RACE TO A GUNFIGHT WITH TWO PSYCHOTIC ASSHOLES WEARING ANIMAL MASKS.
PIECE OF CAKE. RIGHT, AJ?

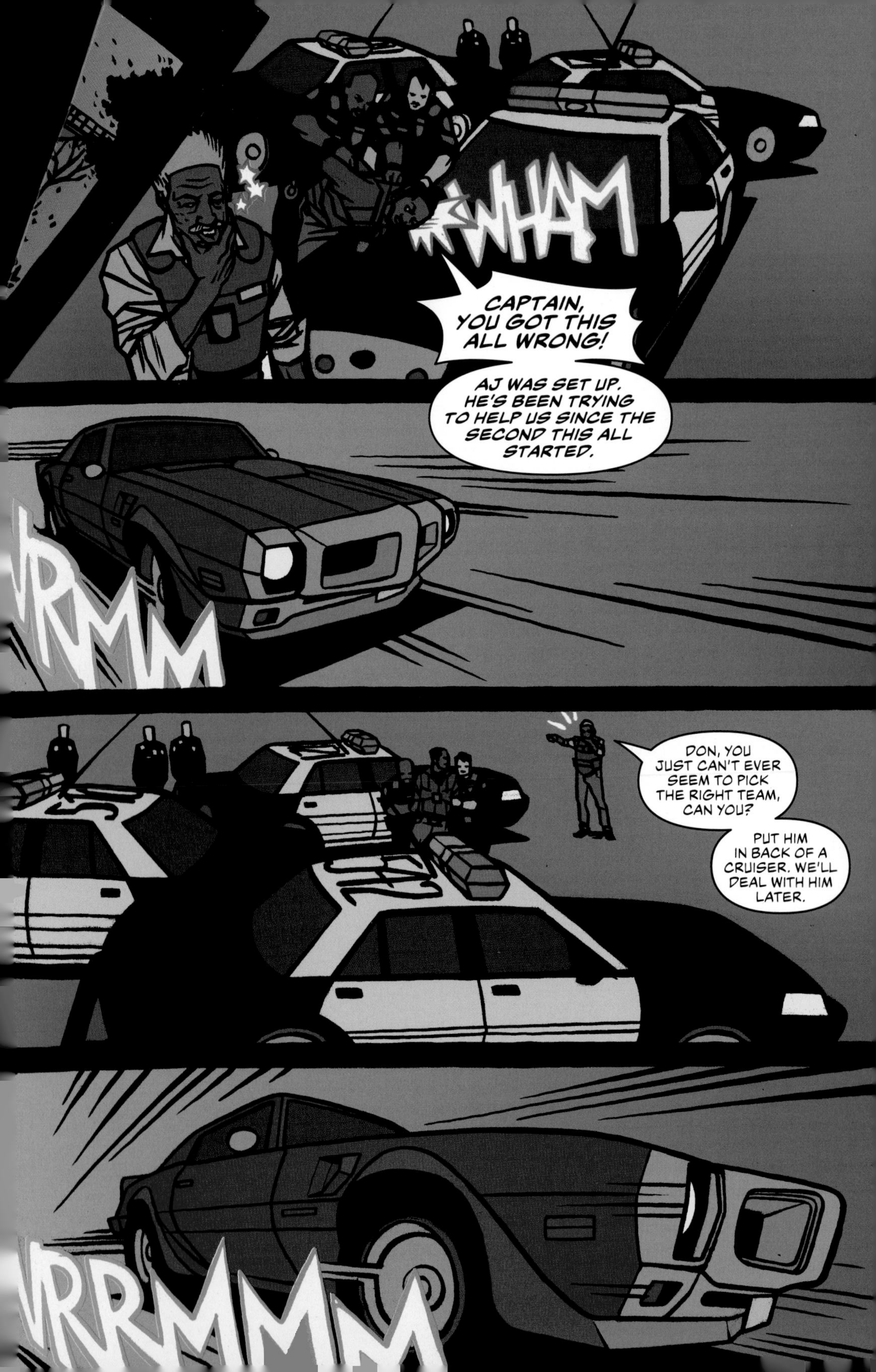
WHAM
CAPTAIN, YOU GOT THIS ALL WRONG!
AJ WAS SET UP. HE'S BEEN TRYING TO HELP US SINCE THE SECOND THIS ALL STARTED.
VRMMM
DON, YOU JUST CAN'T EVER SEEM TO PICK THE RIGHT TEAM, CAN YOU?
PUT HIM IN BACK OF A CRUISER. WE'LL DEAL WITH HIM LATER.
VRRMMMM

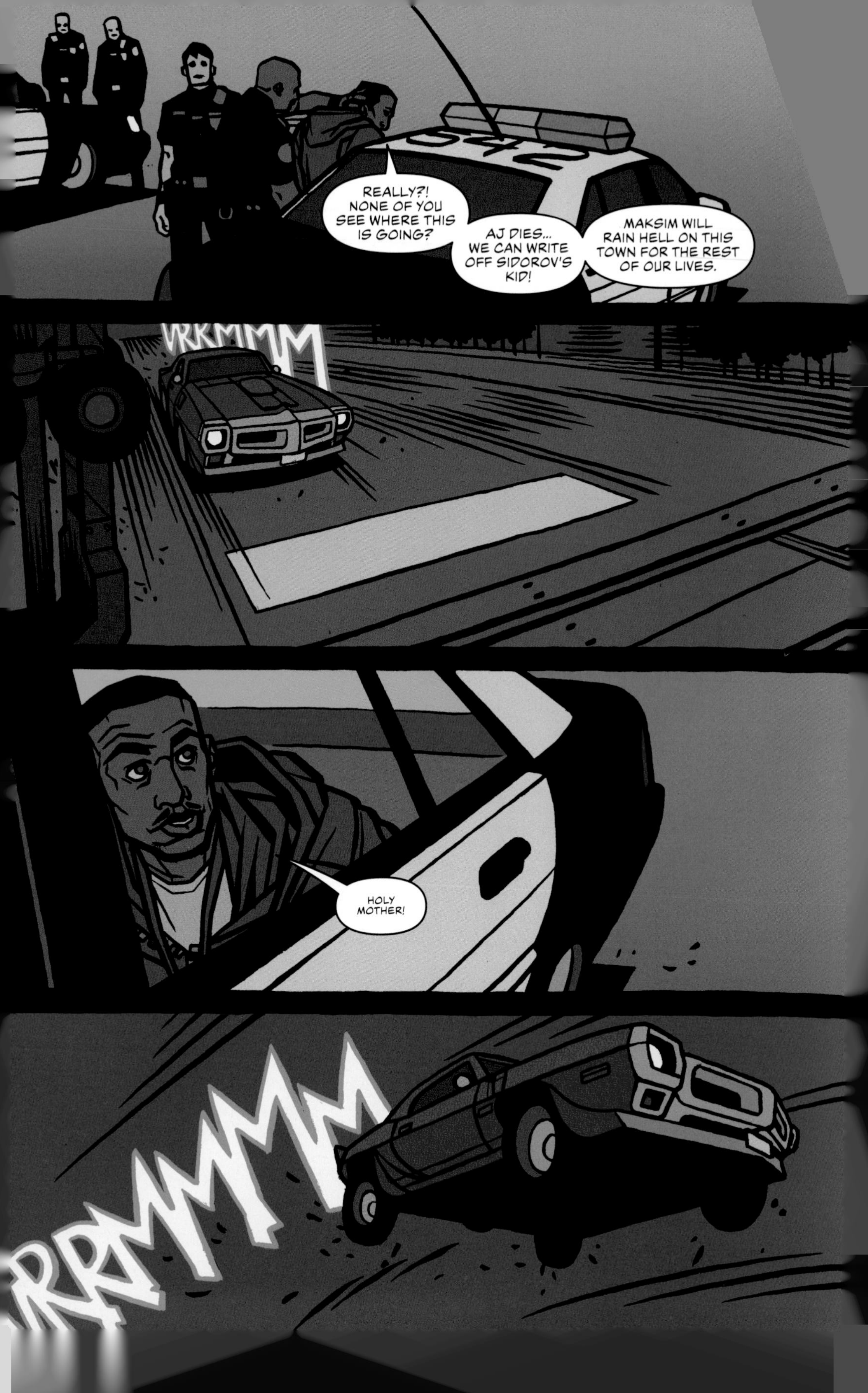
REALLY?! NONE OF YOU SEE WHERE THIS IS GOING?
AJ DIES... WE CAN WRITE OFF SIDOROV'S KID!
MAKSIM WILL RAIN HELL ON THIS TOWN FOR THE REST OF OUR LIVES.
VRKMMM
HOLY MOTHER!

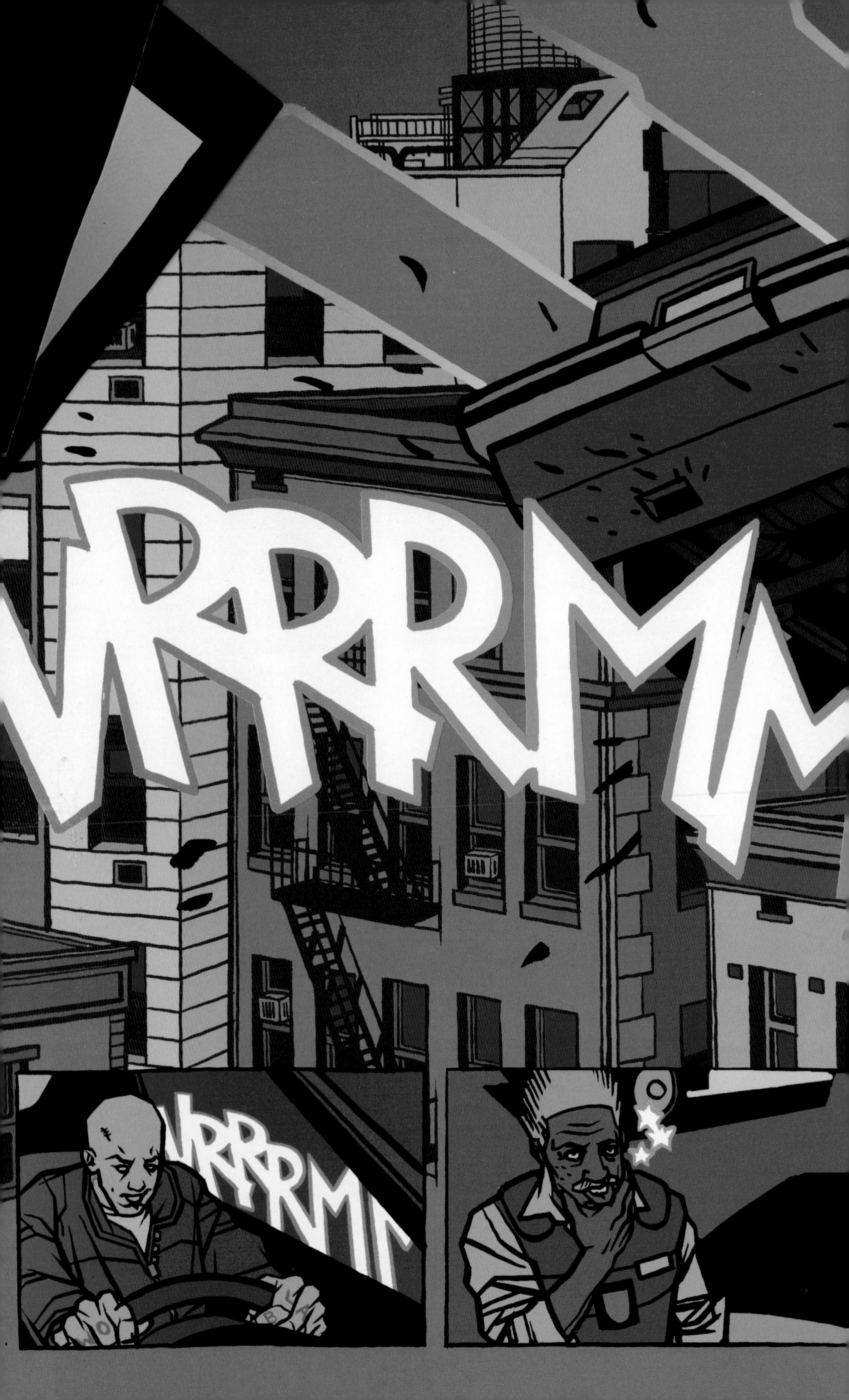
VRRRM
VRRRM

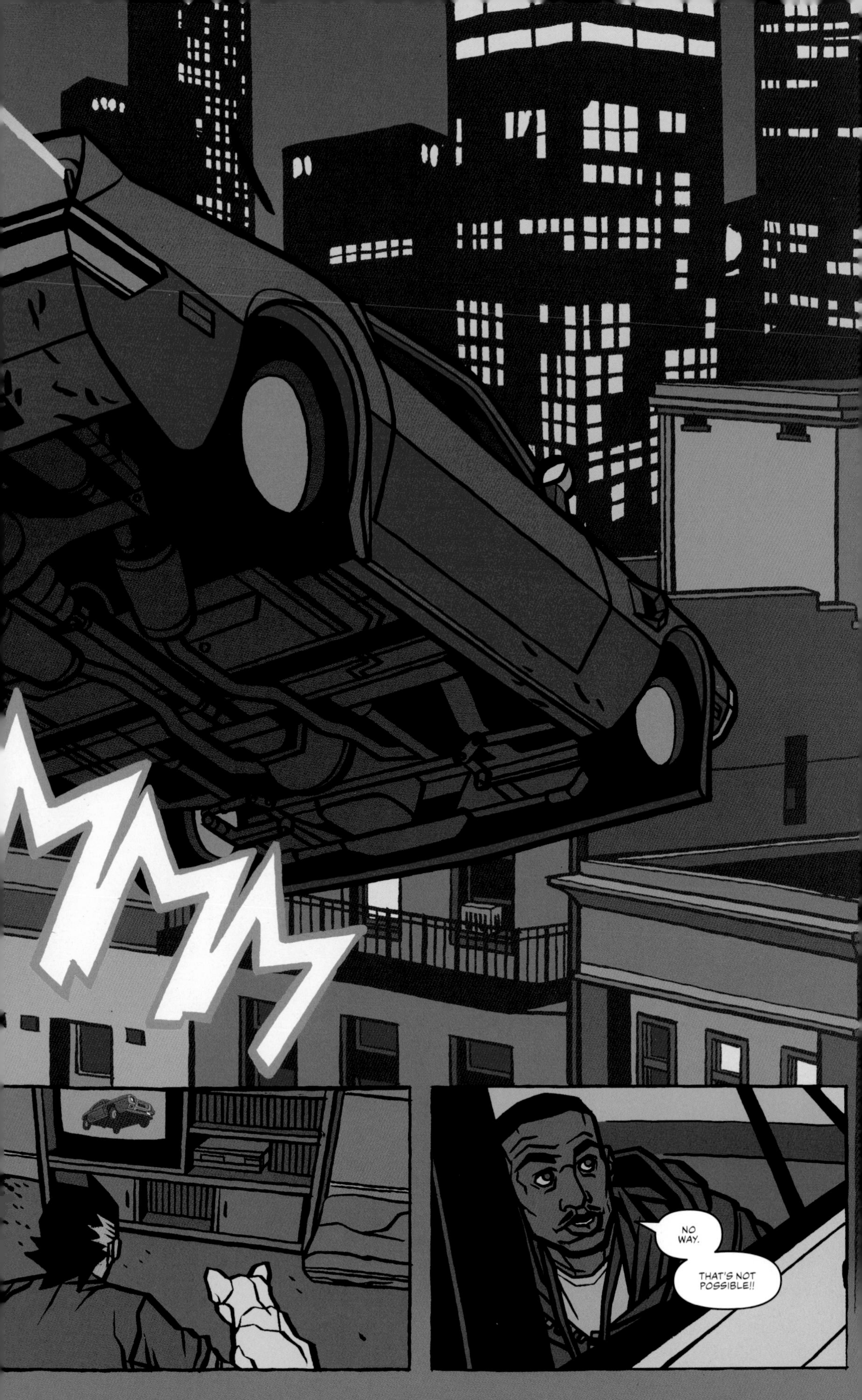
NO WAY.
THAT'S NOT POSSIBLE!!

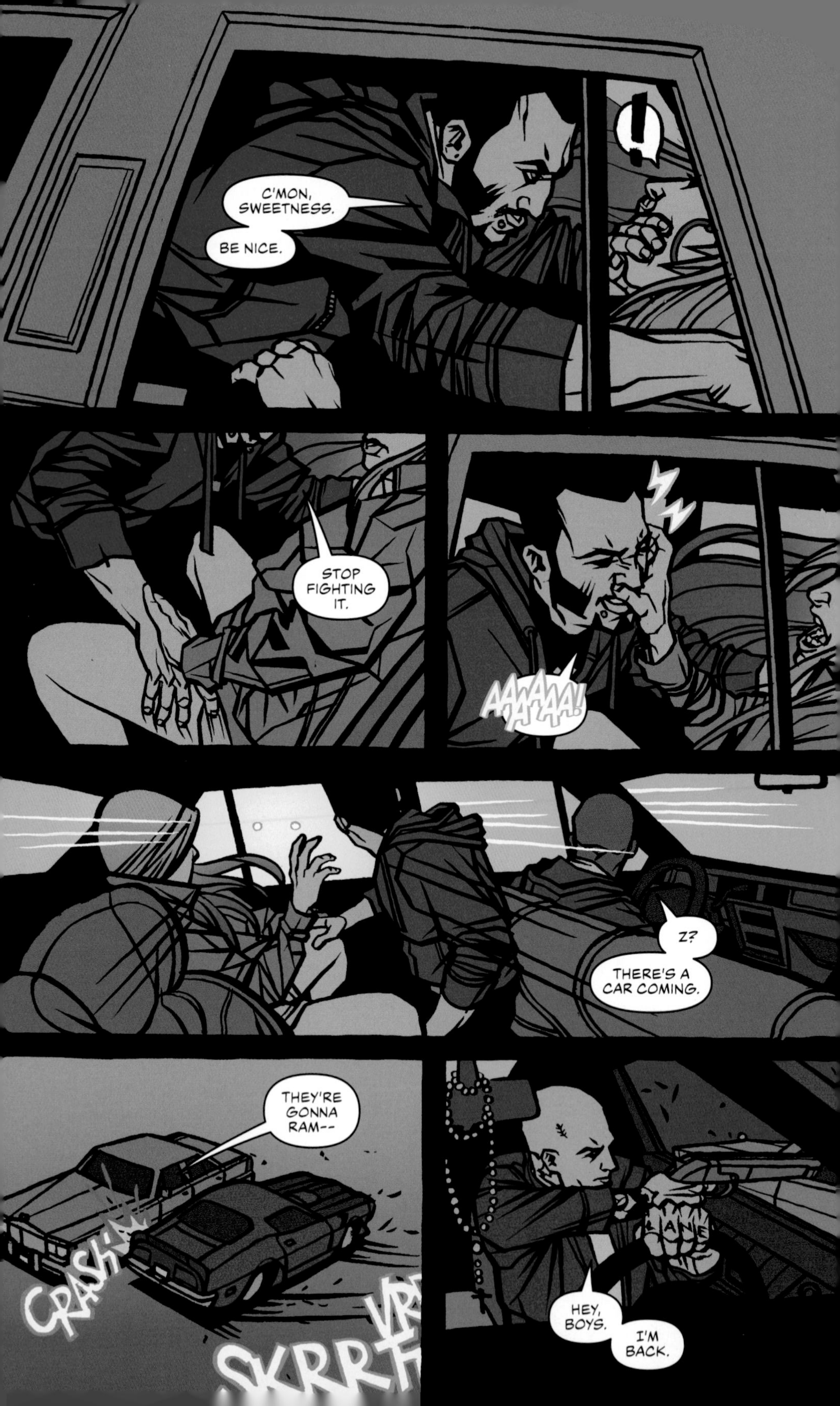
!
C'MON, SWEETNESS.
BE NICE.
STOP FIGHTING IT.
AAAAAA!
Z?
THERE'S A CAR COMING.
THEY'RE GONNA RAM--
CRASH
SKRRT
HEY, BOYS.
I'M BACK.

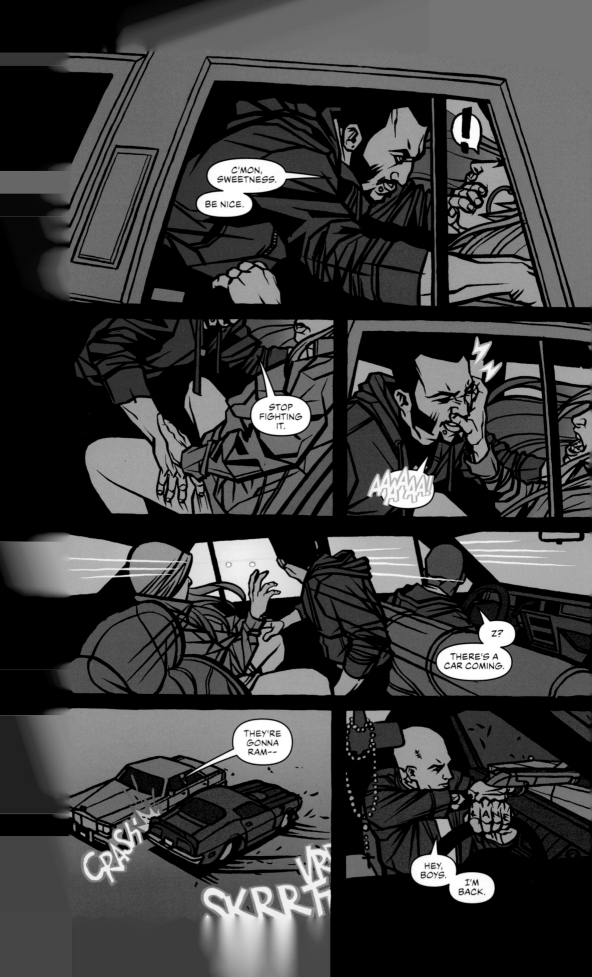

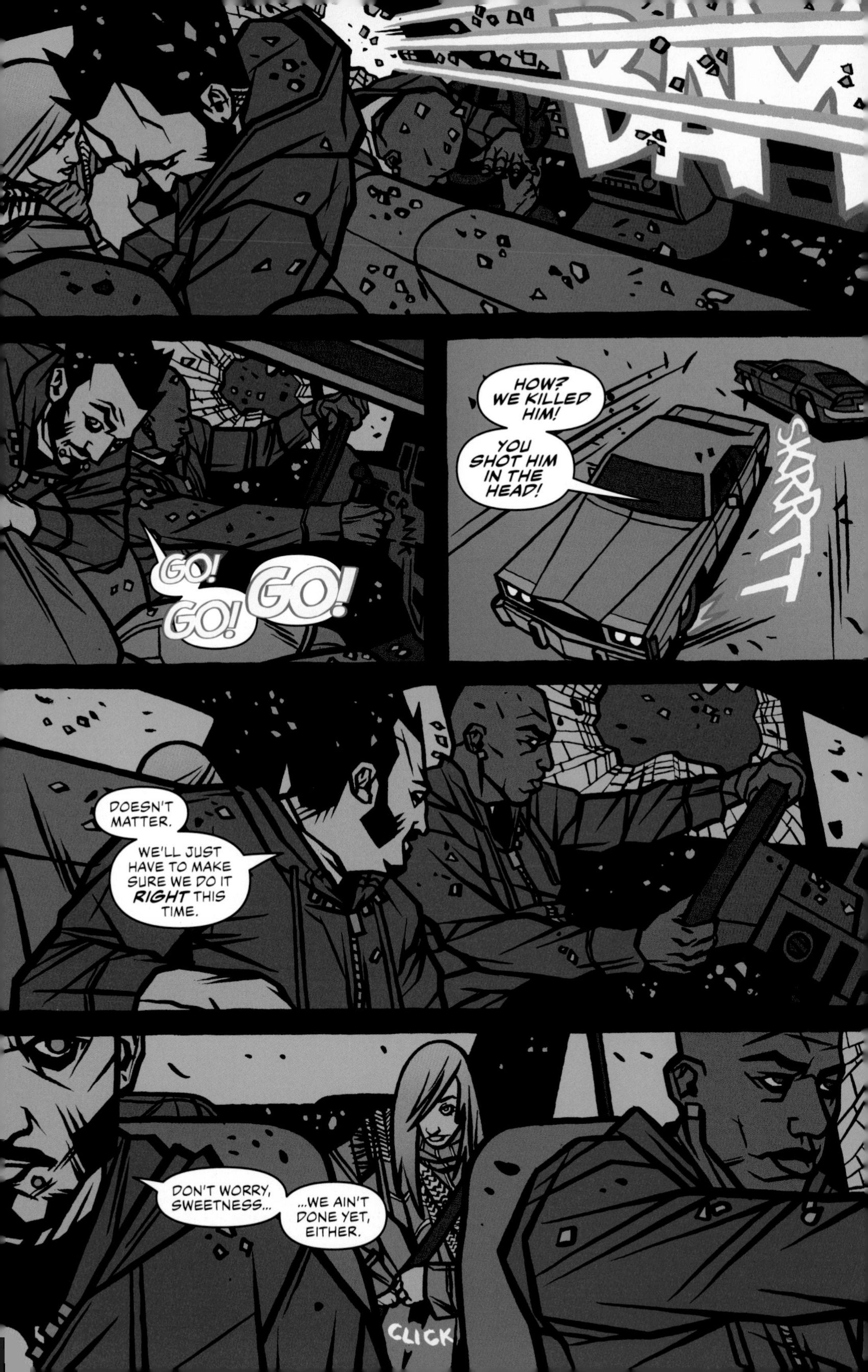
BLAM
GO! GO! GO!
CRANK
HOW? WE KILLED HIM!
YOU SHOT HIM IN THE HEAD!
SKRRTT
DOESN'T MATTER.
WE'LL JUST HAVE TO MAKE SURE WE DO IT **RIGHT** THIS TIME.
DON'T WORRY, SWEETNESS...
...WE AIN'T DONE YET, EITHER.
CLICK

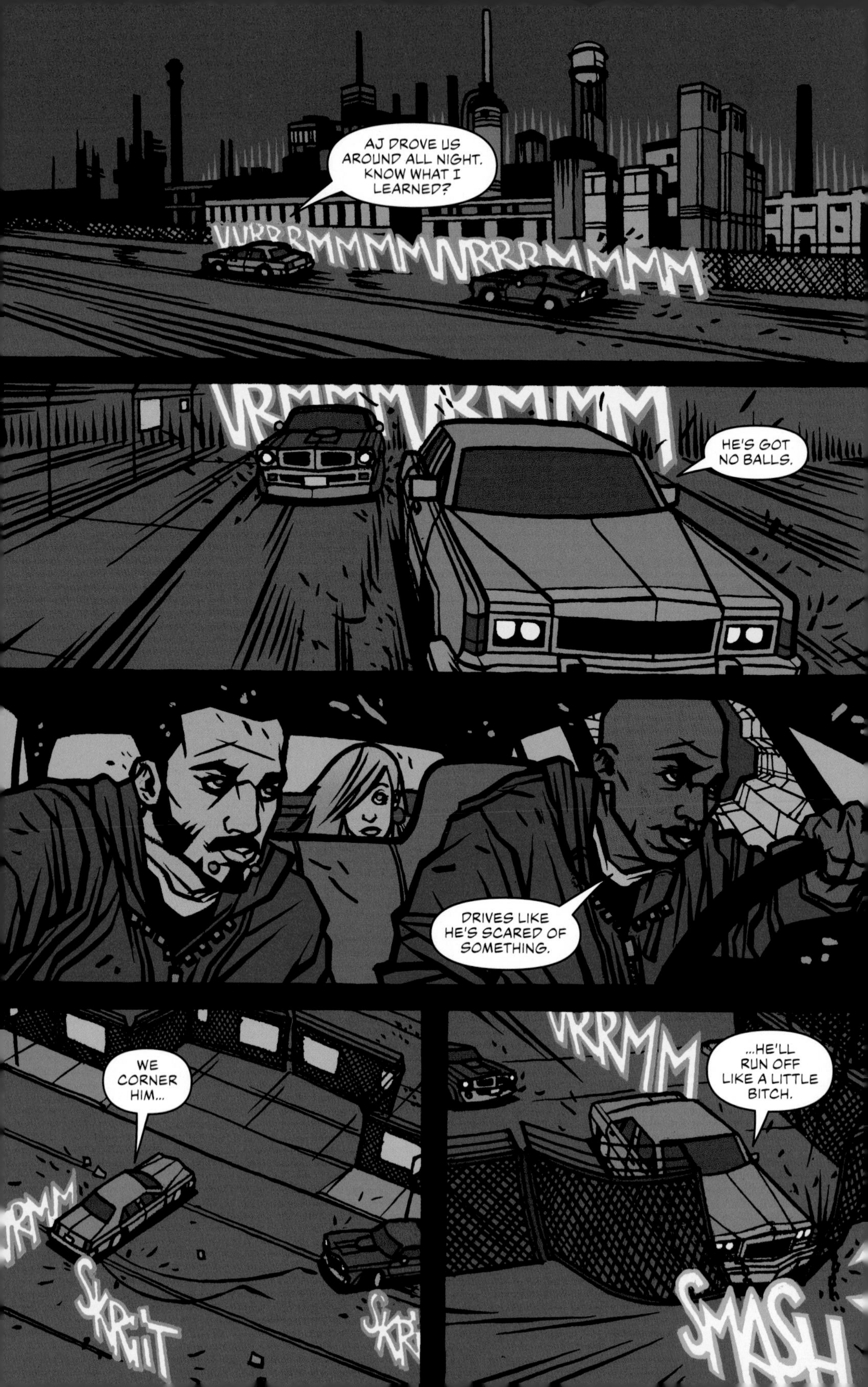
AJ DROVE US AROUND ALL NIGHT. KNOW WHAT I LEARNED?
VVRRRMMMMMVRRRRMMMM
VRMMMVRMMMM
HE'S GOT NO BALLS.
DRIVES LIKE HE'S SCARED OF SOMETHING.
WE CORNER HIM...
VRRMM
...HE'LL RUN OFF LIKE A LITTLE BITCH.
SMASH

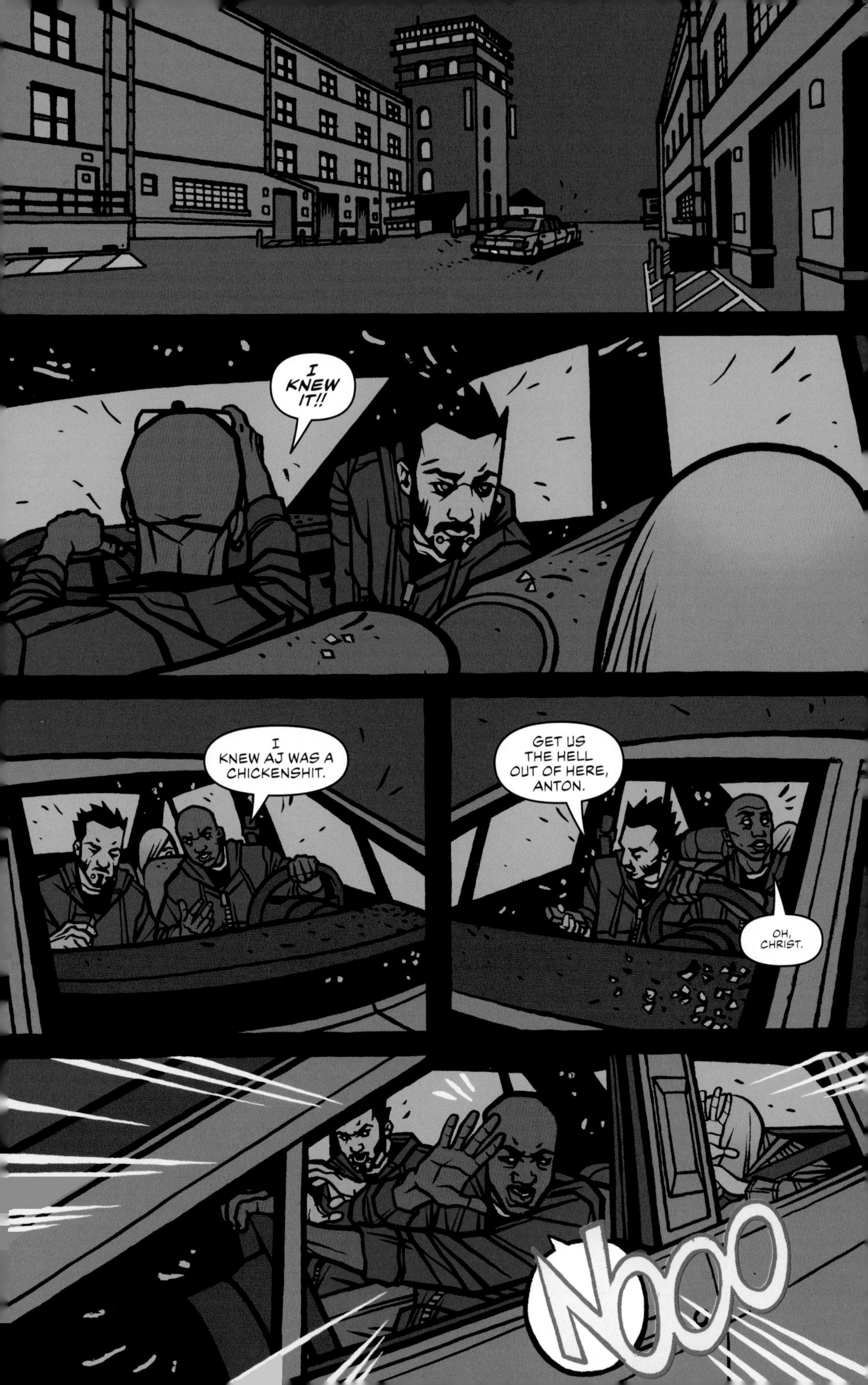
I KNEW IT!!
I KNEW AJ WAS A CHICKENSHIT.
GET US THE HELL OUT OF HERE, ANTON.
OH, CHRIST.
NOOO

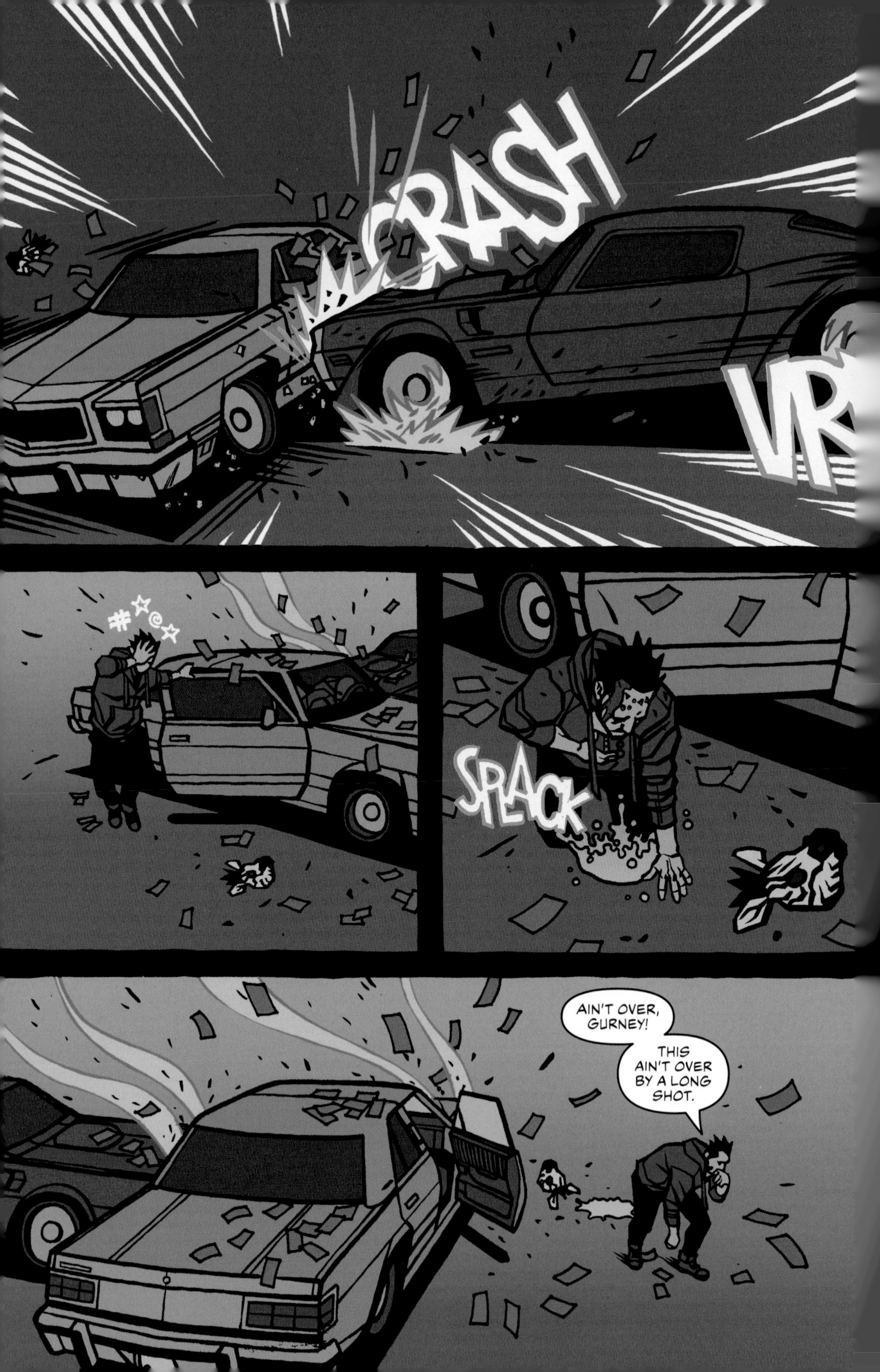
CRASH
VR
SPLACK
AIN'T OVER, GURNEY!
THIS AIN'T OVER BY A LONG SHOT.

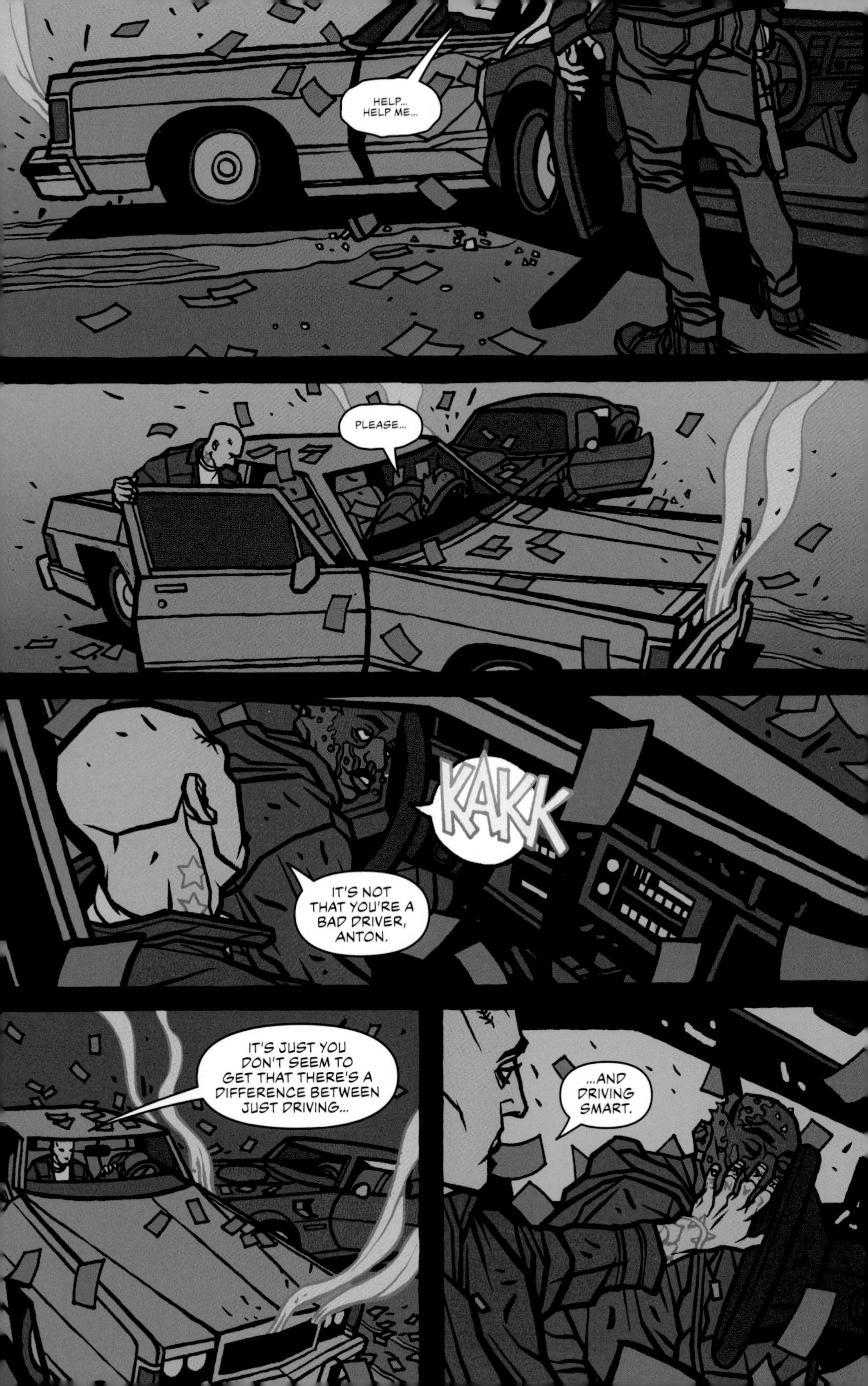
HELP...
HELP ME...
PLEASE...
KAKK
IT'S NOT THAT YOU'RE A BAD DRIVER, ANTON.
IT'S JUST YOU DON'T SEEM TO GET THAT THERE'S A DIFFERENCE BETWEEN JUST DRIVING...
...AND DRIVING SMART.

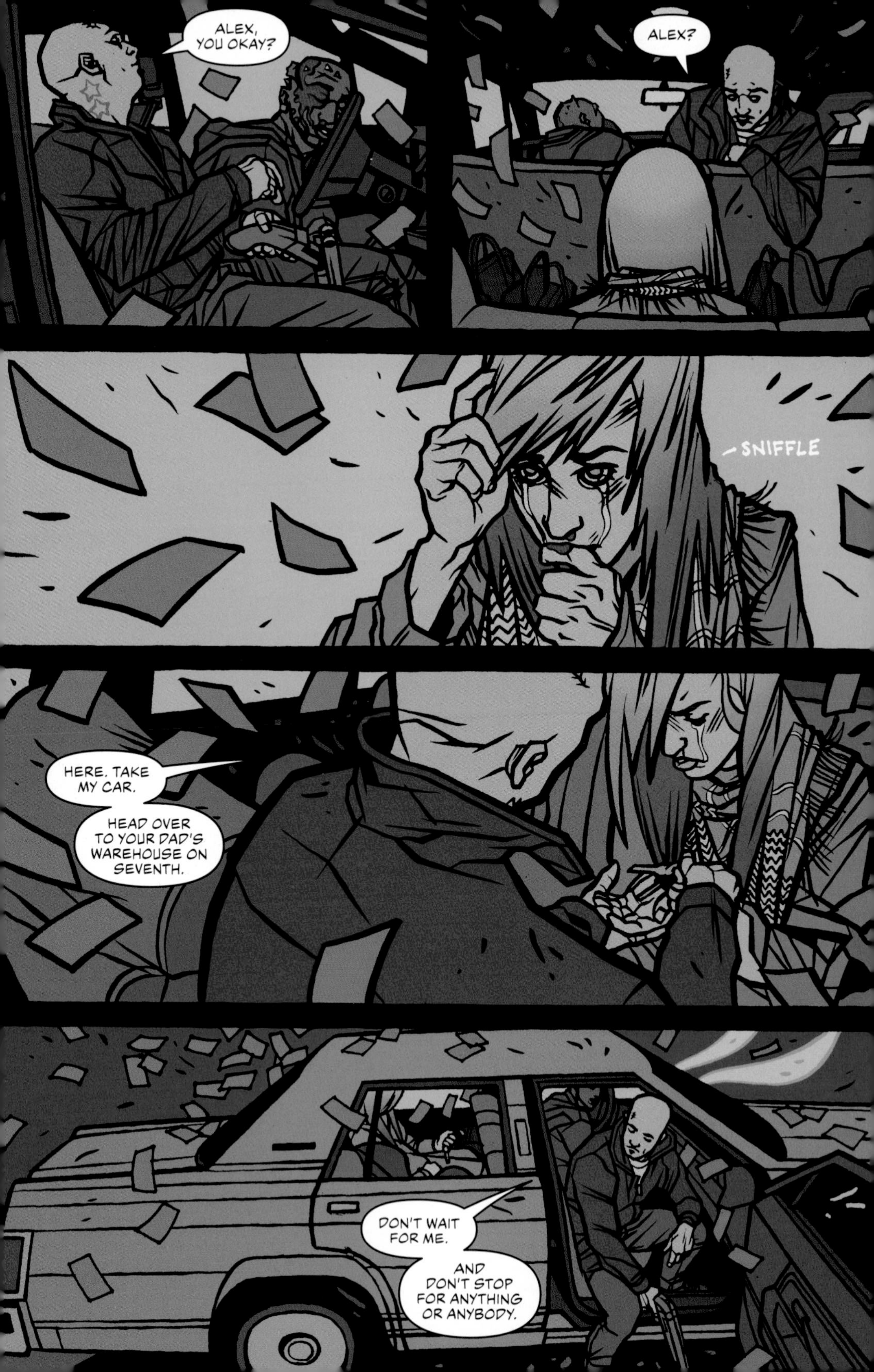
ALEX, YOU OKAY?
ALEX?
-SNIFFLE
HERE. TAKE MY CAR.
HEAD OVER TO YOUR DAD'S WAREHOUSE ON SEVENTH.
DON'T WAIT FOR ME.
AND DON'T STOP FOR ANYTHING OR ANYBODY.

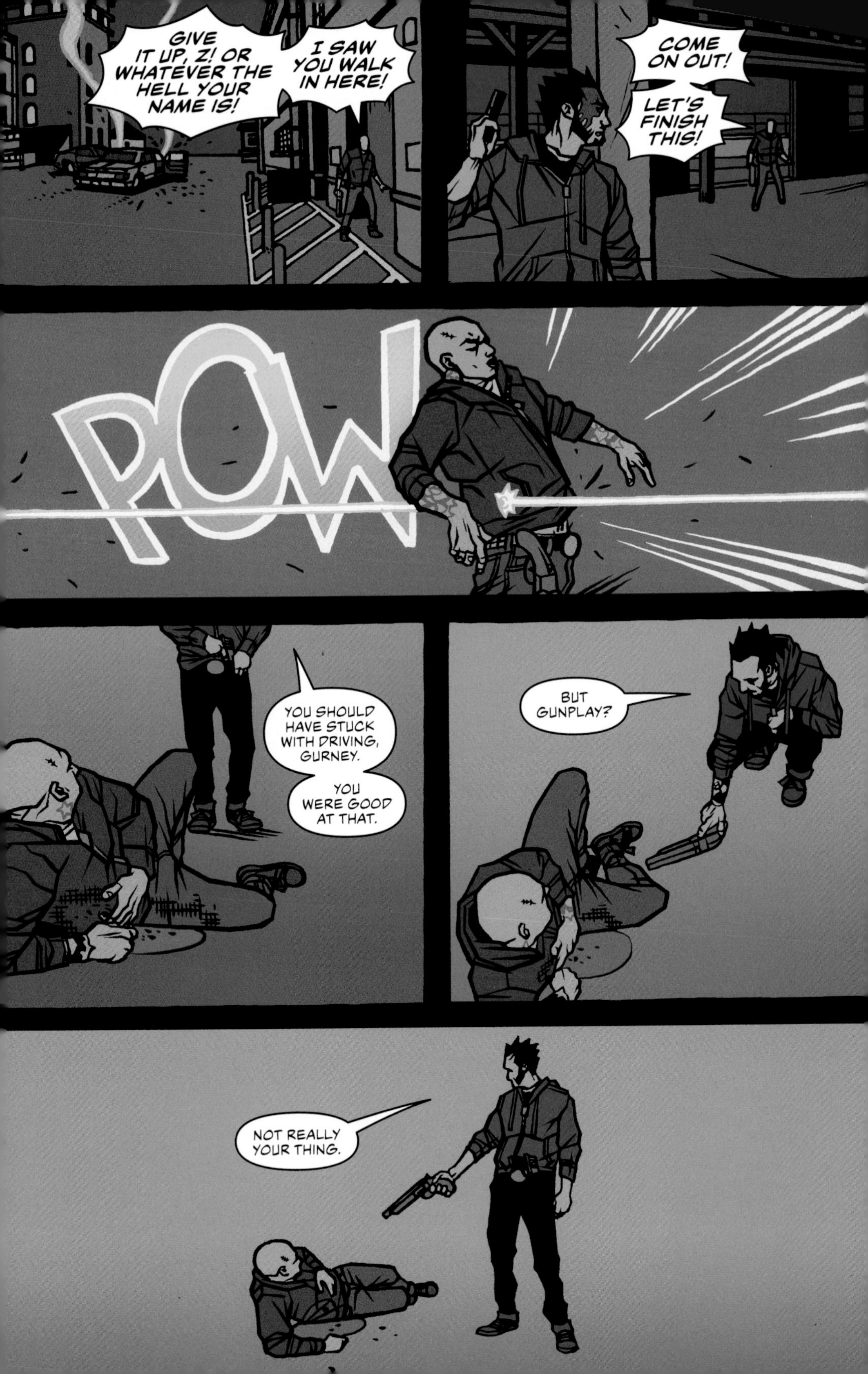
GIVE IT UP, Z! OR WHATEVER THE HELL YOUR NAME IS!
I SAW YOU WALK IN HERE!
COME ON OUT!
LET'S FINISH THIS!
POW
YOU SHOULD HAVE STUCK WITH DRIVING, GURNEY.
YOU WERE GOOD AT THAT.
BUT GUNPLAY?
NOT REALLY YOUR THING.

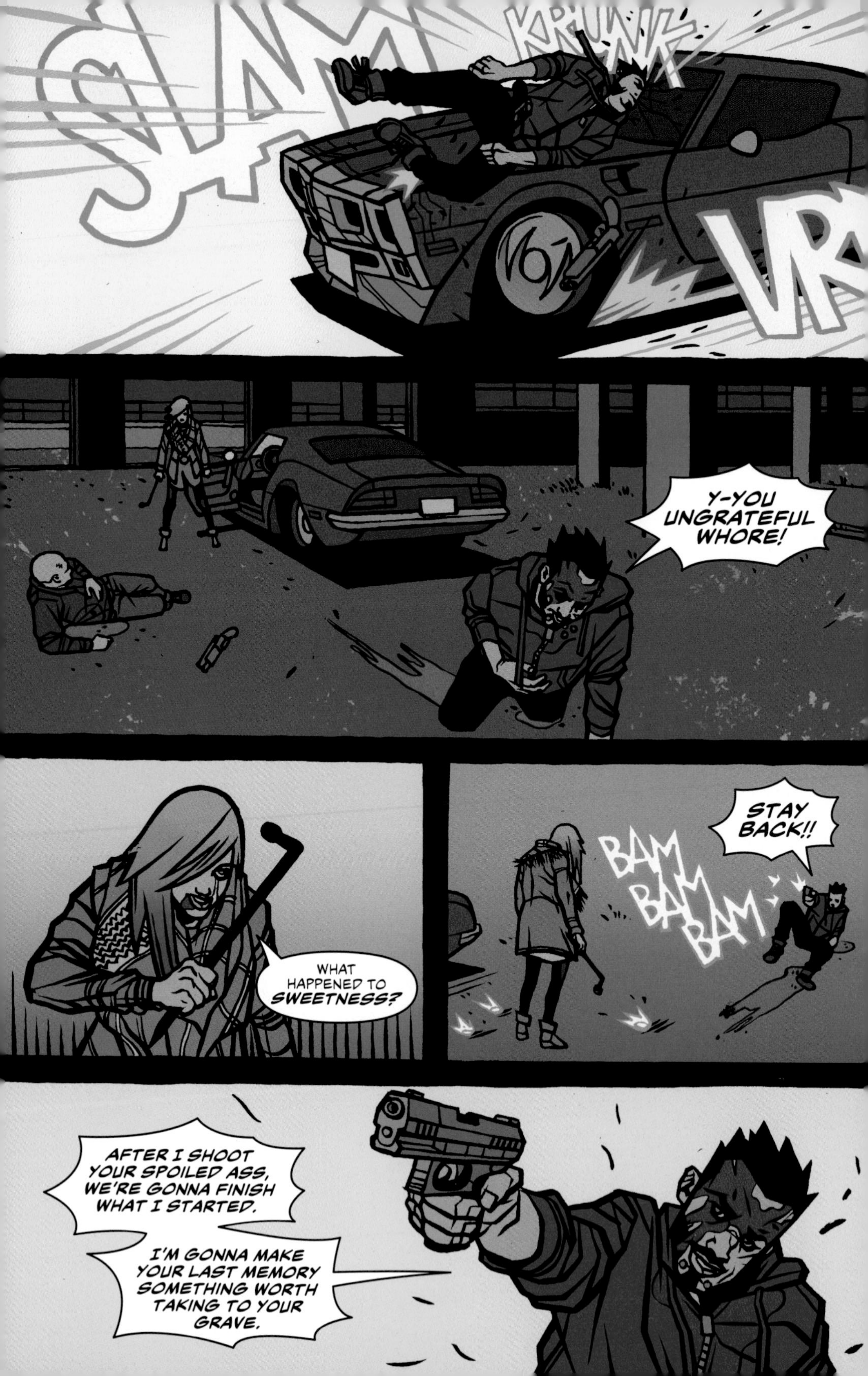
SLAM
KRUNK
VR
Y-YOU UNGRATEFUL WHORE!
WHAT HAPPENED TO SWEETNESS?
STAY BACK!!
BAM BAM BAM
AFTER I SHOOT YOUR SPOILED ASS, WE'RE GONNA FINISH WHAT I STARTED.
I'M GONNA MAKE YOUR LAST MEMORY SOMETHING WORTH TAKING TO YOUR GRAVE.

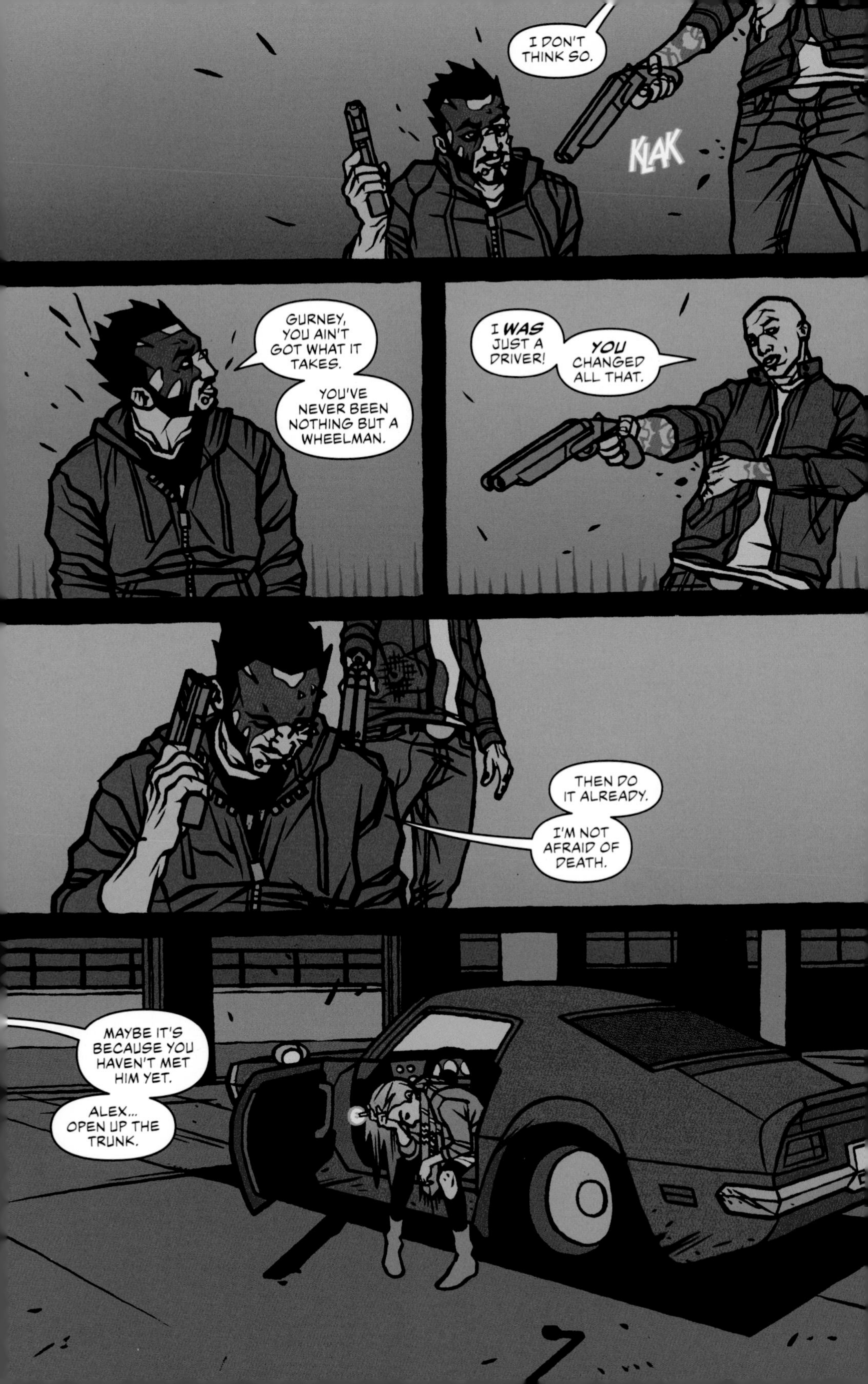
I DON'T THINK SO.
KLAK
GURNEY, YOU AIN'T GOT WHAT IT TAKES.
YOU'VE NEVER BEEN NOTHING BUT A WHEELMAN.
I WAS JUST A DRIVER!
YOU CHANGED ALL THAT.
THEN DO IT ALREADY.
I'M NOT AFRAID OF DEATH.
MAYBE IT'S BECAUSE YOU HAVEN'T MET HIM YET.
ALEX... OPEN UP THE TRUNK.

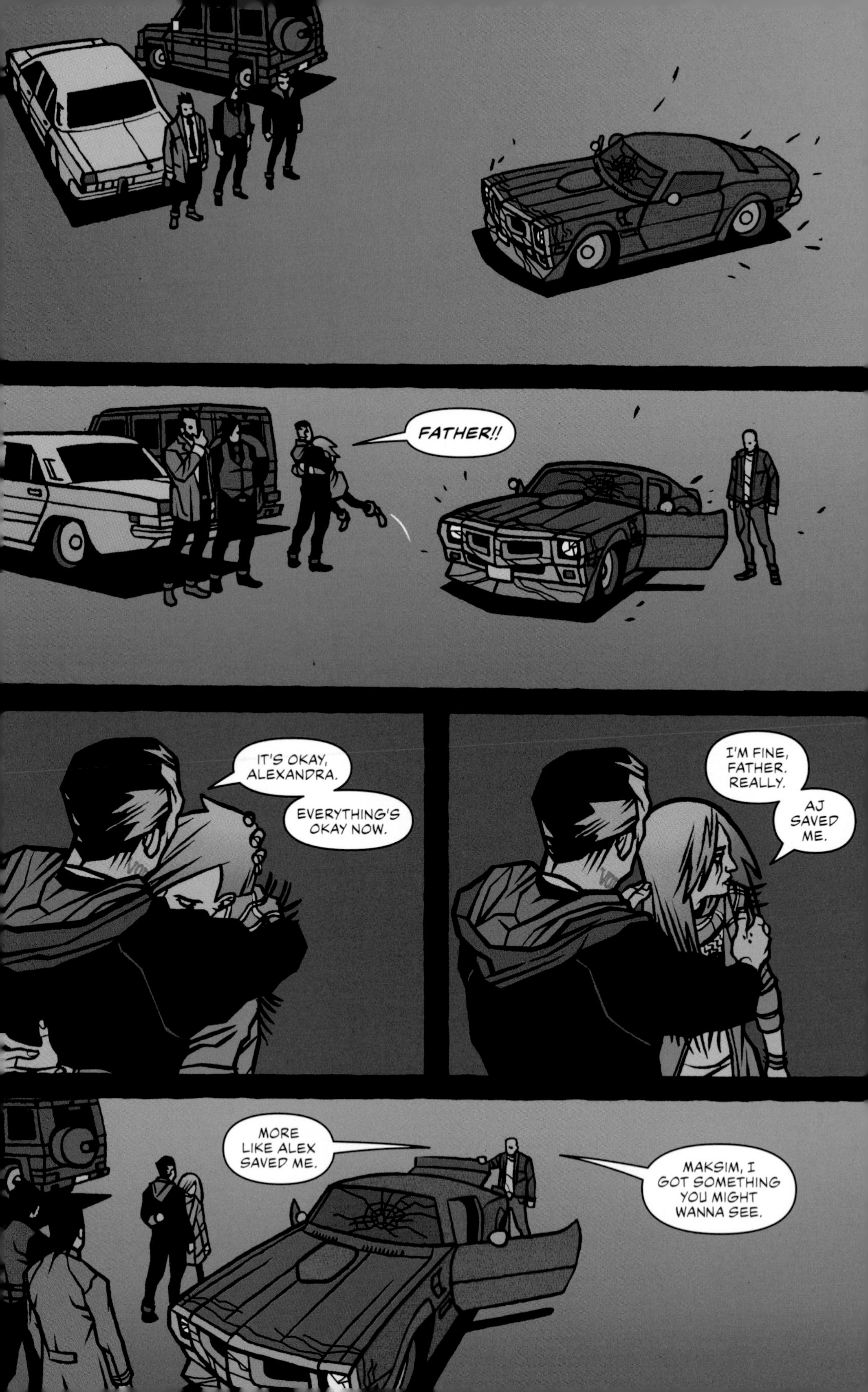
FATHER!!
IT'S OKAY, ALEXANDRA.
EVERYTHING'S OKAY NOW.
I'M FINE, FATHER. REALLY.
AJ SAVED ME.
MORE LIKE ALEX SAVED ME.
MAKSIM, I GOT SOMETHING YOU MIGHT WANNA SEE.

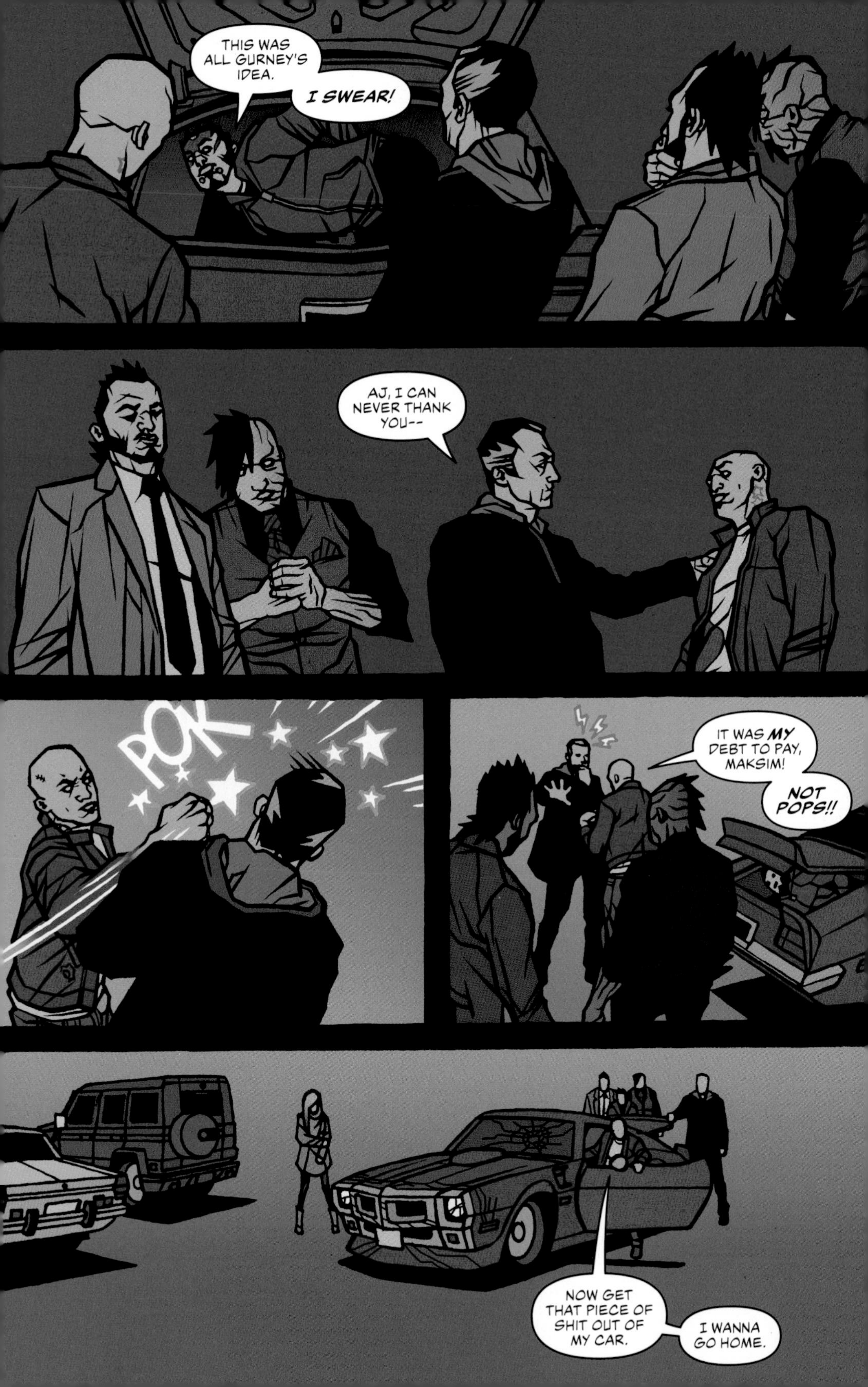

THIS WAS ALL GURNEY'S IDEA.
I SWEAR!
AJ, I CAN NEVER THANK YOU--
POK
IT WAS MY DEBT TO PAY, MAKSIM!
NOT POPS!!
NOW GET THAT PIECE OF SHIT OUT OF MY CAR.
I WANNA GO HOME.

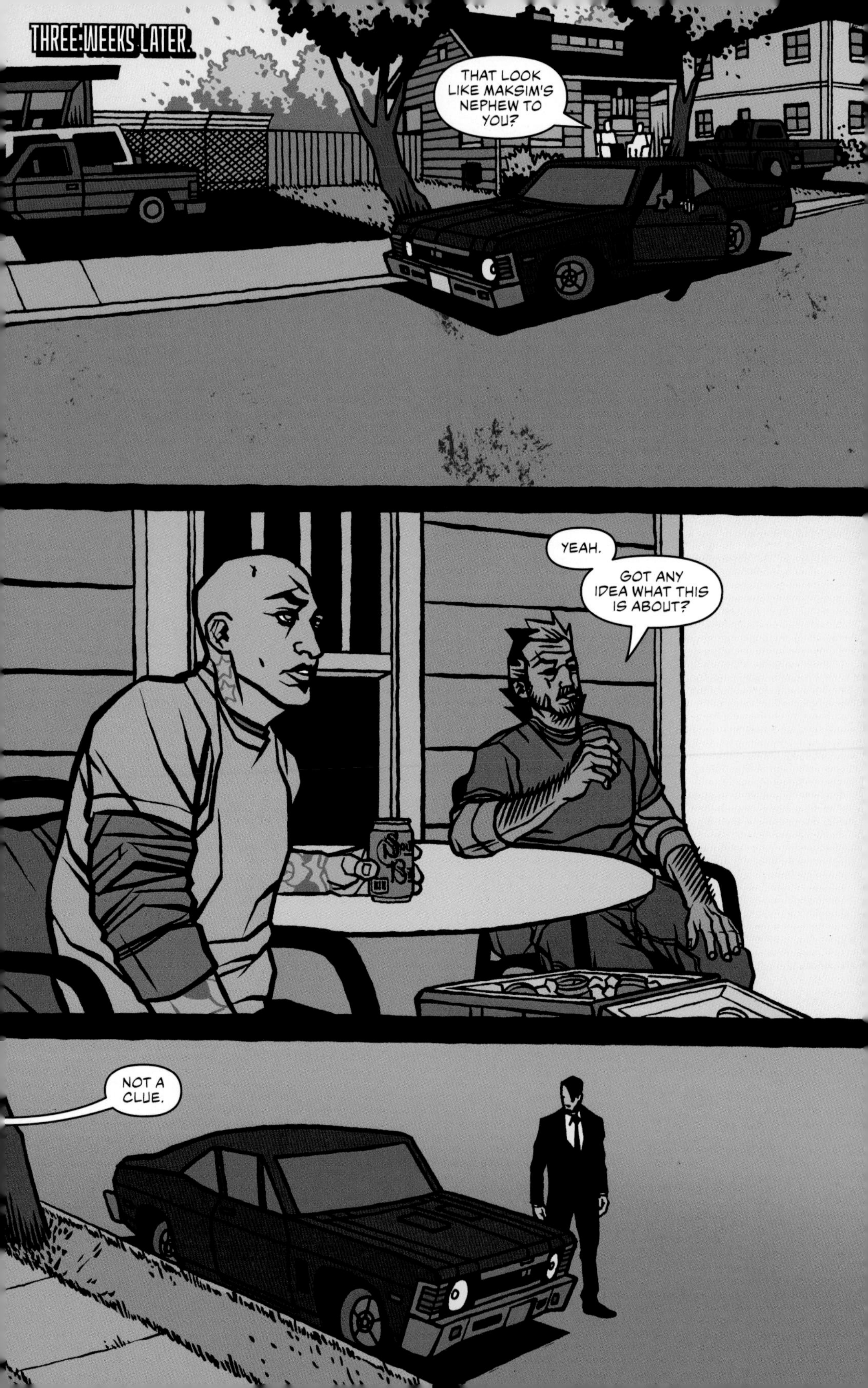
THREE WEEKS LATER.
THAT LOOK LIKE MAKSIM'S NEPHEW TO YOU?
YEAH.
GOT ANY IDEA WHAT THIS IS ABOUT?
NOT A CLUE.

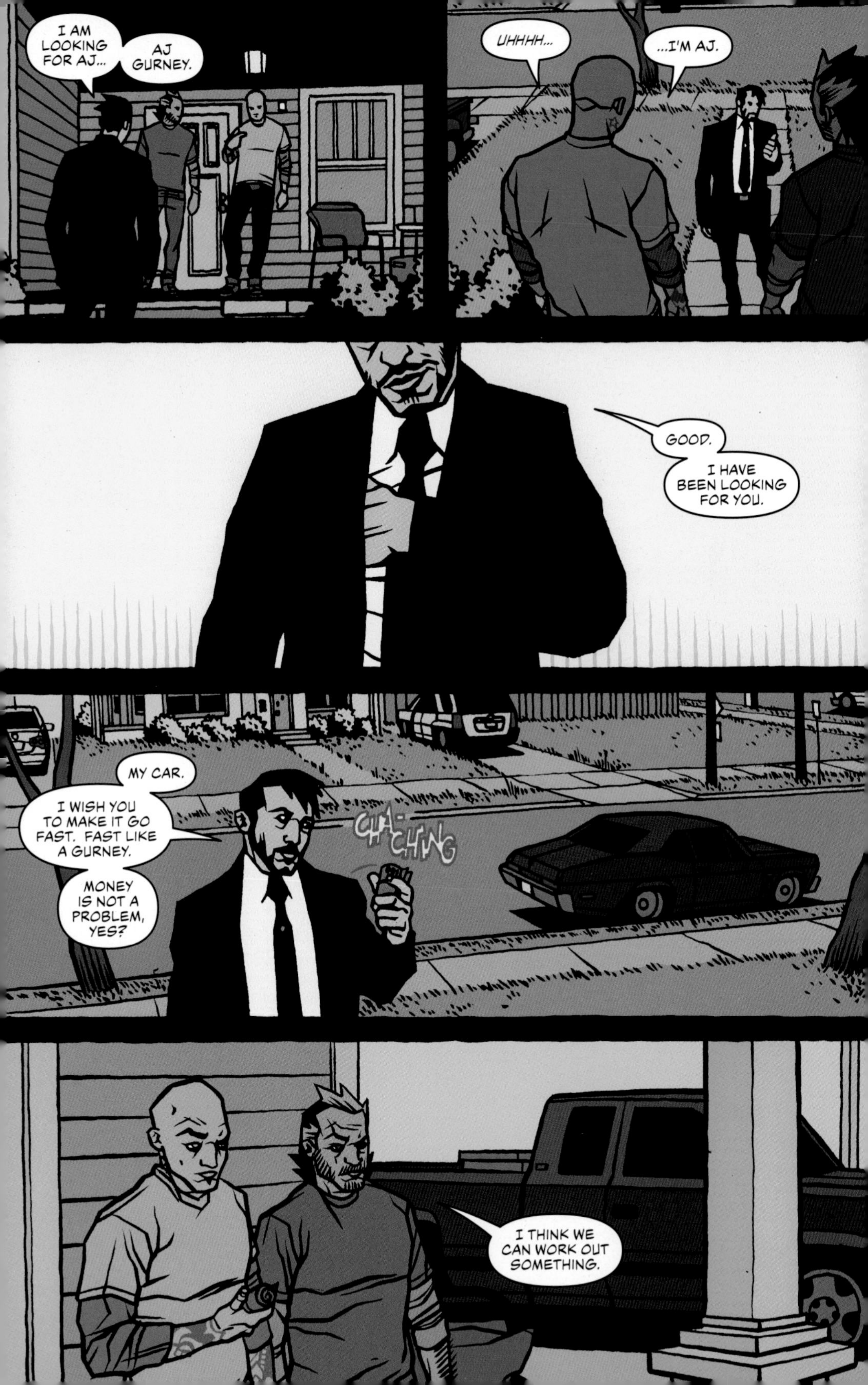
I AM LOOKING FOR AJ...
AJ GURNEY.
UHHHH...
...I'M AJ.
GOOD.
I HAVE BEEN LOOKING FOR YOU.
MY CAR.
I WISH YOU TO MAKE IT GO FAST. FAST LIKE A GURNEY.
MONEY IS NOT A PROBLEM, YES?
CHA-CHING
I THINK WE CAN WORK OUT SOMETHING.

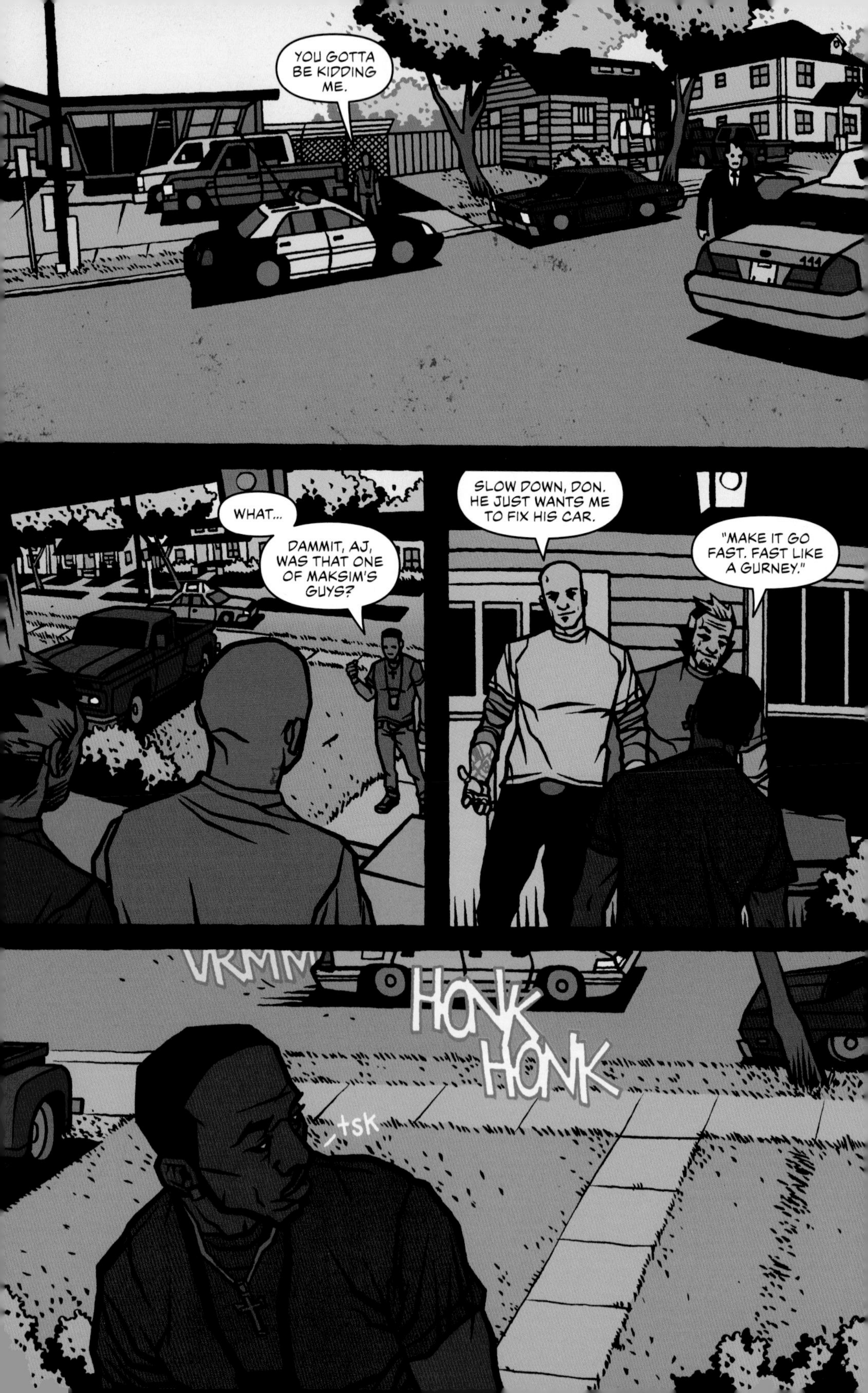
YOU GOTTA BE KIDDING ME.
WHAT...
DAMMIT, AJ, WAS THAT ONE OF MAKSIM'S GUYS?
SLOW DOWN, DON. HE JUST WANTS ME TO FIX HIS CAR.
"MAKE IT GO FAST. FAST LIKE A GURNEY."
VRMM
HONK HONK
tsk

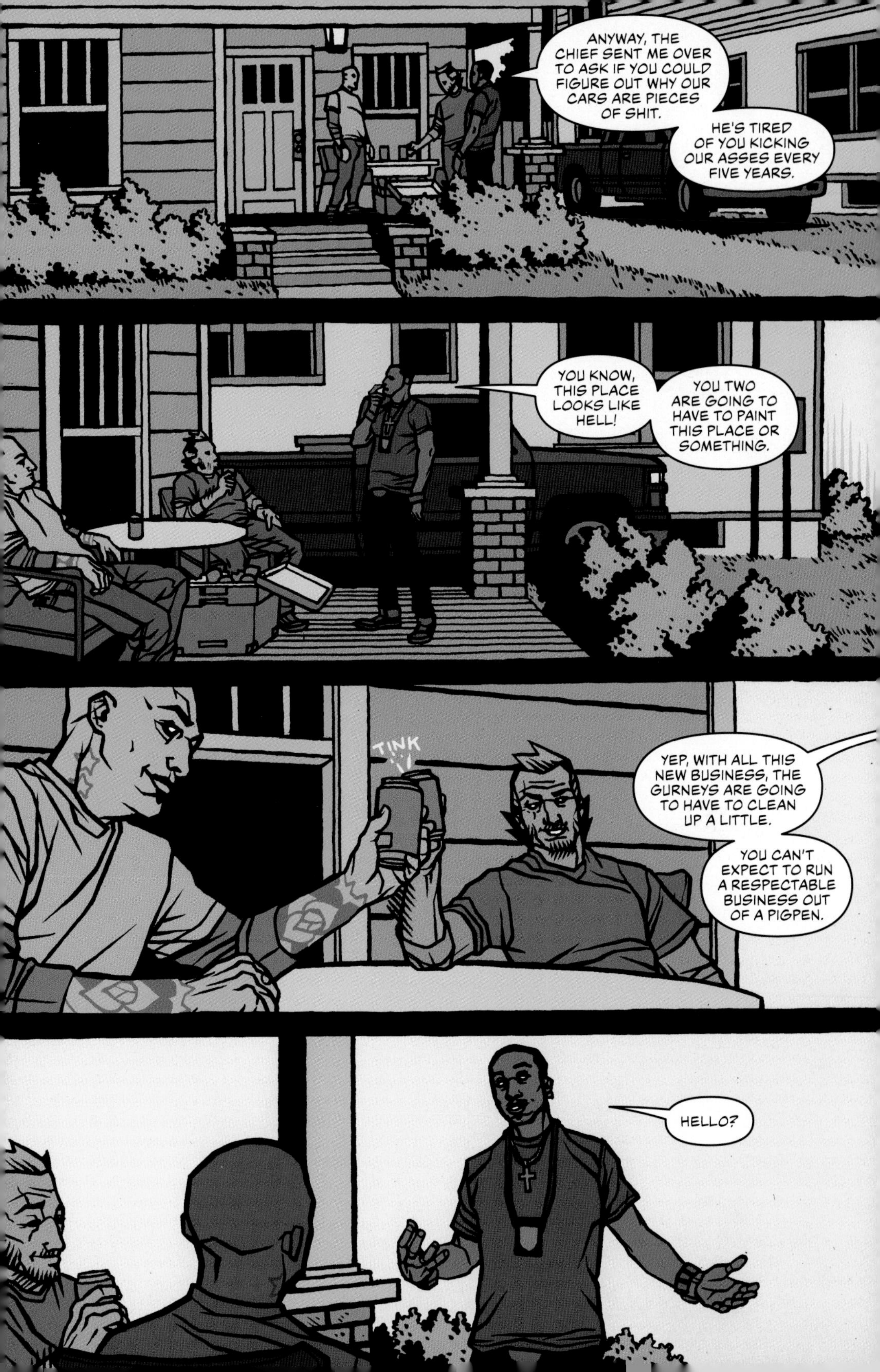
ANYWAY, THE CHIEF SENT ME OVER TO ASK IF YOU COULD FIGURE OUT WHY OUR CARS ARE PIECES OF SHIT.
HE'S TIRED OF YOU KICKING OUR ASSES EVERY FIVE YEARS.
YOU KNOW, THIS PLACE LOOKS LIKE HELL!
YOU TWO ARE GOING TO HAVE TO PAINT THIS PLACE OR SOMETHING.
TINK
YEP, WITH ALL THIS NEW BUSINESS, THE GURNEYS ARE GOING TO HAVE TO CLEAN UP A LITTLE.
YOU CAN'T EXPECT TO RUN A RESPECTABLE BUSINESS OUT OF A PIGPEN.
HELLO?

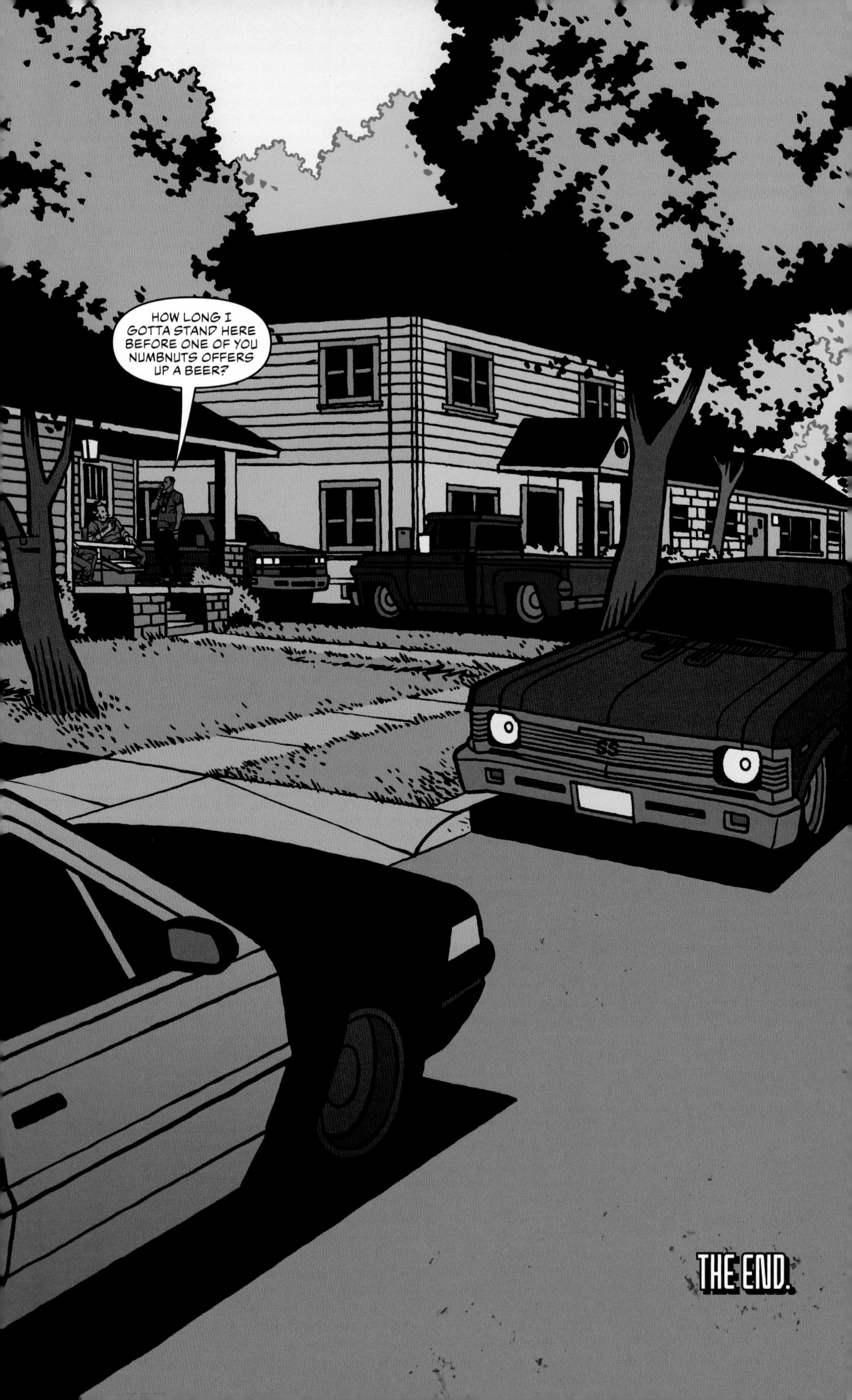
HOW LONG I GOTTA STAND HERE BEFORE ONE OF YOU NUMBNUTS OFFERS UP A BEER?
THE END.

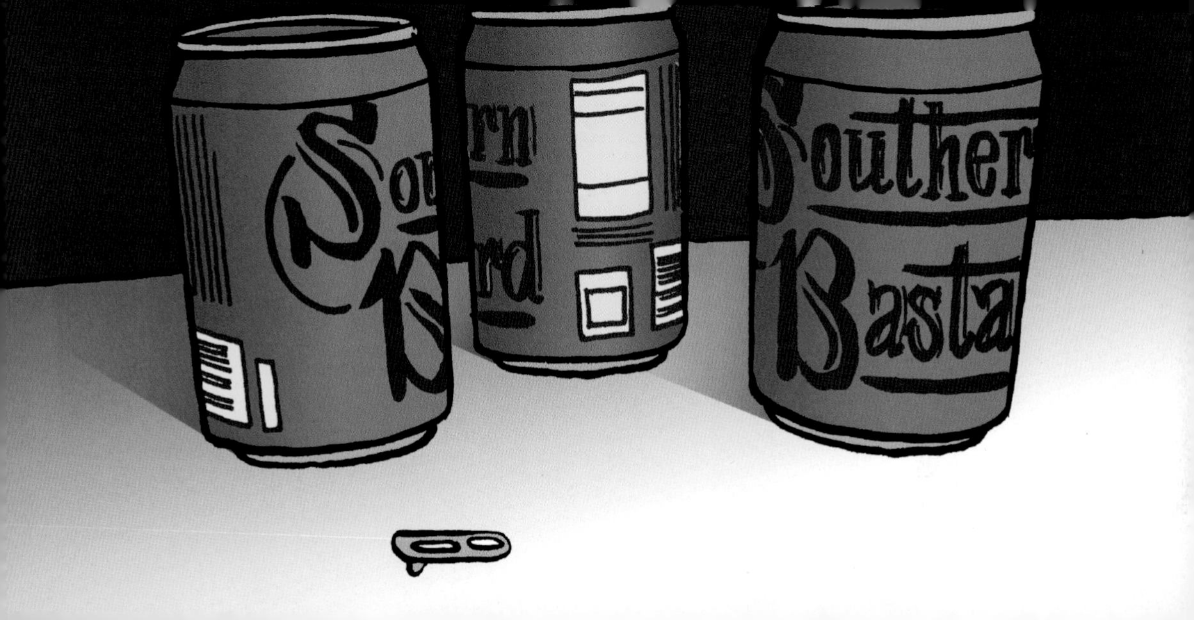

Sou
rn
rd
Souther
Basta

ISSUE ONE

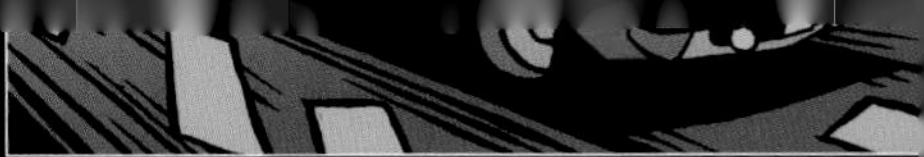

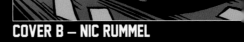

COVER B — NIC RUMMEL

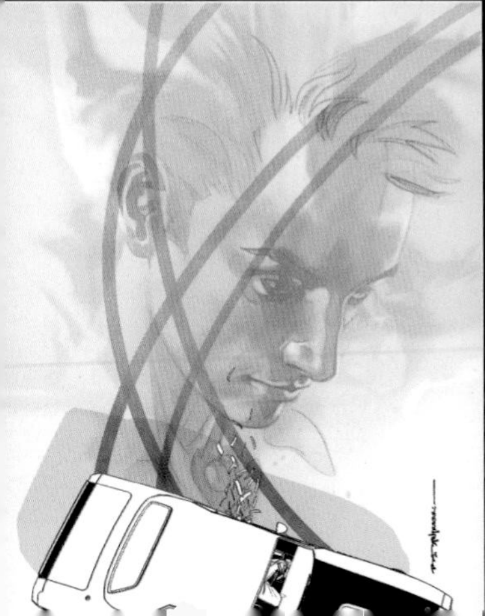

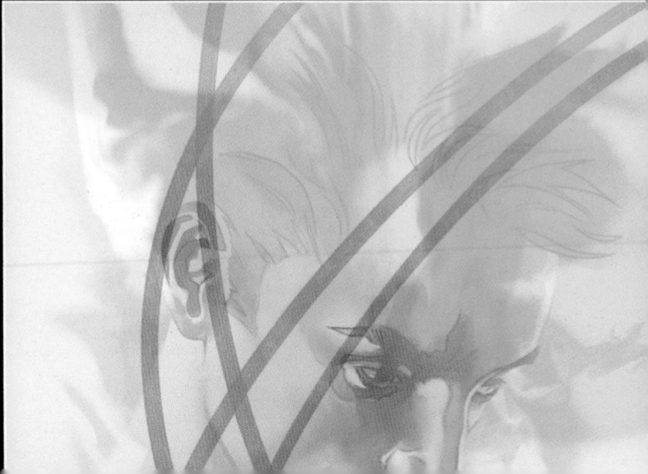

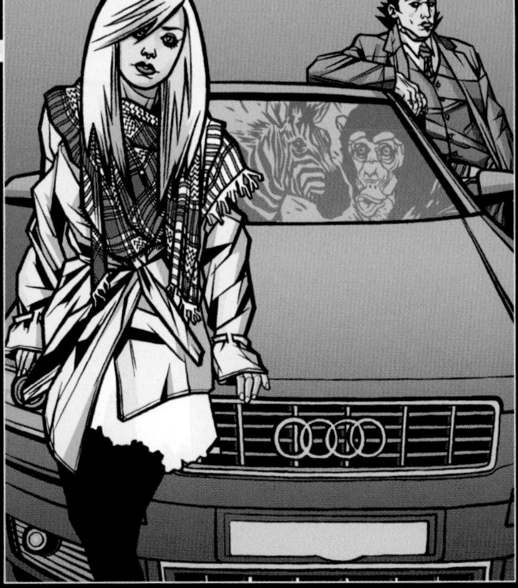

COVER B – NIC RUMMEL

ISSUE TWO

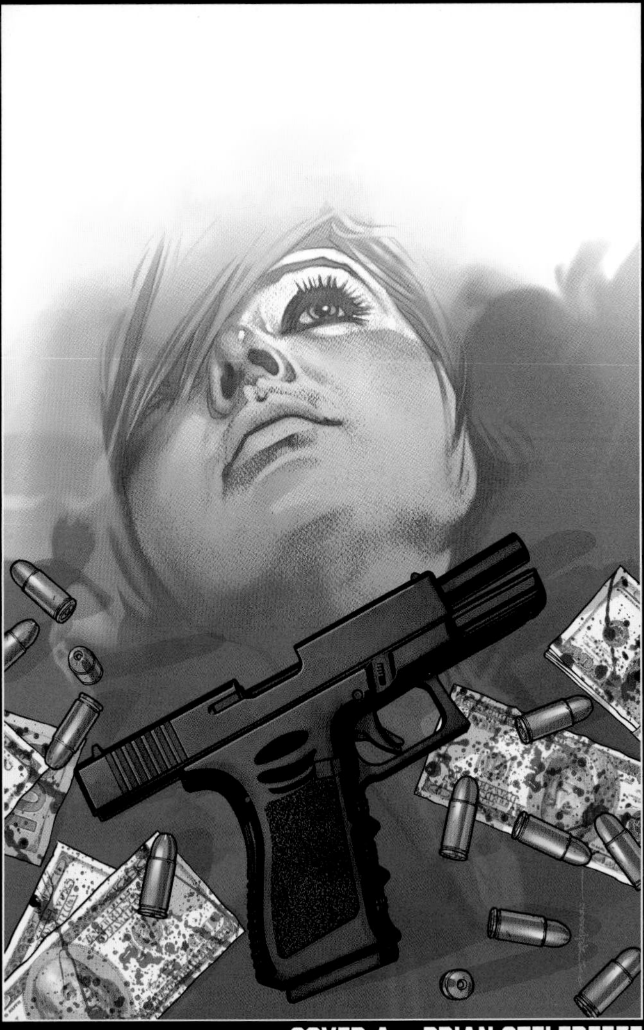

COVER A – BRIAN STELFREEZE

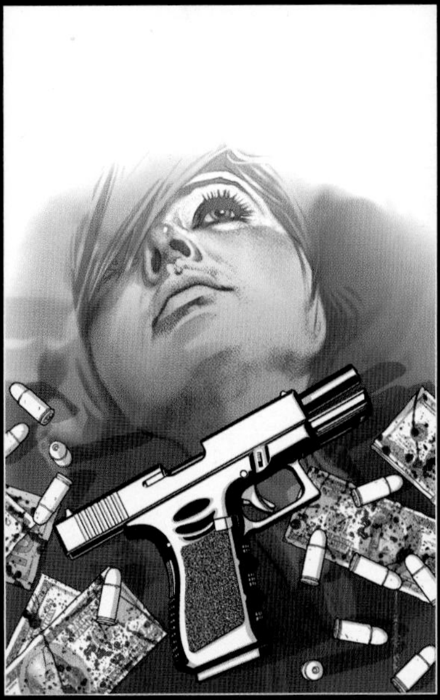

COVER C – BRIAN STELFREEZE

ISSUE THREE

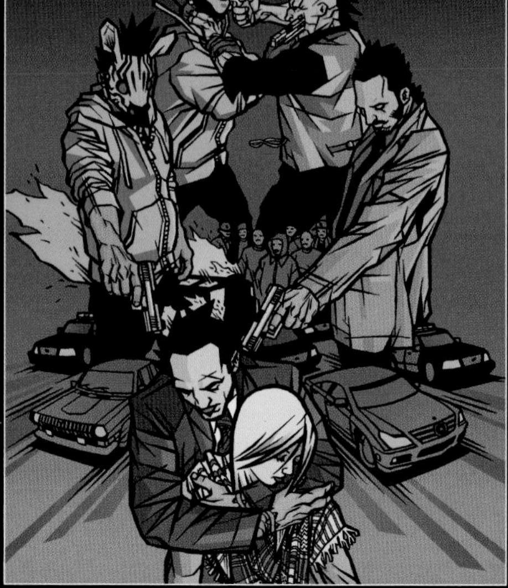

COVER B – NIC RUMMEL

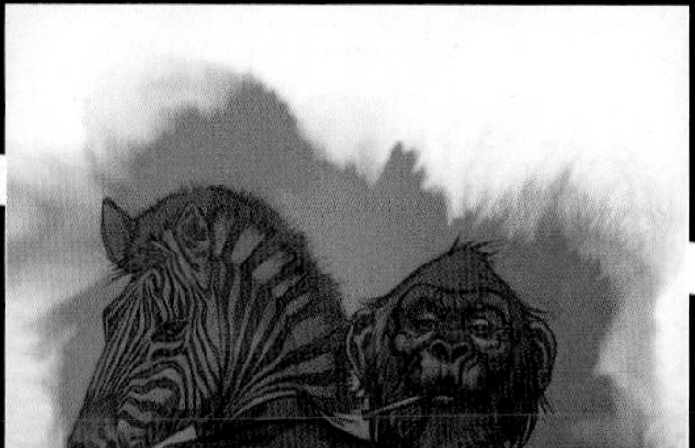

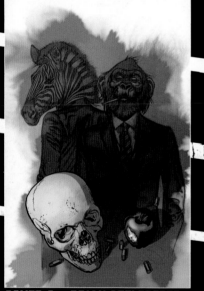

COVER C – BRIAN STELFREEZE

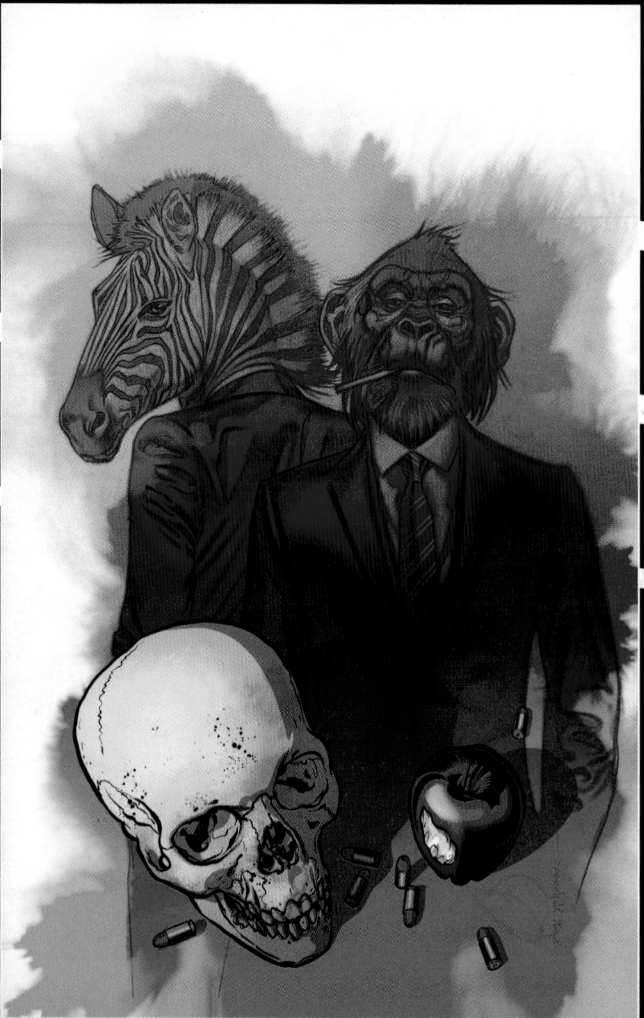

COVER A – BRIAN STELFREEZE

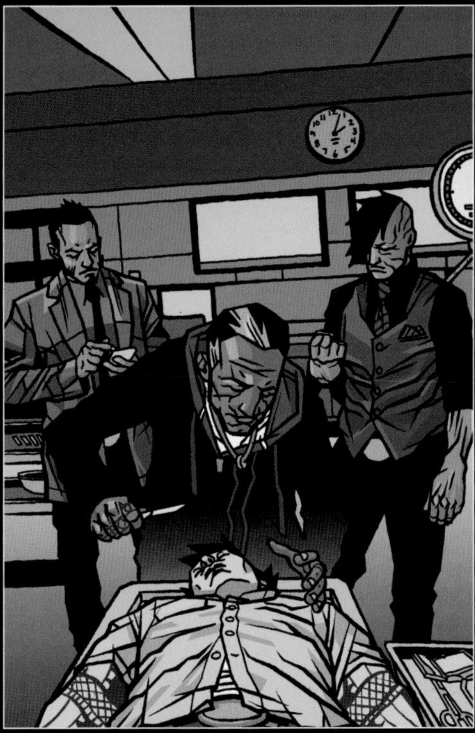

COVER B – NIC RUMMEL

ISSUE FOUR

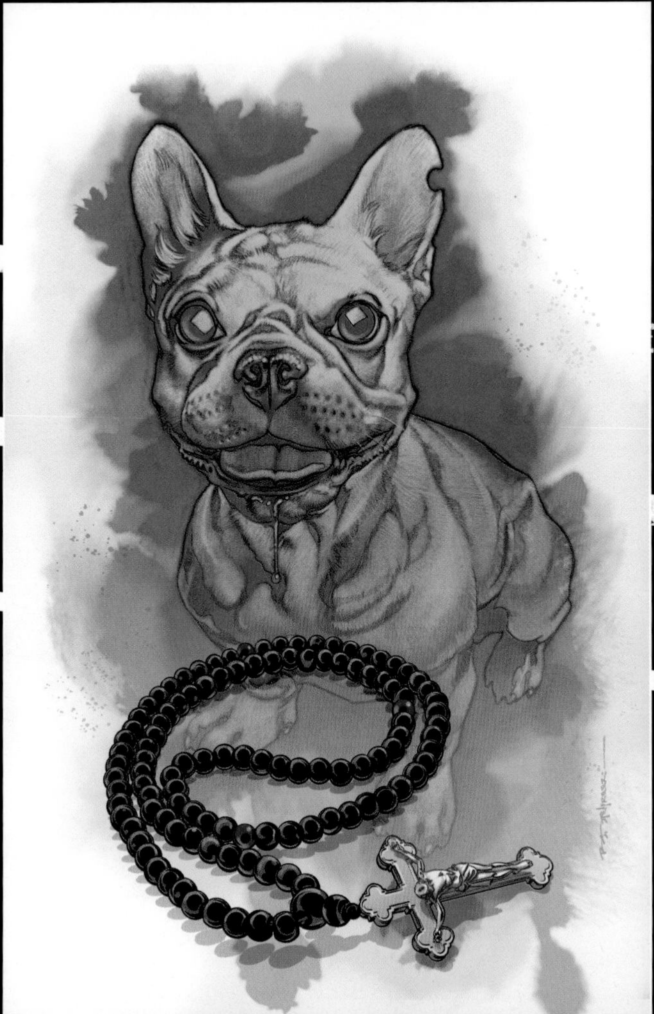

COVER A – BRIAN STELFREEZE

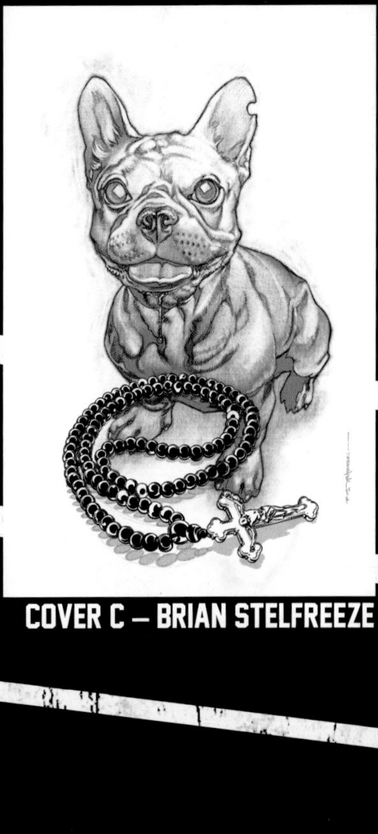

COVER C – BRIAN STELFREEZE

ISSUE FIVE

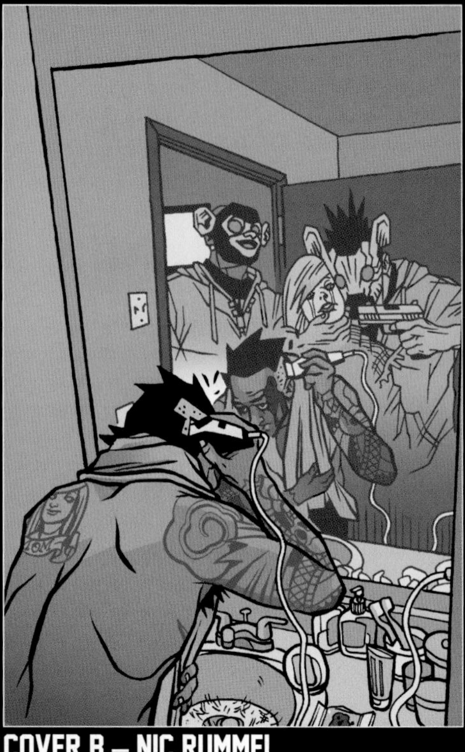

COVER B – NIC RUMMEL

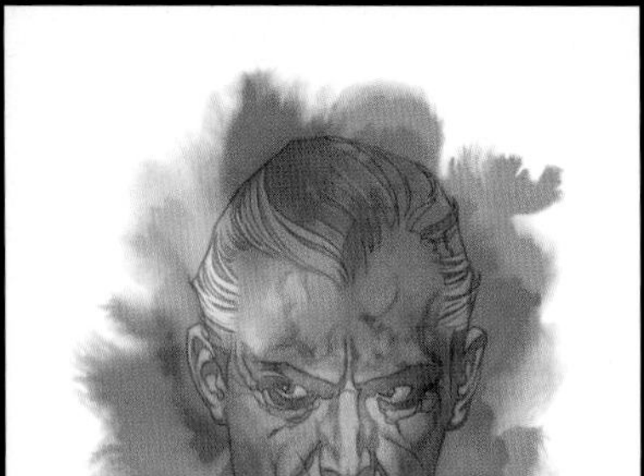
преданность

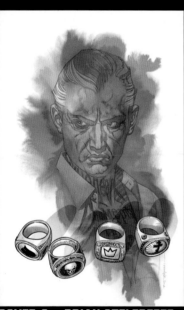

COVER C – BRIAN STELFREEZE

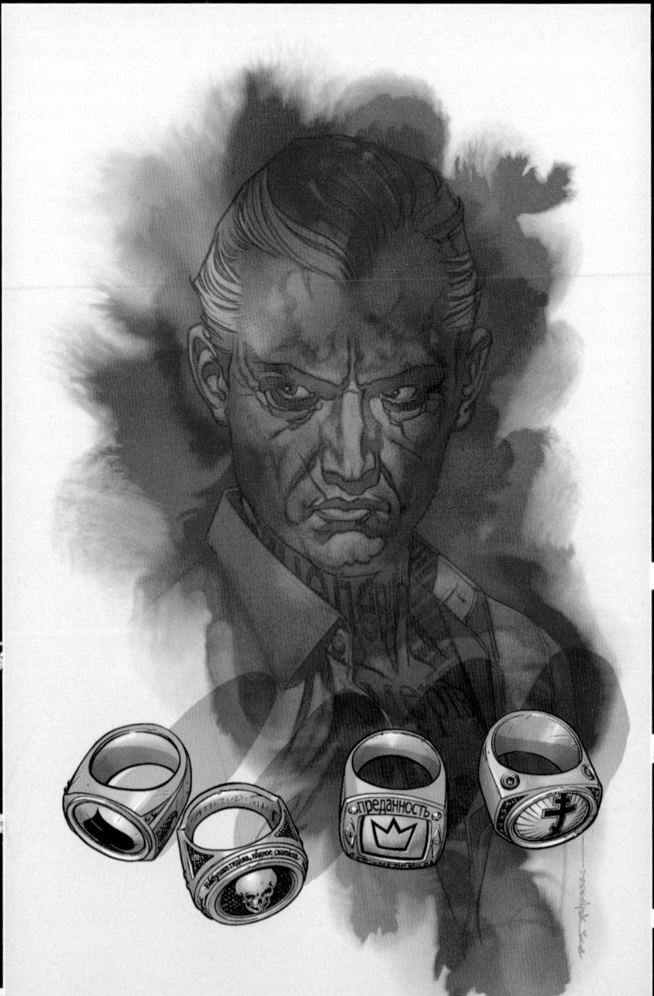
преданность

COVER A – BRIAN STELFREEZE

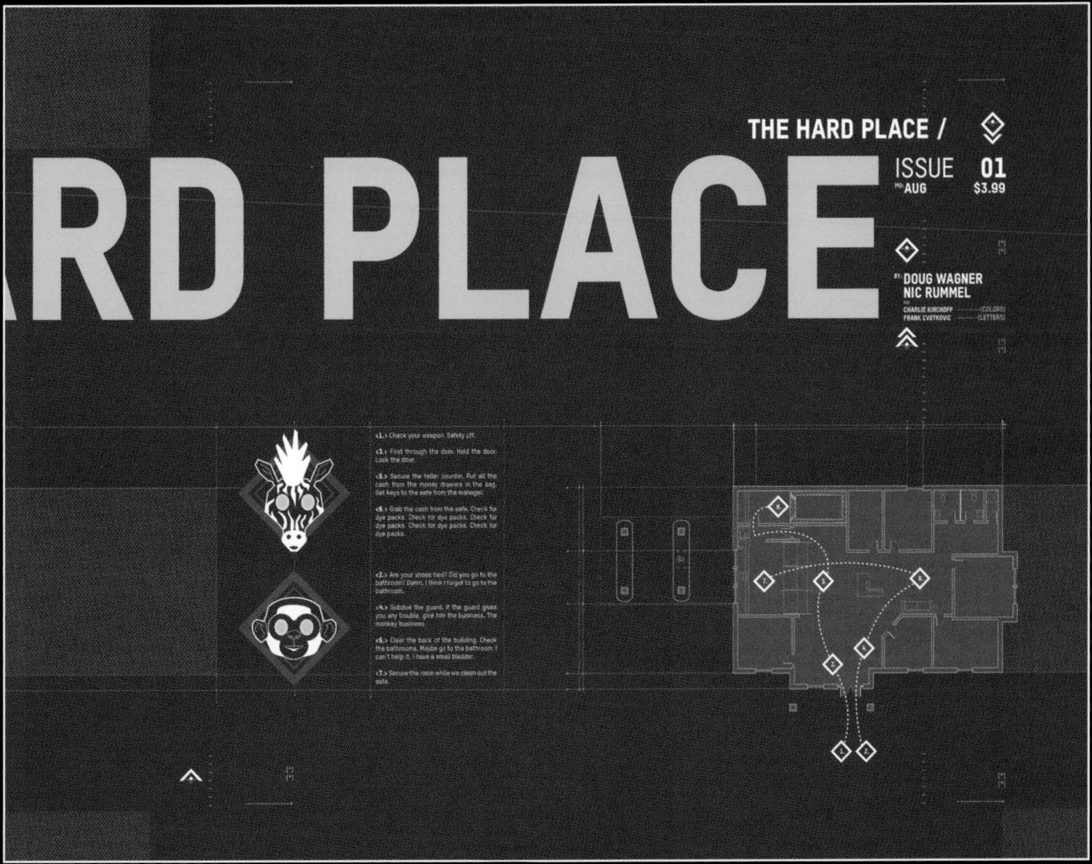
THE HARD PLACE /
ARD PLACE
ISSUE 01
MO: AUG
$3.99
BY: DOUG WAGNER
NIC RUMMEL
CHARLIE KIRCHOFF (COLORS)
FRANK CVETKOVIC (LETTERS)
<1.> Check your weapon. Safety off.
<3.> First through the door. Hold the door. Lock the door.
<5.> Secure the teller counter. Put all the cash from the money drawers in the bag. Get keys to the safe from the manager.
<8.> Grab the cash from the safe. Check for dye packs. Check for dye packs. Check for dye packs. Check for dye packs. Check for dye packs.
<2.> Are your shoes tied? Did you go to the bathroom? Damn, I think I forgot to go to the bathroom.
<4.> Subdue the guard. If the guard gives you any trouble, give him the business. The monkey business.
<6.> Clear the back of the building. Check the bathrooms. Maybe go to the bathroom. I can't help it, I have a small bladder.
<7.> Secure the room while we clean out the safe.

ISSUE ONE

COVER D – JONATHAN HICKMAN

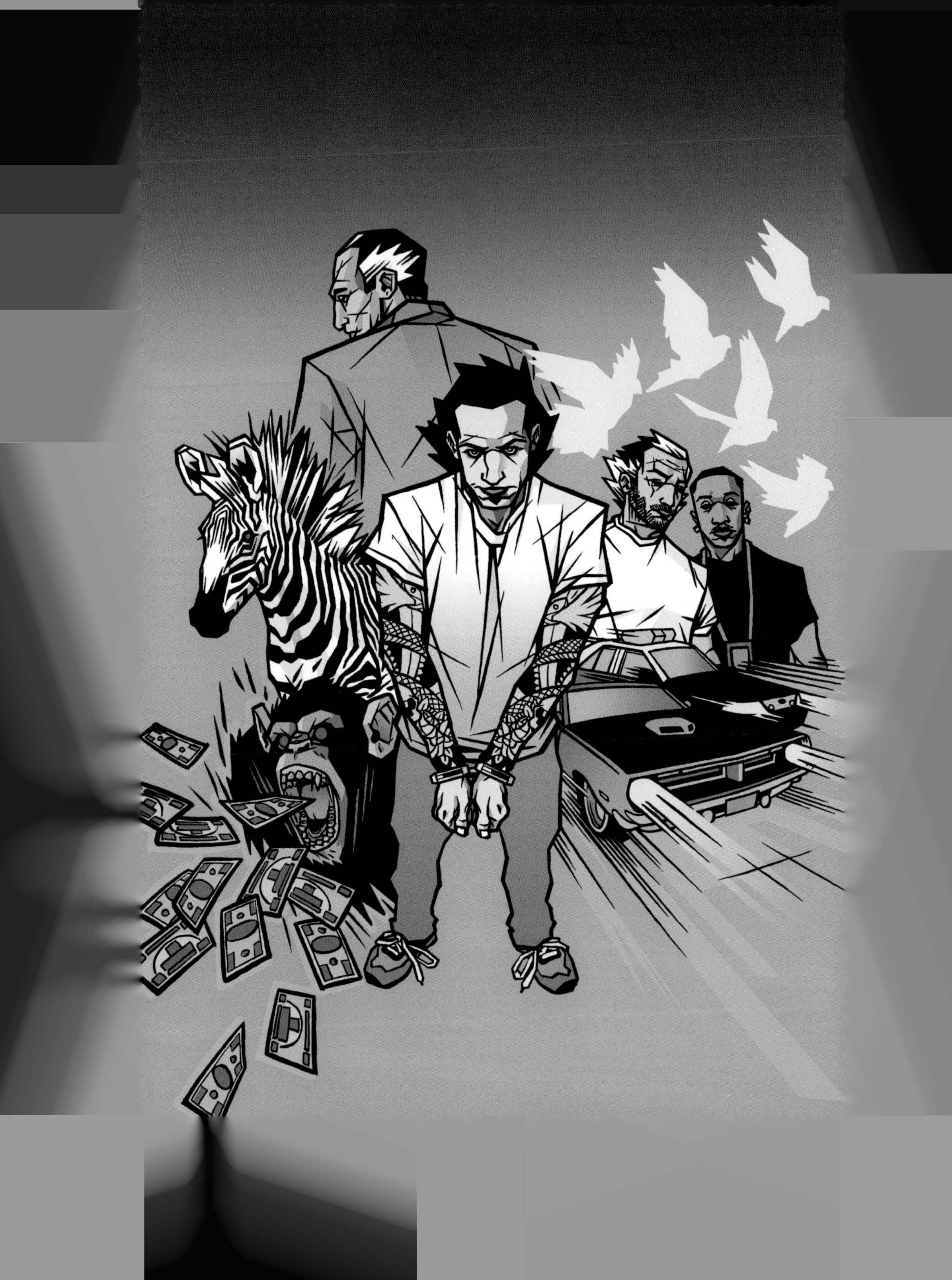

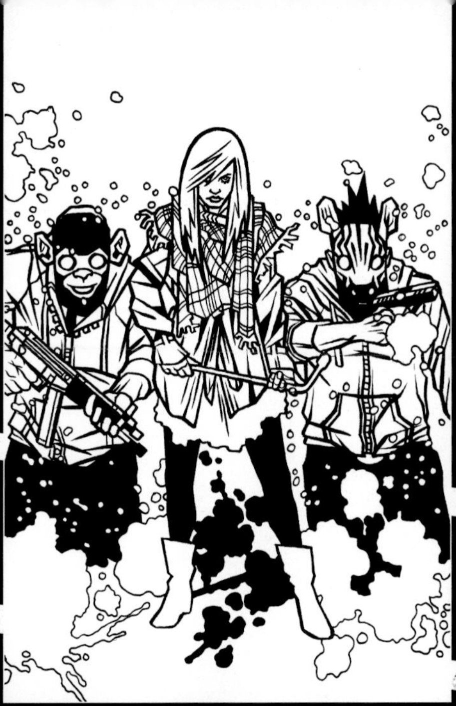

COVER E – THE WALKING DEAD
TRIBUTE VARIANT

ISSUE THREE

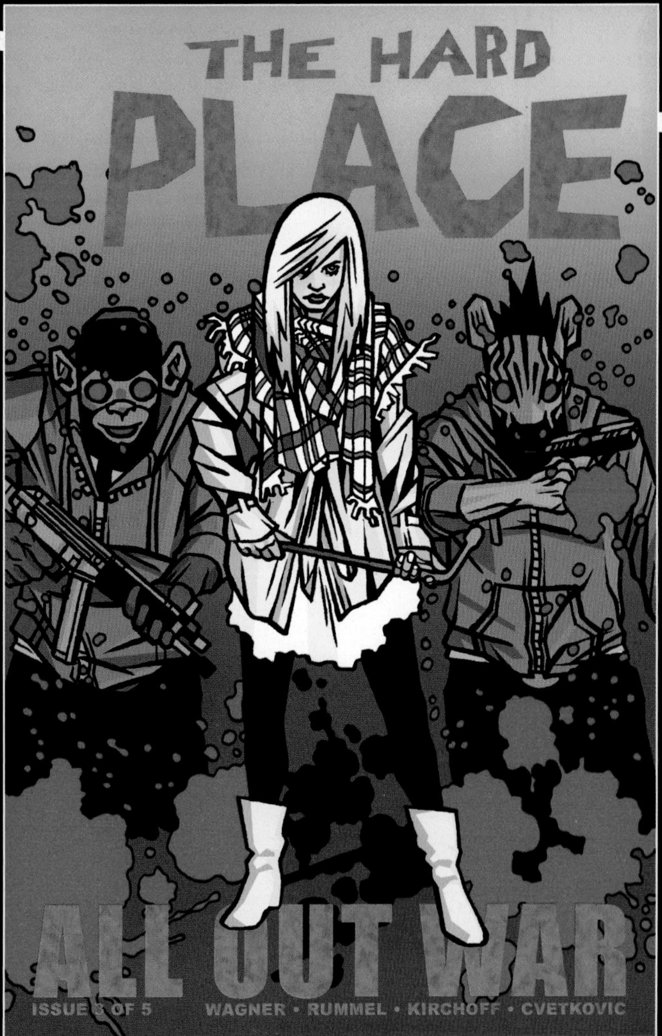
THE HARD
PLACE
ALL OUT WAR
ISSUE 3 OF 5
WAGNER • RUMMEL • KIRCHOFF • CVETKOVIC

COVER D – THE WALKING DEAD TRIBUTE VARIANT

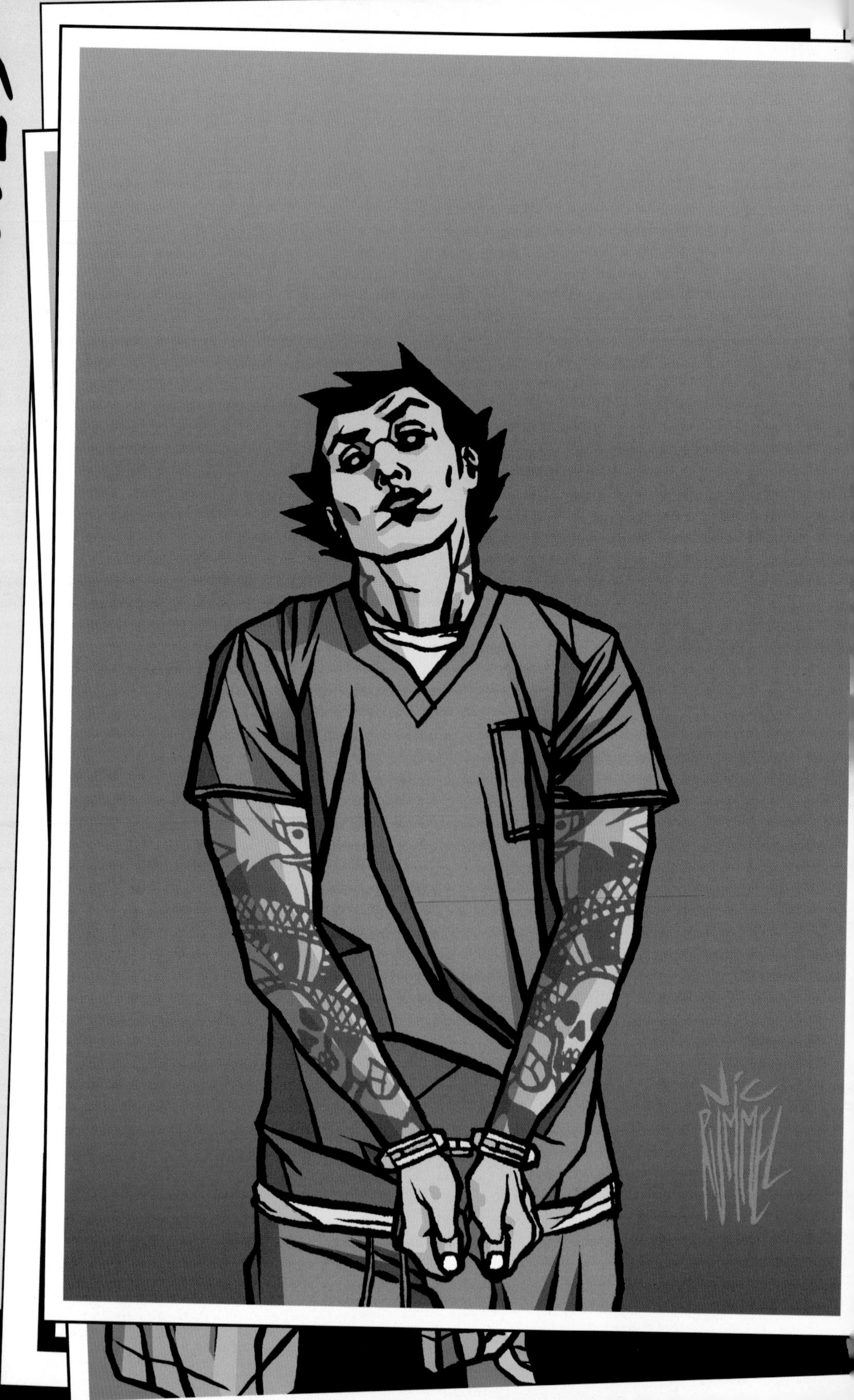

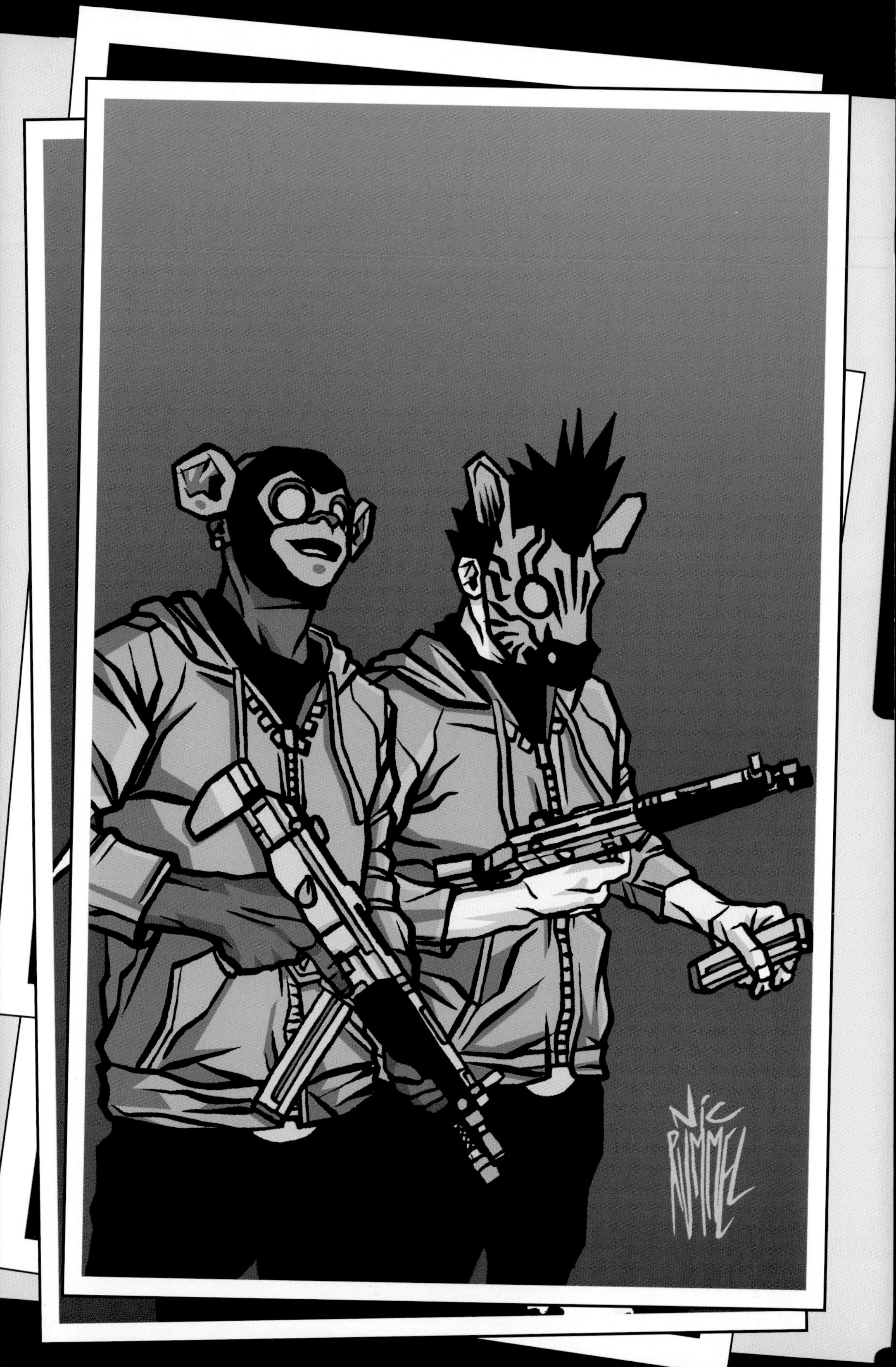
NIC RUMMEL

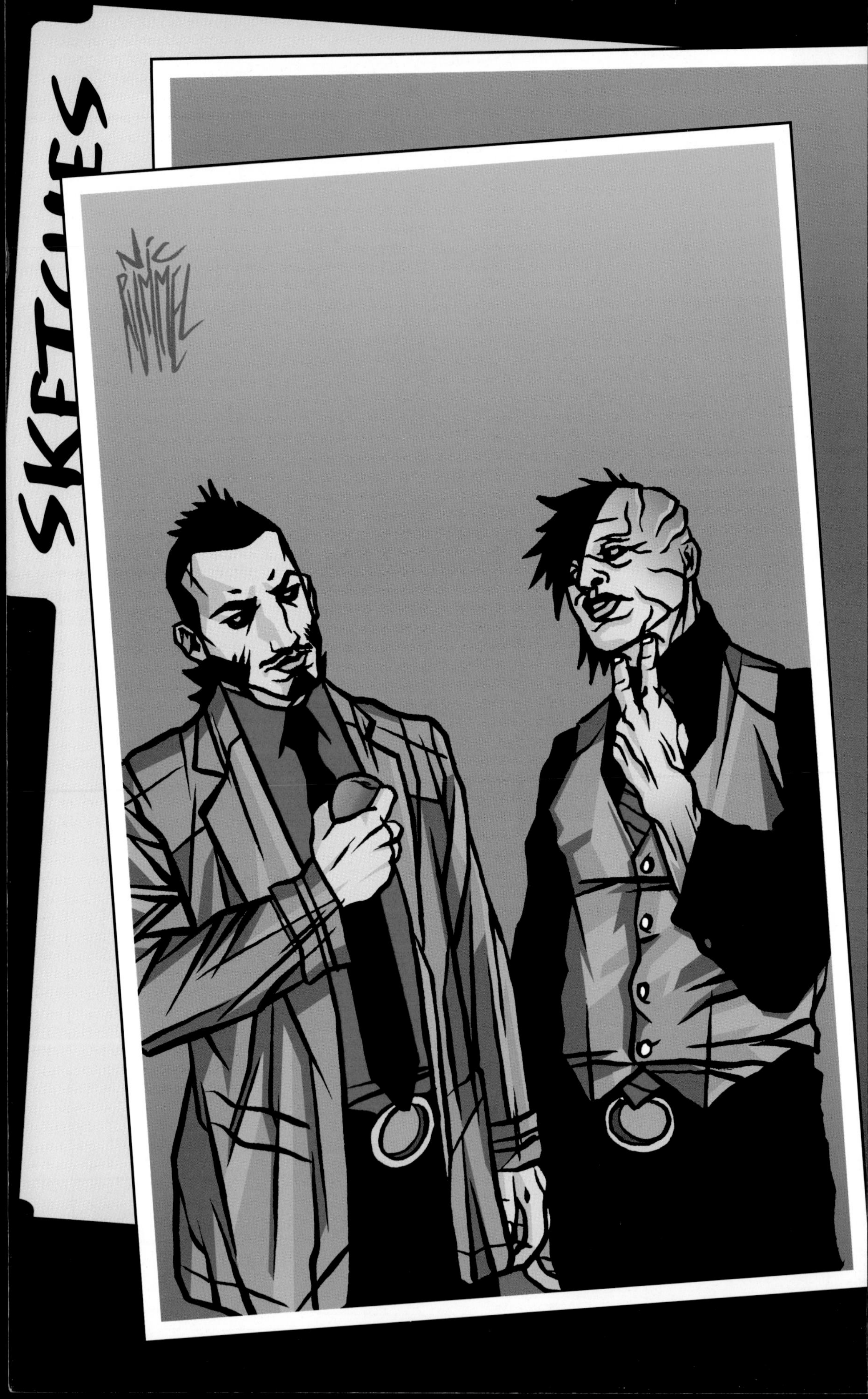

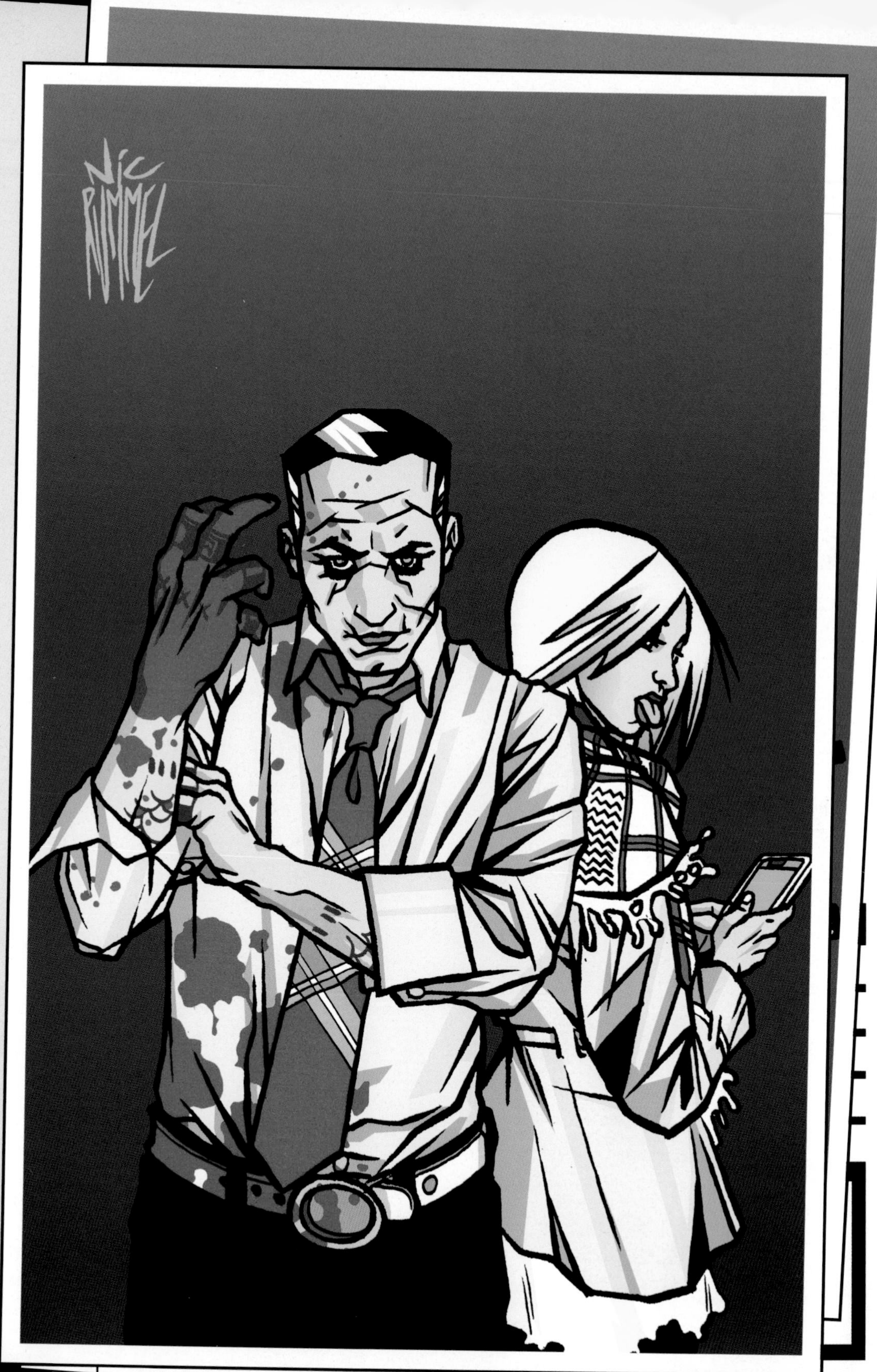

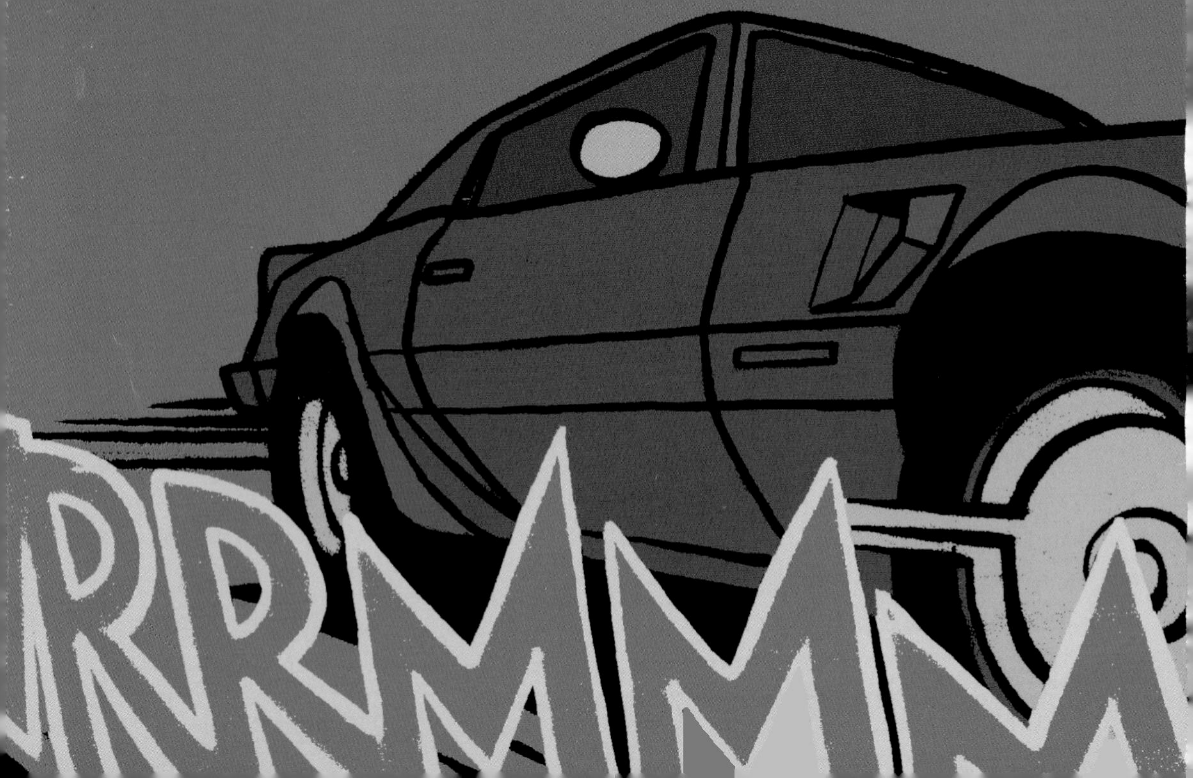
RRMMM